My Mind's Eye

By
Gillian Jones

Copyright © 2015 Gillian Jones
Print Edition

All rights reserved. In accordance with the U.S. Copyright Act of 1976, the scanning, uploading and sharing of any part of this book without the permission of the publisher except in the case of brief quotations embodied in critical articles or reviews is unlawful piracy and theft of the author's intellectual property. Thank you for your support of the author's rights.

This is a work of fiction. Names, characters, businesses, places, events, and incidents are either the products of the author's imagination or used in a fictitious manner. Any resemblance to actual persons, living or dead, or actual events is purely coincidental. Gillian Jones is in no way affiliated with any brands, songs, musicians or artists mentioned in this book.

First eBook edition: June 2015

Edited by Hot Tree Edits and Deliciously Wicked Editing
Cover design ©: Book Covers by Ashbee designs
Image by Dollar Photo
Formatting by Paul Salvette

About the Book

Ryker

She is the epitome of the girl next door, but with a feistiness that makes my dick throb.

I'm drawn to her like no other. She stirs things in me I have no desire to feel, makes me long for things I shouldn't.

This is my game. I choose the players, and I never play for keeps.

I don't believe in fate. I make my own destiny. I work hard and play harder. Luck is for pussies, karma for idiots. Me, I make shit happen.

Meeting her fucked up my plan. Threw me off my game.

I'm now face to face with my karma. Her name is Kat Rollins.

Kat

Ryker Eddison is the epitome of a player. You know the type: Mr. Get In and Get Out.

He's all about the chase, wanting just one night. Everyone knows this—I know this. Still, I find myself craving him, my greedy body betraying what my heart and mind already know: *he will only bring me pain.*

He's the guy who girls like me should avoid. I'm smart; I know better. But when I'm with him, I feel things I've never felt before. Things I never knew I wanted.

I can't deny it … I like the chase. The high is explosive, but I'm afraid if I give in, I may end up losing more than I can handle: my heart.

Dedication

To my incredibly patient and loving husband and son,
thank you for ignoring me while I ignored you.
You guys are my everything.
Thanks for letting Mommy try on this hat.

Table of Contents

My Mind's Eye Playlist	viii
Prologue: Kat	1
Chapter 1: Kat	12
Chapter 2: Kat	16
Chapter 3: Kat	22
Chapter 4: Ryker	37
Chapter 5: Kat	48
Chapter 6: Ryker	57
Chapter 7: Kat	60
Chapter 8: Kat	66
Chapter 9: Kat	72
Chapter 10: Kat	78
Chapter 11: Ryker	84
Chapter 12: Kat	89
Chapter 13: Kat	99
Chapter 14: Ryker	110
Chapter 15: Kat	114
Chapter 16: Ryker	119
Chapter 17: Ryker	129
Chapter 18: Kat	133
Chapter 19: Ryker	139
Chapter 20: Kat	141
Chapter 21: Ryker	147
Chapter 22: Kat	150
Chapter 23: Ryker	153
Chapter 24: Kat	157
Chapter 25: Ryker	160

Chapter 26: Kat	162
Chapter 27: Ryker	168
Chapter 28: Kat	169
Chapter 29: Ryker	180
Chapter 30: Kat	183
Chapter 31: Ryker	188
Chapter 32: Kat	190
Chapter 33: Kat	194
Chapter 34: Kat	197
Chapter 35: Ryker	204
Chapter 36: Kat	207
Chapter 37: Ryker	210
Chapter 38: Kat	213
Chapter 39: Ryker	215
Chapter 40: Kat	217
Chapter 41: Ryker	220
Chapter 42: Kat	223
Chapter 43: Ryker	226
Chapter 44: Ryker	230
Chapter 45: Kat	232
Chapter 46: Ryker	236
Chapter 47: Kat	238
Chapter 48: Ryker	240
Chapter 49: Kat	246
Chapter 50: Kat	248
Chapter 51: Kat	252
Chapter 52: Kat	256
Chapter 53: Ryker	258
Chapter 54: Kat	261
Chapter 55: Kat	264
Chapter 56: Kat	267
Chapter 57: Kat	272
Chapter 58: Ryker	275

Chapter 59: Kat	277
Chapter 60: Ryker	280
Chapter 61: Ryker	282
Chapter 62: Kat	284
Chapter 63: Ryker	289
Chapter 64: Kat	292
Chapter 65: Ryker	295
Chapter 66: Kat	297
Epilogue	300
Acknowledgements	306

My Mind's Eye Playlist

Can be found on Spotify

Ed Sheeran – Thinking Out Loud

Sohodolls – Stripper

Sarah McLachlan – In Your Shoes

Delerium – Silence – Acoustic

The Tea Party – Heaven Coming Down

Queens Of The Stone Age – Make It Wit Chu

Paula Cole – Feelin' Love

City and Colour – Sleeping Sickness

Tyler Ward & Anna Clendening – Stay With Me

Chris Cornell – Can't Change Me

112 – Only You-Bad Boy Remix (feat. The Notorious B.I.G. & Mase)

Disclosure – Latch

Sam Smith – Like I Can

Haim – The Wire

Britney Spears – Toxic

Pearl Jam – Yellow Ledbetter

Kelis – Milkshake

JAY Z – Always Be My Sunshine

Kings Of Leon – Be Somebody

3 Doors Down – Here Without You

Big Wreck – Blown Wide Open

Hedley – Perfect

Hedley – For The Nights I Can't Remember – Live

The Flys – Got You (Where I Want You)

Deftones – Change [In The House Of Flies]

Passenger – Let Her Go

My Chemical Romance – Welcome To The Black Parade

Ray LaMontagne – You Are the Best Thing

Van Morrison – Into The Mystic

Van Morrison – Crazy Love

Edward Sharpe & The Magnetic Zeros – Home (featuring the Gulu Widows Choir)

Mark Morrison – Return Of The Mack

Maroon 5 – This Love

Bruno Mars – Locked Out Of Heaven

Bruno Mars – When I Was Your Man

Zara McFarlane – Open Heart

Ella Henderson – Hard Work

Rita Ora – I Will Never Let You Down

Xavier Rudd – Love Comes And Goes

John Butler Trio – Used To Get High

Ryan Star – My Life With You

Hey Monday – How You Love Me Now

Coldplay – A Sky Full of Stars

Hozier – Take Me to Church

Prologue

Kat

April

MY EARS ACKNOWLEDGE the shrill sound of an alarm blaring in the distance. The annoying sound disturbs the little sleep I was finally getting. "Claire, shut off your bloody alarm clock. It's Saturday, for Pete's sake." I huff annoyed.

It isn't until I turn over on my side, nuzzling deeper into my duvet that I register my best friend and roommate's unfamiliar tone—*panic*. *She sounds panicked.*

Claire is on my bed yelling at me.

"Kat! Kat, come on, come on…fuck!" she shouts, tossing my covers aside. She's trying to jerk me up and out of my bed without an ounce of patience or care.

"Kat, I need you to wake the fuck up." Claire yanks on my arms, and continues to yell at me. *What the fuck?*

"Get the hell up already, Kat. We need to get the hell outta here, like, now!" She uses a force unlike any I've ever known her to possess, and it propels me out of my cozy cocoon an up-and-unsteady position; one that lands me with half of my body on the bed, the other half on the floor.

"For God's sake, what the heck are you doing? Are you drunk?" Without a word or time for me to catch my bearings, Claire pulls me up so I'm standing face-to-face with her.

1

"We need to get the fuck out of here, I said. Let's move. Now, follow my lead and stay close." Before I can respond or ask why, Claire grabs my hand and with stubborn determination, leads me out of our tenth floor Brock University dorm.

Smoke. *Is that smoke I smell?*

I'm still groggy, but as the adrenaline from being awoken so abruptly by this harsh version of Claire starts to weave its way into my system, I'm becoming more alert and aware of my immediate surroundings. I notice more and more students, all moving frantically and rushing in scattered directions, attempting to vacate the dorms as quickly as possible.

"Oh, my God! Do you smell smoke? I smell smoke. Holy shit, Claire, the dorms, I think they're on fire!" I assault her ear with information she clearly already knows. As we walk I begin to fully register what's going on. Desperation is taking over as I try to inch in closer to Claire's back, as if being closer to her will protect me. Instinctively my feet are trying to make my body pick up its pace. My fight-or-flight instincts are kicking in. It's like they know we need to get moving, they just can't seem to cooperate. *My flight instinct always wins.*

Plumes of dark smoke are flooding the halls. I can hear glass shattering in the distance and the crackle of flames seemingly closing in around us; it sounds almost like bacon frying in a pan. I can feel the temperature rising.

"I'm really scared. Claire, please, we need to hurry; we need to run."

"Dammit, Kat stay calm," she orders. "Keep walking, ease up your pace; you're gonna trip us. Just follow my lead," she scolds as she opens the door to the stairwell.

Finally.

"You're right; I'm sorry. I'm honestly trying."

"Try harder, keep clam, we got this." Claire says, her voice full of conviction.

There are a few more people in the stairwell with us, all moving in the same direction. No one seems to be talking as we all file in a line behind each other. Somehow, Claire and I lead the way.

"Please, can we go faster?" I beg her as images of people getting trampled on take shape in my mind and I hear more people moving in to the stairwell to join our evacuation efforts. "It's really getting to me. I keep thinking about getting trampled by the people behind us; can we just let them pass?"

"Stay close and try not to think about it. I'm going to get us out of here. No one's going to trample us; everyone is just trying to get out safely. Keep focused on me. I got you. Please, trust me." She is pleading with me, knowing I'm about to lose it.

As we walk down a few more flights of stairs, the smoke is intensifying, making it difficult to breathe and causing us to cough. "Cover your mouth with your sleeve." Claire commands and I do it without question. As Claire continues to guide us down the stairs, we hear a loud crash in front of us. A huge beam, engulfed in flames, falls from the rafters and blocks our escape route. As it lands, it gives off bright sparks. The lights flicker and a terrible screeching sound begins blasting from the ceiling above us.

"Fucker!" Claire yells while I scream, the severity of the situation hitting me front and centre. "We're gonna have to turn around."

We push through the smoky hallway, and face a growing line of people. My ears are quickly overloaded with sounds of others in the stairwell. People are starting to push one another, and I hear them crying, begging for us to hurry up.

"We're all going to die," some girl yells.

Watching the scene as it unfolds, my heart accelerates and my palms sweat as I fall deeper into hysteria. Claire is coughing deeper, and, oh shit, *it's getting harder to catch my breath...*

"Fuck," Claire blurts, her voice stern, but steady. *How the hell is she handling this so well?* "We need to go back up a floor and leave through the other exit door. I think I know how to get us out...I do; yeah, it'll work," she says to herself then grabs my hand, forcing me to follow as she leads us back in the direction from which we came. It's in that moment when I note just how brave my friend is. I almost smile at the thought. *Almost.*

"Follow me, Kat. Stay close." She stops us for a second, to ensure I'm on the same page. "Others will have the same problem; it might get crazy in here soon. I don't know how many of us are still inside, but with this way blocked, people are going to be frenzied trying to get out. And I don't wanna get separated," Claire instructs me through a hacking cough as she tries to pick up our pace. "We're almost there. Don't you dare give up on me, Kitty Kat," she says, using my nickname while opening the door leading to the fifth floor hallway. I'm starting to lag behind her a bit as my mind reels at the severity of the situation. When we step in to the hall, we're assaulted with the smells of melted paint and scorched wood.

"We're not going to make it! We should run for it!" I shout as the lights start flickering on and off above our heads again. I'm following so close to Claire that I can feel her hair tickling the bridge of my nose. The smoke is black, oily and thick. I'm thinking we may need to crawl the rest of the way. You know the saying 'stop, drop, and roll'? Well I feel it's getting that bad in here.

"Made it." Claire says, and offers me a small smile as she enters the door to the stairway opposite to the blocked one.

"Please don't be blocked. Please don't be blocked," I chant in a low voice as I move to follow Claire down the new set of stairs.

"Kat, stop! Hush with that. It's not helping. I'm scared too. But we need to focus on getting the hell outta here. No more talking. I said we

MY MIND'S EYE

got this." I nod. At her confession I become more worried, because up until now, Claire hasn't acted panicked or afraid.

Claire continues to lead us down the stairs without another word. After what feels like forever, we're barging through the emergency doors on the bottom floor. *Oh thank you, sweet baby Jesus.* Finally, we arrive safely on the sidewalk, metres away from the building.

The night's air is cool on my skin despite the heat radiating from the fire. The feeling of dew covering the grass only helps to coat the layer of chills over my arms and legs, as I take in everything around me. Standing in my bare feet obviously isn't helping the situation either. *Maybe I should start sleeping with socks on.*

I can hear the sounds of sirens in the distance, and I see our campus security doing all they can to contain and deal with the situation until the emergency response vehicles arrive. They really can't do a lot other than crowd control and contacting all of our families. The air smells like a mix of spring laced with that horrible melted plastic smell. People are scattered all over the perimeter in small groups, eyes wide, and mouths agape just like ours. I just can't believe it.

"God, that was fucking crazy shit," Claire yells over the approaching sirens through a harsh set of coughs, dropping my wrist from her strong hold. She trembles, her face flushed and covered with a sheen of sweat.

"You were amazing, Claire. I can't even…what happened?" I ask with a bit of a wheeze.

Claire wipes her eyes with her palms. "I heard the alarms go off, but it took me a second to understand what was happening. Then someone was yelling, *'Fire! Fire!'* I opened the door a bit to see what the hell was going on, and that's when I caught a whiff of smoke. I started to panic, but knew I had to get us out of there as fast as I could. It was scary," she says, tears streaming down her face. "I was yelling and shaking you. Jesus seriously, sleep like the dead much? I was really

5

starting to worry there for a few minutes. I wasn't sure what I was going to do; you wouldn't budge. I really can't believe how deeply you were sleeping. Especially with those alarms going off like that, it's not like you. Are you all right?" Claire whisper-yells to me as we stand in front of our dorm, the glowing flames of the blaze reaching out of almost every window. I can see the fire's glow reflecting off the students as we all stand watching.

God, that fire spread fast.

I half listen to her as she continues, but I'm stuck thinking: *Why didn't I hear the alarm?* I'm usually such a light sleeper. I barely sleep, ever.

Huge angry flames engulf our residence. Each flicker is a slow, powerful movement intent on taking over everything in its path. Windows shatter as the flames reach higher and higher, and smoke fills the night sky. Seething inch by molten inch, this inferno is swallowing most, or rather *all*, of our belongings. *Damn, I hope everyone made it out safely.*

"Shit!" I mutter more to myself than to Claire, but she catches it anyway.

"What?" she asks.

My Imovane.

I have suffered from insomnia since my first year of university. My doctor diagnosed me with what is commonly known as Primary Acute Insomnia. Which, lucky for me, means it's not a result of a medical condition such as asthma or cancer. He also informed me it's likely the result of having elevated anxiety levels, which, in my case, makes complete sense. I am, and always have been, a bit of what people refer to as "a stress ball, uptight, or worry wart." Whatever you want to call it. I'm a stressed-out person. According to Claire, if I were to become a Transformer, I would be called Stressor.

Since the end of first year, it's just gotten worse. By my second year, having realized my sleep issues weren't going away and weren't exactly normal either, I consulted my doctor. The other good thing about Primary Acute Insomnia is that it comes and goes; some weeks are better than others, so I'm not always a walking zombie. This is also why I pick and choose when I take a pill. I'm not a big fan of taking a sleeping aid, as it really makes me groggy the next day and I don't like the idea of becoming dependent. I usually try not to take one unless it's been a rough two or three nights and I know I need the help.

"Last night, I took one of the sleeping pills Doctor. Benson prescribed for me," I say, shaking my head more at the irony of the situation than the fact that such a little pill can pack such a punch. "Of all the times I decide to take one, this happens. It's been a few days now since I've had any sleep, so I figured I should be well-rested for the trip home."

"Well, that explains it. Maybe you should see about getting a lower dose, 'cause, girl that shit knocked you out!" Claire jokes, clearly trying to make light of the situation. "Thank God I didn't stay at Laurie and Jenn's last night like I had planned. I would hate for anything to have happened to you. I can't even imagine…" She whispers the last bit, but I catch it. Her words impact me immediately.

What?

Sirens, accompanied by flashing red and blue lights, approach on the horizon, only solidifying the gravity of the situation. My ears catch the voices of other people in the vicinity; they are coughing, crying, attempting to soothe one another. There are now hundreds of our fellow students here on the sidelines in the middle of the night, gaping in shock at the reality of this situation. This fire is sure to change all of our lives.

Standing beside Claire, waiting for the firefighters, I distantly hear her go on and on about how they'd better be hot. I know she's trying to brighten the mood; however, all I can think about is what could have happened to me tonight if Claire hadn't been home. Goosebumps settle over my skin, as I shudder at the thought.

The fire's glow radiates from the building and I can almost feel the blaze as its heat kisses my skin. *I could still be in there.* That's when I feel it, when the full impact of her words hit me like a ton of bricks.

Suddenly, I'm having a hard time catching my breath. "I…what?" I'm gasping, unable to get the words out. "What do you mean imagine? Oh my God! What if you weren't home? What if I didn't wake up?"

My heart is beating so fast I can feel its heavy pounding echoing in my ears. The anxiety slamming its way in overwhelms me, consuming my mind. I reach for my chest to try and lull the panic that is taking over. Teetering in my stance, everything begins to fade. I feel weak, dizzy. *Fuck, I can't breathe.* I bend over, trying to even out my breathing, but it's no use. The repercussions are too much for me to bear. Then, by some small stroke of luck, I'm pulled tightly into a familiar set of arms before succumbing to the panic. Arms that demand I fight, arms that offer support, comfort. And, thank goodness, it's enough. Slowly, I regain control as a sense of calm washes over me. I silently thank the 'best friend gods' for giving me Claire, who is always there for me; especially tonight.

"Kat, I didn't mean anything by it. I was just thinking out loud. Fuck, you need to calm down. Take a deep breath, just try and focus." Claire faces me, mimicking how I should take calming breaths. "Oh shit, I'm sorry. I wasn't thinking. I'm upset. I was just rambling. You need to keep taking big, calming breaths, Kat, please." I can tell she's upset, but it doesn't help me. I still can't quite seem to stop all of the 'what ifs' from creeping into my mind.

Finally, after what feels like forever, I'm able to even out my breathing. I'm thankful for Doctor Benson teaching me—or rather forcing me—to learn those breathing exercises designed to help me relax. He said to use them on nights when I'm feeling a bit like Stressor, but don't want to take the Imovane. Doctor Benson had warned me on my last visit that if I continue down this path, not only will I need a sleep aid but he also might have to insist on adding an anti-anxiety pill into the mix.

"I'm going to be all right. I just had a bit of a panic attack but I'm okay. I'm feeling better already. I know you didn't mean anything by it. I couldn't stop the scary thoughts from getting to me. Fuck, it's like a feeling of doom took over," I tell her. "Honestly, I'm fine."

Claire squeezes me closer to her while we stand side-by-side. We stare as the firefighters make their way closer to battle the blaze; which has now engulfed everything in a mass of amber light that I can imagine is being seen for miles. A blaze that I could have still been stuck inside of. I shake my head to rid myself of the thought. Again, I think, *Thank God for Claire.* I try to keep that gratitude in the front of my mind, along with or the hope that this night doesn't end as a tragedy for anyone. I silently pray that everyone is safe tonight.

While we're waiting to give our statements to the police, Claire smiles and says, "Well as you often like to point out, I like to find the silver lining to everything. And I've got one for us here, the fact that we just finished our exams and it's summer vacation is a huge lucky break."

"You're right, I can't begin to think of where the hell we would have lived or how we would have been able to study while we finished the year, and how we'd replace our stuff—" I start rambling, but Claire is quick to cut me off.

"Jesus, Kat, stop. You're gonna make yourself have another panic attack. Slow down with that imagination of yours. None of it matters. Your parents will be here soon, I'm sure security got a hold of them by now, and we'll have a few months to deal will all the aftermath. Breathe, Kitty Kat. I was just saying we were lucky to be going home for the summer, so we don't have to deal with this shit right now. I wasn't trying to make you go crazy with those notions of yours."

"I know. You're right. I just can't get out of my head sometimes."

She nods. "I know, young Jedi. We'll get you there, but, hey, just think, we're heading home and we'll have lots of time to replace our stuff, meet boys, and best of all, *neither* of us," she glares at me, "will be doing any kind of studying until September. See? We're lucky." Claire winks.

I know she's trying to distract me. She is more than aware that I'm not fine. Although, I think, *Yeah, she's right. I'm lucky.* I really do need to work on getting out of my own head.

I clear my throat before stepping in front of her, stopping us for a moment on the sidewalk as we're following a security officer who's directing us to one of the many school buses. Buses they've brought in to take us all to the police station, as we all need to give our statements and wait for our parents to come pick us up.

"Claire," I say, putting my hand on her shoulder. "I don't know how to thank you. Honestly, I hate to think what would have happened if—"

"Stop." Claire raises her hand between us, her tone telling me to listen to her carefully.

"Don't say it. Don't even fucking think it," she counters, pulling me into a full-blown hug. "We are both safe, and that's all that matters. From this moment on, don't think about anything other than that."

I nod in agreement as I hug her back, tears streaming down both of our faces.

"I love you" I whisper in her ear. She moves, pulling away just enough so we are now face-to-face.

"I love you too, Kitty Kat. I'll always have your back. Remember that." She gives me a big sloppy kiss on the side of my face.

"Eww, what the hell?" I cringe, wiping my face with my sleeve.

"Tension breaker," she shrugs, and for the first time since she woke me up, we share a small laugh.

I always knew Claire was my best friend, but with tonight's events, I realize even more how special this girl is and just how lucky I am to have her in my life.

Chapter 1

Kat

July

"JEEZ, THAT WAS a lot of work. I usually love to shop, but, man, that was a workout. I'm surprised we managed to get it all back here," I say, feeling overwhelmed looking at the pile of bags, boxes, and suitcases littering the basement of my parents' home. Claire and I have finished another round of shopping; we've been trying to replace as much as we can of everything we lost in the fire before we head back to school next month.

"I think we've got everything we need. I can't think of anything I've missed. You?" Claire asks.

"Nope, I think I've replaced all the important things I needed for now," I tell her, looking around the room. "We sure did some damage today. Good thing we rented the bigger moving truck."

"Hey, Kat?"

"Yeah?"

Claire nudges me. "I guess now we know how Julia Roberts felt in *Pretty Woman*. It's too bad we didn't have a Richard Gere there to help us out. Not that your mom wasn't awesome, but I could have used a little eye candy and muscle to carry my bags." She laughs before sorting her stuff from mine.

I'm lucky my parents bought me renter's insurance for the things I lost in the dorm fire. As for the aftermath, other than a couple people suffering minor burns and a few with broken bones, no one was seriously hurt. I don't think I could have handled it if anyone had been. With the fire being deemed an electrical issue, the insurance company was quicker than expected in sending my parents the cheque; which was more than enough to cover our losses. Shopping for new furniture, clothes, and other items was actually a lot of fun. But I'm glad we're done now.

"You know, as much as I'm going to miss all of my old things, I need to tell ya, I'm pretty frickin' excited about all of our new stuff," Claire says. "Especially the new MacBooks we were able to squeeze in with the insurance money. Ours were way in need of replacing."

"I know. I think I bought mine in the eleventh grade. Definitely an exciting purchase," I agree as I pull the white box out of the Apple Store bag. "I totally need to go to Apple school, though. We both know how non-tech savvy I am."

Claire and I nod in agreement at my comment, because it's absolutely true. My new Mac has way too much power for the likes of me.

The dorm fire is an event that has helped me realize how quickly you can lose important things in this life. Many of the trivial little pieces of our lives, we take for granted, having deemed them unimportant until they are gone. I had hoped to at least salvage a few personal mementos, but unfortunately, the blaze left me with nothing. Not even the building survived; it collapsed. Some of those items are irreplaceable; like the picture of my Nana and me at the school talent show where I had won first place. Or the quilt my mom made me out of all my old concert t-shirts. I loved that blanket; it reminded me of home. I can't dwell on it and I know this. It only stresses me out and won't change the outcome.

I can't speak for Claire, but I know the fire took a bit more from me than just my stuff that night. Now, each day, I will be grateful for my life and will work on trying to 'live a little,' as Claire puts it. I often think about how lucky I was that night. I still get this crazy, tight feeling in my chest and throat whenever I think on it for too long. But, as time passes, the panic is shrinking more and more. I started seeing a therapist shortly after the fire, because I wasn't able to stop the anxiety from ambushing my thoughts, and it was beginning to really affect me. After a few bad panic attacks in the weeks following the fire, and talking with my parents, it seemed like talking to a professional might help.

I started seeing Doctor Lukas, a psychologist who treats trauma survivors, as per Doctor Benson's recommendation. I was seeing him twice a week in order to help me process my thoughts and feelings. It was the best decision I could have made. It turns out, I basically have some form of PTSD. Luckily, with Doctor Lukas' help, I've made so much progress that I no longer have regular appointments. We decided I could see him on a monthly basis if I feel the need, or I can simply call in and book an appointment through Lynn, his secretary. As my own method of self-help, I stumbled upon a really great website that I visit periodically. The Toronto Trauma Survivor Group is an amazing site that I visit when I need some peace of mind. It also helps me to justify some of the extra safety habits I have come to adopt as a result of the fire, such as taking the stairs rather than an elevator, or sitting near the exit door whenever possible. Doctor Lukas tells me it's all part of my PTSD, and that the bouts of paranoia will likely lessen over time; as long as I continue to seek help when needed. Visiting this website also helps reassure me I am still, indeed, normal. I'm a normal person having normal responses to an abnormal event. It's also nice to see there are others out there who take the same precautions after having survived a traumatic event, one I'll never forget.

"Claire, did you see the emergency box? I want to make sure we have it."

"Yes, it's right there on top of the box with my new desk in it," she says. "Don't worry, we won't forget it. I'll make sure. I put it there last night when your dad and I brought the desk down. I figured that way we know it will get put in the truck." Claire rubs my arm. She knows how important it is to me.

I taper down my memories of the fire, uttering a silent thanks to my fairy godmother that no one was badly hurt and for looking out for all of us on that day. *Especially me.* This thanking routine has become something I find myself doing anytime I think back and remember that fiery night.

"I still can't believe how much stuff we've managed to accumulate between us. I didn't realize how much we actually needed to replace," I note, while sifting through the pile after double-checking all the items in my emergency box are, indeed, still there.

"I am so glad we each have our own room this year. How the hell did we ever have space to move around in that damn dorm?" Claire questions as we continue to sort through the bags. "See, there is always a silver lining…a bright side, if you will, to any situation. You just need to let yourself find it." She grins and I nod.

Claire Knox will always be my bright side, my very own silver lining finder.

Chapter 2

Kat

August

CLAIRE AND I are moving back to campus early, with help from the movers and my mom and dad. They insisted on coming to help us for at least half the day. I think my mom is more worried about how I'll react to the new living arrangements than anything. But seeing as I need my dad to install a few things, it actually works out perfectly. We're moving back just over a month before classes start because we were both lucky enough to score waitressing jobs at the popular bar, Pub Fiction.

Apparently, Pub Fiction has just gone through a big turnover in staff, and Levi, the owner, asked if we'd like to start work early. Seeing as my usual summer job fell through, this was just what I needed. With school starting in September, most of our classmates wouldn't be coming back to school for another few weeks. Thankfully, my parents are okay with Claire and me only spending a part of our summer vacation back home with them this year. My mom took more convincing than my dad, but in the end, she understood that we are two twenty-two-year-old women who need to start being more independent.

"Oh, wow!" I say as we unlock the front door and step inside, beaming with relief as we arrive at our new home for the school year. It's perfect. It's crisp and clean and smells of fresh linen with hints of vanilla lingering in the air. The smell reminds me of my favourite candle combination called My Fresh Laundry from CandleWorx. Looking around, I let out a sigh of relief; thankful it's not a dive. I was admittedly worried the house would be run-down, having been lived in by students over the years. It's hard when you move into a place you've never seen, unfortunately that is the life of students living the dorm life…You get what's available. But it's honestly in perfect condition. *Ugh, I really am a stressor, aren't I?*

"Nothing like finishing up our last year in style, hey, Claire? This place looks awesome," I say as I continue to take in my surroundings. I feel a sense of calm at the looks of our new home and neighbourhood. I've heard nothing but good things about these residences and cannot wait to experience it for myself. The house is located on a cul-de-sac, which is one big loop with condo-style townhouses along either side, allowing up to six students per house. It's honestly a little slice of university heaven, especially for us seniors.

The Village, as it's called, has been open for about five years and is in the best location on campus. It's close to everything—always allowing for an extra few minutes of shut-eye—compared to our old dorm room, which was all the way on the outskirts of the campus grounds. The real highlight for me is having my own room and a non-communal bathroom. *That shit is just wrong.* Claire is right; there are a few ways to see some kind of a silver lining to that fire.

"I know! How lucky are we to get a spot in the Village and manage to stay together on top of it? Somebody must definitely like us," says Claire. "I heard from Lucy Scott the other day that many of them ended up with new roommates this year. She and Sue aren't together, and they've been roommates since first year."

Not getting to stay roommates with Claire would have been devastating for me. Between the fire and the 'what if's' still always looming in the back of my mind, combined with the shit from my ass-of-an-ex,

Seth, not having Claire might have been the straw that broke the camel's back.

"Oh, God, I can't imagine not being roommates. That would have been terrible. I don't think I could stand to be away from you, Claire Bear. You're my back-up, the cheese to my macaroni, the fork to my knife, my bestie…most of all you are *my sister from another mister!*" We both end up reciting the last bit. Claire and I have been saying that silly chant since we were little girls and getting into all sorts of trouble.

Claire Knox and I have been friends for as long as I can remember. We've always been thick as thieves; our fathers referring to us as "double trouble." Growing up, our families were practically next-door neighbours, living only four houses apart on Valley Drive in the city of Stoney Creek. We vacationed together and always celebrated every holiday as one huge group. Looking back, I barely have any memories that don't include Claire and her parents, Tom and Maggie.

When she was fourteen, her parents died suddenly in a car crash while driving home from a work function. It was devastating. Seeing that our moms had been best friends since they were kids, it was a no-brainer that Claire would move in with us. With my parents being named in their last will and testament as the ones to care for Claire, the transition of her moving in with us was a non-issue. And, as a team, we coped and supported each other through one of the hardest times in our lives. Without a doubt, Claire and I are better when we are together.

"Okay, Kat, your father and I are going to get out of your hair and let you get on with getting settled," my mom says as she gathers the boxes and packing peanuts from the kitchen where she unpacked our cookware. "He's almost done with installing the extra carbon monoxide detectors. We may need one more for the basement, he said, but other than that, you're all set." She smiles warmly, knowing how important these things are to me.

"Perfect. I can grab an extra one from the store if we need it. Are you sure you don't want to stay, Mom? It's almost supper and I think we're going to order pizza soon."

"No, it's all right, honey. You and Claire have this time, get to know the other girls and finish with the movers. I don't have a clue where you ladies want all this stuff anyway," she laughs. "Besides, your father is done checking all the smoke detectors, and the new fire extinguishers have all been installed in your room and the upstairs bathrooms. I know he's tired, and we have a long drive ahead. But thanks, sweetheart." She hugs me and I revel in her warmth. My parents have been amazing with my crazy need to feel extra safe in our new home.

"Thank God the girls all seem really nice, too, eh?" I say, as we're unloading the rest of our belongings from the moving truck. Having met our roommates, (we all decided to move in early so we could spend time getting to know one another before the school year) I have a very good feeling about them. I'm relieved. I've been agonizing about whether or not we would get along, or if they'd be a bunch a rowdy freshman girls.

As soon as we all met, I was instantly put at ease; especially since Amanda, Kym, Beth, and Radha seemed to have been just as nervous as I was, which caused me to relax big time. The last thing I need is to be having battles on the home front.

"Yes, I was really worried," says Claire. "More for you than me, though. You know me, I love a good party, and I have amazing stamina."

Love to party, does she ever, I laugh to myself before she finishes.

"I know you were worried they'd be a bunch of freshman party animals, and how you need to keep your focus on school, so I'm glad they are more on the quiet side," she continues. "I think we'll get along well. I'm excited to be the resident party girl. Maybe I can corrupt you all."

Claire beams, the smile on her face giving off a look I know all too well. She is already cooking up raging party plans in her head. I grin at her comment, because over the years, Claire has definitely helped bring me out of my shell. I can only imagine how serious she might be about the notion of corrupting some new blood.

"Hey, Kat!" she says.

"Yeah?"

"Now that I know you're feeling better about the new roomies situation, I have to say, since you don't have to worry about the girls, you'll be able to focus on school and boys this year. I mean, come on, Kitty, have you seen some of the hotties walking around here? Yummy!" Claire yells, as she heads inside with another box. "I say we forget the unpacking and go introduce ourselves to the neighbour-hood." I know Claire is essentially egging me on. She knows my priorities, but she's just enough of a little shit to test my resistance anytime she can.

"Absolutely not, no way. The last thing I need is to get caught up in a relationship. I have enough going on with a new house, unpack-ing, the new job, new friends, and our final year and placements. Oh, and let's not forget to throw in that shithead, Seth. That ass is still trying to win me back. I am done."

"Oh, come on, Kitty Kat. You can't deny yourself fun forever. And nothing says fun like hot sex with a super-hot stud," she says with a smirk on her face.

"You're relentless," I say, offering a scowl at her suggestion. "Listen to me, chick. This year is all about school and work. Only work and school. What I will not be adding to my year is more boy troubles. Fuck. That." I cross my arms over my chest, levelling her with a glare, which I hope shows her I am not backing down on this one.

I'm by no means a prude or a Debbie Downer, but I'm certainly not a drunken sorority girl looking to hook-up and marry the beyond-too-cool, popular quarterback. I have goals and a plan, and some cocky player isn't going to mess that up. The last thing I need is more pressure. Besides, Seth is all the boy trouble I can handle as it is.

I shake off the image of my ex, who has become a pain in my ass, trying to wear me down, to give him the chance to let him "explain" things to me. I've been ignoring his calls and texts for months now. Shuddering at the thought of Seth, I offer to take Claire over to Starbucks for a well-deserved moving break, to which she agreed instantly. "Hell yes, I could totally go for a java fix. It's almost nine o'clock. I am done for tonight, chick. Let me grab my purse," Claire replies before heading to her room.

"I'll meet you outside, Claire Bear," I shout. I ask the other girls if they want to come, but they're all busy unpacking. Standing on the little porch, I notice how the sky seems lit up with what I imagine is millions of stars. I smile while looking up, admiring them and thinking of how all these stars could be symbols of the good things to come. *I sure hope so.*

I spend the next few days settling into our new place, getting to know the girls, and happily embracing the fresh start to the school year.

Chapter 3

Kat

A week later

"DUDE, YOU REALLY need to paint your room; this yellow is terrible. How can you sleep in here?" I ask Claire. I'm sitting on her bed flipping through *Cosmo* while she's destroying her already mess of a closet, looking for clothes.

"I haven't had time. I've had better things to do with myself." She exhales a deep breath. "Besides, I like it. I think I'm going to leave it, actually. I feel like it's my homage to the sun, and you know how much I love the sun and all things hot." She giggles while looking through her closet.

I laugh at her because she's such a dork sometimes. "Well, it's ugly if you ask me, but I guess it does kinda suit you and your sunny disposition," I tease.

I continue to flip through my magazine, sharing the odd tidbit of gossip with Claire. I'm waiting on her to need me, as I've been entrusted with the very important BFF job of "outfit checker." The job where you tell them how great their outfit looks, just to have them change in the end again anyway. Well, yeah, that's what I've been summoned to do for Claire tonight.

"Who'd have guessed that the fire would have actually turned out to be a good thing?" Claire asks as she's zipping up her dark wash jean skirt. She's on her tenth outfit now, I swear. She's dolling herself up all

22

sexy for her date with Colby, the hottie next door.

"You didn't just say that, did you?" I question, rolling my eyes at her comment before continuing to read the article on the latest hair trends.

"What? Silver lining remember? We're always looking for the silver linings."

"Whatever," I say. "I'm not really sure boys are considered a silver lining, but I'll go with it." I can't believe how boy crazy Claire can be while still finding time for school and her friends. Sometimes I wish I was more like her, and less like the worrywart I tended to be.

"Are you nervous to start work at Pub Fiction?" Claire enquires as she's deciding on what shirt to pair with her denim skirt.

Pub Fiction is located downtown and is pretty much the hottest hangout for the locals and university students, as well as the younger working-class crowds in the area. I landed a shooter girl position, while Claire will be working as bartender at the main bar. While she's getting ready for her date, I'm supposed to be getting ready for my first training shift, but I'm clearly sidetracked. Starting work at Pub Fiction is something I'm pretty stoked about, to be honest. With a few weeks to go before the fall semester, I want to make as much money as I can. My goal is to save up enough to make a big payment toward my loan. It's a bit of wishful thinking on my part, but it would be nice.

My family is your typical blue-collar, middle-class household; but my parents have recently taken a financial hit with my brother Wes and me being in university at the same time. My parents are very big on us getting an education. They have always made us the deal that as long as we work part-time, they will pay half of our tuition. I have been very lucky to have that help. I do have some student loans that I will be paying back after graduation, but not nearly as much as a few of my friends. My parents are really great and have always been supportive of us, but they can be a bit overbearing when it comes to school. They've raised us with the idea that a good education should always be our main priority, which will help to better ensure we find ourselves good jobs. Jobs that will, hopefully, allow for the freedoms that go along with financial security. Plus, with me being in my last year, it's probably a good idea to start trying to support myself as much as possible. Clearly, I can't depend on my parents and their generosity forever. I'm a grown woman and they have done way more than necessary for me. My grandparents left money in their will to help toward our education, but my parents have struggled regardless. My father often works overtime at the steel plant and my mother teaches summer school and extra classes in the fall. Besides, with Wes in his first year, my parents will be paying tuition money for a few more years to come, so I think the least I can do is to start trying to pay my own way. And from what I hear, there is a ton of money to be made in tips at Pub Fiction.

"I am a little. I mean, I've waitressed before, but Molly's Grill is no bar, and I was never a shooter girl. Maybe I should have applied to be a bartender like you. I really should have taken that mixology class with you last year; then I would have had that along with my Smart Serve waitressing certification. At least that way I wouldn't have to think about falling flat on my face while carrying a tray full of drinks."

"Oh, my goodness, you'll do great. I would think carrying a tray full of shots will be a lot lighter than all those plates of food were," she says. I nod at her point because she's probably right. Toting trays of shooters should be a breeze compared to lugging those heavy plates. I think it's the bar atmosphere that has me more worried. God, I'm my own worst enemy at times. Seems I can always find something to stress about.

"Maybe you'll meet a nice little cutie who you can hook up with tonight after your shift?" Claire teases. I shake my head at my friend always trying to pimp me out. I ignore her comment, moving right along without entertaining her suggestion.

"How about you? Are you excited for your hot date tonight?" I ask. We have only been here a week, and already Claire is announcing, "Boys, I'm here!" to any potential prey living within our little neighbourhood. "I swear you might as well get a squad car megaphone and call the boys outside for a meet-and-greet," I tease her while laughing at the face she makes. I actually think my comment may have shocked *the* Claire Knox.

"Listen here, friend. It's not my fault if I attract the opposite sex. If they happen to find me, you can't possibly blame me for that." She smirks, feigning innocence. "It's totally not my fault. All I was doing was sitting on the porch, reading one of my smut books on my Kindle, and taking a much-deserved break from unpacking. He was walking up to the house next door and we just happened to spot each other. Turns out he lives there, so naturally, we struck up a conversation, and by the end, he offered to help if I needed it. See, not my fault," she says, shrugging.

"Uh-hmm, whatever you say, Claire Bear."

"I consider myself quite lucky for finding such a gorgeous man so quickly. Have you met anyone yet, Miss Snotty McUptightface?"

"Oh, sweet Claire," I mock, hands on my hips. "I think, by definition, unpacking means opening boxes and actually putting things away, not just rifling through them whenever you need something. Besides, maybe you should spend less time focusing on me and my lack of a love life, and more time unpacking all of your damn stuff." I glance over to the back corner of her room before adding my last dig.

"Oh, whatever, Kat." She sticks out her tongue at me. "There's time for that shit later. You need to get your priorities in check, woman. It's time to focus on adding some fun in there. I think your priority list should be: Boys, boys, parties, then boys again. Who cares about all the other shit? There's always time for that stuff," she insists

25

while following my eyes to the back corner of her room.

"I'm thinking the crazy, leaning tower you have over there needs to be your top priority, Claire Bear," I say. "That is a huge safety hazard; one that is going to cause you some serious pain when it falls on you." But it's true; she's got boxes stacked so high that they're almost taller than me.

"Dude, you really need to unpack that stuff." I grin before singing, *"Honey, we're home, time to knock the tower down!"* At the sound of my lameness, we both fall into a fit of laughter.

"She is right you know," Radha says, popping her head in the doorway. "That thing is scary over there." She nods in the direction of Claire's tower.

"Yeah, yeah, I'll get to it." She waves us off.

"Kym and I are heading out to grab some groceries. You wanna join?"

"No, sorry, we can't right now. I wish I could, but I have work tonight and Claire has her date with Colby. Thanks for asking anyway."

"But, please let us know how much we owe you guys. How about Kat and I go next time? Maybe we can all take turns? We can talk about it together this weekend when we're all around."

"Oh, right, I didn't realize how late it was already. I've been busy getting all my stuff put away. But yeah, that sounds good. Text me what you want, and I'll be sure to grab it." She smiles before leaving. "I'll see you ladies later. Kym is waiting outside already. I better get moving," her voice echoes from down the hall.

Sighing, Claire finally looks around at the mess. "I'll try to tackle it this weekend. I should have time between my date tonight and my shift at Pub Fiction tomorrow, that is, if I make it a priority anyway." She grins.

With the unpacking plan all hashed out, Claire continues to give me all the juicy deets about Colby.

"He's super sweet. As soon as I mentioned we had just moved in the day before, he straightaway offered his help with moving stuff and whatnot; of course I totally took him up on his offer. Especially with that damn desk. There was no way I was getting it together all by myself. Besides, have you seen him?"

"Yes, I sure have. He is definitely your type. All looks and muscles."

"Well, then you should also know, girl," Claire says, "that you never turn down that kind of help."

I chuckle in response. *Oh, Claire, totally boy crazy.* She always has been; it's just part of her charm.

"I don't know where this will go, but we really hit it off. Colby and I have a lot in common. I've really liked getting to know him. I'm actually excited about this one."

"Well, I'm glad. I hope you guys have a great time and are a match made in Village heaven. Who knows, right? Maybe my Claire Bear is growing up and will have a real-life relationship with a man. Maybe you'll actually show this guy the real Claire Knox, eh?"

"Oh, my God, Kat. Let's not get crazy. I mean, jeez, I can't go showing just any guy the wizard behind the curtain, now can I? The reality of that is just too great for any mere mortal of a man."

With this, she smiles, but for a fraction of a second, I see doubt in her eyes. Sure, Claire is tough as nails and has overcome great personal tragedy, but I know she hurts. She doesn't talk about her parents too often, but I *know* her. She isn't always the girl she portrays herself to be. One day she will break, and I will be there for her as she has always been for me. Thick as thieves, *me and my sister from another mister.*

Claire has always been the more outgoing of the two of us, especially where the opposite sex is involved. I prefer to be chased rather than put myself out there so openly. But right now, I just don't need the hassle of a relationship, or feel the need to rely on anyone other than myself, especially after Seth. I'm a bit more reserved than Claire. I would never have the guts to ask a complete stranger for help, let alone initiate a conversation with a random person. If it had been me, I probably wouldn't have said a word to Colby, even if he is our neighbour. I might have offered a smile and maybe a wave. It takes me a bit longer to trust men, thanks again to Seth, the cheating dickhead. Since we broke up, I've been watching from the bench. I'll get back in the game soon, I'm sure. However, it will take the right guy to pull me from the comfort of the sidelines.

Claire thinks I spend too much time worrying about getting my school assignments done and working, rather than cutting loose and having a string of dates lined up each week. She and I are like day and night sometimes. It's amusing how different we can be, but to me, we're simply the perfect balance. She's the yin to my yang. And I wouldn't change a thing about her.

"We're just going to dinner and a movie," Claire says. "We've been spending time together here and there. But, yes, before you ask, I am kind of nervous and excited to actually go out on an official date with him and see if there is anything more than friendship and sexual attraction between us. I mean for now, it seems we're compatible in the important areas, but I want to see if he's committed dating material," she quips as I start heading toward my bedroom realizing the time. I need to get ready for my shift; I hadn't realized how long we'd been chatting.

I walk into my room—my *own* room, let me remind you—and I take a moment to breathe and admire my haven. I love it! I've painted the room in light lavender, which is beyond the perfect colour. It makes me smile every time I look at the walls.

After rooming in a small dorm for what seems like forever, I enjoy retreating to my private space to read, do homework, or to simply relax in peace. I'm still super social with the other girls, but to be honest, there are times when I long to bail and just hide out in my room. Deciding I really do need to focus and get ready, I jump to it. Lord knows, I don't want to be late on my first day; definitely not the impression I'm aiming for.

I grab my new uniform off my favourite black and purple armchair; the one my mom insisted would just "make my space." *You'd think she hosted her own show on HGTV.* I slip on the uniform Claire picked up for me last week, look down, and end up doing a double take. After putting it on, I stand staring, a bit in shock to be honest, at the very barely there shorts, which I'm to pair with the seriously small and low-cut matching V-necked shirt.

Oh, shit. I move to stand in front of the mirror, staring at my reflection. I try to convince myself there must be some mistake as I look at the way they mould to my body like a second skin. *This can't possibly be mine. There is no way Levi wants us to wear this?* I quickly duck my head out and yell down the hall.

"Claire! I think you have my shirt, or you grabbed me the wrong shirt size, for sure, 'cause this shit is tight. *Way* too tight!" I wiggle around, trying to stretch it out.

"Oh." She laughs, coming into my room, staring at me in my tight-ass outfit. "I assume this is the first time you've put them on, then?"

"Clearly," I say, waving my hand down the length of myself. "I've just been too busy unpacking and spending time with the other girls, trying to get to know them better. It just completely escaped my mind," I explain, knowing what she's thinking—it's really unlike me to leave stuff like this to the last minute. But, honestly, I wasn't expecting the clothes to be this tight.

"Yes, uh…sorry to be the bearer of bad news, but there is no mistake, my friend. That is definitely your top. Mine's just as bad, if it makes you feel any better. Well, my boobs are smaller, so mine isn't as tight, but these shirts sure do hug the girls, better get used to it." Claire shrugs like it's no big deal. "You actually lucked out by getting those shorts you have on there because the other choice for bottoms was a skirt that would make a stripper blush. You're probably going to be more covered than some of the others so that's good news."

Awesome. Leave it to Claire to always try and find the bright side of things. I laugh at the visual of her stripper comment, but I'm still not impressed. *How did I miss that this was the uniform?*

"You should be thanking me. After all, it's your fault. It was your lazy-ass who decided to sleep in rather than pick up your uniform. And you should have tried it on. Who waits until the day of to try their uniform on, anyway?" Claire adds, in a mockingly bitchy tone. "I'd go as far as saying you owe me. You almost got stuck with the shortest skirt I have ever seen, and you know me, I like my stuff short, but I can admit they were way short. But seeing as I'm the best person you know, I saved your snatch from being on display during work hours."

At that, I have no choice but to bow down to her. "You're right. My apologies, oh Great One. I definitely owe you, and shall it be my first-born? Or is me paying for our next mani-pedi enough? I mean, after all, it's not like I get a ton of regular sleep. But yeah, yeah, rub it in. You're my snatch-saving hero." I move my arm across my forehead and feign a dramatic sigh.

Claire snorts. "Well, if it means your tight ass will get laid, then I choose your first born. Yes, yes, that'll square us," she says, tapping her finger to her chin as if in contemplation. "Best get on that right away, like, tonight. I've got no immediate plans after this year, so, yup, mom it is." She beams.

"Oh, sure, I'll get right on it. How about this, think this will work? Hello there, my handsome. My name is Kat; it's my first day. You're hot. Wanna fuck and, hopefully, impregnate me to pay off my snatch debt to my asshole of a bestie?" We both laugh and quickly continue getting ready, despite how reluctant I may be about it.

I decide to make the best of what I've got, despite knowing it's never going to be enough to make me comfy. I try my damnedest to tuck in all my lady bits. *God, this shit is tight.* I glance at myself one last time in the full-length mirror. I note that, despite being tight, it's very flattering actually, hugging me in all the right places. Places I'm not used to having hugged, I guess. That's the part that makes me the most nervous. I just don't want people thinking this is me. I'm definitely more of a jeans and t-shirt type of girl.

I move to my dressing table to put on some makeup. I'm not a huge makeup fan, not because I don't like it, but more because I don't really know what the hell I'm doing. I mean, I can do the basics, but getting all dolled up isn't really my forte. My mom doesn't wear it; therefore, I missed out on that whole makeup bonding experience where she might have taught me Face Applying 101. According to my mom, we Rollins ladies just don't need it, which isn't really too far off the mark. I do have to admit; I've been blessed with a clear complexion, rarely having breakouts, which allows me to usually get away with only a tinted moisturizer.

I'm a simple 'dab of foundation and lip gloss' girl, but seeing as my goal is to make good money in tips, I decide to go into 'full face' mode. I smooth on foundation and cover-up, brush on powdery pink blusher, and smudge on some grey eye shadow and dark eyeliner; which helps my green eyes stand out. I finish off with some mascara and lip gloss, then spray on a bit of my favourite Viva La Juicy perfume. I give my hair one last look over in the mirror as I make my way to the door, shutting off my light before heading to see Claire in the living room.

"Jesus, Kat, you're gonna make a killing in tips tonight! That shirt sure shows off your best assets. Those other waitresses are going to hate you!" she says.

"That's perfect, just what I needed to hear. Way to help me squash my already fluttering nerves, chick," I reply, giving her a dirty look. "I'm already feeling super awkward, like I'm showing off all my wobbly bits. I don't think I can handle worrying that I'm overstepping or anything with the other girls." I sigh, dropping my hands to my sides in defeat. "Do you think they're going to think that? Like I'm there to poach their tips and stuff?" I'm starting to ramble now, my nerves getting the best of me. "I'm not like that. Oh, maybe I can't do this; maybe working in a bar isn't for me..." I trail off, pacing the living room now.

"Calm down—" Claire starts but is interrupted, thank the stars.

"Wow, Kat," Beth says, coming into the living room with a bowl of ice cream. "Don't panic; you look very pretty all done up. I agree, you will definitely stand out, but I do think it's a bit sexist you having to wear that, to be honest, especially in this day and age," she quips. "Please don't get me wrong, you look amazing, and that seems to be the norm for bars. Tight and sexy. As for the other girls, they will love you. You're too sweet for them not to. Don't listen to Claire," she says, sticking her tongue out in Claire's direction.

"Thanks, Beth." I let out a relieved breath. "I'm glad you think I look okay. I'm just nervous. It's not what I'm used to wearing. Tight clothes aren't really my thing," I say while tugging the shirt out from the inside, trying to stretch it again. She smiles.

"Just leave it; it's not as bad as you think," Claire assures.

"I do have one question, however," Beth begins. "Do the guys at least walk around shirtless to make up for your uniform? Like, will I get some man-candy when we all go there drinking?"

I laugh at her question because I doubt it. "I don't think they do, but they should, shouldn't they?"

"Hell yeah they should, especially if the guys are haw-t." Beth drawls, making me laugh. I'm really loving this girl so far. She's a perfect mix of level-headed with a side of spunk.

"You're too sensitive. Please don't worry," Claire interjects. I think she realizes I took her comment about the others hating me the wrong way. "I know they are all gonna love you, trust me. It's impossible not to. Beth is right. It's just you look slammin'. Your makeup looks great, those beautiful green eyes of yours are popping, and your hair looks fab. I'm just stating the obvious. Take a compliment, would ya? All I'm saying is, with you in that outfit, those other shooter girls might as well go home, for real." She laughs. "No dude is gonna want a shot from them with you in sight."

"Oh man, you're hopeless. I give up." I wave my hand flippantly in the air. "I'm gonna be late if I don't get out of here. This conversation is over, lady. You're lucky I love you," I say, patting her head, before making my way down the stairs.

Despite knowing I need to get going, I get in one last comment, feeling like I need to get a last dig or two in. "Maybe it'll be you who causes the biggest stir?" I shout up from the landing. "I mean, between that pretty face, those longs legs, and of course, the winning personality to go with it," I deadpan, pausing for reaction. After a beat, the sound of Claire's fake laughter is all I get. "And just maybe the other bartender's will hate *you*, seeing how cute and oh-so-lovable you are. I'm sure the customers will be flocking to your end of the bar."

"Looks like Pub Fiction is in for a little double trouble, if you ask me," she hollers, her tone cheeky.

Dammit, of course she takes it as a compliment.

But then, I hear a loud thump from where I'm standing by the front door, looking behind me I see Claire. "Oh God." She's standing at the top of the stairs and it surprises me. I look toward her and see a worried look on her face. "I sure as shit hope we're working on the same nights, or that will really suck. I didn't think we might not be. I mean I knew we were training on opposite days, but I didn't once think we might not be working together." She's all but yelling now, waving her hands all around as she talks, and I secretly enjoy her and her little panic attack.

"What if we're not on the same shift pattern? If that happens…how often will we get to go out on the odd times you do let us party together? Or catch up on all our shows? You know, hang out Claire Bear and Kitty Kat style." At this, I let out a full-blown belly laugh.

"I'm serious. Don't laugh at me." Claire crosses her arms. "You need to look at your schedule when you get it and call me ASAP, so we can check them. I mean it, lady. I will be expecting your call, text even…well, if your phone isn't dead." I shake my head at her last little dig; she knows me too well.

"Oh, my goodness, relax, we'll have a ton of time for that stuff. It's not like either of us have late night classes. I actually thought something was wrong there for a minute. Besides, I'm sure we can swing a few weekends off together, so really, calm your farm. You're starting to sound like me, *Stressor*. Maybe I'll start calling you Stressossaurus if you keep that shit up." At that, she shoots me a dirty look.

"Hmph, no you *re-lax*," she enunciates slowly, pointing her finger up and down at me. "You will manage fine at work. You'll see, sooner than later, my beautiful friend; there will be plenty of time for normal, stuffy clothing on school days. For tonight, embrace your assets. Go forth and be sexy!" she shouts. Then, with a small curtsy, she turns and walks away; surely thinking she's so damn smart.

I know I'm pretty, but I'm not a super-confident person. I have insecurity and flaws just like everyone else. I like to think that, despite being a bit high-strung, I do have the ability to be easy going; well sometimes anyway. I've really been trying to be more social and laid back since the fire. It isn't always easy, but I am getting better. I've missed out on too many opportunities by being a chickenshit. According to my younger brother, being able to "go with the flow" is a must-have quality in a chick, and high-maintenance girls are a turnoff. According to Mr. Chick Magnet, Wes, this is a trait I really need to work on. Not that I would ever listen to a thing he says about relationships, but I do smile when he gives me advice. He's too cute thinking he's a ladies man. He and Claire have no qualms about giving me advice on how to loosen up.

Wes calls me at least once a week, to make sure I'm not being a societal troll. Seeing as I do easily get attention from the opposite sex, they both think I should be serial dating my way through university. But, just because I happen to get male attention, does that mean I should think I'm God's gift? Absolutely not. Do I enjoy getting male attention? Of course, who doesn't? Does that mean I want to flaunt myself, or my goods, for the world to see? Ah, no. Does it mean I have to date the male population to be considered fun and going with the flow?" Hell no. Needless to say, I hate it when Claire and Wes chat. I do just fine on my own.

Annoyed by my thoughts of Wes and Claire, I slip on my black ballet flats before putting on my jacket. It's summer, I know, but I'm trying my damnedest to cover my chest, which I feel is on blatant display. Despite how sticky and hot it may be outside, I opt for the little grey jacket. I'm willing to suffer through the heat if it means I can keep my modesty for a while longer. I also make one last attempt to pull the shorts down over more of my ass. *It's no use.* I sigh before grabbing my keys and cell phone and head out the door.

Walking to my car, I check my phone. I have to admit, I am the worst person when it comes to having a cell phone. I'm constantly losing it or letting the battery die, without noticing until days later. Like I said, not being a tech-savvy person, I'm not really dependent on my phone like some people. I really only bought it in case of an emergency while away at school. My friends and parents are always giving me the business for being a cell phone dud. Once Claire and I replaced our phones, I agreed to put more effort into checking it, as well as to responding; especially since we both got iPhone 6s with the insurance money. Wes told me if I didn't actually use mine, he'd take it and give me his crappy outdated one that he still has a year's contract on. Apparently, according to my little bro, I don't deserve this kind of phone.

Glancing down at the screen, I notice I have a text message. I stop in my tracks when I realize it's from Seth. Groaning, I slide my finger across the screen to see what that son of a bitch has to say. I know I'm most definitely going to regret this already. Texts from the ex are never good, especially ex-boyfriends turned annoying like mine.

Seth: *Kat doll, I miss you. Please call me. We NEED to talk. X*

Reading this just pisses me off. The guy is relentless. It's his fault we broke up in the first place. He made it clear I wasn't enough. I roll my shoulders, trying to relax, letting out a sigh as I begin to text back.

Me: *No, stop texting, don't call me…we are over, Seth.*

I make a mental note to call my provider and get my number changed during my break tonight. *See why I don't care for cell phones?*

Dropping my cell into my oversized purse, I continue to walk to Bertha, my red Beetle Bug. She was a hand-me-down from my mom that I love, one I gladly adopted from her when she wanted to get a new car. Settling in, I take in the scent that lingers in the air. Nothing beats the smell of old leather and patchouli. The combination always reminds me of my mom, the little hippy, and I take in a deep breath and relax. All notions of Seth suddenly dissipate with what I think is a fantastic idea to rectify my shirt problem. As soon as I get to Pub Fiction, I'll simply exchange my shirt for a bigger size, claiming I was given the wrong one. With this plan fresh in my mind, I start to relax and smile, pleased with myself. *Well, at least I think it's a good excuse. Now to convince my new boss, Levi.*

Chapter 4

Ryker

I KNEW COMING back to campus early was going to be a fucking mistake. Not even back a full day, and here I am, already headed to help out my older brother, Levi, with his club. I know I get paid to work there, but times like this I feel it's more a favour than part of my job. It's not like I could tell the fucker no, especially after all he's done for me. Levi bought and opened Pub Fiction three years ago, right out of university, his business degree in tow. Our mom, Patricia, agreed to co-sign a loan for him, and already he's managed to pay her back along with a hefty bonus for believing in him and his dream.

Luckily for me he hired me as a part-time bartender. The gig gives me enough money to pay for tuition and living expenses while I get my degree. I'm studying sports medicine here at Brock; it's one of the best programs in Canada. I know Levi was hoping I'd partner up in the club with him, but at the end of the day, he knows that lifestyle just isn't for me. Don't get me wrong, I love the bar scene, but dealing with the day-to-day operations is not my thing.

I don't believe in handouts, the idea that things happen for a reason, or any of that other karma bullshit. I know it's me who will make my dreams come true, not some bullshit called fate. *Me. It's all ME.* Like my job at the bar, sure, Levi gave it to me, but I have worked my ass off both to maintain it and to be good at it. I took mixology classes and Smart Serve training, not only to show people that I've done my time, but that I deserve the job on my own merit, not just on kin. I'm keeping my options open, and it helps Levi too.

One day, I'd like to open my own sports clinic, called The Locker Room. It'll offer a wide-range of sport-related therapies, as well as a variety of medical services ranging from ortho care to strength training and recovery options. Although Levi is willing to share his dream with me, I'm going to chase my own.

I do have to admit that bartending at Pub Fiction is the best job I could ask for as a student. On top of my hourly wage, I bring in a shitload in tips. I think the good tips come from the fact I give extra attention to my customers, *especially the hotties.*

Levi called our mom this afternoon to check in on her recovery, and she let it slip that I was already back in town. I pretty much got an immediate text demanding I come to work to help train and supervise the new hires starting tonight.

August and September are always crazy months for us. Every new school year brings in a few new workers to replace the ones who graduated and moved on.

Being the good, reliable brother that I am, I grab everything I need for my shift as fast as I can before heading in. Lucky for me, it doesn't take me long to get ready. The guys wear a simple uniform of jeans and a t-shirt with the Pub Fiction logo across the chest, unlike the servers and shooter girls who have to dress in short skirts or shorts and low V-necked shirts. Not that I'm complaining at all, but it's definitely nice knowing I'll make good tips regardless of my clothes. I tidy up my room a bit, as well, because I know the chances are pretty good that I won't be alone when I get back to my room later tonight.

The idea of jumping right back into working again, after having the last month off, doesn't exactly excite me. I wish I could say I was away on holidays for the last month, but actually, I've been living back home with our mom in Oakville, helping her while she recovers from knee surgery. It's been some great practice for me, too. I've been able to use some of my skills on my mom. She played soccer for years, and went pro for a while, until her knees got too bad. I guess you could say she helped spark my interest in sports medicine. I'm the one who went home to help her out because Levi had to work. With me being on summer vacation, it was a no brainer. It's been my brother, my mom, and myself ever since my dick of a dad bailed on us five years ago. The piece of shit up and left my mom for a younger model; remarrying no more than six months after their divorce was finalized. He married a chick named Sandy, who is exactly the woman you picture when you hear her name. Yep, that one. The one with the perfectly altered face, huge fake tits, complete with a Valley Girl voice shrill enough to drive you fucking crazy.

Levi and I don't really spend too much time talking or visiting with our dad. We do, however, make sure we are always there for our mom. She's the best and didn't deserve what our asshole father did to her. The one thing I could never condone is cheating, and for that alone, I rarely speak to him.

Shaking off the angry thoughts, I grab my keys and lock the door before walking to my car.

Man, how I wish the summer would stay. I can't believe it's mid-August already. Images of school starting in a few weeks begin to plague my mind as I trudge down to my car...well, that is, until I happen to glance to my right and notice my very friendly neighbours, Missy and Sarah. I offer them a wave as they sit on their porch soaking up the sun and drinking what looks to be some fruity frozen shit with one of those annoying umbrellas decorating the cup, all the while showing off their assets in slinky bikinis with their tits almost spilling out. I have no doubt they realize they're driving half of the men in our cul-de-sac crazy. Women with bodies like that always know exactly what they are doing. *Yeah, I'm sure gonna miss the summer.* I grin to myself as I hear Sarah calling out to me.

But looking past Sarah down the street, I see what looks to be one fucking hot-ass brunette rushing to a little red Beetle that's parked on the side of the road. *Is she wearing a fucking coat? It's summer.* Fuck me, those legs alone have my full attention, as she's wearing a pair of black shorts that show nothing but legs for miles. And here I figured my pervy brother had found the shortest shorts possible. *Damn.*

Squinting to get a better view of her, I realize I've never seen her around here before, and this is my third year living in the Village. I wonder if she's some fresh meat who's just moved in, or a visitor passing through. I tend to have a thing for brown-haired women, and this one's a babe. Who am I kidding? I tend to have a thing for brunettes, blondes, redheads—I'm not picky. I have a thing for women, period. I scan this new girl to memory, and remind myself to revisit this little situation later when I'm not running off to work.

"Hey, Ryker," Sarah purrs in a low sultry voice, one I assume is her 'sexy' voice, bringing me back from my thoughts as she inches closer to me. *When the hell did she move off the porch?* I take in her long strawberry blonde hair along with the trace of freckles gracing her nose. She really is pretty.

"We're having a small get-together tonight with some of the other early arrivals. You should come over and join us," she adds, while looking me up and down, a knowing smirk on her face. I take in her perky tits; the ones pretty much on display for all. Tits she's clearly using to entice me as she bounces up and down as she goes on about the party. She also manages to move her cold drink along her nipple so it's now protruding, taunting me as we talk. I stare as she smiles, knowing she's gained my full attention.

"Thanks for the invite, sweetheart, but I'm heading to work. Believe me, I'd rather be here with you girls tonight. I mean, you're so fucking sexy right now, Sah," I say as I pull her closer. Sarah is hot and

I know she's into me. We've been flirting with each other since at least second year. Maybe it's time to say fuck it and just give in.

"Well, sexy." She pretty much moans into my ear as she leans up on her tiptoes. I can smell the coconut of her sunscreen mixed with the alcohol on her breath. "We'll be here when your shift is done. Why don't you come on over after? I promise I'll make it worth your while."

"That sounds really good, Sarah, but I don't think us hooking up tonight is a good idea. I'm going to be closing the place down, maybe another time." I tap her nose, giving her tits one more glance before walking away.

The reason we've never hooked up in the past has been me. I think she lives too close. You know that old saying about dipping your pen into the office ink…well, I think that applies to neighbours, too, especially ones who live right next door. The last thing I need is a complication if she doesn't get my rules.

"Well, if you change your mind, you know where to find me," Sarah calls out in a last-ditch effort.

See? She's already showing herself as a needy, clingy chick. Yep, decision made. Avoid Sarah Richards at all costs. There is no way she could handle my golden rule.

One night only.

See, this is a game for me. One where I make the rules, choose the players, and never play for keeps.

Hopping into my car and making my way to work, I admit to myself that I really do need to get laid. It's been way too long. Visions of how Sarah's lush body would feel come to mind. I laugh as I think back on how living at home with Mommy for the last month hasn't really helped my game at all. *Mom, you're a huge cock-block.*

I mean it's not like I could bring a one-night stand home and give it to her while my mom is asleep in the next room. *Nor would I want to.*

Besides, I wouldn't want to chance some girl accidentally running into my mom. Any girl meeting her is completely off limits. I've never brought a woman home, not even Melissa, my ex. Although we dated for a year, I just didn't feel Melissa was worthy of that honour. Fuck, am I ever glad for that now. For me, meeting the family signals a huge commitment; one I'm just not ready for. The idea of being with one woman is not appealing to me at this point in my life, and it's something I intend to steer clear of for a very long time.

Luckily for me, Pub Fiction is always ripe for the picking when I need to bury myself in the warmth of a woman's tight, hot body. It's a hangout for the type of women I'm looking for right now. Women who are looking for quick, no-strings attached hook-up just as much as I am. Ones who know and respect the score.

We tend to get a lot of regulars at the bar, groups of girls who have made Pub Fiction their stomping ground. This is great for business, but not always great for my extracurricular activities. Which means I need to be extra careful when choosing who I hook up with, like making sure I don't end up with a crazy stage-five clinger. You know the type, the one who will be there every week, drunk with her girls, trying to convince me to take her home one more time. The type who would make it look like I'm taken to the other prospects. And that shit is the last thing I need, some chick that thinks she can change me…to be the one to tame Ryker Eddison. *It ain't happenin'.*

Don't get me wrong, it's not like I'm this super douche or any-thing. But, truth be told,

I'm…a guy; A guy who, like all men, likes to fuck.

Like most other guys my age, I'm a horny motherfucker and I do not do relationships. Not serious ones, anyway. At best, if you're something extra special, maybe we can be fuck buddies for a while. But the number of girls to hold that status is currently zilch. I haven't had anything other than a one-night stand in years. Not since my ex,

Melissa, anyways. That girl did a real number on me. She really messed with my head and, honestly, my heart, too. Melissa and I dated somewhat exclusively for just over a year during my first year here at Brock. I use the term exclusively loosely, because apparently, people have different interpretations as to what the word actually means.

In the beginning, things were great. I couldn't have been happier. Melissa was smart, attentive, sweet, and drop-dead gorgeous, to top it all off. Complete with a sexual appetite that rivalled my own. Yeah, she was a dream…until she became my nightmare.

Now I refuse to put myself in that position again, not unless she is my perfect girl, my very own Holy Grail: *The future Mrs. Eddison.* And right now, I can safely say I'm not looking to meet her. One day I want a wife and family, the norm I guess, but not anytime soon. I can't allow myself to get so caught up in a woman like that again. I simply want to fuck. A lot. It's never more than fucking. I'm only looking for Ms. Right Now.

Walking into Pub Fiction, I immediately spot my brother behind the bar. God, I love the smell of this place—lemons and leather with the slight hint of beer—always lingering in the air.

"Hey, man, we've missed you around here," Levi says, shaking my hand and giving me a typical man hug. "It's nice to have you back. I think a few of the regulars will be happy to see you, too. They've been sulking without their main eye candy behind the bar. They've had to settle for the boss and Lukey. We aren't nearly as fun as you, buddy," he adds with a wink.

Levi and I have always been close, even though he's two years older than me. We've always hung out in the same circles, especially once I hit high school and he realized how cool I am, so being away for a month has sucked for both of us. "Well, of course you missed me. I'm the one who gets you all the tail. How the hell have you and Luke survived without me?" I deadpan.

"You wish, man. I'm the one with the big dick, and you know it, you little fucker. You're just the tagalong, and always have been," he says, tossing the towel at me.

"Asshole, is what you are," I say, throwing a bar lime at his head.

While neither of us would ever admit it, Levi's my best friend. He knows me better than anyone, and he shares the same mentality when it comes to women and commitment. I'd say he's more committed to not being committed than me. I can't name a single woman Levi has dated, not ever, not even in high school.

"Ryk, dude, you must be dying! A month at Mom's with only Palmela and Handula to tide you over must have killed you." He chuckles. "Good thing you're back. The girls are going to be all kinds of batshit to see you tonight. They've been going stir-crazy waiting for their favourite bartender to return. I actually think Naomi had to replace your message cup with a bowl behind the bar."

I laugh, picturing Naomi with a message bowl. With so many girls trying to give Luke, Levi, and me their numbers, many of the staff were done with "being our receptionists," as they eloquently put it. One of the main shooter girls, Naomi, thinking she was funny, set up two stations at each end of the bar with three labelled cups and a sign saying, *"If you wanna get a HOLD of Levi, Ryker, or Luke, drop your sales pitch here."* Despite it starting as a joke, you wouldn't believe how many chicks actually put their info along with a blurb into those cups!

"Good, that's what I was hoping for," I say, reaching for my bowl, sifting through the messages. "I'm hoping to find a girl to make myself happier later tonight."

I put the bowl back on top of the bar and quickly turn to face Levi with my hands in front of my face, studying them intently. "After all, I need to give these blisters some healing time." I laugh, and then display my pristine hands. He just shakes his head. I clasp his shoulder, squeeze his neck, and give him an all-out, shit-eating grin.

"How's Mom? She sounded like she was doing good on the phone. She told me she's been a lot more mobile than she figured she'd be."

I quickly fill him in on how well our mom's doing, sharing how the doctors are pleased with her progress to the point where they might begin her physio sooner than expected.

"You should go see her, Levi. I can hold down the fort here for a few days." I look around the club. "I mean, really, this place is a well-oiled machine. Besides, with my easy course load, I have some extra time, so I can cover you no problem."

"Yeah, I'll leave you in charge for a week while I go see her. I think I can trust your ass to take care of the place for that long. Thanks, Ryk—"

"Aw, shit!" someone yells from the front entrance, followed by the sound of something clanging, interrupting us.

"Who the hell is that?" I laugh. "Naomi being her klutz-assed self again? Shit never changes around here," I say, shaking my head and picturing Naomi all flustered.

Levi shrugs as he polishes glasses for tonight. I crane my neck to see what the hell is going on. I freeze, not at *what*, but rather *who* I see. It's not fucking Naomi. *Shit, this girl is gorgeous.*

"Holy shit, Levi, I'm serious, man. Who the fuck *is* that?" I nod toward the door again. My eyes are glued to the girl who's just come barrelling in. "Fuck me," I mutter, more to myself than to Levi. I feel like I've seen her before, and the more I look at her, the sooner I realize it's the same girl I saw not twenty minutes ago. She's still wearing that fucking jacket in the middle of summer, but those killer legs, I'd recognize them anywhere. Shit, I wonder if she spotted me too and followed me here? It wouldn't be the first time a girl has followed me to work. *Goddamn clingers.* But as she unzips her jacket, I catch a glimpse of the Pub Fiction logo stretched across her impressive rack. *Fuck, are you kidding me?* She works here. "Levi, dude, again, who the hell is she?"

"Newbie shooter girl," Levi says, then growls the next bit, "and keep your fucking hands off her, brother. I need this chick, and I can't afford to lose her 'cause you're an asshole."

Asshole. I slap his back. "Ha, okay. Whatever, man. Like you've never fucked your own staff." He ignores my jab, but shakes his head.

Turning back just in time, I smile, 'cause I'm such a lucky bastard. I catch the sweet curve of this chick's ass as she bends over to retrieve her keys. Fuck me, that ass is perfection, instantly giving me wood, even from a distance.

I'm staring, completely rooted in place, unable to peel my gaze from her. She is, without a doubt, the most stunning creature I have ever laid eyes on.

I see her pausing, nervously taking in her surroundings. The reaction I'm having to this girl is not one I've experienced before. Never have I been this stunned by a woman to the point of near immobility. *Yep, I'm gonna need this one beneath me. And soon.*

As if he can hear my thoughts, Levi leans in. "Easy there, fella. Don't go scaring off my newly hired help before she gets through the door. Like I said, I need her, man. I'm short-staffed as it is," he says, turning toward the dishwasher, beginning to empty it.

"No, I know Levi, it's a crazy time. I'll be good."

"I hope so, Ryk. Marie moved back to Toronto for work in her field, and Stacey quit because Luke doesn't want to give her the time of day after they slept together." He raises his eyebrows, knowing I'm shocked he knows about those two. "Yeah, yeah, don't think I don't know. Fuckin' Stacey told me when she quit. Told me how she was in love with the little shit and he didn't want her. Said she couldn't bear to look at him every day. So yeah, I need the new girls, especially this one and the new bartender, Claire, who happens to be her roommate."

"Okay, okay, man. I get it. Relax, Levi," I tease, "I'm just looking...for now." I grin.

"Ryker," he grits. "Believe me, I know she's some real eye candy, and you can thank me later, little brother. I think I'm actually going to be getting a lot of thank yous for adding these two to the staff. I can only imagine the cock parade that will start once the men around here feast their eyes on them. Big Jim and the team are gonna be extra busy for a while," he adds.

Levi prides himself on security and his staff feeling safe. Sure the girls might wear short shorts and tight tees, but he won't take anyone messing with his crew. Levi has hired the best security staff he could find. Big Jim is just that, *big,* and his team of Big John, Ruck, Sam, and Dalton are just as tough and scary. We've never had any real issues. I think just their presence alone is enough.

For some reason, the idea of other guys checking her out, meeting her, doesn't sit well with me at all. *I want to be the one to check her out, to meet her.* I clench my jaw and glare at Levi. *Whoa, shit, I don't know this girl and I'm starting to be all kinds of pissy. What the fuck is that?*

I listen to Levi go on and wonder if he's noticed my little freak out. If he has, thank Christ, he hasn't said anything. I don't need Levi busting my balls about some girl I don't know.

"I mean, you don't need to tell me twice, she's smokin' hot," he says, "but if you ask me, the new bartender is hotter." I simply nod, unable to find the right thing to say. He laughs, shaking his head, as we continue watching from behind the bar.

Jesus, she's gorgeous. She stops just inside the bar and looks up at the ceiling, checking the place out from top to bottom. It's clear she hasn't noticed us watching her yet. Well, I'd like to think not anyway. I know I should be here to introduce myself when she finally makes it to the bar, but my instincts kick in, telling me to flee while I still can. I bolt just as she catches me staring and our gazes lock for a few seconds too long. *Shit.* The last thing I want is for her to see she has any effect on me.

Chapter 5

Kat

"AW, SHIT!" I yell, without having intended; it just slipped from my mouth. I dropped my keys while walking through the front doors of Pub Fiction, and I absolutely hate when I drop stuff. My butterfingers are my biggest pet peeve. I cover my mouth and glance around. Thankfully, I don't think anyone heard my trucker mouth. That would not make a great impression at all. I'm flustered and my hands are shaking. I need to stop for a minute and take a deep breath in order to recompose and calm myself down.

It really isn't that big of a deal. It was just a stupid text, and it's just a goddamn shirt. Seth is hours away, so I really shouldn't let him get to me like this in the first place. And I'm almost laughing at myself because, let's be real, I know what sells, and that's sex. With that, and this being a bar, I know there isn't a chance in hell of me getting a bigger shirt. *Breathe, Kat. Just stop and breathe.*

Claire is right. I really do need to work on not being too uptight. I let things get to me way too easily. Claire is always telling me not to let little things stress me out, and I normally just shrug her comments off. But now, I'm actually starting to see her point. My current situation is a perfect example of *one* of those instances where she would no doubt call me out for being an idiot. I can hear her: *You're turning into Stressor again.*

I know I'm on time, like right on the dot, even after having stopped for gas—. *I really need to stop playing the red line game.* I wasted too much time gabbing with Claire. Getting caught up like that again is not an option. I don't like cutting it close. At least I'm not late, and that was my goal, I remind myself. So why I'm totally rushing and letting my nerves get the best of me, I'm not sure. It was definitely a close one between all the bullshit and traffic. I just barely made it. What I need to do is shake off this mood, and get excited to be here. *You got this.* I decide to put everything out of my mind. With renewed excitement, I move into the bar area.

I quickly scan this place where I'll be spending most of my free time over the next school year. I make a mental note that the fire exit is, indeed, to my left, as I remembered. *I'll need to check where the other ones are, too.* I wonder what type of evacuation plan they have here. I'll have to ask Levi. I'd hate to not be prepared, should anything ever happen while I'm working.

It's actually quite a breathtaking place. I can see why it's popular. I take in the huge vaulted ceilings, which are painted completely black, and notice tiny fibre optic lights embedded throughout, which turn the black abyss into how I imagine outer space would look with millions of stars scattered in constellations. I love it immediately. I tilt my head back and seriously gawk at it. It's so beautiful and unique; I've never seen anything like it before. The starry space feature must not have been turned on the day I came for my interview, because I definitely would have noticed. Best of all, I spot the tiny sprinkler heads hidden between the stars. I feel my shoulders relax a bit more as I spot them all over the ceiling now.

I must look like an idiot, standing here so enthralled with a ceiling, my mouth hanging open.

I don't think I will ever get over how cool the ceiling looks. I note how the club's decor is also very modern, with dark black wood flooring, that compliments the ceiling perfectly. The walls are painted a deep oxblood red with smoky grey undertones. I notice a small seating area to my right, which has black leather couches with a few small glass tables for drinks. I take a deep breathe in as I inch in closer. It smells like leather and lemons—two scents I love. Along the wall with the fire exit, there are six large booths, which are roped off with what looks to be black velvet ropes. I assume these booths are reserved for parties, guests looking for bottle service, and VIPs. Each booth is illuminated with a dimmed amber spotlight, giving off the perfect amount of light to set the mood. The next thing I see is the enormous bar. It's also sleek and very modern, made out of cherry wood, which matches beautifully with the floor and walls. Whoever decorated this place has great taste.

As I take a better look at the bar itself, I find two men standing behind it, joking. One I recognize as Levi, the owner, the other is the hottest specimen I have ever seen. And he's staring at me, no, rather gawking. His gaze is so intently focused on me that I begin to feel uncomfortable, yet it's also making me feel kind of excited at the same time. He's looking at me as if I'm the only thing that matters at this moment. Well, at least that's what I was thinking, until he quickly turns and walks away without waiting to introduce himself to me. This reaction confuses me and makes me feel a bit irritated. How weird is it to stand there and stare at me like that, then take off before introducing yourself? I mean it's clear he works here from the Pub Fiction t-shirt he has on. *Jeez, nice to meet you, too, asshole.*

Quickly shaking off the weird vibe from The Asshole, I walk over to greet Levi with renewed composure and a big smile on my face.

"Welcome, Kat," Levi says warmly as he happily greets me.

"Hi, Levi!" I extend my hand to meet his. "I'm very excited to be here. Thank you for giving me a chance. I'm really looking forward to jumping right in."

"Not a problem. Ben and Molly went on about how strong your

people skills are and how you're a quick study. After talking to them, and with how well you did in your interview, I know you'll do a great job."

This makes me smile. I had worked for Molly and Ben at Molly's Grill all throughout high school and for the last three summers. They became like family to me, I was sad when they decided it was time to retire last year, selling the property to a woman who turned the restaurant into a bakery, which specializes in what are honestly the most amazing ice cream cakes ever. Rose's Frozen Delights has the craziest flavour combinations and, I swear, the whole street smells of caramel, cake batter, and sugar. It's such a unique smell; it's enough to overload the senses.

Rose didn't need waitressing staff, only a full-time counter helper at the bakeshop, so I found myself jobless for the first time this summer. That's how I ended up applying at Pub Fiction. I needed a job, and Claire had already applied and been hired. I'm thankful for the awesome recommendation Ben and Molly gave me because I know it helped me a lot.

"Well, I just want to make sure you know I really appreciate the job. I know I don't have much in the way of bar experience, but I promise they're right. I am a quick learner, and I can handle a fast-paced environment like this." I wave my hand, gesturing around the bar.

Levi offers a lopsided grin. "I have no doubt you'll be a great fit at Pub Fiction. I know the customers will be fighting to get your attention as soon as they set their eyes on you. Be sure to tell me if you have any issues, and Big Jim and his team are always here to help if I'm not. You're beautiful, and from what I hear, very sweet. A lethal combination. Just stay safe and don't take any shit," he affirms. "And, hey, Naomi and Brooke will be happy to help, too, if ever you need a hand with anything. They can be a bit standoffish at first; but trust me, they are the nicest girls once they get to know you. We've just had a lot of changes here lately, so bear with them."

The last thing I want is any trouble with my co-workers or customers, so I'm happy Levi has told me not to put up with anything I'm not comfortable with. I'm used to a small staff that easily got along, worked well together, and was genuinely nice to one another. I'm relieved to hear everyone is nice here. *Well, maybe not everyone.*

As Levi is telling me the lay of the land, giving me a tour, while guiding me to the staff room where I can hang up my stupid jacket and belongings in any unused locker, I'm building up the nerve to talk to him about my uniform shirt. I don't want him to think I'm difficult or anything, like I'm going to be a prude or a pain in the ass employee who complains about everything, but I really do need to make sure there wasn't a mix-up. As he hands me a lock, I decide to just get it over with. I already know the answer, but I need to ask him about it before he leaves me. I'll regret it if I don't. It's worth a try, right?

"Any questions before I go get ready for tonight and the meet-and-greet staff introductions?"

"Uh, actually, yes, I do have one quick question. I was wondering if, um, if…it…*would it be possible to get a bigger shirt?*" I say it so fast I'm not sure if he heard me properly. I continue to stammer on. "I mean, mine…my shirt is just feeling a bit tighter than maybe it should. I, um…I just don't want to look bad while working, you know what I mean?" I trail off, having done my best to sound convincing that there is something simply unprofessional to about wearing a shirt so tight.

But as soon as I ask, as soon as the words leave my mouth, I already know there isn't a chance in hell that I'm getting a new shirt. Levi's smile is sweet as he informs me, "No, sorry there hasn't been any mix-up or mistakes. All the girls wear the same uniform; it's standard. I realize it's a bit more form fitting on some than others, but we chose them with the male customers in mind. I hate to say it, but they're the majority of our customers. Think of it as a way to *entice* the customers, a way to maybe help with better tips?" I can tell he's trying to find the right words. Enticing customers? Well, it's a good thing I've heard nothing but good things about the work environment here. I'm probably just blowing this whole uniform thing out of proportion. I mean, in reality it's not Levi's fault I don't prefer tight clothing.

"But, ah…" I don't really have a response, but it doesn't matter, because Levi cuts me off anyway.

"And believe me, Kat, you will definitely be happy with that uniform come the end of the night when you're adding up all your tip money. In fact, I think you will come to love my uniform selection." He laughs as he writes out my lock combination on a yellow post-it.

"That being said please don't worry at all about your safety. We have the best bouncers in town, and any customer who gets out of line will be dealt with immediately, I promise you. You're in excellent hands here. I won't put up with any bullshit, and if you are still uncomfortable with your shirt at the end of the shift, let me know and we can look into ordering you a bigger size. It might take a week or so to come in. I just went by what you ladies wrote down. I really don't want you to worry about it, but I do think it looks great."

I mentally high-five myself for having the nerve to ask and decide Levi is going to be a fair boss, which makes me relieved. "That's great, Levi. I appreciate that. I guess I wasn't expecting to feel this exposed. It's nice to know there's help nearby if there's ever a need. I have to ask, has there been many problems here?"

"Not at all. I can't remember the last time we had a bar fight or a time when the girls needed to call Big Jim."

"Big Jim, you've said that name a few times now, how big is he?" I ask curiously.

"He's a beast, but a huge teddy bear. I'll introduce you to him and everyone else soon. Why don't you settle in and I'll see you out by the

53

bar in a few." With that, he places the lock and staff room key on the table before ducking out of the staff room, leaving me with my thoughts while I put my things away.

Putting the lock on my locker, I reflect on my conversation with Levi. I decide to give it a go. I'll do as Claire suggested and embrace my inner sexy. I mean, fuck it, I want to try and loosen up; this is a great start. So what if my boobs are on display a bit more than I'd normally be comfortable with? It's not like Levi said no. He was actually awesome about it. Worst case, I go a few shifts until a new bigger one arrives. *I'm over it; time to move on.* I just hope the customers he was talking about aren't a bunch of sleazebags and I make it through my shift unscathed. But, based on Levi and the look of this place, I'm more than positive he runs both a tight and clean ship, so I know I've got nothing to get riled up about. Shit is about to get interesting, that is for sure. *Kat, we are definitely not in Kansas anymore.* I look down at my girls one last time, hoping they stay in place tonight—and every night I wear this way too revealing of a shirt. "Time to perk up, ladies." I laugh to myself. Despite my unease, I suck it up before meeting the other staff on shift tonight.

As I open the door and go to walk out of the staff room, I hear what can only be described as... *a growl?* Yes, it was definitely a legit growl. I look up at the source of said growl, and I'm met with a pair of the most incredibly set of magnetic eyes I have ever seen. They could suspend time by their beauty and uniqueness alone. They look like, what I would imagine to be the result of warm butter and sweet, golden honey perfectly colliding with one another. Its result creating this balance of colour perfection; eyes that will forever be known to me as *honeybutter.*

Standing there in the doorway, almost face-to-face, I decide we're clearly at an impasse. He's not talking and neither am I. I breathe him in, and he smells of sandalwood and what I can only describe as man.

It's a clean smell that I want to bottle and stick under my pillow for a rainy day, a smell unique to him. We're both staring and it's getting intense, our eyes analyzing and taking in the other. No words are uttered, but it's clear a conversation is happening. The intensity sends shivers down my spine. I feel as if he's trying to figure me out, and it's nerve wracking and frustrating at the same time because I sense he wants to speak, but for some reason he holds himself back.

Finally, after what feels like we've shone a light into each other's souls, exploring one another, I decide to not allow him the satisfaction of knowing he has had any kind of effect on me. Even though he has the most beautiful eyes I have ever seen and he does affect me, I refuse to get involved with a fellow employee. Whether I'm interested or not, messing around with a co-worker would be unprofessional, on top of being the last thing I'm looking for. That being said, I will also not be a pushover who some asshole can intimidate. It's time to put this guy in his place. *God, my big girl panties have been getting a workout today!*

"Um, hey there. I'm Kat. Today's my first official training shift," I share with him. He just watches me, almost urging me to go on with his eyes. "I'm really excited, but a little nervous, too, actually," I add, hoping he might join in the conversation. "I'm one of the new shooter girls. What do you do here?" I ask and get no answer.

I stare nervously, waiting for a reply from the man who chose to growl at me instead of speak. He says nothing and continues to stare, making me more and more nervous. His now hooded eyes blatantly take me in from top to bottom. I now understand what Claire means when she refers to an "eye-fuck." I feel as if time has frozen. Standing there, all I can hear is my own heartbeat. All I can feel are the tingles running along my spine as he brushes by me, making his way into the staff room. That is, after he's knowingly raked those honeybutter eyes over me again and again.

He is the same guy who'd been standing with Levi behind the bar when I first walked in; the one who'd looked at me, then turned around and left. I'm not sure of his name, and at this point, I don't care to find out. As he stalks past me, I swear I can hear him mutter, "Hot was an understatement." I shake it off and stick with my original assessment. *Asshole.*

I turn to face him, because I'm clearly a glutton for punishment, only to find him staring back at me once again, his eyes penetrating mine. I really do try to think of something to say, but I'm so flustered that I draw a blank as my mouth hangs open on its own accord. I feel I'm being scrutinized, so I say the first thing that comes to my head: "*Pfft…* well, okay, it was really nice talking to you. I, uh, hope we can d-do this again sometime." *Not!* "It's been really nice to, uh, *not* meet you, I guess?" I whisper the last part and congratulate myself for choosing what I think is the high road. Well, maybe not entirely, but at least I decided to say something. This time, I'm the one who turns around and marches out, slamming the staff room door. *Fuck him. I mean, who growls, anyway? What is he, a damned animal?*

Chapter 6

Ryker

*D*ID *I JUST fucking growl at her?* I'm pretty sure I did, but I couldn't help myself. Smooth, asshole, real smooth. I place the rest of my stuff into my locker after I finish with all the crap Levi had me doing to help him catch up.

When I was on my way to the staffroom to change my shirt, she opened the door just as I reached it, and caught me totally off guard. She really is breathtaking. I couldn't find my goddamn voice.

What the fuck is wrong with me today? If hot girl didn't think I was a dick earlier at the bar she sure as shit will now. She no doubt thinks I'm a buffoon as well as a creep who clearly can't speak the English language, but instead growls at her while at the same time fucking gawking with drool pretty much spilling out of my mouth. What a loser I must have looked like. Shit.

The best part is that once I got over the initial shock of my guttural reaction to seeing her so suddenly again, instead of introducing myself like a normal human being, I walked right past her. Then I turned and gawked at her all over again. *And she saw me do it.* Yeah. Talk about being a creepy motherfucker.

How the hell am I supposed to train her, or work the same shifts with her, when she no doubt thinks I'm a giant douche? Or what if she *always* has this effect on me? I'm going to have to ask Levi to make sure we aren't working together; that's my only choice. I cringe as I picture

Levi's face as I try to explain why I need opposite shifts of this girl's. *Fuck me.* He's going to enjoy this way too much. Maybe I should lie and say we've slept together and she's a clinger? Nah, Levi isn't dumb. He knows by my reaction to her alone that I've never seen her before. Shit, I might have to take the hit on this one.

Despite my earlier hopes of fucking her later tonight, I think it's safe to say that idea is a bust. There's no way my plan to convince that hot piece of ass to come home with me is going to work, especially after that shitshow in the hallway. Unhappily I resign myself to the idea, accepting I won't be burying myself deep inside her tonight, which is too fucking bad, 'cause man, she is smokin'.

This might actually turn out to be a good thing. I need to listen to Levi and not shit where I sleep, as they say. Just like I wouldn't screw Sarah, she's too close to home. The last thing I want to do is fuck shit up for him with his staff.

Damn.

I shake off my disappointment; it's actually not such a big deal. It's Friday night, and there will be plenty of other chicks to choose from. I'm still confident I'll find the perfect honey to sink balls deep into tonight.

Noticing the time, I quickly grab a clean uniform shirt from my locker; thankfully, I have a few extras. It seems I'm always spilling shit on myself when I stock this place. and today is no different. Of course, the last case of beer I brought up from the storeroom had a broken bottle, shit leaked all over the front of me. Levi loses it if our uniforms aren't clean. He's made sure we all have a few extra shirts onsite. It's a simple black t-shirt with the Pub Fiction logo across the front. It hugs my arms just enough to showcase I work hard on them. I workout at least four times a week and make sure to eat properly. Being in sports medicine has taught me to take care of my body. It's a machine that has needs, just like my dick. An added bonus is that chicks seem to dig my muscular arms. I have no problem with showing them off and choose to wear a snugger fitting shirt. *Shit.* Thinking of my shirt makes me think of hot girl and also how I need to thank Levi again for the girls' sexy shirts. Fuck me, does she ever have a stacked rack, which was seriously on display in her tight top, taunting me, just begging for my hands…my mouth.

I am so fucked. I make my way out of the staff room to the bar for the meet-and-greet.

Chapter 7

Kat

AFTER THE MEET-AND-GREET, I'm so relieved to learn I'm not being paired up with Ryker for the training portion. Ryker, I've come to learn, is the mystery man's name. It turns out he's Levi's brother, and will be overseeing our training, plus helping out behind the bar when needed. Thank goodness Ryker and I won't have too many interactions by the looks of things. I think that would have been way too awkward. I can't believe the way I spoke to him; he's practically one of my bosses. But come on, who doesn't acknowledge a person when they are speaking directly to them? Jerks, that's who. Total jerks. And I thought I'd only have to worry about warming up to Naomi and Brooke. Stupid me. Apparently, Ryker might be an issue for me. Too bad because he sure is nice to look at. Why does it seem the hot ones are always the assholes?

"Hey, Kat, I'm Luke. I'll be your trainer extraordinaire this evening," a super cute bartender says, sliding up to me as I reach the bar, holding out his hand. Luke is definitely a sex on legs. He isn't overly tall, but he has the strong build of a rugby player, complete with broad shoulders and very large hands. His sandy brown hair is a bit longer and spiked on top, while short and trim everywhere else. He has vibrant blue eyes, a sexy line of stubble gracing his jawline, and a shit-eating grin to complete his player status. He really is a good-looking man. I've heard from a few girls who know him from school that he is very sweet, but a total flirt. According to the rumours Claire has shared with me from a few of the girls, he and Ryker play the same game of love 'em and leave 'em. I can see Luke giving me a onceover as we shake hands. I offer a sheepish smile because I basically did the same to him.

"Hi, nice to meet you, too. I'm glad to be working with you. I don't have a ton of bar experience, as I'm sure Levi has told you, but I am a quick learner, so I'll be the perfect student," I tell him, hopefully convincingly, despite my nerves.

He grins at me. "Well, lucky for you, you've been paired with the best teacher in the joint. Don't you fear, lovely, you're in good hands. Really good hands." I look at him skeptically, and he lets out a deep belly laugh. "Oh, Kat! We're gonna get along great. I didn't mean those kinds of hands though. Sure, you're beautiful—stunning really—but something tells me you and I are better off as friends. I think we're gonna have a lot of fun together. I love a girl with a sense of humour, who can take my innuendoes in stride." He continues to laugh and I join him.

His cheerful manner and flirty, fun demeanor has me feeling instantly at ease. It's clear he's completely harmless.

"Now, come on. Let me show you how we run things here," he says, while leading me to the storage room. "I need to stock the bar a bit more, so I figure we'll tackle that first."

We quickly fall into a relaxed banter while I learn the ropes. Luke is very easygoing and funny; it's understandable why women would be drawn to him. Not only is he easy on the eyes but he can also be completely charming. Good thing we've got zero attraction to one another, so I won't need to worry about things being awkward. It's clear he was right in his assessment; we'll have a great time working together.

As he's showing me how to stock the bottles on the shelves, he cautions, "Now make sure you always use the stepladder when stocking the higher shelves, not only for Health and Safety Regulations, but also for your overall safety. And please do not ever use a barstool to reach the high-shelved bottles. Ask one of us or, again, use the stepladder. The last thing we need is for you to get hurt."

"Stepladder, got it." I nod.

"Why don't you shelve these last bottles on that top shelf and I'll spot you. That way, I'm close by for your first time." He smirks, knowing I catch his entendre.

I laugh. "Oh, God, Luke, it's going to be a long night isn't it?"

"What?" he says, feigning innocence. "I'm just being helpful."

"Sure, sure. If that's what they call it these days. Now hand me that bottle and get outta my way."

"I gotta tell you again, I'm pretty happy we've been partnered up."

"Well thanks, Luke. You're okay, too, so far, I guess." I snicker and he rolls his eyes.

While I'm perched on the stepladder, Luke is below me handing me the bottles of wine, vodka, and rye to shelve along the overhead shelving unit. I'm feeling pretty confident and I'm pleased that I haven't faltered in my footing much since I've never done anything like this before. It's only about eight rungs high, but when you're not used to balancing your weight while having your hands full, it can really be a bit daunting. Yeah, I'm feeling pretty happy.

Well, that is, until he hands me the last bottle.

Perched high on the ladder, I have the top shelves fully-stacked with premium liquors, like Patron and Hennessy, and the generic brands perfectly set, except for one empty spot far to my left. "Awesome job you got them all to fit in perfectly. It's kind of like a puzzle sometimes, but you're a pro." At his compliment I beam.

"Thanks, it wasn't as scary up here as I imagined. I was kind of nervous I'd fall or break something."

"Nah, piece of cake, now one more set and we're done. We've just got the bottles of Bailey's and we can take a break."

Luke passes me the last bottle of Baileys, and I stretch over, trying to fit it neatly in the gap. I should have just stepped down and moved the ladder, but thinking that would only waste time, instead I press my tiptoes harder into the ladder rung to make the most of my 5'6" height and decide to make a reach for it. Luke doesn't say anything so I assume this move will work.

Judging from the cool breeze suddenly hitting my mid-back, this *graceful move* has obviously caused my shirt to ride up much more than I would like. But with my hands occupied, I'm forced to ignore it for the time being.

As I start to slide the bottle into place, I sense someone other than Luke watching me. I know it's not Luke because I've felt this kind of stare before; it does things to me. I feel holes being bored into my back. I know without a doubt it's Ryker.

My skin comes alive, making me all too aware of him and how ridiculous I must look up on a ladder in this awkward pose grunting, shirt hitched up, with my ass sticking out of my shorts. I'm sure; trying not to fall off while doing a simple job doesn't make this situation any better either. I become unnerved and feel my ballet slipper skid roughly through the ladder and lose my footing, which causes me to tumble off the stepladder.

"Shit," I yell as I fall, and of course, meet Ryker's eyes on my way down. As I fall, so does the last bottle of Bailey's. *Dammit.*

Luckily, I land safely in the arms of Luke, who laughs at me. Unluckily for the bottle, however, it wobbles out of my fingers and hits the floor with an explosive smash, leaving the smell of the sweet liquor infusing my senses as it spreads all over the bar floor.

"Jesus, Kat, I know I checked you out before, but that isn't a reason to throw yourself at me. You want me, baby, you got me!" He laughs that deep belly laugh of his.

I find myself giggling nervously before apologizing, hoping I haven't injured him. "You didn't hurt me girl, but please, next time move the goddamned ladder. Not that I didn't enjoy the show, but we're not really that kind of place." He winks at me and I slap his arm, while laughing harder, in spite of myself. "Now let's get this cleaned up. I'll go grab the broom and shit." He gestures toward the opposite end of the bar before tossing me a rag.

The next thing I know, Ryker is standing in front of us, but on the opposite side of the bar. He's snarling.

"Luke," he seethes, then repeats it, "*Luke*, we don't pay you to flirt with the help, especially ones who seem to need all the help they can get. Just train 'em. Make sure she doesn't get hurt and she's trained properly. I don't have time for another useless staff member. Quit fucking around and get back to it, eh?" His eyes shoot daggers at me. Then he stalks off, shoulders tight, jaw rigid.

I stand, stunned, but also kind of turned on by Ryker's forthrightness. *What the hell is wrong with me? Did he just refer to me as useless? What a dick!*

"Good thing you'll be working on my shift instead of his, eh?" Luke says, as I sweep up the glass, my face hot and, no doubt red. "Don't bother yourself about Ryk. He's a moody fucker, but his bark is bigger than his bite. Guy probably just needs to get his dick wet."

"That is disgusting Luke, and waaay too much info," I say, giving him a dirty look.

He just laughs and says, "It's true!"

Luke continues to train me and we don't see or hear from Ryker for the rest of the shift.

Thank God, Ryker and I have ended up scheduled on opposite

shifts after this awkward start to my training. There is no way in hell I would work with that ass. The moment he gave Luke shit and made the useless comment, I was more than convinced that, although he might be the hottest man I've ever seen, Ryker Eddison is an asshole!

Chapter 8

Kat

September

CLASSES HAVE BEGUN and I cannot tell you how much I love life now that I'm in my final year. My course load is pretty heavy, but still leaves me enough time to work and have a bit of a social life when I choose. I managed to schedule my classes so that I only have one evening course and it isn't bad because it's over at 7 p.m. I'm also getting along with all my roommates, even though Amanda can be a bit of a slob sometimes. I'm working on having a bit more excitement in life, too. I haven't gone on any dates or anything, much to Claire's dismay, but I have let the girls drag me to a few frat parties. Where I actually had fun!

This time next year, I will, hopefully, be teaching in an elementary school. I'd absolutely love to teach in a primary classroom, with my preference being either second or third grade. I think it's the perfect age group; still needy but with enough independence to make for a great teaching and learning environment.

I'm so very grateful my mom convinced me to take the four-year Concurrent Education Program that Brock offers. By the end of this year, I will be completely done with both my undergrad degree and Bachelors of Education saving me almost an extra year of schooling. *Thank God!* I'm so ready for the real world.

Claire and I have always talked about working at the same school and living within walking distance of each other. I now know that's not quite as realistic as we dreamed it would be when we were sixteen, but, hey, I know we'll always be friends and see each other as much as possible.

As for work, it's been great. Other than my first day run-ins with that Ryker guy, I haven't seen much of him at all. However, I do have to admit, him and his honeybutter eyes have definitely crossed through my mind more than a few times.

Since I have some time before my next class I pop into Pub Fiction to pick up my work schedule as well as Claire's. Pulling up, I notice that the only vehicle in the lot is a suped-up truck. *That doesn't seem like the kind of ride I pegged Levi to own.*

The club's doors are unlocked. Since it's only three o'clock, I wasn't sure he'd be here; I'm not too sure of his schedule yet. But I know he posts our hours every Sunday for the upcoming two weeks.

I walk into the open bar area, but then stop when I hear the sounds of two male voices. They sound like they're having a lot of fun. Curious, I step closer in the direction of where the voices are coming from. I end up stopping in my tracks to take in the scene in front of me.

"Awesome, Jacob, you did it," I hear a vaguely familiar, gruff voice boom with excitement. But it isn't until I get closer that I see who Ryker is talking to. He's sitting in one of the booths with a young boy, who looks to be about twelve, giving him a high-five. He has a genuine look of pride on his face, and I can see what looks to be math homework spread out on the table.

"It's all because of you, Ryk. I never would have gotten that equation right if it wasn't for your help. I'm glad my mom convinced me to ask you to help me." *Oh, my God, Ryker as a tutor, a mentor? How sweet is that?*

"No way, Jacob. That, my friend, was all you. It's been all your hard work over the last few weeks. I have no doubt you'll ace this test." The little boy's smile is huge; I stand there to eavesdrop for a bit longer.

"How about I grab us some ice cream to celebrate?"

"Yes! I'd like that, but my mom will be here soon. We better hurry up. She'll be pissed if I ruin my dinner."

"Language, Jacob, not cool," Ryker warns and I hide a giggle at the pot calling the kettle black.

Jacob raises his hands in mock defeat. "Oh right, coming from Mr. Holier-than-thou," Jacob taunts back. I stifle another giggle at his witty comment.

"Let's go, you little pain, before I change my mind and move on to fractions," Ryker says, scruffing Jacob's hair as they head toward the kitchen.

I smile at how cute they are; at how cute it is to see Ryker in this light. Who would have thought a guy like Ryker would be patient enough to tutor? From what I've seen so far, he kind of comes across as a hothead. Maybe there's some depth to him after all. Not wanting to be seen, I move quickly down the hall ducking into the staff room.

As I round the corner, coming from Levi's office with our schedules in my purse, I begin to text Brooke about a possible shift change. I'm right in the middle of hitting the send button when the next thing I know—BAM!—I'm on my ass and my cell phone is skidding across the hardwood toward the bar.

"Dammit!" I shout, sitting there stunned for a few moments before getting my bearings. As I right myself, I look up because I hear a familiar growl. *You've got to be fucking kidding me.*

Standing in front of me with a scowl, and again this fucking growling sound, is none other than *Ryker Eddison* with a dented container of ice cream at his feet.

I am so annoyed at this point; it doesn't matter if it may have, in fact, been my fault for not watching where I was going. Again, why I don't love cell phones.

"Um, well…I hear sorry is popular," I tell him with a glare. He gives me nothing, just stares back at me but it's intense and I feel it deep within my bones. "Er, you know, like, usually when two people collide, the brute force apologizes…" Still nothing. "That would be you here, Ryker. You are the brute who took me out. You should say,"—I air quote—"'Sorry, Kat, are you all right?'"

Again, not a sound.

"Are you familiar with the concept?" I ask, annoyed.

Radio silence.

I wait for his response, a reaction, but he continues to stare at me with what appears to be a hint of a smirk forming in the corner of his lips. *Jesus, he's pretty.*

I take a better look at the entity standing intimately close to me now, causing my pulse to race. He really is one mountain-o'-hotness. *Too bad he's an ass. Well, to me, anyway.*

"You can't talk to me? What, I'm so 'useless' to you that you don't want to waste your words on me? Fine." I start to move around him, but the next thing I know, I'm pressed flat against him, chest-to-chest, nose-to-chin. His hands are gripping my waist, puling me against his rock hard body, his hard-on pushing into me.

"Not sorry, not fuckin' close to being sorry," he growls in a deep baritone voice that has me clenching my legs from its intensity as the impact of his words vibrate into my neck. He keeps us still for a few moments as he breathes me in deep. "I like you close like this, so I am *not* sorry," he says, before laying a kiss to the side of my lobe, tracing his lips down to the juncture of my neck. He releases his hold on me and walks away without another peep. *Fuck me.*

PULLING OUT OF Pub Fiction's parking lot, I watch as Ryker's truck gets smaller in the rearview mirror. I think about what just happened or about how good-looking he really is. I know I'm not supposed to refer to a man as being "beautiful," but, hot damn, if there's a better word to describe Ryker right now, it's beyond me. *How did I not notice the rest of him before?* I mean I saw him my first day, but didn't get a chance to really check him out. Between the growl and the asshat comment to Luke, how could I? Yes, he was clearly good-looking, but up this close is completely different. On top of those killer honeybutter eyes, his face is flawless with smooth, tanned skin and a strong jaw with a light casting of stubble along it and his chin. And those lips…full and taunting. I feel as if they're teasing me, begging for my touch, waiting for me to kiss them…oh, God, how I could suck on them for days!

It's obvious he takes pride in the way his body looks because, man oh man, let me tell you, a girl could lose weeks thinking about the things she would like to do to that body. I'd love to climb up that man, that's for sure. *Oh, my gosh, where did that come from?*

Holy hell his fucking cut biceps alone could make me forget my name and leave me panting—maybe even begging—for just one lick, one taste, one touch. Seriously, Ryker Eddison is *hot!*

I can't deny that, besides being all kinds of delicious, there's something about him that intrigues me. It's like he calls to me on another level. When I think of him, I get this desire to explore why he affects me the way he does, especially because I don't know him. Is he safe? A good guy? But I can't lie, despite any reservations I may have, I'd really like to know him, the real him. I'm curious to learn what makes him tick, what makes him happy, what makes him Ryker. The one thing I do know is I need to proceed with caution with whatever I decide where he is concerned. Ever since that first day, I can't seem to get over this feeling that he wanted to get to know me, too. With the way he looks at me, and the few interactions we've had, I think it's obvious we're attracted to each other. That is what I think scares me the most. I don't know him and he affects me like no other and I hope, just maybe, I affect him on the same level. I smile at the thought as I pull into our driveway.

"What the hell happened to you? Did you meet a boy? You met a boy!" Claire immediately greets me as I open the car door and step out.

"Were you voluntarily taking out the garbage?" I tease her, as she's holding a recycling bin in her hand.

"Ha, ha, don't bother trying to deflect, Kitty Kat. I saw your face as you pulled in; you had on your 'I'm so friggin' excited' smile." she raises her hand to stop me from talking, "I know you better than you know yourself sometimes. Something happened." I can't hide the smile on my face at her excitement.

"Nah, I'm just happy to see my best friend dealing with the garbage, that's all it is," I say and she smacks my arm as we make our way inside.

With Claire on to me and Ryker taking up my thoughts, it's fair to say that *I am so fucked.*

Chapter 9

Kat

I

T'S WEDNESDAY AND I'm working with Naomi for the first time since I heard about her from Levi during my training shift. I've heard she's really nice from Brooke, who has been nothing but welcoming. I'm not as nervous as I assumed I might have been. I'm hoping I can get some info on Ryker from her, too.

Ryker's kind of become this anomaly to me. From my experience, I know he's a jerk, but maybe I'm wrong. After seeing him with Jacob the other day, I wonder if it's all a front; the whole asshole gig he's got going. Maybe he really *is* a nice guy? I haven't seen much of him lately because we work on the complete opposite shifts. *Thank goodness.* I say this because I could see myself giving in to this attraction even though I really don't think he's the type of man I need to let into my life. He's one I'd easily get myself worked up over. It's clear he likes to send mixed signals and he's not looking to get into a committed relationship.

"Kat! I'm so excited to work with you," Naomi hollers with a huge smile on her face as I make my way out of the staff room and head behind the bar. "How has it been going? Do you like the job? The staff?" she asks excitedly.

I quickly tell her how great the place is, how the tips have been incredible, and how I can't believe I've already been working here a few weeks. As Naomi and I are logging ourselves into the new Point Of

Sale system, a girl storms up to the bar.

"Excuse me," the girl says, "I'm looking for Ryker. Is he here?"

Naomi gives me a knowing smile, and says, "Um, no, he's off to-night. Can I take a message for him? He should be in tomorrow I think." Naomi pauses, waiting for the girl to respond. The girl just stands there scowling as if contemplating something. This causes Naomi to sigh, clearly irritated; it seems this isn't the first time Naomi has had to deal with this sort of thing.

"Son of a bitch, I knew he was lying to me. What an asshole. Do you, uh, can you give me his number? He forgot to leave it with me last night when we were chatting when I stopped in to see him. He said he would call me, but then I realized he forgot to get my number."

I hope that maybe Ryker didn't really forget her number, that maybe he's not interested in her.

"Sorry, what did you say your name was?" Naomi asks.

"Taylor," she sighs, while tapping her nails on the bar's surface.

"Well, Taylor, I'm sorry," Naomi says, "but it's not my place to give out Ryker's number. If he wanted you to have it, he would definitely have given it to you." I smile, mentally giving Naomi a high-five. "But I'll gladly give him a message for you."

"Well, okay, but I know he'd want me to have it. You see, a few months ago, we were a thing, if you know what I mean," she says, raising her eyebrows, "but then I had to go away for a while. Now I'm back. I really need to get in touch with him. I have a welcome back present to give him," she says proudly, and I assume she means a sexual present considering the way she's leering. That idea is one that doesn't sit well with me. I dismiss it just as fast.

"Like I said, Tay-lor," Naomi says, over pronouncing her name, "I've worked with Ryker a long time and trust me, if he wanted you to have his number, he would have given it to you last night when he saw you." Naomi laughs, then reaches under the bar for a bowl full of post-it notes and little papers loopily scrawled with what looks like names, numbers, and messages. "See this, Taylor? These are all Ryker's messages from ladies like yourself. So, as I said, feel free to write your info on this Post-it and I will be sure to add it here." Naomi shakes the bowl, and despite my better half, there is a little part of me that is enjoying Naomi's cruelty, because in the end, it's women like this who make me realize there is no way Ryker could settle for a girl like me.

"You can tell him Taylor stopped by, and you make sure to tell him I have a surprise for him." She pauses, then points to the bowl. "And be sure to keep mine on top. I'm important."

Naomi just smiles. "Again, hun, just write it down and put it in here. I am not Ryker's secretary. I don't give verbal messages and I always shake the bowl, equal rights and all that."

With that, the girl huffs, then mutters, "Fucking bitch. Just tell him Taylor will be back." She turns on her heels and thunders back out just as fast as she came in. Naomi doesn't let it faze her.

Picking up the pen off the bar top, Naomi writes 'Taylor' on the yellow Post-it note, and says, "One more ho for the bowl. God, you'd think between Luke and Ryker that they were the last two dicks on Earth. The way some of these bitches toss their snatches at them; fuck, ladies, have some class, please!" Naomi laughs again, and drops the newest Post-it into the bowl and gives it a solid shake. "You know what? Ryker is an ass sometimes and can be a total player, but I have to say, he isn't as bad as Luke. I honestly think Ryker has potential. He just needs the right motivation. One day he'll meet his match and be the man I've seen glimpses of."

"Um, is this something that happens often? Casualties of the one-night stands coming in, demanding to see the guys? Do I need to do anything with that?" I ask, nodding at the bowl. Its existence makes my stomach coil.

"Hell, yes! It happens all the fucking time. That's why we made the bowls. We got tired of dealing with their leftovers and *pick-me's*. This way," she points to the end of the bar, "during shifts we just set them here and direct enquiring minds to them. See, I made a sign to sit with each one then taped them with duct tape so they'd be all secure and shit."

The rest of the shift goes by without incident, and I see a few ladies dropping messages in the bowls; some go so far as putting a note in each. I can't imagine being that desperate to get a guy's attention that I'd reduce myself to putting my name in a bowl with a bunch of others. *I wonder if he's really that good? Oh, my God, no, Kat, he is not the type for you,* I scold myself and finish my shift without thoughts of Ryker and his hoochies.

DESPITE WORKING OPPOSITE nights to Ryker, I still manage to get the lowdown on Mr. Honeybutter himself, without actually seeing him in person. This is, of course, thanks to my chatty little bestie who ended up on the same shift pattern as Ryker, and quickly formed a friendship with the man himself. Claire works the bar with him on Wednesday and Friday nights. I'm always hearing about his antics, as well as how sweet and fun he is; how well they get along. It seems she always has a new Ryker story to share after each shift she works with him.

I listen, trying hard not to let Claire see just how interested I might be, but I also think back on how nonchalant he can be and, well, it confuses and irritates me. Plus, just thinking about the way he spoke to Luke while he trained me—which Luke let slip the other day, was supposed to be Ryker's job—only serves to prove that he isn't the one for me. I have yet to see this funny or sweet side of him that Claire claims exists. Okay, well, maybe I saw a glimpse of his sweet side the other day with Jacob, but he's been nothing but an ass to me. Therefore, I remain skeptical of its existence. My first encounter with Ryker

Eddison is when he couldn't be bothered to introduce himself to me, which served to show me what a big jerkface he can be.

Claire has no idea about my awkward encounters with Ryker, and I intend on keeping it that way as long as I can. Not that it's a big deal, it's just that Claire is always trying to hook me up, or trying to convince me I need a "fuck buddy" to tide me over until Mr. Right comes along for my next relationship. She tells me to think of fuck buddies as weekly appointments to help keep me de-stressed and relaxed. Claire is big on women exercising their libidos as much as men do, so her pressuring me to hook up with Ryker would make me a bit uncomfortable because my feelings about him are all over the place right now. The last thing I need is her pushing the idea of Ryker and me hooking up every chance she gets.

Here I am, harbouring thoughts of Ryker while Claire is clueless as to how hearing about him affects me. Between the memories I've stored, and Claire's stories, my brain is filled with enough Rykerisms to torment myself on almost daily at this point.

"I'm telling you, I have never seen bigger players then Ryker and Luke. They are seriously delicious to look at, like clenching yummy, and I can only imagine what good fucks they must be, especially Ryker. That one's always fending off the ladies; it's hilarious when he has to deal with chicks wanting repeats."

I sit in our living room one night after her shift, cringing at how this makes me feel. I hate to admit it, but even though I shouldn't, I still want him, but I really wish I didn't, and it bugs me. A lot.

"Then, tonight, this chick—Paula—comes up to him, *demanding* to speak to him, and he reminds her of his rule, pretty much *tsk*-ing her for thinking she'd be any different."

"Rule? What rule does he have?" I ask.

"One. Night. Only." Claire says, enunciating each word slowly. "And believe me, some chicks just do not get it. Just the other night, some chick was almost removed by Big Jim for trying to come around the bar to make him talk to her."

See? This is why I cannot allow myself to think about this man.

"But being honest, I really do think he's great, and maybe he just needs to meet the right girl to get him on the straight and narrow. I see the real him under the player front, and he's got a lot to offer."

Funny, that seems to be an opinion Claire and Naomi both share, why can't I see it?

"Like what?" I challenge.

"Well, aside from being gorgeous, he's funny, super sweet, and he really does have a good head on his shoulders. He's ambitious and, best of all, I heard he's hung and could give you the ride of your life."

With that, she pats my knee before uttering goodnight.

Chapter 10

Kat

"**K**AT, OH MY God. You're hot and Ryker's hot. Holy shit, you two need to hook up! This would be your perfect opportunity to have fun and experience the world of no strings attached," Claire practically squeals, like she's had the best idea ever. We're sitting around the kitchen table with our other roommates, Kym, Amanda, Radha, and Beth eating Chinese food, drinking beer, chitchatting, and laughing.

Claire was sharing a bunch of funny work stories. Seeing as she works the bar, she gets to meet some pretty interesting people, ones who think she has time to listen to their life stories and ones who like to pour their hearts out to her. I meet some interesting characters too, but the ones I meet tend to try and talk more with their hands. Right in the middle of a story, in mid-sentence, she'd turned to me as if she'd had a revelation, and blurted out that crazy idea of Ryker and me getting together. *Where the hell did* that *come from?* It was as if she'd finally pieced together some great puzzle in her little matchmaker mind; her brain had concocted this little epiphany of our pairing clicked into place. And, Claire being Claire, of course felt compelled to blurt it out in front of everybody the second it hit her. I immediately feel myself flush.

"Hmm. Who's this Ryker guy? And does he have any cute friends? I swear, I'm dusty from living at home most of the summer, and I haven't gotten out much yet to meet anyone," Amanda asks, joining this bullshit of a conversation.

"Count me in, too, ladies. I could use a little dusting myself," Kym adds, brows raised with interest.

"Well, Ryker is just this total fuckin' mountain o' sex that Kat needs to climb and conquer, 'cause I am telling you, they would be H-O-T together, I just know it," Claire shares, way too enthusiastically. "And yes, I'm sure he has a whole entourage of hottie progeny that we could infiltrate."

"Claire! Did you just really say that? 'A mountain o' sex,' really?" Radha can't help but ask after she chokes a bit on her beer. "Well, hell, count me in, too, then. I'm not dusty, but I like a good shag, too." She coughs, still recovering.

"Yep, I sure as hell did say it." Claire raises her hands in mock surrender. "What? It's the truth. Ryker Eddison is *hawt!* Wait 'til you guys come to the club, you'll see he's the perfect specimen for our little Kitty Witty Kat. Hopefully, he'll have some friends there, too. If not, we could always take up stalkin' *his* ass."

"Well, you have been crabby lately, maybe you should listen to wing-woman Claire. She seems to think you're kinda dusty, too, from the way she's been going on," Amanda teases.

"I totally agree," adds Kym before I can say a word. "I'd love to see you doing the walk of shame, sneaking into the house all tousled hair, trying not to be seen. I'd pay money to see that!" She laughs, as do the others.

"You guys are sooo hilarious," I quip, but can't help but laugh along with them.

Unfortunately for me, the girls are enjoying this way too much to let it go now; they continue to joke regardless of the dirty looks I send their way. *Assholes.*

"Are you insane? No way! Aren't you the one always telling me what a player he is?" I laugh. "I have zero interest in him whatsoever. You need to give up on this idea right the hell now, missy. Girls, do not let Claire Knox try to set you up. Trust me, you will create a matchmaking monster."

Claire just shakes her head, and we all have a good laugh.

"I'm telling you, Kat, you should get in there—and fast—if you want a turn. And I so think you need a turn, 'cause let me tell you, that man is like catnip to some of these bitches."

I shake my head at her. "No way. Not happening, my friend, there is no way I want to be somebody's next bitch."

"I honestly think you should be all like, 'Hey, Ryker, my body has 206 bones in it, but I could use one more,' then blow a kiss at him."

"Oh, God, what is wrong with you? You are so crass! There is no way I'd ever repeat that! I don't really want to talk to the guy, let alone proposition him! Where the hell do you get this stuff from, anyway?"

We all laugh. I can barely believe the shit that comes out of this girl's mouth. Claire should've been a guy.

Standing proudly as she grabs more beer for the table, Claire tells us she thinks it was from an article in Cosmo about raunchy pick-up lines for girls.

"But, for real think about it. A little Ryker might do you some good; you sure could use some release, right? I mean, you' haven't been with a guy since you-know-who, and that is not okay my friend," she says before sitting back down and pouring her Shock Top into her favourite BrockU beer mug. I manage to steal her full mug and take a huge gulp of the tasty cool blonde goodness, the taste of citrus dancing on my tongue.

"Maybe you're just what he needs. And maybe you'll be *that girl,* but regardless he's what you need, which is one hell of a good fuck. Come on, at least take a ride on the Ryker Express: *Toot, toot!*"

Did that bitch actually just fucking toot *at the thought of Ryker and I hooking up? Jesus!* Then she tries to high-five me. *Not a chance, lady.*

"No way don't talk to me about me wanting *'a ride.'*" I air quote. "I know he's fucking hot, but I'm not interested in being a notch on a proverbial bedpost."

I go on with my rant. "Like I've said before, I might be ready for a one-night stand or two eventually, but not with Ryker; that would just be intense. I'm definitely not in the market for getting myself all caught up in the girl drama that I can only imagine attaches itself to 'catnip' like that, as you call it," I say, directing the last comment specifically to Claire. I hope I've done a good enough job concealing my reactions to the man in question, especially from Claire. If Claire or the other girls caught wind of my true feelings, I'd never hear the end of it. Already I'm feeling my chest get a bit tight when Claire goes on and on about Ryker and me hooking up or with her pressuring me to just hook up with anyone for that matter. I have no idea how she thinks casual sex is something I can easily handle; she knows me better than that.

Finally, the topic shifts to Beth's sister's wedding, which she's dreading going home for. "I love my sister, don't get me wrong, but she has turned into Bridezilla on 'roids," Beth giggles, popping a handful of nuts into her mouth before going on. Beth tells us all the crazy things her sister has been doing over the last few months, from wanting live doves flying around the venue to demanding the brides-maids learn a choreographed routine, which they will perform in front of all the guests. I sigh, starting to actually relax as I sit at the table, sipping my beer, listening to Beth and the others ramble on about boys, work, and everything else.

Sitting here now, listening to them chat about I couldn't even tell you what, I think about *him;* how strong and sexy he is. How when he held me close the day we bumped into each other in the hall, just how well I fit into him. I remember his scent—the traces of laundry detergent mixed with hints of sandalwood that tickles my nose. Taking a sip of my drink, I remind myself of his firm grip and how his solid body wrapped me in a safe cocoon. How he felt nice...right. Thinking of him like this makes me question everything Claire has told me about him. Maybe I just need to give in and see what happens? Maybe I need to put myself out there with him, take the lead? *God, I need to stop drinking before I do something crazy, like tell her I want to hook up with Ryker Eddison.*

God, he is hot. Maybe Claire's onto something...

"Hello? Earth to Kat. Dude, are you *even fucking listening to me?*" I hear Claire shouting, breaking me out of my Ryker-induced thoughts, which, against all normal logic, seem to be creeping into my mind more and more. *God, that man confuses me.*

Asshole.

The few times he showed up at the pub unexpectedly, it was uncomfortable, but also so...something else entirely. I would try to avoid looking at him, but of course every time I did sneak a peek in his direction, he'd catch me. He'd stare back at me, as if he was calling me out, and then he'd smirk, which in turn only left me standing there among all the staff and customers, blushing like an idiot for having been caught. Not that anyone seemed to notice our interactions, but still, I don't want to take the risk.

"Kat," Claire calls in my direction. "Well, will you?"

"Uh, sorry, yes! Yes, of course I will," I reply, hoping to make her think I was, in fact, listening.

"Oh, good! It's this Friday coming. I can't wait for this party with Colby. Thanks for covering my shift. You're the best!" Claire gushes and gives me a sloppy, beer-soaked hug.

Oh. Hell. No.

I pat her shoulder awkwardly and try to not act as annoyed as I am after realizing what I just agreed to. *Friday night. Working. Great.* I had been planning to study at the library, and then go for dinner with Jenn this Friday, but I guess not. I sigh and watch Claire bounce into the living room, already sharing the good news to Colby on her iPhone. We decide to call it a night and begin clearing off the table and cleaning up. I really do need to get these wayward thoughts under control before I end up agreeing to something truly awful, like allowing Claire to set me up on one of those blind dates she's always threatening me with, or—even worse—hooking me up with Ryker.

But then I realize that's exactly what she's just done. Ryker is scheduled to work every Friday.

Shit.

Chapter 11

Ryker

IT'S FRIDAY NIGHT and I walk into Pub Fiction for my shift about forty-five minutes early, after hanging out with Jacob. I've been tutoring Jac now for over a year, and lately I've been taking on more of a mentor role. I like the kid, and seeing him make progress has been pretty rewarding. His dad bailed two years ago so I try to do things with him now and again. He's thirteen and going through a rough time. Levi and I met him and his mom, Cheryl at The Centre, where we both volunteer with their youth programs when we can. The Centre is a non-profit organization that focuses its resources on helping and working with troubled youth. They offer a variety of programs that range from simple homework help to organized sports and counselling. It's an amazing organization, and Levi and I both really enjoy helping out. Not having had the most positive male role model in our lives, we figured it was a great way to make sure that at least some other kid will get one. It was a good fit, seeing as he needed help with math and basketball and I'm a whiz at both.

Passing the bar as I make my way down the hall toward the staff room, I expect to see Claire, but then I remember Levi mentioning she needed tonight off and was trying to get it covered. Brittany suddenly pops her head up. "Hey, Ryk, looks like it's you and me behind the bar tonight, bud. Ya ready for a good time?" she jokes.

"I sure am, but the real question is, are you gonna be able to keep the pace? I mean, it's been a few months since you decided to ditch us to work as a shooter girl."

She mutters, "Whatever," and I tell her I'll be back in a few minutes to help her with prep. *But if she's working the bar for Claire, who is going to cover for her tonight as shooter girl?*

Shit. I hope Levi reminded Claire to cover the floor for Britt, too. Friday's are busy.

Not thinking twice about knocking on the staff room door like we normally do, I skip it because: a) I'm early, and b) I know Brittany is already behind the bar working and the other staff aren't due to clock-in for another hour yet. Well, let me tell you, apparently a) and b) don't apply anymore with all the new staff we have working here now. And, apparently, our knocking rule needs to be followed at all times.

'Cause *Holy Fucking Christ!* As I come through the door, I'm quickly met with the sexiest scene I have *ever* laid my eyes on.

Sitting on the black leather ottoman in the middle of the lockers, while bending forward toward me with an abundance of mouth-watering cleavage spilling out of her black lace bra, is none other than hot girl. *Fuck, I bet her rack is amazing.*

Well, fuck me sideways 'til Sunday! She doesn't see me right away, since she's busy slipping up her black pantyhose over her legs; legs, I might add, that don't seem to quit. With this vision in front of me, taunting my senses—mainly my sense of *I-wanna-fucking-touch-taste-and-smell*—I do what all men in my position would do. Yup, like a fucking perv, I stare. Actually, no, I full-on gawk at what's unfolding in front of my greedy eyes, the way she slides the silky material up to her thighs and just as I think she will stand up, she pauses and fixes her bra instead. And again, like the lucky bastard I am, I swear I see a glimpse of her pink nipple as she adjusts her tits. I am fucking greedy for this girl; greedy to take her all in, every motion and every curve. Jesus, who knew a simple act being done by Kat could be that erotic? Her brown waves dance along her chest and shoulders, covering her face as if it's trying to tease me, concealing those jade eyes from finding mine, not that I'm ready for her to see me. Hot girl is just that, goddamn smokin'. My cock is throbbing, straining against my underwear, pulsing against my zipper, aching to be set free. *Shit*. Stifling a moan, I adjust myself, thinking of my next move.

Even if I wanted to leave, *I couldn't*. It's as if I'm rooted in place, my feet encased in cement trapping me, my brain convincing my body it's actually stuck. And, truth be told, I'm totally o-fucking-kay with it. There's no place on this earth I'd rather be at this moment than right here with this woman as I silently wallow in her beauty. This, this in front of me, is what wet dreams are made of, a pure erotic fantasy come to fruition. I knew this girl was hot, but fuck me. Man, am I grateful my brain and body aren't on the same page right now. You know, the page where my legs would be walking away, like I know I should. I know the right thing to do is to turn around and walk right the fuck back out the door. But there's not a bloody chance of that happening, 'cause...*this view is spectacular*. And there is no goddamned way I'm missing this opportunity.

As if she suddenly senses that something in the air has changed, Kat looks up and sees me standing there, rooted in place by the door, virtually drooling at her. Rather than freaking out like I assumed she might, she simply smiles, her face a bit flushed. *I'd like to make all of you flush, baby.*

"Oh! I'm uh, umm, sorry. Thought I'd locked the door," she says. Our eyes meet and she continues to blush the sexiest shade of pink I have ever seen. I'm thinking about what other body parts of Kat's might match that colour. Shaking these images from my head for now, I focus my attention back to Kat, who is rising from the ottoman. "I'll just, uh... uh, duck into the bathroom and finish," she adds in a shaky voice.

I should say something. I know this, I really do, but for some fucked up reason, I can't form a response. It's like I'm one of those assholes who gets all tongue-tied around pretty girls. Shit, I look like such a dick right now. Here I am, staring again, mouth agape waiting for her next move, waiting to see if she'll lose her shit on me. However, in this moment with Kat, I've never been thankful for not having a voice before in my life. I have no clue why she makes me tongue-tied. It's never happened before. I mean, fuck, I'm Ryker Eddison, the king of one night. But with her, things are different. I don't want to be a dick around her. I can feel this girl is different, that she deserves better, and for some reason, I want to be the *better* she deserves. And as fucked up as it is, I kind of like the way I react to her; it's a rush and I cannot wait to see how things play out between us. As Kat stands, yanking her pantyhose off as they've fallen down, I can tell she's actually quite nervous and shy. *Don't be shy, baby; you're incredible.*

My instincts are telling me to comfort her and, honestly, the idea scares the shit out of me. It's a new feeling that messes with my mind. I want to call her *baby,* and reassure her she doesn't have a goddamn thing to be nervous or embarrassed about, but I don't. I want to tell her how sexy and completely thought consuming she has been, but I don't. I want to tell her she is fucking hot. But again, I don't. I decide to stay quiet. I want her to continue leading how we're going to play this thing out, which again is a new concept for me. I like control, to dictate how things go in my life and in the bedroom. Truth be told, if it were up to me, we'd be fucking like animals while I had her pinned against the lockers, but I don't think Kat's ready for that just yet. I see her as timid and shy, and the last thing I want to do is scare her away from me, or have her think I'm an asshole. I want to be respectful to Kat, do whatever will make her feel most at ease. This is why I stand in silence, watching and waiting for her to call the shots.

She starts to fumble as she pulls her t-shirt over her head, and rather than staying quiet like I had planned, guess what happens?

I fucking growl.

Yup, a big deep-throated growl that honestly could pass for a full-blown moan this time.

What the fuck is wrong with me?

Chapter 12

Kat

OH SHIT, OH shit, fuckity-fuck-fuck! Are you fucking kidding me? I swore I locked that door! Oh, God, when I heard the door open I knew I had obviously not locked it properly.

I sit, hoping it's just Naomi or Brooke and not a big deal. But after a few moments of silence, followed by the door closing, I know it's not them. If it had been one of the girls, they would be whistling and catcalling at me by now to mock me for changing with the door not fully secured. A door they have both already warned me doesn't always lock, one I should make sure I test before undressing. Clearly, I need to heed this warning in the future. *Come on, don't people knock?*

Due to the lack of sound, along with a feeling I'm being watched intently, my skin begins to prickle, causing the hairs along my arms and neck to rise and my face to warm as it flushes under the scrutiny. My body is reacting to the watcher, but it's not in fear, it's with excitement. I know right away—I know with every fibre of my womanhood and the vagina goddesses below—that, of course, it's none other than Ryker himself standing there and gawking at me. With half of my body on display, he's not making a sound.

This is so not happening.

In hindsight, I knew we would be working together tonight, but since I was early I figured I could get ready and make myself scarce before he arrived. That way we'd have little to no interactions, other than me having to pick up drink orders. I figured we'd be forced to be at the pre-shift meeting together, which would no doubt be uncomfortable, but if I had to talk to him, I planned to do my best to be professional no matter how weird he might be. I resolved to be composed, even if there is some palpable awkward tension between us. I wish our interactions could be as easy and fun as they are between Luke and me. I smile at the warm feeling that consumes me as I consider this type of easygoing relationship with the gorgeous Ryker. *Ha, you wish, Rollins. Fat chance, he's Ryker. I mean, look at him and what he does to you.*

I feel his heated stare boring into me as I lean over to finish pulling on my pantyhose.

Seeing him in the room, I quickly figure there's no point in freaking out. After all, I simply didn't lock the door as I presumed. I decide to fake nonchalance and toss back on the baggy t-shirt I was wearing before coming to work, then move to the washroom to finish dressing. Why give Ryker the satisfaction of thinking he's making me uncomfortable? "Sorry again, I'll just go..." *Shit, stop apologizing. Be casual, Kat. Be chill...*

But then, as I stand and make eye contact with him I hear it. He fucking growls at me.

At that, I swear, all I see is red. *Holy shit! He's fucking growling at me again.* I've had enough. Fuck it. It's time to show him my big girl panties. It's time to end this little intimidation game.

"What the hell is your problem?" I ask through clenched teeth.

Silence. Staring. Smirking. *Bastard!*

Jesus, this man is infuriating. *Don't show him any weakness. Don't show him how he affects you.*

And, believe me, he does affect me, not in the 'I'm scared of him' kind of way either. No, it's a full-on 'What the hell are you doing to me?' way, one that makes me want to let my inhibitions go and explore what type of woman I'd be with a man like him. He makes my body buzz like never before and brings out a side of me that I hate to admit is really relishing in our game of cat and mouse. A game I think I want to play. Part of me is hoping to be the one to bring him to his knees.

Shaking these memories from my mind, I'm brought back to the here and now.

"Oh my God, Ryker. Are you kidding me? You're driving me crazy! What the fuck are you *growling* at me for? Are you just a cosmic asshole?" I ask. However, my last question gets lost in the void because just as the question crosses my lips, as I'm putting my arm through the shirt, it tears at the seam, creating a huge split along the side. *Are you fucking kidding me right now?* Frustrated, I let out my own growl and attempt to throw the shirt out of anger, but it only lands in a small pool at my feet.

Shit. It's now very embarrassing for me. After trying to play this whole situation off as being cool and unaffected, I lose my shit and basically throw a temper tantrum, which is sure to let Ryker see how, he does not only impacts me physically, but also emotionally. Perfect, now I'm standing in front of Ryker Eddison, the boy of my incessant thoughts, in nothing but my black lace bra and panty set. *Where's my fairy godmother when I need her?*

I give my head a shake and quickly bend down to retrieve my shirt to use as a cover, deciding again to try to carry on like it's nothing. *It's no biggie, Kat. Just breathe,* I tell myself as a familiar tunnel vision begins to make its way to the forefront and my palms start to sweat. *I need to cover myself and get away from this man. I need to compose myself. Breathe, just breathe, you're safe. You're fine; it's just Ryker. Gah! Ryker the man I just might want to see me, to really see me, all of me.*

Once calm, I retrieve my shirt, but before I can stand, I'm quickly swept off my feet and pushed on my back on top of the ottoman. Ryker is now directly above me.

Holy fuck!

I'm caught so off guard that I only yelp in response as Ryker's massive arms pin my wrists above my head. His cheek drags up and down the side of my face, ever so gently.

"You smell too fucking good, baby," he says, his voice hoarse. "Jesus, you are…"

God, that voice. My heart is beating so loudly I cannot be sure how he ended that statement, exactly. All I know is, just as quickly as I was pinned, I'm released and left there in a daze, more confused than ever. I lay there dumbfounded, wetness running down the inside of my thighs from the excitement of his actions and words. I watch Ryker stand and adjust the front of his pants before heading to the door. He glances back with what looks like an apologetic expression on his face and, as usual, he leaves without another word.

I finally manage to compose myself enough to get dressed and make my way out to the bar for the pre-shift meeting. As I walk, I give myself a little pep talk and a reminder to remain calm, seeing as tremors of excitement are coursing through my body from just thinking about what happened. *Holy shit, that was hot!*

I CATCH UP to Brooke and Naomi as they discuss who will work what section tonight.

"Kat, do you have a preference? 'Cause I really like working the VIP section," Brooke says.

"No, I never care what section I have; you guys can work it out. I really don't have a preference yet. It's all still new, I'm easy," I answer, "but thanks for asking."

Thank goodness these two have been nothing but nice. Levi had really made me nervous that maybe they wouldn't be, because of that comment he made back when I first started. Lucky for me, we get along great; there is no cattiness at all.

"Well how about you work the front section just off the main bar?" Brooke suggests. "Seeing as it's 2-for-1 bar shots tonight, it's gonna be crazy in every section, honestly really it doesn't matter where we all end up." She giggles. "We're all gonna get paid."

"Yeah sure, I can do that section, no problem," I say.

And, of course, I'm sectioned closest to the main bar…Ryker's bar. Not only will I be back and forth a million times tonight, but we'll also be in each other's view the whole time. *Perfect, just bloody perfect. Who am I kidding? I'm totally okay with it as much as I wish I wasn't.* Naomi must hear my mutterings, or sees it on my face, because she asks me if everything is all right. I tell her everything is great and maybe I'm just a bit nervous about working a busy Friday.

"Just you wait, you will be begging Claire to permanently give you this shift. Friday nights are the best. Everyone is in the mood to wind down, the hotties are all out, and with the 2-for-1 shooters the tips are insane. I wouldn't be surprised if you make more in tips tonight than you did all week," she comments with a smile.

Luckily for me, my shift flew by. But best of all, it ran by nice and smooth, giving me very little time to worry about Ryker or what happened between us earlier.

Naomi was right. It was crazy busy and I did indeed make a small fortune in tips tonight. I think Levi might have been right, too. These tight shirts definitely help, not that I would ever admit it to him.

Ryker and I did manage to have our fair share of not so stolen glances throughout the night. Every time I'd try to steal a look, I'd find his honeybutter eyes already looking my way. Honestly, it was a little unnerving, but hot at the same time. There were times I would venture to say it felt like he was looking out for me, making sure I was okay, especially when I was out serving the bigger groups of men. A few times, I could feel his gaze boring into my back. It was actually a nice feeling having his eyes on me tonight. And I swear, the few times his hands brushed mine as he handed me my full trays, actual sparks could have been seen. Geez, I sound like a smitten schoolgirl with a crush on the popular boy. Wow, that doesn't really sound too far off, actually.

I'd be very interested to see just how caught up in this boy I could get. *If only I could get Ryker to talk to me in full sentences,* I think as I collect my things from my locker. Just being back in here makes my skin comes alive, and all I can think about is him. Walking back out to the bar, I wave to the girls, but don't stay to see if I can find Ryker. I'm not brave enough yet to try and talk to him about what's going on between us.

Smiling at the thought of him, I make my way out to my car. Walking out, I breathe in the fresh air, taking in the sounds of crickets in the distance. I love the cool night breeze as it kisses my arms and legs. It was hot and stuffy in the bar tonight and I'm a sweaty mess. I'm beyond looking forward to getting home and unwinding with a long bath and delving into *Malevolent* by Cassia Brightmore. I could use a good creepy read tonight. This is one of the pros to having insomnia, lots of reading time. 2 a.m. is nothing to a girl like me.

Someone's leaning against the back of Bertha, legs crossed.

"What the hell—*Seth?* What the hell are you doing here?" I say, and stop in my tracks. I'm shocked, and somewhat panicked, wondering what he wants and how he knew I'd be at Pub Fiction tonight. He looks the opposite, relaxed, like he hasn't a care in the world. It's an odd look for him, really, because he had always been agitated, well, around me anyway.

"How…how did you know where I work?" I question, my voice shaky.

"Hi, beautiful. I told you we needed to talk. So, I'm here. I got shit to say, and you're gonna hear me out," he says, making his way toward me.

My eyes dart around the mostly vacant lot, noting a jacked-up truck to the left of us and a few stragglers waiting on cabs off in the distance. *Phew!* At least we're not alone. Not that Seth ever hurt me physically, but I want nothing to do with him. At all.

"You're supposed to be in Ottawa, Seth," I remind him. "And we're done. I've...I've moved on," I stammer, clutching my keys tighter, but he doesn't balk. He's moved right in front of me, blocking the driver's side of my car. "We've been over this. Stop calling, stop texting, and, as a matter of fact, don't come near me again!" My breathing becomes heavy as I'm getting upset that he has the nerve to think I want anything to do with him.

"Oh, doll, don't say that. We're gonna work it all out," he says, his eyes serious as his blond hair falls across his forehead.

"No, we're not. I am *d-o-n-e*," I spell it out for him.

I try to move past him to get into my car, but he grabs my arm and pulls me against his side. "I said I had shit to say. I need you to listen. You're going to fucking *listen*. I need you, sugar," he says. I cringe at that pet name.

"No, Seth!" I yell. "You had me. You changed us. Not me!"

Pulling hard, I manage to break out of his hold, but the momentum causes me to fall backward, and I land on my ass. And just as my ass kisses the asphalt, I hear *him*.

Ryker.

"What the fuck is this? Are you okay, Kat?" Ryker asks, while helping me up. He places his hand on my cheek and waits for assurance, but I find myself unable to make any words come out. He gestures in Seth's direction, seething. "This asshole giving you a hard time?"

"No, no, everything's okay, thank you. I'm fine. I just tripped is all," I lie to him and I don't know why. Maybe I don't want him to think I'm weak. Useless.

"Besides, I was just leaving," I say as I open the driver's door with purpose, knowing Seth won't try to stop me with Ryker here.

"Kat," Seth seethes, "we need to talk. We're not done here."

"Oh, no, bud. I believe you *are* done. Way past fucking done. Kat, go on ahead, sweetheart, I got this," he says and offers me a small smile before turning back to Seth.

I really don't want to leave. A part of me wants to stay and make sure Ryker is okay, to stay and deal with Seth myself once and for all, but I know Ryker can take care of himself…and me, too, for that matter. Seeing Ryker quick to defend me sparks a familiar emotion in me, one I've gotten from Claire, and that feeling is trust. For some reason, it feels like I can trust him…already.

Without another glance, I get in my car and peel out of the lot as my tires slip a bit at my speed.

What the fuck was all that?

How the hell did Seth know where I work? I'm shaking as images of Seth plague my mind.

What the hell was he thinking?

Oh, God, what the hell will Ryker think? Shit.

HALF AN HOUR later, I'm home and comfy in my boy shorts and black tank top. I'm too hyped up to read my book, instead I'm unwinding from this strange night by watching TV. I'm trying not to think about Seth and everything else that happened, when I hear a light knock at the door. I'm home alone. Claire is still out with Colby, and as for the girls, I assume they are partying somewhere after the bar they all went to closed. Obviously, I'm a bit reluctant to answer it. *Shit. It better not be Seth.*

I quietly tiptoe across the living room, cell phone in hand ready to dial 911 if needed. I make my way to the top of the stairs and wait to see if the person is still there in the dark. Damn, I wish I had left the light on. *Maybe it's just a drunk student at the wrong house?* I stand there, my legs feeling a bit like jelly, palms sweaty. I hate being home alone at night sometimes, and this is exactly why. I stand perfectly still and hope they've got the wrong house, or whoever it is will just give up and go away.

Suddenly, there is a series of harder knocks, and I startle, letting out an embarrassing yelp.

"Kat, it's me, Ryker. Open up."

I immediately calm, letting out the breath I hadn't realized I'd been holding, relieved at the sound of concern in his voice.

Holy Shit, Ryker is at my door. I check myself over in the mirror, making sure I look okay. *Whoa, girl, who cares what you look like at 3 a.m.?*

Opening the door, I'm met with Ryker's honeybutter eyes staring down at me intently. Ryker is at my doorstep at almost three in the morning. He scans me from head to toe and I swear I feel it everywhere. *Jesus, what is it with this guy?*

Stepping closer, he cups my face again like he did in the parking lot. My breathing hitches and he smirks. "I was just on my way home. I needed to make sure you were okay. I didn't like that. Not one bit. You are going to explain it to me one day." He drops his gaze to my lips, to my chest, and then back to my eyes.

Like an idiot, I'm frozen. I'm caught off guard at his gesture, his kindness. I can't seem to find my voice, but I'm even more surprised at how I do want to tell him. I want to tell him everything about me. *That's twice tonight he's shocked you, Rollins. Maybe you're wrong about him.*

Staring up into his concerned face, I manage to utter a few words, "I'm all right, Ryker. Thanks to you. Thank yo—" Before I can finish, he pulls my face closer and kisses my forehead.

"You're welcome, sweet girl," he says before kissing the side of my mouth. I will my brain to make my face turn that fraction it needs for full contact, but, of course, my whole being is so overwhelmed that it doesn't cooperate. "We'll pick this back up soon. Go and get some rest. It's late."

And with that, he's gone just as fast as he came.

Well, I'll be damned.

Chapter 13

Kat

THE ONE THING I can't seem to do like most people my age is sleep in, like ever, even before I had insomnia. I have the internal alarm clock of a child. Regardless of how late I go to bed or how many days my insomnia has affected me, after five hours I'm wide awake, all bright-eyed and bushy-tailed, with no hope of going back to sleep. Especially when I have nights that end like last night did. There was no way I could shut my mind off.

As Saturday morning rolls around, I'm the first one up. I might be the only one home. I pad down the stairs with a plan of action in mind: Netflix and coffee! I give the place a onceover, noticing their shoes and bags are strewn everywhere as if a tornado roared through the condo sometime early this morning. *I guess falling asleep with my headphones on was a good thing. I can only imagine how loud the girls were coming in.* I can see they're all home, with the exception of Claire; her purse seems to be the only one missing from the cubbies in the front foyer. This, however, doesn't surprise me in the least. I figured Claire would be spending the night at Colby's.

After a few hours of an *Orange is the New Black* marathon, Claire finally shows her face. The other girls are all still sleeping, so it's pretty quiet. I end up scaring Claire with my greeting as I pop my head up over the back of the couch as she makes her way up the stairs from the front door.

"Morning, sunshine! Did we have a good night?" I welcome her home in a singsong voice.

"Gah! Jesus, Kat, what the actual fuck! You scared the piss out of me!" Claire yells.

I giggle; add a "Gotcha!" and point at her after she completes her mile-high jump.

"Why the hell are you up this early, anyway? It's Saturday, and didn't you work until 2 a.m.?" she asks.

I answer her question by giving her a *'really?'* look.

She quickly makes her apologies. "Oh, buddy, why didn't you take a sleeping pill? You need to get some actual sleep. Isn't this the fourth day this week?"

"Yeah, yeah, I know, but I can't seem to want to take any Imovane. I'm still nervous it's going to knock me out and I won't wake up if I need to, even with the new dose Doctor Benson prescribed."

"Okay, but I think if you can't sleep tonight, you should at least try taking half. I'll be home, you won't need to fear not waking up. I've got your back," she says with a reassuring smile.

"Thanks, lady. You are seriously the bestest friend a girl could ask for, Claire. I hope you know how much I love your face."

"We-ell," she muses, dragging out the word, "seeing as you love me tons right now, what would ya say to hitting pause while I put my shit away and we'll have us some Best Friend Forever TV time?"

"I guess I could do that for you, but hurry up. I'm dying to see what happens next."

After quickly running upstairs to put her things in her room, Claire hits the kitchen to get coffee and grab some of her full of sugar cereal that she can't live without, before returning to join me on the couch. Plopping down beside me, a huge smile on her face, she slouches with her feet propped up on the coffee table.

"What are you waiting for? I'm ready, press play bee-yotch!"

"Clearly you had a good time last night." I grin.

"Oh, my God, you have no idea. The party was lots of fun. I seriously think we should have joined a sorority. *I mean they were, like, so awesome. Like, everyone was just, like, so nice. Like, oh, my God,*" she adds in her best valley girl imitation. We both laugh as she tells me about the party.

"Colby was super sweet and fun. It's weird; sometimes I feel more of a friend vibe, but that's okay. We still get along great," she shares. "I met a ton of super nice people and I would hang out with them again. They definitely know how to throw a party, that's for sure. Kegs, kegs, and more kegs. We totally need to go to the next one and bring the other girls, too. There were a lot of hot guys there."

"Well, I'm not sure that's really my scene. Frat parties are always huge, Claire. You know how I feel about too many people packed into small spaces since the fire. We'll see when the time comes, okay?"

"Sounds good, grasshopper. At least you didn't shoot me down right away. Progress, young Jedi! Thanks again for covering my shift. I might just be willing to pay you back one day."

We're watching our favourite show, when Claire breaks the silence. *I'm surprised she lasted this long.*

"Now, about last night. Tell me, tell me. I am dying to hear all the details from start to finish," she says, nudging my arm and raising her eyebrows in a suggestive manner. I laugh her off as she continues to torment me with her sharp elbow. "Did you get to work close to Ryker? Do you need me to hook you up, or did you get in on your own? Will you be paying off the saved-your-snatch-debt?" she crows.

I laugh at her by this point.

"Could you now be preggers with what would be the most adorable baby ever? She asks.

"Oh, my God. Let's slow things down a bit, eh? It was one shift and we barely spoke," I tell her, thinking how she's going to flip when she finds out what really happened last night. She will totally lose her shit when I tell her about Seth showing up. Claire hates Seth with a passion because of the way he treated me and how he still won't leave me alone. I decide to talk about the shift itself first.

As I get ready to tell her all about my night, I think back on Ryker and how his touches made me feel, as well as how incredible he was with the whole Seth incident. I can no longer deny how badly I want him. No longer deny it to myself, or to my best friend. More so now after the way he helped me with Seth and how he cared enough to stop by to make sure I was okay. But still, I'm scared to go down that path. He'd be no good for a girl like me. I'm not the one-night stand type, and I have a feeling that the more I get to know him, the more I'm going to want to keep him, which is not something he does. Ryker doesn't do relationships.

"The shift itself was both hectic and a lot of fun. I have to admit, I might have overreacted about the uniform after all; it appears to have its uses. I can't believe how much I've been making in tips! I actually told Levi the other day not to bother ordering me the new size."

"Oh, yay, I'm glad. See, I'm all-knowing it would seem, eh?" she gloats.

"Yeah, yeah, I get it, you're a savant, but I have to tell you, you were totally right about working Fridays, Claire. Friday nights are crazy, and I was like the shiny new toy; all the boys wanted a shot from the new girl," I say.

"I knew you'd come to appreciate the look. You need to listen to me more often, lady. When will you learn that I'm always right?" she adds.

I give her yet another 'yeah, yeah' response, then decide to woman-up and finally tell her about the interesting part of my shift. The part I have been dying to share with her since she walked through the door this morning. So I begin to tell her what happened with sexy honeybutter after a six hour shift; one that was filled with sexual tension and recurrent thoughts of Ryker that were leaving me weak in the knees and wired as I hustled around the bar all shift. Then I share how I've been thinking about it all night and how it's like a constant movie reel replaying the highlights of the staff room incident over and over in my head, and how I am no closer to figuring out what the fuck happened than I was before. I need Claire's advice. I know she jokes, but she really can be a great sounding board when I need her to be, and right now I need her opinion and guidance on how to proceed. All I have so far is that I'd like to have Ryker mount me like that again...but *naked* next time.

"Jesus, Kitty Kat, that is sexy as hell. I can't believe you didn't pass out with him staring at you practically naked. I guess you'll be checking the door like a person with OCD now, eh?" Claire says, and I laugh nervously because she's right on both accounts.

"I don't know what the hell was going on," I tell her, exasperated. "I was just too stunned. Then I was trying to play it off all cool, and, well, you heard how well that turned out," I say, making a pouting face, and she just smiles.

"Well, chicka, once again, I'm proven right. I did tell you that you're one hot piece of ass, and I'm sure seeing that rack of yours in your lacy bra only helped Ryker to react like that when he opened that door. I can only imagine his face; I would have loved to have seen both of your faces, actually."

As we chat a bit more, she is a perfect ear. She listens to everything I tell her and reassures me it will all work out. She convinces me that my little tantrum is the last thing Ryker will remember.

"Now speed it up." She taps my knee as she rocks up and down with excitement while sitting on the couch. We're now facing each other, and she's pushing me to move on to the good part. "Okay, enough shop talk, I wanna hear how Mr. Mountain o' Sex ended up on top of you. I cannot believe you didn't start with that shit, now go. Eeep, this is killing me. I'm glad you worked for me last night. But before we go on, I need to take a quick pause to ask a very important question. One I really need you to consider, okay?"

"Oh no, do I really want to hear this? You are being way too giddy about this," I reply, my voice skeptical.

"Well, because it's clear it's inevitable." She grins at me before continuing. "Well, are you going to tap that?"

Oh brother, this girl is way too much sometimes, but, unfortunately, I roll my eyes while I scowl at her. "Ah, Claire, just a reminder: You're a girl. I don't think we call it 'tapping that.'"

"Meh, equal rights," she replies, rolling her hand impatiently. "Get on with it."

I continue with the part I consider the *good stuff*, the part where my arms are pinned above me with Ryker whispering in my ear: *You smell too fucking good, baby. Jesus, you are...*

"Wham! There it is! The part I couldn't make out," I say, louder than I intended to. I'm clearly more affected than I was hoping to let on to Claire, but I can't help it. I'm pretty giddy and radiating excitement. I'm not going to be able to deny it anymore. There will be no more trying to hide my real feelings on the subject of hooking up with one Ryker Eddison. My voice has started to fluctuate all over the place. "And, that's all I got." I've been trying so fucking hard to guess what the last word he whispered in my ear had been before he bolted out the door.

"Fuck, that is hot but why didn't you hear what he said? I mean, he was whispering words into your ear, how the hell didn't you hear? You're killing me!" Claire states, annoyed. *I'm killing* her, *ha!* Meanwhile, I'm dying a little inside.

"Damn it, I know. But it's like as soon and I heard him call me 'baby,' I melted. It was like that word and his growling tone caused me to short circuit. Maybe he was mumbling, or maybe it was just that him growling 'baby' like that caused me to go half-deaf at the worst fucking time, and that's why I didn't hear the last part?" I say with a long, deep sigh, now restlessly prowling around the living room.

I'm not a virgin by any means, but sex has always been very...*vanilla*. "Vanilla" seems to be the term everyone uses to mean *boring*, right? So, yes, it's definitely been vanilla. Boring in the sense that it has never been an all-consuming, 'I need you *now*' kind of act. Sex for me has always happened when I was in more of a relationship situation, never one-night stands, and it's been mostly plain old missionary, which is sweet, I guess, but not how I imagine it would be like with a man like Ryker. God, just thinking about Ryker evokes a kind of wantonness I've never felt before. *Jesus.*

"I'm not really sure why it's hard for you to understand why I can't be sure what he said to me. I mean, after all, Ryker was pinning me down, whispering in my ear. You try having that man pin you down like that and see how much you can focus."

"Relax. If I didn't know better, I'd almost think you liked it and wanted more," she taunts and smirks at me.

"What the fuck did you expect to happen? A girl can only take so much, you know. I think my brain just shut down. Fuck, *look* at him!"

It doesn't go unnoticed that I have now let on just how much into Ryker Eddison I might be.

Claire starts bouncing up and down on the sofa, and squeals, "ERMAHGERD, O-M-G! Kitty Kat, you soooo want to tap that! I knew it! You lying bitch! I knew it. You can't deny what's written all over your face. Hellooooooo! Kitty Kat needs her catnip, people." God, I love to hate this bitch sometimes. My bestie howls and holds her stomach as she enjoys my squirming way more than is strictly necessary.

Part of the problem I have with admitting to Claire that, yes, I might be finally warming up to the idea of having a one-night stand…and with *Ryker*, is that I'm inexperienced. I'm nervous and not really sure how to even go about it. I've never been that type of girl. Don't get me wrong, I'm not judging. It's not that I think one-nighters are wrong, it's more that I'm not sure I could pull one off. Truthfully, I'm not sure I'm built to be the 'love 'em and leave 'em kind. I think I'm too much of a stressor to not allow my emotions to become involved when I think I'll always want more than a one-night stand. Besides, I kinda really like the idea of being wooed and all that fluffy stuff that I've never had. I've just always been the relationship type. However, that route hasn't always worked out for me either; at this point, who the hell knows which is better?

I attempt to get Claire to drop the current topic of conversation, but to no avail. She is relentless about hooking me up with Ryker.

"Claire, Ryker and I haven't talked much yet. All I know about him is hearsay and rumours and, of course, the weird interactions we've had, but I admit that, yes, there is something there. I do feel it. You were right. I think we might be great together. Even if it's…if it's just for one night. But the hard part for me, Claire, is can I do one night?" I ask, leaving it in the air.

"You little minx," Claire shouts, but then looks me in the eye, like really looking at me for the first time since all this shit with Ryker started, realizing I'm considering all the facts. She's looking at me like she's really contemplating my words, her words, and the situation. Like she knows I might be about to make one of the biggest changes to myself, and it's with her help. I just smile as she watches me in silence for a few more minutes.

Then I take a deep breath and get ready to tell Claire about the next part.

"But before we keep talking about Ryker, I need to tell you what happened after work. And I need you to stay calm. It's not really a big deal, but—"

She cuts me off immediately. "Fuck that what the hell happened? You never start like that unless it's something big or something bad. Just tell me, but you know I can't promise not to react. *Pssht*, please. You know better than to ask that shit of me."

"Okay. It was Seth. He showed up after work. He was waiting for me at my car," I say, broaching the subject of Seth with a calm voice, trying to show her I'm okay. Because honestly, I am. Other than a few texts and phone calls, this was Seth's first time showing up in person; well, as far as I know anyway. And I'm pretty confident that after Ryker talked to him; it will be the last time.

"What the fuck! What a shitface douchebag!" Claire yells, pacing the living room now. She's going on about what an ass he's always been and how I need to call my dad and Wes so they can deal with him once and for all. She hates Seth and always has. Claire tried to tell me how he was a controlling asshole, but of course, I was too blind to see it.

Once she calms down, she makes me repeat the Ryker parts over and over. I swear, she's getting a kick out of this now. Hearing how Ryker is a hero, how Seth got shut down, and blah, blah, blah, yes, yes, he is a pretty fucking hot—all hero—caveman of a being.

"Now tell me again, please, why the hell—after last night—you aren't convinced this could work with this hunk of a man? I mean, he came to check on you. Come on, that is major swoon."

Putting my hands up in surrender, I cave and tell Claire my true thoughts about him.

"Yes, Ryker Eddison does seem to have some sort of powerful pull on me, one that is starting to make me and my lady bits go crazy, and I'm realizing that, yes, maybe there is more to him than the player status. And, yes, seeing him last night has heightened his likability, a lot. He was all superhero-like, swooping in to save me from that asshead, and it was pretty fucking sexy."

"Shit, yeah, that is such a sexy visual. I can picture him being all hot and seething. Now to think of a name and design his costume." She strums her hand on her chin as if contemplating this. "Nah, but honestly, Kat, I really think you should just go for it, just put yourself out there and take a chance for a change. You can do it. You know deep down you want to. Shit, I can see it written all over your face." I sigh, preparing to share my final decision with her.

"With all this having been said, I've been thinking, and I really need you to really hear me now. Are you listening? Because this attraction, these feelings are something I will be *ignoring*. Us hooking up is not something that will never happen. I need to focus on other things, like school and work. Besides, I'm really not build for that kind of relationship. It can never happen. It won't ever happen. In fact, I will deny having *ever* felt attracted to him from this point on. I felt what I felt, but in the end, I know he's just a player, and so I'm going to leave it alone."

"Uh-huh," she says, and smiles. "I completely understand."

"*Claire,*" I draw out her name after seeing her sneaky smile. "I mean it, you got me? Please. Listen to me for once. I will not be, like I've said before, another notch on his bedpost. I refuse." I go on, rambling now.

Claire just stares at me, smirking.

"For real, Claire Bear. I need you to tell me you understand. Seriously."

Smirk.

"Honestly, I don't want to have to worry that you're saying stuff to Ryker about me—and how we should hook up—when you're working together." I sigh and stare at her, waiting for confirmation. "Okay?"

"Argh, okay, I got you, Kitty Kat, don't you worry. I gotcha loud and clear," she sasses back at me, her eyes shining with mischief, brows raised with interest. "But I can thank him for coming to your rescue," she taunts before she says good day and heads to her room for a nap.

After shutting everything in the living room off and cleaning up our mugs and bowls, I head up to my room too, but to think. My conversation with Claire helped a ton, but I seriously feel overwhelmed and I need to reflect more on what the hell I'm going to do with the Mr. Honeybutter situation.

Chapter 14

Ryker

October

FUCK ME! MY dick has been hard for over a month now, ever since Kat barged into my life. Not hard in the 'I can tug it out in the shower to make it better' way, either. No, I mean hard for that sweet little thing, Kat. Fuck. Ever since the time I practically broke her when I bumped into her, and then when I walked in on her in the staff room. Shit! I have been harder than Wolverine's adamantium claws. Anytime I think about her, it's like—*bam!*—my dick's at full attention. Her pouty little mouth and that fucking attitude she tries to give me, just make me crazy. God, I swear, a guy can only eye-fuck a chick so hard for so long before needing the real thing. *She's fucking beautiful.*

Thank Christ we don't work together; I don't know what I would do. *Yeah, I do. I'd be fucking her in the staff room, supply room, maybe even on Levi's desk? Fuck.* That last Friday shift in August nearly killed me. Thinking of that shift, I would have killed that son of a bitch had he laid a finger on her that night. Since that incident, I've had Levi make sure all late-night employees are escorted to their cars by security. That way I can make sure she—no, *all*—of the female staff are safe when leaving work.

I wonder who that asshole was? Fuck, why do I care? *'Cause she gets to you.*

It doesn't fucking matter who that asshole is, anyway. I told him if

I saw him sniffin' around Kat or the bar again, he'd live to regret it. He tried to tell me she was *his*. I laughed in his face. It was priceless. *"You're not man enough for that girl, asshole. You probably wouldn't know what to do with a fine piece of ass like Kat."* I grabbed him by the collar, stood toe-to-toe with him. *"She's fucking sweet and MINE. My advice from this point on...fuck the hell off. I protect what's mine. Now get the fuck outta here before I change my mind and kick your ass."* I don't know why I told him she was mine, but I did. And if I'm being honest, I like the way it sounded. *A lot.*

"Matty, you 'bout ready to get the fuck going yet or what, pretty boy? You need me to come do your makeup?" Justin, my roommate, yells out to Matt, our other roommate, and my best friend. We're sitting in our living room sipping beer before heading to the bar, waiting on Matt like always. "Let's fuckin' go, dude." He shouts out again, shaking me free from my reverie. He turns to me. "You all right, brother? You seem preoccupied. You itching for some sweet pussy like I am? It's been a slow week. Between work and school, that's all I've done. I sure as shit need to relieve some tension tonight," he admits with a grin.

"Naw, man, I'm good. Was just thinking about work shit, is all. Yeah, of course I'm ready. I'm always fucking ready. I could definitely use a distraction." I stand and nod at his beer. "Another? Seeing as Princess isn't fuckin' ready yet..."

Man, I just need to get laid. I realize this the more I think about Kat's tight body.

It sure as hell doesn't help that Claire, her fucking roommate, can't seem to stop talking to me about all things Kat and showing me pictures. She's taunting me on purpose, I swear. She gave me the biggest hug and thanked me for helping Kat with her ex. It's almost as if she really is on to me. Like she knows, despite my aloofness to her ramblings, how affected I am by Kat, that I'm actually quite interested in learning about her.

Thank God the boys and I are headed to the bar tonight. I'm sure to find a hot piece of ass there to take the edge off. It's only been this long because Levi's needed me to work a few mornings when I don't have classes on top of my usual nights. Two full-timers up and quit mid-September, leaving us short-handed. *Liar.*

"Dude, let's fucking go. The Beaver and Bulldog is gonna be jammed with the hotties by now; it's almost eleven. I am not coming home alone tonight. Let's fuckin' *go*, man. Five more minutes and we're leavin' your ass behind," I yell up the stairs as I grab two more beers for Justin and me from the fridge.

Tonight my plan is to get myself back into the game. Back to thinking about taking care of me and my needs. Seriously, no more thoughts of hot girl for this guy. Like I said, I don't do relationships. *Why the hell am I letting this girl get to me?* Visions of her have been distracting me non-stop, her beautiful smile popping in my head at the wrong times, all the time. I don't like not being in control. Well, tonight I'm taking that control back.

It's not that the opportunity for a serious relationship hasn't presented itself since my breakup two years ago. Believe me, if I wanted a steady girlfriend, I'd have a bevy of choices. Cocky or not, it's the truth. But like I said, it's been all about release for me. I don't have time for feelings and emotions or idle chitchat about shit I couldn't care less about. I have goals and a life plan that I intend on seeing fulfilled. It's not like I'm here to find, meet, and marry the head cheerleader. No, for right now, it's all about getting my dick wet.

I've been totally consumed with being at work and school all the time that I guess thoughts of her have been able to seep into my mind's eye through the cracks, taking up spaces that aren't usually reserved for only one girl. And after tonight, she will slip on out just as quickly as I slip my dick inside the pussy of the chick I allow to grace my bed for a

MY MIND'S EYE

few hours. *Goodbye, Kat.*

There's a thunder from the stairs and, suddenly, Matty bounces into the room ready to go.

"How do I look?" Matt twirls in front of us, like the chick he is, once he's finally downstairs, ready to get the night on.

His signature cologne clouds the room and I notice he's spiked his short hair up in the front tonight.

"Aww, Matty, you look very pretty. I just love your hair all spiky like that." I point and he calls me a douche.

"Nah, fuck, man, you still look like a dick. What the fuck? We thought you were changing," Justin razzes Matty, and we share a good laugh at his expense.

"Sorry I took so long. My room was a mess. I needed to make it pussy safe. I don't need some chick-repellent smell making my night's fuck change her mind suddenly because my room smells like Eau de hockey bag, you know? This guy needs to get laid tonight." He points double fingers at himself, and I can't leave it alone.

"Dude, your face alone is a pussy-repellent. It's not your room you need to worry about," I say, downing the last swallow of beer.

"Fuck you, Ryk, you pretty boy. Let's fuckin' go. I'll show you how the ladies love Matty. I ain't no repellent. I'm like a fucking magnet...a chick magnet."

"Oh, for fuck's sake, dude," says Justin, "that was lame. Do not say shit like that again. And maybe if you cleaned your room on a more regular basis, you wouldn't be wasting our trolling time. Let's fuckin' go already."

Bring it on, says my cock.

113

Chapter 15

Kat

CLAIRE AND I are finally off together on a Saturday night. We decide to take complete advantage of the weekend.

Thank goodness tonight we are heading out for a night of fun along with our roommates and two other friends, Jenn and Laurie, who we met in our teacher's program. We are in for a night of drinking, dancing, and what is sure to be a shit-show. I seriously cannot wait!

I rush home from studying at the library to grab a bite to eat and get ready. Knowing Claire, she will have the house set up like a beauty salon, armed to primp and pimp us all out.

Making my way through the front door, I stumble on the mess of shoes that greets me as I make my way inside. *Of course the festivities have already begun.* I hear laughter and Taylor Swift on the stereo singing about how a player will always play. *Isn't that the truth,* I think as an image of Ryker pops into my mind.

"Hey, ladies," I call, kicking off my runners. "I see you started without me."

Amanda is stationed at the blender, making what looks like margaritas. I see her adding in tequila to the slushy concoction before turning it on, once again drowning out the sounds in the kitchen. Once she's done, the smell of fresh limes and Cointreau lingers in the air and I wet my lips in anticipation. That girl makes a killer 'rita; it has me salivating just thinking about it.

"For you, my lovely. It's about fucking time you got here, ya book worm," Radha says and hands me her drink.

"We were starving. I hope you don't mind, we ordered pizza. We've been sitting here chatting all things boys, sex, and margaritas," Kym adds. "Glad you're finally here to join us. Pizza?" She hands me a plate and napkin and a slice of pepperoni pizza that oozes with cheese.

Glancing at the clock, I'm surprised to see it's already six o'clock. *Wow, that paper took me a lot longer to research than I expected.*

"Kitty!" I hear a shriek from an excited Claire as I approach her putting my pizza down before taking a sip. "Amanda, get this bitch another 'rita; she's got some catching up to do!"

I laugh as Kym passes me another salt-rimmed glass oozing with liquid perfection. Doubled fisted now, I take a seat next to Radha and Jenn, and lift my two glasses to utter a toast my brother taught me, which I know they'll all love.

"Attention! Attention! In honour of our first official girls' night out, I'd like to make a toast! Amanda, get your skinny ass over here and join us." I raise my glass higher, prompting the others to follow. "Ahem, okay, ladies. A toast to kick off the night. Thank you, Wes Rollins, for teaching me this." I clear my throat again before loudly expelling the rest of my toast. "Here's to you, here's to me. Friends forever we shall be," a collective *awww* ensues before I can finish, but I raise my glass higher and clear my throat. "And if ever we should disagree, then fuck you. Here's to me!" I take a huge gulp before bursting out laughing at their faces.

"Oh my God, Kat!" Radha smiles. "I did not expect that from you."

"Cheers. That was the best toast ever, you bitch." Beth smiles.

"You can be such an ass, my dear Kitty Kat," says Jenn.

We begin the production of getting ready for our night out on the town, but before we head upstairs to join the others, Claire and I decide to grab everyone another drink. While I pour us all our fourth round since I've been home, I keep thinking that it's a good thing our glasses aren't too big or else I'd be a mess right now. As I even them out, Claire starts on about her vision for my night. *I love the effort this girl puts into my love life.*

"Kitty Kat, I'm looking forward to getting our dance on tonight, and getting you laid! No more waiting for Mr. Right; we need Mr. Tonight!" She laughs at her stupid joke while carrying the tray up the stairs to where all the girls are.

I opt for a sexy little black number that hugs my girls amazingly, perfecting my line of cleavage. I compliment my outfit with a pair of silver heeled sandals with straps that wind around my legs, stopping just above my calves. Beth finishes my sultry look with some smoky eye shadow in a beautiful violet, which makes my green eyes really pop. I complete my look with silver hoop earrings and a wristlet, apply some tinted lip-gloss, and am ready to go after spritzing myself with my favourite scent.

I have to admit; we are a hot group of girls, all dressed up in our sexy outfits with our makeup and hair all done. It's smells like a beauty salon in the house, but that's to be expected with all the primping that's gone on. After taking what feels like a million pictures and uploading them to Facebook, while we indulge in one more margarita, we finally pile into a taxi van and head out to the bar at 10:30 p.m.

Walking into The Beaver and Bulldog with my girls, I glance to the emergency doors and relax. It's a habit I still do everywhere I go, like a tic. Doctor Lukas assures me this is normal and should lessen over time. We spot a few other students from our classes and greet each other. Everyone's dressed up, happy, and beautiful. The music is blasting from the speakers, and the vibe is positive all around. Seeing my glowing reflection in the mirror over the bar, I feel full of my own power. I look damn good I think, and decide that tonight I'm going to cut loose for once. I am not going to be my usual uptight self. I plan to get my drink on even more and maybe, just *maybe*, listen to Claire and get myself laid. Say fuck it, let me be the player tonight.

It has really been too long, like way too long. Claire is right and I know it. But since Seth and I broke up, I just haven't been feeling it. I think Seth's incessant texts and emails claiming how he wants me back haven't exactly helped either. Since the night at the bar, he still texts me at least once a week. It's tough when you're constantly being made to feel guilty by the person in the wrong, like he has no clue why I don't want to hear what he has to say anymore. I'm being made to feel like I'm the one responsible for pushing him to cheat on me. As if it was me who took his dick and shoved it into that whore. But still, after being cheated on, you can't help wonder. *Is it really me? Am I that bad in bed? Am I too demanding? Or am I just not good enough?* Needless to say, after some soul-searching and lots of Claire-therapy, I discovered it wasn't my fault at all. He chose to cheat. I've since changed my number and email again, hopefully, the asshead cannot reach me and just gives up.

Moving past the crowd, I lead us closer to the bar and the table section. I might not like to go out clubbing very often, but I welcome the sounds and smells around me as we walk. I love the mix of cologne and perfumes battling for dominance; it's the perfect reflection on life. I smile at the analogy I've just made.

Now, months post-Seth, I finally feel a change in views. My body is awakening and it's wanton, craving things it never knew it wanted. My libido seems to be coming out of hibernation with a roar, yelling at me to feed it. Truthfully, I can't blame it. My body's sexual energy has been sparked by Ryker, and it seems the fire has no intention of dwindling any time soon. I note the correlation between this new energy since I began working at Pub Fiction. I chalk it up to me getting comfortable with wearing the sexy uniform and the constant male customers attention that, honestly, has me buzzing with desire at the end of each shift. *Ha! Who am I kidding? I know with certainty there is more to it than just that.*

Standing here now, scanning the room as I'm taking in the scene of the huge dance floor, the sexy dim lighting, and the crowd as a whole, seeing people dancing so close and intimate, helps me realize it's definitely time. Especially when I think about how much use my Rabbit has been getting as of late. A lot of use, by the way. I'm like an addict. I'm in some denial and will not willingly admit to myself that this abuse of my buzzy little friend, as well as my impure thoughts, have anything to do with a certain honeybutter-eyed boy. *Liar.*

As part of my current state of Ryker-denial, I think it's most definitely time to trade up for an anatomically correct, real, lifelike model. *I can do it.* I can set my emotions aside and be like normal girls my age. Fuck it. *Adieu, Rabbit…w*ell, maybe just for tonight, anyway.

Chapter 16

Ryker

YOU'VE GOTTA BE fucking kidding me! As soon as we stroll into the bar, Matt notices a sweet little number sitting on a barstool with her girlfriends.

"Dude, blonde chick, black dress, sitting at the bar. Check her out, man. Fourth chair on the left toward the washrooms, the one sandwiched between the two brunettes. Yep. That's mine for tonight," he bellows over the music, which is pumping out the bass and lyrics of Pitbull and Ke$ha's "Timber."

This place is jammed tonight. I'm shocked he spotted someone who caught his interest so quickly, to be honest. Me, I'm planning on scoping out the selection a bit more slowly. I need an extra hot piece tonight. I'm not settling on the first girl to catch my eye, that's for sure.

"It's as if she's calling out to me. Can you hear her? She's calling to my cock, whispering, 'Come to me, Matty. I will be yours.' And my cock is never wrong about these things. Besides, you know how I'm a sucker for blondes!" Matty smiles with an excitement that has me laughing as he stalks off in her direction before I even get a chance to check her out for myself.

"You coming, Ryk?" he turns and shouts as he keeps pushing through the crowd ahead of me.

"Yep, but all I care about, buddy, is if she's got a friend who's pret-

119

ty, stacked, and willing to play a little round of hide the stick with me tonight, if I happen to deem her worthy of my time. Lead the way, my friend, lead the way. Let's see the offerings."

I get a better look at the girls he's leading us toward. From behind, the girl Matty has picked for himself for tonight seems smokin', and is wearing a tight black dress, the ass-end of which would make any man drop to his knees. Especially the way she's perched up on that barstool. She starts to turn. I struggle to focus, because there is no way in hell I see what I think I do. *Fuck me!*

It's Melissa. Fuck. Me.

Once I manage to get over the initial shock, I try to catch up to Matty. "Shit," I mutter. He's almost made it to the bar. *Damn it!*

I tried, but with Matt's one-track mind, there was probably no stopping him anyway. I wanted to warn him before he made a huge mistake. But now, I guess, I'll just have to stand by and watch this train wreck play out.

I laugh at his earlier "my cock is never wrong" comment. *I can't wait to rub his face in this later.* I will get sweet pleasure from it.

Matt clears his throat behind her; he's practically rubbing up against Melissa's back. Yep. Karma is an asshole.

I stand beside Matt, leaving a good amount of distance between the group of girls and myself. There is no way I don't want an easy escape route once this scene turns to shit, but with the bar jammed packed, I know it's not going to be a quick getaway, so I distance myself as best as I can.

"Hey, sugar, care to allow me to buy yo—aahh…*shit.*" He barely finishes his sentence because as she turns around. Matt instantly realizes his big mistake, looking to me for a clue about what the hell to do. Shrugging my shoulders, I simply grin, as if to say, 'This is all you, buddy, all you.'

We broke up because I caught her cheating on me with some older guy. I had walked in on them while she was riding him as he sat on one of her kitchen chairs, a chair upon which I had once sat, enjoying the same act, not to mention breakfast from time to time. Obviously, when I'd seen that balding, fat fucker with a ton of gold around his neck enjoying sex with *my* girl, I'd lost my shit and made my presence known before slamming the door as I stormed back out.

And now, her eyes find mine, and all the hate and animosity of our breakup comes barrelling back.

Melissa wanted to be a model and actress; to her, it was all about the *connections*. According to her, this guy, Quinton, was some bigwig at one of the top modelling agencies in the area. He was helping her, giving her some tips on things she could do to help her stand out compared to the other girls. Yeah, clearly his biggest tip was the tip of his dick inside my girlfriend's pussy. The bitch went so far as to try and convince me it was *me* who was the problem, that I was an asshole for not supporting her dreams.

Fuck. That. Shit. Cheating is a deal breaker. Always.

I ended it with Melissa in a face-to-face blowout after she showed up at my place later that same night, as if everything was okay between us. However, Melissa turned into this crazy stage-five clinger who relentlessly tried to convince me we still belonged together. It took my brother threatening to call the cops one night, when she showed up at Pub Fiction and made a scene, to finally get her to back the fuck off.

I haven't seen Melissa Foster in almost two years. *Thank God.*

But now I hear Melissa's voice, like nails on a chalkboard, irritating as fuck.

"Oh, *hey*, guys, fancy meeting you two here. It's been forever since I've seen either of you," she says, leaning in toward us, eyeing me up and down, focusing on the front of my fly. "Ryker, baby, you look really good. How are you?"

Oh, fuck me. I need to get the fuck outta here, now.

"I'm great, Melissa, really good. Just out with the boys," I curtly tell her.

"I'd really love to catch up. It's been way too long, Ryk, and I'm sure we could have a little fun while getting reacquainted," she says with a flirty tone and a familiar gleam in her eyes, a look that brings back memories. Memories I'd rather forget than revisit.

"No. That's the last thing that's going to happen, Melissa. You know that." She gives me a pouty face, but lets it go nonetheless.

"What were you going to ask, Matty?" she asks, batting her eyes, trying to come across seemingly sexy and innocent, rather than the whore she really is. Too bad both Matt and I know better.

Fuck me. This little act just goes to further prove what a schizoid bitch she turned out to be. Looks clearly can be deceiving; that's what I've come to know for sure. In spite of her cheating on me, she had always been possessive as fuck. Possessiveness, now that I come to think of it, was something I'd never really felt toward Melissa, even though I cared about her a lot when we were together. Even when I caught her fucking that other guy, I was just more disgusted than anything else. I never really gave a shit at all when other men checked Melissa out; it didn't bother me. But I suspect possessiveness is a trait I have lying dormant within me, just waiting for the right girl to awaken the beast. If I think about the way I feel when I see other dudes checking out Kat at work...*Fuck, where the hell did Kat come from?*

In the end, I think she did me a favour. I'd been too caught up in her, naïve and blind. Seeing her cheat on me had been, I admit, a kick in the guts. Being too starry-eyed is a mistake I will not repeat again, ever.

"Oh, hey, Melissa, actually, Ryker and I were just looking to move in closer to order our beers," Matt stammers. "This place is hoppin' tonight! We didn't realize it was you. It's been a long time, eh? But, hey, this works out perfectly. You mind scooching over a bit or flagging down the bartender for me? If you get him before me, I need two Stellas."

Melissa looks at us with uncertainty, but then waves the bartender over our way. With a huff, she places the order, staring as if she's thinking of something to say.

Matt hands me my beer as he tosses some bills on the bar. I manage to stifle a laugh as I take my glass from Matt. I nod to Melissa before she can continue her attempts to engage me in conversation. I made it more than abundantly clear where we stand, so I'm pretty confident she won't follow us if I move fast enough and get the hell out of there.

Matt slaps my back. "Dude, did you know that was Melissa? Fucking psycho. That chick is all kinds of crazy. No man deserves that shit. I have the fucking jitters now, just thinking how I thought she was hot. Fuck, clearly my cock is in need of a stern talking-to."

"Naw, man, I didn't clue in until it was too late. Believe me, I would have stopped that shit on the spot if I had realized. That chick is nothing but trouble." I chuckle before making a jab. "Maybe your cock was really just trying to help find you a beer? 'Cause clearly no sane cock would whisper in that bitch's direction."

"Ha ha ha, you're such a dick, man," Matt shouts.

"I see the guys; they've got a booth," I say, pointing. "Come on."

Once we're a safe distance from the whore, I turn back around to face the crowd after fist bumping my buddies and chatting about how busy it is. My eyes roam, scanning the crowd for the night's endgame, the chick I'll want in my bed. Then I see *her*.

OH. MY. FUCK.

Right in front of the stage, wearing a sexy-as-sin black dress that fits like a second skin over her curves, is none other than hot girl. Immediately, my cock catches up with my eyes at the realization of her presence and I'm hard—like 'a teenage boy seeing naked boobies for the first time hard.

I need to sit my ass down before anyone sees what I'm sporting in my pants. I would never live that shit down, especially with these assholes. *Fuck me,* she is all kinds of luscious, and those amazing tits of hers are calling out my name as they bounce while she sways her hips in time with the music.

I can't stop staring.

OPENING THE DOOR to exit the washroom, I'm met with a very drunk Kat.

"Shit, Ryker, sorry. I wasn't paying attention. I didn't see you there," she slurs, stifling a giggle. Looking around to make sure no one was watching I pull her inside the men's room, locking the door behind us. I want some alone time with her. I need to make sure she's okay, seeing as she's drunk; I know this because my gaze has been set on her and her alone—her curves, her smile, her eyes…everything that makes her Kat—since the second I spotted her tonight.

"Kat," I whisper, looking into her jade eyes before walking toward her. Her back smacks into the countertop as she tries to back away from me. I end up pinning her hips against the counter, my arms trapping her on either side. I lean in close to her, but I want to be closer. Her hands have nowhere else to go, so she rests them on my chest, and I feel her touch pulse against me.

"Are…are you actually talking to me now?" she stammers, then gives a small hiccup, and I swear it takes everything in me not to carry her out of this place caveman-style to my bed, where I know she'll be safe. I don't like seeing her like this, drunk and vulnerable.

I smile at the shock in her question. *I know, I've been a dick, baby.* "You're drunk. You'd better be a good girl tonight, baby. No guys are to touch you. Get me?"

"What do you care, Ry-*ker?*" Kat enunciates my name in a cute slur. "I mean, you can't talk to me in full sentences most of the time, or at all in over a month now. Then you're hot one second, then cold the next..." she trails off. "Speaking of hot, you're so *hot*, did you know that?" Her drawing out my name like that was sexy as fuck and has me imagining her screaming it out in ecstasy. And her calling me hot makes my dick ache and my heart pound.

"I don't care that we haven't talked in a month. I just don't wanna see anybody get hurt tonight, believe me, sweet girl, just behave. You and me, we'll talk again. Soon. I promise, beautiful." And with that, I kiss her nose before guiding her out the door. I wait there, watching her for a second, making sure she makes it to the ladies room before I disappear into the crowd.

She never looked back at me, which only makes me smile. *Stubborn thing.*

In spite of myself, knowing I should just leave her alone, I can't stop myself from looking out for her, watching her after she emerges from the washroom. I keep my eyes on her all night. Running into her by the washrooms served to make me all the more aware of her, and her every move. From that point on, I was sunk. Game over. I can't help it. My dick is straining my pants so badly; I couldn't stand up even if I wanted to.

"I'm just gonna stay here," I tell Matty and Justin, who want to take a prowl around the other side of the club, "and have a beer or two and chat with Roger and Bryce. You guys go on. I don't see anything I'm interested in yet. Besides, Bryce needs a job, so I'm gonna tell him about Pub. I'll catch up in a bit."

"Okay, man, we're gonna hit the head then do a walk-around. I saw a sexy little thing by the stage I wanna get closer to," Matty says before walking away.

Damn Kat and her sexy-as-fuck self.

125

Once Matt officially ditches us for *that chick,* there is no way I'm leaving my spot at the table with the guys, especially since Justin came back to join us.

"Ryk," Justin shouts, "Matty says we can go on home, he's found his for the night, and we are in no way to expect him home tonight. He actually told me to tell you that if he can help it, he won't be seeing our—well, he meant *your*—ugly mug 'til Sunday."

"Cool, glad he's hooking up," I say as he shows me the chick Matt's picked. "What about you? Doesn't Matt's girl have any friends you can hook up with?" I ask as I look where he's pointing.

Are you fucking kidding me? This is perfect.

I feel relieved as Justin points out the group Matt has decided to infiltrate, pointing out Claire as his night's conquest. Matt being near Kat could be beneficial to me. Hopefully he spends some time getting to know her, too, which will in turn give me his opinion about her. Maybe another guy's perspective would help squash these feelings she gives me.

"Hey, Ryker, check out this chick getting up on the bar, man. She's fucking hot," Bryce says, nudging me.

What the fuck is this? With perfect clarity, I see Kat being lifted by a couple of guys up onto the bar, yelling out to the DJ to play "Stripper" by SoHo Dolls. With a sexy, lopsided smile down to her friends, she slowly unties each of her heeled sandals, unwrapping the straps weaved around her calves before tossing them aside. Then Kat begins to sway her hips in time with the sexy beats pouring out of the speakers, and my breath hitches. Her hips and legs grind lower and lower down as the lyrics kick in.

I'm stunned, mesmerized, and just cannot take my eyes off of this girl who is affecting me like no other before her. Affecting me in a way that I'm not okay with at all. She is consuming my mind, and I need to end this bullshit. Not only am I noticing her effect on me, but so are my buddies, just as she's rubbing her hands ever so slowing down between her ample cleavage as Maya Von Doll sings in whispers the words about moving, being in the mood, and teasing.

My wettest dream comes to life in tunnel vision before my very eyes, but then is abruptly interrupted.

"Hey, stalker, drool much? You wanna napkin to catch all that drool there, bud?"

Justin, the asshole, asks from beside me, a knowing smirk on his face. "Dude, she is one hot piece of ass, that chick right there. Look at those fucking titties," he says, handing me a napkin, watching her sway those sexy-as-fuck hips to the music.

I'm pissed that he's watching her, commenting on her. Without warning, I turn to him and scowl, tossing the napkin back, hitting him in the face with it. "Don't even think about that chick, Justin," I all but growl. "She's not for you. Ever." I realize my teeth are clenched, my eyes trained on his, sending off a 'do not test me' vibe. And, oh boy, does he get it. It's at this point I know I've just outed myself where this girl is concerned, not to mention I feel like an ass. Justin is my friend after all.

He raises his hands in defeat. "Whoa, man, Jesus! Look, I'm sorry. I didn't realize you were into her. I didn't know you fuckin' knew her. So, tell me, lover boy, who is that sex-on-heels and what are you going to do about the way she's got you all twisted up? 'Cause, dude, you almost took me out over some chick."

"You're a dick. There's nothing going on. I think she's hot. Yeah, so…sorry. She's nothing. She's just some chick who works at the bar with me. I'm not trying to sound like a dick I, uh…I just know I'll be sinking between those thighs pretty soon, and need you to back off, man, that's all. I just don't want there to be any confusion. I'm the one who's going to fuck her, and not any of you douchebags," I say, then add "and you know me. You can go for it once I'm done; I don't care for repeats." I hope he's buying it. *You'll never have her, dude. I don't think I will ever be done with her.*

Where the fuck did that come from? I. Am. So. Fucked.

"As if I'd want your sloppy seconds, dude," Justin says, then just stares at me with a 'you're full of shit' smile. It's obvious I'm failing to hide or deny the impact Kat has on me. Fuck me. The last thing I need is the guys razzing me about Kat and how I'm acting like some kind of whipped pussyboy over some girl.

Once I realize what a tool I just was, I decide it's time to get the hell out of there before I lose my shit even more and do something stupid. Something I know will prove I'm losing my damn mind. Something like stalking up to Kat, throwing her over my shoulder, and walking out the door with every intention of finishing what I started in the staff room. *Fucking her 'til she can't move. Please her like she's never known.* I want to make this girl tremble at my touch, teach her that only I can satisfy her, that I am what she craves. I need this girl like I need air, and it's crazy, because I barely know her.

Thanks to Kat Rollins and that sexy-as-fuck dance on the bar, I think I'm going to lose my mind completely. The worst part, I don't think she realizes how truly stunning and sexy she is.

Never has my cock been as hard as it is just from watching a woman dance. *Fuck me.* It's like this girl has a one-way ticket to my cock and she keeps taunting me to convince her to get on, so she can take the ride of her life. Jesus Christ, what a sight that would be. Kat and her amazing tits moving up and down over me, her wet pussy milking me for all that I've been saving for her. *Shit! I'm gonna come all over myself if I keep thinking like this.*

Damn, what a fucking vision, one I plan on bringing to fruition very soon. It's at this moment when I decide that. I am going to get to know every single part of Kat Rollins.

Chapter 17

Ryker

I WAKE UP in my own bed the next morning, alone, staring at the ceiling and feeling nothing but pissed off and irritated as hell. I lay here while image upon image of last night rocks through my mind like a movie reel that's stuck on repeat. Groaning, I roll over in utter frustration, gripping my pillow as I scan the empty space beside me. "Fuck!" I mutter into my pillow, as my arms and legs starfish out, again noting the bed's cool emptiness. It's a space that should be alive with recent memories of me pounding into a willing pussy and a smell of last night's sex. Instead, I wake up to this bullshit feeling, a feeling that karma is mocking me, out to get me, forcing me to re-evaluate these feelings I'm having.

Fuck! I feel like a pussy, which is a feeling foreign to me, a feeling I don't like at all. A feeling I need to deal with, and fast. I'm not used to my bed being empty after a night at the bar, especially when it's been empty as long as it has, and when I had firm plans last night to get some much-needed release. No, I'm used to waking up to either a warm body, which I'm quick to dismiss with a 'Thanks, it was fun', or at least the smell—I love the smell of fucking, breathing it in the next day. Nothing beats waking up to the smell of sex.

But this morning, waking up to this emptiness, this feeling I'm having, it's pissing me off. I'm losing my game; I need to remember the stakes. Need to remind myself what chicks like Kat can do. No way will I allow some girl to take over my world again. I can't let there be another Melissa. I can't allow Kat to break down my walls. I can't risk being left with a feeling of emptiness again. I can't allow myself to become devoted to just one woman, not when there are many to choose from. Why the hell anyone would limit themselves is beyond me.

Last night clearly didn't go as I had planned. I should be feeling sated and happy, not pissy as hell and hornier than fuck. Looking back on last night, I realize I acted as my own goddamn cock-block. I need to shake my head, rid my thoughts of a certain green-eyed beauty. I need to up my game. I need to fuck her out of my system, like I'd planned to last night. Kat is affecting me too damn much.

I mean, in all actuality, could I have gotten laid last night? Abso-fuckin-lutely. I had a ton of chicks to choose from, which was all working out just great until my little encounter with Kat in the washroom.

God, the look on her face when she bumped into me was priceless. She looked fucking beautiful; her green eyes round from the shock of seeing me and the way her body responded to my proximity, she really is striking.

Kat was a very good girl. Whether she remembers our talk or not, she heeded my warning and stayed away from any guys trolling, looking for a hook-up. She saved some guy's face last night, that's for sure.

Well, until that fucking dance she was a good girl anyway. Little vixen. I swear it took everything for me to stay back. That dance, fuck me, that's what changed my mind last night, solidified my choice. I didn't just want any girl. No, I wanted that girl. Last night I wanted— I needed—Kat.

Lying here, I play out last night more times than is good for me, but I can't help it, I keep pressing rewind. Apparently, I feel the need to torture myself. I'm a glutton for punishment this morning, and I just can't shake the images of Kat running through my mind. I'm like an addict needing one last fix.

I groan in frustration because she was right, about me not talking to her. I wipe my hands over my face. Irritated with myself, I think about how I should have gone over to her last night. Realizing that Matt being with Claire would have been the perfect reason for joining them, giving me the excuse to talk to her, to get close. But with this unpredictable growling reaction I tend to have toward her and the ramrod hard-on I get at the mere idea of her, there was no way in hell I was going anywhere near her last night. Not that I didn't want to; believe me, I wanted nothing more. But I need to have better control over myself when I'm around her. No wonder I feel like such a puss.

With these relentless thoughts of Kat, I realize I'm wound way too fucking tight to function normally. Irritated, I whip out of bed, throwing my covers to the floor and pulling off my boxers. I head into the washroom and directly to the shower with my dick beyond angry, throbbing for release I crank the water on without paying attention to its temperature. In fact, the colder the better; I need to relieve this tension.

Once under the spray, I stand still, trying to let the pulse of the cold water take the edge off me as it cascades over my shoulders, neck, and back. But it doesn't. I succumb to the need pulsing through my body. Using the visions I've stored of Kat dancing up on the bar and laying under me on the ottoman as ammunition, I take my swollen cock in my hand. I tug it over and over, slow to fast, then fast to slow, teasing and taunting myself, imagining what I'd do if I were sinking my cock inside her tight pussy. *God, I bet she's so fucking tight. Shit, I need to sink myself deep inside this girl.* With that, I close my eyes, bracing myself as I come hard into my hand, overflowing down onto the tiles.

As I finish pumping it out, I watch my cum flow down the drain. Leaning against the cool tiled wall, I try to catch my breath while thinking about how this fucking chick is killing me... killing my game. As soon as I talked to her last night, I knew I would be going home alone. No one else could elicit the sexual cravings I was having, and it pisses me off. I need to deal with this shit and soon.

Chapter 18

Kat

OH, SWEET BABY Jesus. I wake up in my room the next morning with my head feeling all kinds of fuzzy. My body is chilled to the bone as I realize I'm completely hungover and stupidly wearing nothing but my bra and panties. Apparently, I cannot dress myself for bed properly when I am tequila drunk. I pull my dark purple duvet off the floor onto my bed and snuggle into it. My head is pounding. Gosh, am I ever happy I unpacked this baby the other day. I lay snug as a bug, thinking back on the night, at least what I remember of it. We had such a blast; it was a much-needed night out with friends to decompress and let loose. Despite having a feeling of being watched all night—a feeling that I just couldn't seem to shake—the night was otherwise epic! I haven't laughed, drank, or danced like that in forever. It was awesome to cut loose. I definitely need to let myself do that more often. Well, maybe go lighter on the tequila next time.

I know without a doubt that we will absolutely be heading back to The Beaver and Bulldog. The music was a perfect balance of new and old hits, the atmosphere was positive, and the drinks went down all kinds of smooth, especially the tequila, which was also the reason I couldn't be bothered trying to hook up for the night. I was way too drunk to start any kind of meaningful conversations with the opposite sex. Plus, I was having way too much fun with my friends to really care.

Close to an hour later, I finally force myself to get up out of bed. Having thrown on a hoodie and my favorite pair of Lululemon's from the day before, I cover my freezing body. But before exiting my room, I come to a halt in front of the mirror. *Oh fuck, I'm a mess.* Mascara is caked in little clumps along my eyelids, my hair's a bird's nest, and there is crusty lime 'rita drool dried on the side of my face. *A sure sign of a good time, if you ask me.* "Thank God this is not a regular thing, Rollins," I mutter as I grab a yellow hair tie, scooping my hair up into a knot on the top of my head. *I'll deal with my face in the washroom.*

Opening my door, I have every intention of making my way down the hall to the washroom, but I'm sidetracked by a deep voice booming in the distance. *What the hell?* I'm pretty sure this unfamiliar voice is coming from the kitchen. Confused and curious, I forgo the washroom, cautiously heading to the kitchen. I'm not too concerned, as I know it's probably a guest of one of the girls; I'm just a bit jelly that he's not mine. *Yeah right, like you could handle a one-night stand.* As I approach the archway, I end up stopping stock-still, awestruck with what I see in front of me. *Jesus, Mary, and Joseph on an airplane! Who the fuck is that sex on a pole of a man standing in our kitchen? Wow! Did one of the girls score big time last night, or what?*

I make my way closer to confront this unknown hunk, this shirtless wonder. But as I get closer, I laugh at a voice I hear and the person I see lapping up this guy's every word—*Claire*. I should have known. My little bestie is, of course, sitting on a barstool grinning like a Cheshire cat at Pole Guy.

"Oh, there you are!" Claire calls out as she spots me smirking in her direction, glancing between her and her hottie, who is not only half-undressed, but also cooking breakfast. "I hope we didn't wake you, Dancing Queen," she says. I shake my head, smiling sheepishly at Claire's name for me this morning.

I stop in front of the fridge where my goal was to grab the cream for my coffee, a much-needed staple this morning. A vague image from last night's festivities flashes into my head. "Oh my God!" I shout as I leave the cream and march over to the stool next to her, the need to suddenly sit taking over.

"Did I, uh, did I dance on the bar last night?" I ask, nervously thinking *Please say no, please say no*, as memories start flooding back to my mind.

"You sure as hell did, you little sexpot. And fuck me, was it a sight!" Claire laughs back at my question.

"Yeah, you were hotter than Hades, by the way," adds Pole Guy. Wiping his hands on a dishtowel, he reaches over the countertop for me to shake his outstretched hand.

"Hey, the name's Matt. We met last night, but I think it's safe to say you may not remember," he chuckles as we shake hands.

"Oh, God, no," I moan and they both laugh out loud, proceeding to tell me how Matt, no longer to be referred to as Pole Guy, was walking by on his way to the bar and noticed Claire and decided he needed to talk to her.

"Kitty Kat, you, my sexy friend, were on fire! You practically drank a bottle of *ta-kill-ya* by yourself!" she seems to yell, making me wince in my current state.

"Okay, okay, you don't have to yell, Claire Bear. I just need you to talk in whispers right now. Please be my friend, and *shh,*" I say as I head to the couch to listen to the rest of this wonderful recount of a night I have no clue about. *Damn tequila fuzzies.*

From there, I gather that a whole bunch of shots and a game of bar-dare ensued and I, of course, being the competitive type, lost a few dares and ended up tequila-drunk and dancing a dare off on the main bar. Matt and Claire, my ex-best friend, seem to be enjoying my misery way too much, if you ask me.

"Man you are hilarious. You had Brad drinking Rocky Mountain

Bear Fuckers while sitting on the floor with his hands behind his back. It was awesome. He was so drunk; we had to send him home in a cab." Claire and Matt then go on to tell me how we ended up sitting at the bar daring each other and people around us to do all kinds of crazy stunts.

Suffice it to say, I got my justice for my dare to Brad. I'm mortified as I listen to Matt and Claire tell me how, apparently, no one knew how sexy one could manage to make tequila-drunk look. With that point being shared, I start to feel my face turn beet red. I start to apologize for my behaviour, but as I begin to speak, Matt and Claire quickly squash my apology, telling me I have nothing to be embarrassed about and I was sexy as hell, putting on quite the show, which ended in nothing but hoots and hollers all around. No wonder I woke up remembering a feeling of someone watching me all night. *Oh, God, I am dying!*

"Did Laurie and Jenn stay over last night?" I ask, not remembering how I got home, come to think of it.

"Oh yeah. They actually ended up leaving before your performance. Laurie hooked up with some hottie and left with him. Jenn got a ride home from Matt's buddy Max who was their DD last night. She wasn't feeling too hot after you made her down a couple of shots for losing her dares."

Pointing to a vase of flowers beside her, which I'd been too hungover to notice until now, Claire slips it over to me. I scrunch my face in confusion. "These were delivered for you this morning. I think someone may have an admirer," Claire says while raising her eyebrows in a teasing manner. I take the flowers from her and find the attached card, it simply says:

My little tiny dancer...I enjoyed the show. x

Showing Claire and Matt the creepy card, they try repeatedly to convince me it's nothing to be worried about, both listing off all the people it could be from.

"I'm pretty sure it's just a joke. Don't stress about it. Besides, they're beautiful and smell amazing. I know how much you love lilies. Just enjoy them, 'tiny dancer'." Claire says with a warm grin.

After listening to her, I immediately think it's Seth. He knows how much I love lilies. I shake the thought, knowing he's probably back at school, so really there's no way he'd be here again. He'd never miss classes for me twice. Seth never really chose me when it came down to things anyway. I'm still shocked he even showed up that night at Pub Fiction. I mean, he never did make me his main priority like he'd been mine. That was definitely another sore spot in our relationship. Besides, it's not like I've seen him since that night, and after I changed my number, I'm pretty sure he got the message.

I really do appreciate their efforts as they keep trying to convince me the flowers are probably just from one of our friends playing a joke on me, trying to embarrass me about my bar-dare, and to just relax.

After reading the card over again a few times, I decide to toss the flowers in the trash, regardless of who they're from. I just can't shake the bad vibe I'm getting from them. At least this way, they're out of sight, out of mind.

LATER THAT NIGHT, while sitting at the kitchen table working on lesson plans for our in-class placements, Claire and I get a chance to catch up on some much-needed girl chat. Claire fills me in on all the things I've clearly missed.

"So, chicka," I ask, "mind telling me how Matt came into play? What the heck happened to Colby?"

"Oh, yeah, about Colby. We decided a few weeks ago now that we were much better as friends. We just clicked that way. He's a great guy and we have a lot of fun, but after a few dates, there wasn't much of a spark, so in the friend zone he shall stay." She shrugs her shoulders. This revelation makes me feel a bit guilty, as I have obviously been a bit too wrapped up in myself to have noticed.

"I'm sorry, I had no clue, and I've been busy with work and school; it's honestly been consuming all of my time. I promise to be a better friend. I hope you know I'm always here."

She smirks at me. Hell, even I don't believe the shit coming out of my mouth.

"Don't sweat it. I know you're *consumed*," she chuckles, which doesn't go unnoticed. "Like I said, Colby and I are friends, it's not like we had a bad breakup. In fact, I've been helping him to get in there with Amanda. Apparently, they met and really hit it off. Please, don't worry; everything is good."

I nod before closing my laptop, done with my plans for the week.

"Besides—oh, my God, woman—did you see Matt? Jesus. That man is F-I-N-E. I swear, when he came up behind me to dance last night, my vagina started reciting a soliloquy about how badly she needed to meet his cock. Shit, that man can dance. And he fucks like he dances, hence my vagina and I are very happy girls," she says, before sauntering up the stairs.

I let out a laugh at my bestie; she really is something else. I have to say, I'm pretty impressed with Claire's ability to have casual sexual relationships with men and her ability to remain friends once the relations end, for the most part anyway. There have, of course, been one or two exceptions.

Chapter 19

Ryker

WORKING WITH CLAIRE over the past few months has been great for getting insight into her, as well as Kat. I feel like I know them both. Claire is sweet, smart, and beautiful, too. I think she's totally Matty's type. I had even thought about introducing them myself one day soon. Looks like I may have been too slow, but still correct in the sense that they'd be a good fit, I think, as I look over and see Claire, busy texting with a grin on her face.

"It's Matt, sorry. He wants to pick me up," she beams.

"No problem, just be sure to put the phone away when we get busy," I say.

I find myself enjoying getting bits of information about Kat whenever possible. When Claire and I work together, I indirectly try to steer the conversation to topics where she would be forced to bring up and talk about Kat. Wednesday, Claire brought her up without my help.

"You need to hook up with Kat, Ryker. She could use a little fun in her life. I love the girl, but man is she way too uptight. I think you and Kat would really hit it off."

The comment piques my curiosity about why Claire would call her uptight. From what I've seen of her, she seems pretty balanced. My heart starts pounding and my pulse quickens from Claire's words, and for the first time in a long time, I want to find out for myself. I really do want to get to know Kat on a deeper level, but I'm scared shitless to let her in. From what I know, not only is Kat beautiful on the outside, she is even more so on the inside. Everyone here at work loves her; they're always saying how kind and loving she is. Apparently, she wants to be a teacher; maybe I should see if she'd like to volunteer at the rec centre. *If I could only manage to form complete sentences around her.*

I try to downplay my interest in Kat to Claire, so I deflect. "Yeah, but does she put out? 'Cause really, that's the kinda fun I like best." I wink.

"Ryker, you're such an ass. I see the way you look at her whenever your paths cross. Believe me, I'm all-seeing and knowing." Claire tosses the bar towel at me before she resumes serving customers. The rest of the night flies by with no further mention of Kat at all.

But she's right; I do want her friend, more than I care to admit to her or to myself. Now if I could just figure out what the hell to do about it.

Chapter 20

Kat

"WHERE DO YOU want to sit, Kat?" Beth asks, and I scan the library for an open table closest to one of the exits. The girls are more than aware of my little quirks since the fire, so they usually allow me to choose our spot when we're out together. We've all been spending a lot of time together; it's something I've been very open about. I'm lucky to have met them, because they have all been more than understanding about everything; including my dad adding the extra safety gear around the house.

Once we're settled at the long study table, Radha, Beth, Jenn, Laurie, and I pop open our laptops with the intention of finishing up our research notes that we need for our essays.

"God, this inquiry stuff is killing me. I feel like we've been working on it forever. Have you had any luck finding good journal artic—." Jenn interrupts her own words and I look to where she's staring. "Holy cheese monkeys! Look at that fucking guy over by the reserve desk; holy rainbows, he's pretty," She all but drools. I see who she's talking about and immediately my heart begins to pick up its pace.

Really? Really? Does he need to be everywhere I am?

"Oh, shit, guys, look down, and just keep looking down. Please, do not draw attention to us."

"Are you batshit loopy or what? 'Don't draw attention?' Hell, girl, I wanna rip my fucking clothes off and ask him to go bag me in the stacks over there, 'cause hot damn, woman, that man is fine, and I would like to fuck him—a lot," Radha shares while she's fanning herself, sinking further and further into her chair.

"First of all, you need to stop hanging around Claire, Radha. You just freaked me the hell out with that Claire-ism. Next thing I know, you'll be calling me Jedi or grasshopper." I try to stifle my laugh because it was really quite funny. "Second, that over there is none other than Ryker Eddison; the torturer of all things Kat Rollins. So, yeah, keep it the fuck down, ladies. I do not need him to see me." I sigh in defeat as the fuckers do exactly what I just asked them not to.

"OH, MY GOD, KAT!" Beth shouts.

"No way! He is sooo fucking hot," Beth and Laurie practically yell in unison. Perfect. Draw attention to us, to me.

"Guys, this is a *library*. Please shut up! I said I do not want him to see me," I plead a bit louder.

"Holy snickerdoodles. Claire is right; you need to tap that!" Laurie is now looking right at him.

"Please, Laur, keep your voice down. Stop gawking," I mutter, my eyes still looking downcast at the keys of my laptop.

"Ohh shit, Kat, he's on the move. He's looking this way. Jesus, he really is fine with a capital F for fuck me," laughs Beth.

I want to throat punch her. *Please don't see me. Please don't see me.* Unwillingly, my brain is an asshole and shuts down as I seek Ryker out. I can't help it. It's like I just need to see him. Lifting my head, I gasp in an immediate breath as Ryker Eddison is staring at me. He's like ten feet in front of our table, and he's just standing there, like the beautiful Adonis he is. Finally, as my eyes make their way from his shoes back up to his eyes, I suddenly feel the urge to smoke, because for the first time in my life, I, Kat Rollins, *Miss Uptight,* just eye-fucked a man. Not only did I do this in public, but also with my friends sitting beside me giggling at my blatant display of appreciation. As our eyes meet, his go wide before he nods and gives me the biggest shit-eating grin known to man. All before he mouths, *I see you too, baby*, without anyone seeing him and saunters out the library doors, leaving me speechless.

"Well, that was just all kinds of hot. Jesus. That was the sexiest eye-fuck I have ever seen. Tell us again how you don't wanna tap that," Laurie basically calls me out.

After telling them all about my recent Ryker experiences, we finally manage to get a bit of work done. Well, they do.

EVER SINCE WE left the library, the girls have been teasing me about Ryker. They all seem to think he's absolutely interested in me, and they've been going on and on about him and I all evening. After dinner, I've finally had enough and decide to get away from them for a bit; there is only so much pressure I can handle, especially when it's five against one. I know they mean well, but come on, there is no way a guy like that would have any interest in a boring girl like me. Besides, I have a huge math assignment due that I can't seem to wrap my head around and I need some me-time. It's just too loud at home tonight with all the girls there at the same time. It doesn't happen often that we're all home, but when we are, it can be like a circus.

Walking into a little coffee shop across from campus, called The Bean, I instantly take in the aromas of fresh coffee and baked goods. God, I love that smell. I have a serious love for lattes, well, maybe more of an addiction. I'm excited to have found this spot. I had been driving by, deciding where I should go, when I passed the plaza and spotted it nestled in the far corner. After placing my order, I look around while waiting for my drink at the end of the counter. I smile thinking this little gem of a cafe might just become my new study hall. It's homey, comfortable, and, best of all, quiet. There aren't too many people sitting inside; I assume because it's well hidden from the main street. The decor is perfect. There are a few steel tables scattered around the small space and a beautiful seating area with oversized leather chairs, which are nestled around a brown brick fireplace. Yeah, it's definitely a place I see myself visiting often.

Thanking the barista for my latte, I find a small table by the side exit door. Placing my cup and bag down, I take off my jacket, placing it behind me on the chair's back before taking a seat. I decide to sit facing the entrance door, that way I can people watch between studying, as well as be aware of my surroundings.

I'm lost in my own little study bubble when suddenly a deep voice startles me, infiltrating my peace.

"Kat," the voice calls and I feel it in my bones. It's the smooth baritone I've come to register with Ryker. I glance up from my laptop to find him standing in front of my table. *Oh, my God.* He's here, standing right here in my new little coffee shop. Gah! The same one I thought was going to be my safe haven. The same one I figured most wouldn't bother with, seeing as Starbucks is much closer. *I guess that theory can go jump out the window.* What is he doing here? My hands begin to sweat a bit as I compose myself, getting ready to speak to him. God, he's big.

"Ah, hi, Ryker, how are you?" I manage to sputter out, and I know I sound timid, nervous. "What are you doing here?" I ask him, looking around the coffee shop, and he grins, obviously aware I'm a dork. "Other than the obvious." I let out a small giggle because I'm such a loser. *He thinks you drool over him. Make sure your mouth is closed.*

He smiles and his eyes radiate as we take each other in. "I mentor over at the community centre and I just finished. I was popping in for a coffee. It's been a long day," he shares, and I practically melt in my chair. *See, maybe there is more under his player persona.*

"Wow, Ryker, that's amazing." I breathe deep in awe of all the things he does with Jacob and the other boys at The Centre. "I'd love to do something like that. I love kids. I'm in school to be a teacher."

"Yeah, I know that." He shifts on his feet like maybe he's nervous, too. *Yeah right.*

"Claire," we both say at the same time and laugh. Our eyes catch and something passes between us. *God, those eyes.*

"Well, we're always looking for extra helpers down at The Centre. You should give me your number and I'll pass it on to the coordinator, Robin. And I should add my number into your phone, just in case you ever need it." I give him a questioning look. "I promise," he holds his hands up in surrender, "I will guard your number with my life. I won't even use it myself. I'll just pass it on to Robin...unless you'd like me to."

I blush at his comment. *Did he just say that?* I turn my phone on and hand it to him.

"It was off?" he asks, confusion lacing his tone.

"Yeah, I'm like the worst person ever with any type of technology." I sigh. "I'm more a pen and paper, snail-mail kinda gal." He gives me a chuckle and types his number into my phone.

"What is it you're doing here, anyway?" he asks. "You looked deep in thought before I came in and interrupted," he says, then nods down at my laptop and the worksheets askew all over the table.

"Oh, believe me, you don't even wanna know," I reply, exasperated.

"Actually, I do. I'm very interested." He smiles at me, and I feel there is more behind those words. "It looks like math."

"Oh, yeah, it sure is, and I'm the worst at math. It's always been my worst subject. I just can't seem to grasp the concepts, especially this crap." He's now sitting beside me, looking over my work. "Like, how am I supposed to teach this if I don't really get it?" I say, tapping the page in my notebook with my pen.

"Well, you're in luck, sweet girl. I don't have any plans tonight, so I'm all yours. Lay it on me. I'm a math whiz," he says and gives me a panty-dropping smile.

Holy hell, would I love to lie on you.

"You don't have plans? *The* Ryker Eddison doesn't have plans?" I ask.

"Naw, none I'd give up this chance for."

Holy shit.

And with that, Ryker Eddison helps me learn proportional reasoning in just a few hours.

I spend that night replaying every one of our shared looks, stolen glances, accidental touches, and the tummy-flutter moments he gives me over and over. It turns out there is a lot more to Ryker Eddison than meets the eye. Maybe, just maybe, Naomi and Claire were right. Needless to say, I didn't get much sleep, but at least I had something good to think about.

Chapter 21

Ryker

I WALK INTO The Bean after finishing at The Centre, and I falter in my step. Sitting to the left of the front counter is Kat. Shit, she looks good. She's sitting facing me, but she's completely oblivious to anything but her laptop right now. She's wearing her hair in a high bun and barely a trace of makeup; I like it. All I want to do is go over and rub my face along her neck and collarbone, because I remember how sweet she smells. After placing my order, I decide, *fuck it, I'm going to talk to her,* especially after the way she stared at me today in the library. I know she's just as interested as I am and from our last few encounters, I'm hoping she's sensing I am, too. I've been exercising self-control, proving to myself that I can talk to her after all, but not get too tangled up with her to the point where I lose myself, not that I think Kat would let me anyway. She is unlike any woman I've known; she's too caring and compassionate to intentionally hurt anyone.

As soon as she looks up and notices me, I know she's happy to see me. Her eyes light up and her breath hitches. *Yeah, baby, you take my breath away, too.*

She smiles and we begin talking about Jacob and the other boys and teaching. Kat's genuinely interested in The Centre, we chat about it for a bit, and before I can think twice about it or stop myself, I suggest she volunteer. *What did I just do?* We really could use the extra hands. And I'd like to see Kat around more, even if I think I need to keep her at arm's length. *Jesus, what is this girl doing to me?*

As soon as Kat tells me she's struggling with math, I'm relieved. Here is my chance to spend some time with her and practice keeping things cool. Thank fuck I'm a virtual math prodigy. Kat just gave me the in I was hoping for, allowing me to spend some time with her, giving me more insight.

I'm all yours? Holy shit, I sound like a pussy saying that to her. My comment doesn't seem to faze her. So I sit and take a look at her work.

I did have plans tonight. Of course I did. But as soon as Kat was in my sight, I willingly cancelled. When I programmed her number in my phone, I shot a text message to Grace cancelling. Honestly, I don't know who I'm trying to kid here, there hasn't been anyone since Kat came into my life. I like to think I would've hooked up with Grace, but I think, deep down, I know better. Kat is who I want, and I'd rather be right here with her, getting to know her better.

"Wow, Ryker, you're a genius," Kat says, all excited, leaning in and grabbing my arm, thanking me. "How can I ever repay you?" She smiles, leaning in closer to me and I swear to everything that's good that all I can think about is the many dirty ways she could pay me back. "I can't believe how easy you made that! And here I've been thinking you hated me," Kat almost whispers, breaking me out of my sexually induced thoughts.

"What? Why?" I ask, trying to play dumb. I know I've been a dick and I need to make it up to her, big time.

"Oh, please, Ryker." She rolls her eyes, but I don't care because all I think in that moment is how my name falling from those pouty lips is a huge fucking turn on.

"I mean, after all of the crazy runs-ins we've had, you can't really tell me things aren't always awkward between us." She laughs it off as if it's nothing. "I mean, you growl at me and make me feel useless. Then I get bitchy thinking how crazy you drive me." She giggles and it's such a sweet sound.

"Kat," I command her attention a little harsher than I intend, "the last thing I do is hate you. I—" The sound of my phone blaring interrupts. "Damn it, sorry, gimme a sec; it's my brother." I answer it only because it's Levi; I'm not sure why I wanted Kat to know this information, as well.

"Shit, I'm sorry. I gotta go," I tell her unhappily, getting out of the chair. "I guess Luke needed to bolt, Levi needs me to come in and close tonight. We'll finish this conversation soon, baby," I say, rubbing her cheek with my index finger. *Fuck, she's soft.*

With that, I leave Kat right in the middle of a conversation that I'd wanted to explore, in spite of myself.

Chapter 22

Kat

CLAIRE AND MATT have become quite the item since the night they met at the bar. I should know because *they are always here*.

Heaven forbid they go to his place. No. Apparently, Matt's room-mates, unlike us girls, are slobs and way too obnoxious to be around when they want alone time. Luckily for us girls, we get to watch the lovebirds go at it.

Claire and Matt are here almost every day. Well, except the days she works, that is. But sure enough, every day after I get home from either work or school, lo and behold, Claire and Matt are either going at it in the living room or can be heard from her room. Not that I really mind—well, other than the constant PDA. I could do with a lot less of that. Matt is a super great guy. And on top of being very easy on the eyes, his best attribute is that he makes Claire happy. Very happy, from what I have seen and heard thus far, which is all that really matters.

The one major benefit for me is that Matt loves to cook, which is just fine with me because cooking is not my forte at all. I'm a Lean Cuisine girl most nights; therefore Matty's culinary skills are always welcome.

Ever since The Beaver and Bulldog, Matt has jumped on Claire's bandwagon, and *both* of them are now being pains in my ass about me getting laid. Claire and Matt have decided that, "Any girl who dances like that is essentially screaming, *I need to get laid.*"

I've told them both they're crazy and that is absolutely not the case at all; not wanting to admit how right they actually are. But I know Claire is on to me. And she knows I still want Ryker; she hints at it by dropping Ryker comments here and there when we're alone. At least she knows better than to mention him around anyone else. Still, it doesn't matter whether she knows my truth or not; I simply deny, deny, deny. "Guys, for real, I don't need your help. I'm more than capable of meeting someone on my own. You really just need to mind your own business. The last thing I need is for you two," I point to them both, "to embarrass me every time we go out. I don't need a pity party."

The three of us are in the kitchen cooking pasta, and rather than talk about my love life—or lack thereof—I'd like to focus on eating. Dinner smells really good and I'm starving.

"Sorry, Kitty Kat, but you absolutely need a life outside of the library and work," Claire says, grabbing Matt by the waist, a smug smile on her face. "Matt and I," she smiles up at him, "we've decided we're implementing *Operation: Kat Needs a Man,*" she belts out like it's no big deal, before leaving Matt's side to grab plates and cutlery from the cupboard. "We are going to help find you a perfect specimen with who you may fuck your brains out, m'lady. It will be amazing, just wait and see." She beams and I can't fathom if she is serious. *You have got to be kidding me.*

"Actually," Matt offers his two cents while serving us each a huge bowl of spaghetti, "I think I have the perfect guy. His name is Jay. He's one of my roommates. I really think the two of you will hit it off. And the best part, we live close, it's the perfect booty call situation…if that's all you're looking for. I'm sure he'd be down with dating, too, if that's more what you're after."

Are these two kidding me right now?

"Please, guys, listen to me again. I'm good. I can find a guy on my own if I really want. Believe me. I do know how to socialize. The way you're talking is as if I'm some old crazy cat lady who needs an intervention and a makeover. So, please, let it be. No hook-up help. I got this." I spend the rest of dinner drinking a few glasses of wine, eating, and listening to these two go on and on about stuff I can't even remember.

I'm used to Claire being all up in my business, but her boyfriend? Oh, heck no. However, her allowing Matt in on her assault only makes me smile, because it shows me that Claire is serious about this one.

Chapter 23

Ryker

"OKAY, LEVI, YEAH. Will do, brother," I say, holding my cell phone to my ear. I'm trying to listen to him and the TV's continuous coverage of the major storm that has hit the area tonight.

"Yes, most of them are gone. I sent all the customers home, too. No, man, they were cool about it. Really, we weren't all that busy. Most people knew we were getting this, I guess." I jot shit down on a list of things he wants me to check before I lock up, but I'm distracted—Kat is standing by the door. It's just her and me left here tonight. I didn't want to tell Levi that; he'd only lecture me. I wasn't supposed to be here tonight, either but Luke called in sick and Levi had a date, so, of course, Levi called me. Truth is, I didn't mind at all. It meant I'd get to work with Kat.

After I hang up the phone, I decide to go talk to her. We haven't really spoken all night, but we've spent a lot of time staring at each other; that's for damn sure. Ever since that day at the coffee shop, I feel like we've made progress. I think we're both afraid of whatever this may be between us.

"Shit, come on, Claire, text me back. Answer your damn phone. Where the hell are you?" Kat is muttering aloud to herself as I approach. Just as I'm about to ask if she's okay, there is a huge crack of thunder in the distance. She jumps a mile high and I laugh at her.

"Scare much?" I say as she startles again at my proximity.

153

"Jesus, Ryker, I didn't see you there. Yes, oh, my God, that totally scared me. I hate these kinds of storms; I always have." She looks down at her phone again.

"Everything okay, baby?" I ask her, moving close by her side to look out the window as the storm moves in closer.

"No...yes, yeah, I guess. I've been trying to get in touch with Claire for the last hour since we closed up early. My car wouldn't start so she drove me. She's supposed to pick me up later, too. I can't get a hold of her now to tell her to come get me. She isn't supposed to be here for another few hours."

"You should have called me, Kat. Me, you should have called me. You have my number. Remember, I said if you ever need anything, you should call, and I meant it," I say, brushing her hand as bolts of lightning illuminate the sky before the thunder pounds. Kat jumps again and I grab her hand, entwining it with mine. "Don't be scared, sweet girl; I'm here with you." We stand like that for a few minutes, in silence, just staring at the storm as it takes over, wreaking havoc. The winds are blowing telephone wires around like rag dolls; leaves and garbage are being tossed around over the streets. The rain is teeming down.

"It's really bad out there. I hope Claire's okay. I'm going to try the house. Now I know how she feels when I don't answer my phone," she says.

"We should probably move away from the windows. The Weather Network is saying it's going to be bad; I have a few things to do here; then I'll drive you home, Kat. Just call Claire and leave a message. I got you." I kiss her hand before letting it go. At my gesture, her eyes grow wide, but she nods in agreement before dialling who I assume is Claire or her roommates. I leave her sitting at the bar and make my way back to the supply room to put some shit away and double check the doors. Suddenly, there is a loud explosion and the lights go out. After a few seconds of pitch black, the emergency lighting kicks in, giving a pale red glow to the place. It's enough to see by, but barely.

"Fuck," I say, grabbing a few flashlights from the supply room before heading back to Kat. *I'm sure she's gonna need some comforting; she was already scared.*

As I'm making my way back to the bar, there's another loud *boom*, which must have tripped the fire alarm because now it's blaring overhead. *Motherfucker.* I'm just about to turn back to go shut it off at the alarm panel, when I hear Kat shrieking.

"Ryker, Ryker! Help me, help, please, Ryker! Where are you? Oh, God."

Shit, I knew she was scared of storms, but come on; it's just an alarm. *Great, now I gotta deal with her on top of listening to this fucking thing.* I figure I'll go check on her then go shut it off.

I round the corner and can't believe my eyes. Holy shit, Kat is sitting under the bar bawling, rocking herself back and forth. Her knees are up, tucked tight to her chest. Her arms are hugging her legs in close and she's chanting my name over and over.

A *"What the fuck?"* slips out; I can't help it.

"Kat, baby, it's me. I'm here, sweetheart." I crouch down low right in front of her, resting on my haunches.

"God, Ryker, there's a fire!" she yells over the alarm. "We...we need to get out, oh God. Ryker, it's a fire, another fire."

Another fire?

"I can't...I can't breathe."

Jesus Christ, what the hell is going on? I manage to scoop her up and she immediately latches on to me for dear life. Her legs hug my waist, and her arms are wrapped so tight around my neck that my own breathing is becoming laboured.

"There's no fire," I whisper in her ear. "You're safe; we're safe. I promise you. I got you." I'm moving us back down to where the

155

emergency panel is; I need to shut this fucking thing off and fast. Kat is trembling in my arms, her body heaving with uncontrolled sobs. "Almost there, brave girl, almost there." Seeing her vulnerable like this sheds the last of my resolve to try and keep my distance from her. There is a depth to her that I want to explore and support. I want Kat Rollins to be mine. I want her to be my endgame, my Holy Grail.

With one hand, I manage to shut the fucking thing off, and the silence is heavy after the screaming alarm. "See, baby, it's off; we're all right," I say, rubbing her back as I move to sit her on top of the freezer. "I'm going to put you down, okay?" She nods and allows me to place her on the freezer top. I open her legs and step between them; she pulls me in close.

"I'm so sorry, Ryker. Thank you, I…just…I couldn't do it again," she sobs.

"It's okay, sweetheart; don't even worry about it." I stand there rubbing her back.

"I'm so sorry," she says again, and burrows into my chest. She's crying softly now; it seems her body is working to calm itself down. I like to think I've helped to console her, too. I like the feeling of her this close to me. But seeing her like this, it's honestly breaking my heart. I'm just glad it was me here with her tonight and not one of the other guys. *I want to be here for her, only me.* Obviously, something has happened to make her react this way. I will get her to tell me, but not now.

"Let's move into Levi's office, sweetheart. There's a couch in there and I want you to relax. Grab onto me again, baby; I'm gonna take you for a ride." Kat looks up and, for the first time in a while, gives me one of her beautiful smiles before attaching herself back to me. "Attagirl."

I kiss her cheek and walk us to the office.

Chapter 24

Kat

I'M BEYOND EMBARRASSED. I can't believe that just happened. I'd been doing so well these past months. I obviously need to make an appointment with Doctor Lukas. Ryker sets me down on the couch then lights a few candles that he finds in Levi's desk drawer.

"You feeling better?" he asks, handing me a bottle of water before sitting himself in front of me on the small coffee table.

Sighing, I tell him I'm okay. "I think I'm more worried about what you must think of me," I say, lowering my head.

"Hey," he says, placing his fingers under my chin, forcing me to tilt my head back up. Ryker is looking at me, really looking at me. "I don't think anything. All I know is that you were scared, and I'm glad I was here for you. And that you know you're all right. Yes, I want to know what all that was about; I want your trust. But I know we've got a long way to go before that happens, I won't pressure you," he says, now rubbing his thumb across my lip, and I swear it makes me tremble. He's being exceptionally sweet. I want nothing more than to jump into his lap and nestle in close to this man. "But I won't let it go either; we *will* talk about it, Kat, okay? And, please, say you'll call me if you ever need a ride or help again, sweet girl."

"I will, I promise. Thank you so much for helping me tonight. I really didn't expect the storm to affect me that much," I lie and we both know it, but he lets it go. *For now.*

157

"I'm gonna go check the rest of the stuff for Levi."

"No," I shout, louder than I intended. "Please don't leave me."

"Okay, I'll stay." He sits beside me. "Lie back and put your feet across my lap, I want you to relax." I do as he says, and now I'm freaking out because I'm so close to Ryker. I can feel the muscles in his legs and the strength in his arms as he grips my feet, taking my shoes off.

"How did your math with the proportional reasoning go after the other day?" he asks while rubbing my feet. I know he's trying to keep my mind off of what happened, and my stomach flutters with how sweet he is.

"Thanks to you, it went really well. Jeez, you always seem to be helping me, Ryker."

"I want to help you. I don't know why, but I like it. I like the feeling I get when I'm rewarded with one of your smiles. You have a killer smile." *Oh, holy shit.*

"Th-thanks. I think you have a great smile, too. Well, when you're not growling at me and I actually get to see it." I smile at the look on his face. It's almost as if he wants to explain something but stops himself.

Ryker and I spend the next hour talking about our families, school, volunteering, and what we want out of life. I decide I'll call Robin to set up a time to come in and enquire about volunteering. Listening to Ryker talk about Jacob and all the other kids makes me all the more ready to put in some time. And, hey, if I get to see Ryker a bit more, all the better.

I will always be grateful for this night. It really gave me the opportunity to see yet another side of the anomaly that is Ryker. *Huh, another silver lining. Maybe Claire's onto something with that bright side shit.*

As for Claire, it turns out she fell asleep on the couch at Matt's house. She apologizes a billion times, but let it be known how happy she is that I got to spend time with Ryker.

Chapter 25

Ryker

"NICE SHOT, RYAN!" Man, that kid's got a wicked three-point shot. It's Saturday, and Levi and I are hosting the annual basketball tournament with the kids. We have been organizing this tournament for the last three years. Teams from surrounding rec centres all come to The Centre for a day of basketball, awards, fun, and a barbecue.

I'm just about to change the line-up when I spot Robin coming out of her office with a brunette I recognize immediately. Kat. *Jesus, she's pretty.* They're smiling while talking and heading this way. *Perfect.* I'll get a chance to make sure she's okay. I've wanted to call her, but I promised her I wouldn't use her number for personal use. After the time we spent together, I was pretty confident she'd be all right with my calling, but I guess I'm still a bit nervous. This girl makes me nervous unlike anyone before. I need to bide my time and take things slow, build a foundation before I make my move.

"Levi, take over for a sec, would ya?" I'm already handing off the clipboard as he agrees. "I'll be five minutes."

"Take your time, bud; I got them," he says with a knowing smirk. I haven't come right out and said anything about liking Kat, but he's not stupid. He knows.

As I'm making my way over, Robin calls out to me. "Ryker, the tournament is another success. The kids are all having a great time. I was just telling Kat what wonderful work you and Levi do here."

I smile at her praise. "Thanks. Yeah, they're loving it. We had a great turnout this year."

My eyes land on Kat. "Hey, how are you? I'm glad you took me up on my suggestion to come."

"Hi, Ryker," her eyes meet mine and she smiles, "me, too. I'm going to start helping out on Tuesday evenings and Saturday mornings. Robin and I decided I could run a homework club, and maybe I could recruit some of my classmates to help out if we get a good turnout."

"Wow, that's a great idea. I'm sure there will be a ton of kids who will join in. Hell, I'd come to something like that knowing you'd be there." *Shit.* I didn't mean to say that out loud. Kat blushes and Robin clears her throat.

"Well, then, Ryker, we'll let you get back to the tournament. I'm just going to take Kat on a little tour."

"Sounds good. I'll catch you later, Kat," I say, brushing her hand with mine before running back to the court.

I think Saturday mornings just became my favourite day of the week.

Chapter 26

Kat

"**N**O FUCKING WAY! Not a bloody chance in hell, no, nope, nuh-uh. *Oh! Hell! No!*" I keep saying to Claire about the supposed *costume* she's trying her hardest to convince me to wear tonight to the big Halloween party over at Matt's house.

Obviously, my happiness isn't a concept she cares about. Clearly, she couldn't give a shit, because at this moment, she is making me very unhappy.

"Oh, come on. You know you look hot. Haven't I proved to you before that I know when you look hot? Stop being a little baby! You know damn well I would never, ever steer you wrong. And right now, Kitty Kat, you are fucking smokin'. Wowee! If Ryker could see you now."

Pretending she did not just say his name, I listen to Claire say this little *shtick* of hers over and over again while we stand in my room getting ready.

"Come on, Kat, its Halloween. It's time to get our slut on. You can't possibly think you'll pick up a guy in that hagwear of a witch costume. Skin, you need to show skin. You, my friend, need to get laid, and that is *not* going to happen with you in that getup all green-faced and hiding that body. Now, look in the mirror and tell me you don't think it's the hottest costume and that you honestly want to change back into a hag."

162

I knew I shouldn't have trusted her to get us costumes. I should know better by now. Claire is standing behind me wolf-whistling, trying her damnedest to convince me to wear what's she's bought me rather than the witch costume I wore to my grade four placement yesterday for the class Halloween party. The costume, I feel, that would make me feel happiest.

I look at her in contempt before I look at my reflection one last time, trying to decide what I want to do. Of course, I know she's right. I know I'm being silly. It's not that I don't think I look hot, I know I do. It's just once again, it seems there could be a bit more coverage to the costume. I'm always nervous putting myself on display. I don't want to be one of those girls with big boobs that other girls assume I'm flaunting all the time. Believe me, I love my girls, but sometimes I would love it if they were smaller and a whole lot perkier.

"Fine, you win. You always win. I'll wear it. I don't have to like it, but I'll wear it. It's Halloween, so, whatever. I can pull it off for one night." I cringe, not believing I'm agreeing to this willingly.

"Good. Come here, you little she-devil. I told your mom I'd send her a few selfies of us all ready to go." Claire pulls out her iPhone and takes a few pictures before we head down to meet the girls, who have been waiting on my ass for the last forty-five minutes.

Walking into the kitchen, I'm met with whistles and catcalls and a bunch of, "It's about fucking time." I shrug them off. "I know, I know, I just wasn't sure I could pull it off. I mean, come on, guys, it's pretty revealing. I feel like I'm going to work…" I hesitate "…on a street corner." Being a dork, I do a little twirl before handing Claire a fresh drink. We raise our glasses in a toast to a fun night ahead.

I eventually gave up the costume fight because I know there's ultimately no use in fighting Claire about most things. Unfortunately, I seem to have a hard time sticking to my guns, and tend to give in to her quite often. Good thing she's right most of the time. *Damn her.*

"Woohoo, now the night can begin. We are all ready and Kitty Kat can cut loose, allow herself to have some fun and, hopefully, find some sexy man to fuck that stick outta her ass," Claire roars. I take another gulp of my drink, but not before giving her a little cut-eye.

I think I might actually agree with Claire. I really do need to let go and possibly have a little fun with some über-hot guy. *But I want Ryker.* Downing the last of my drink, however, I decide for myself that tonight I will at least go through the motions and embrace Claire's Halloween ideals as my own.

Claire describes Halloween as the one night when women band together to drive the male population to the brink of sexual fantasy and frustration.

"Hey, Claire, tell us all why Halloween is important to the women's movement, please. I really think the girls would love to know your thoughts," I say, putting my wings on.

"Oh, I'd love to enlighten all of you on the importance of Halloween," Claire begins, hopping up on her invisible lectern. "Halloween is the night to be brazen and bold. The night where girls can let their inner sluts shine and know that no matter how slinky and sexy the costume you have on is, there will always be some chick dressed even sluttier. The end goal is to bring the boys to their knees!" God, this girl makes me laugh. I could not imagine my life without her.

Hence, why I reluctantly and nervously agreed to wear a damned costume that consists of a headband with a halo attached to its top, and a super tight white sequinned tank top with booty shorts. The top, of course, dips in a low V at the front, revealing a ton of cleavage. It's like a second skin. It's extremely tight and the wings aren't helping at all; they pull the back down, making the front shorter and even tighter. But, I hate to admit, it actually does make my girls look pretty amazing. It also has a pair of fishnet stockings with garters that only serve to further drive the point that this outfit is completely out of my element. But the best part, the real *pièce de résistance,* are the white high-heeled hooker boots! Yep, I am the epitome of an angel. *Maybe a fallen one.*

Matt and his roommates, who live at the end of our cul-de-sac, are throwing a big Halloween party. They are all in the same sports medicine program and have been friends for years. Apparently, it's been tradition since they moved in together back in their first year, and it's the place to be every Halloween.

I'm pretty excited for another night of fun with my girls, and am secretly hoping to find a hottie with who I could—if the mood strikes—try my hand at a purely sexual relationship. One on my terms with a partner that I, not my friends choose. Despite what they may think, I am capable of finding my own one-night stand. I secretly wish it were with Ryker, but I'm still not sure where we stand.

But tonight is Halloween, and I have bigger things to stress about than Claire and Matt working on 'Operation: Kat Needs a Man'. I need to worry about allowing myself to have a good time, and trying not to stress about what I look like in this scrap of an angel costume or the fact that Halloween is such a dangerous celebration; with so many candles, the risk for fires is much greater. Taking a deep breath, I give myself a little pep talk. It's all good; it's all in the name of fun. *Breathe out. And, most importantly, remember to embrace your inner Halloween slut,* I giggle as I remind myself before touching up my hair.

Matt has already messaged Claire like fifty times. He's way too excited to see his girl in her costume, the one she's been teasing him with all week. I swear that guy would have done anything I asked him to do this week if I would have told him what Claire was wearing to the party. But like a good friend, mum was the word. It's really cute seeing how close these two have become. Honestly, Matt is perfect for Claire.

With Claire as my sexy counterpart—a devil, of course, in more ways than one—we check ourselves out, making little adjustments here and there, applying one last layer of lip gloss; then we're finally all heading out the door.

My phone goes off as I'm about to lock the door. I look down to my hand to retrieve the text, and I notice it's from an unknown number. Not thinking much of it, I swipe across the screen in order to read it and am shocked at what I see.

Unknown: *Beautiful, I miss you. I need you. I want you. Happy Halloween, angel.*

Seth xox

Quickly shaking off the irony of his use of the word "angel," I read over the text a few more times before finally showing it to Claire. *How the fuck did he get my number, it's supposed to be unlisted?*

"Who the fuck does he think he is? What a douchebag." She goes on, getting heated. "Forget about that guy; he's all the way back in Ottawa. There's no need to even pay him any mind. He's probably sitting alone in front of his computer masturbating, the little fucker. Knowing his dick is close to falling off, he probably couldn't find a chick who was willing to let him stick that filthy schlong near any orifice." I laugh at Claire's tirade and decide she's right. Before locking the door, I quickly throw my phone on the table, leaving it behind. I'm not about to allow that ass to ruin my night! *Fucking Seth.*

I feel sick, instantly. An uncomfortable feeling takes over my entire body. I hoped Seth would get the message by now. I figured he'd move on. I mean, wasn't it him who cheated on me? I just don't think I can keep dealing with this shit. I wonder about those flowers again. *Shit.*

"Come on, Kat, fuck him and fuck this. Please don't let him ruin your night. Let's go out and have a good time tonight, and we'll figure out how we're going to deal with that asshead tomorrow." I nod, trying hard to be agreeable with what she's suggesting. I really just think he's messing with me anyway.

Claire is right; I need to let it go. I need to not let Seth dictate my choices and decisions like I've allowed him to do in the past. Listening to him has only left me with a bunch of missed opportunities and regrets. Because of his possessiveness, he manipulated me into missing a Spring Break trip to Mexico with my girlfriends. According to him, *"Those kinds of trips are for single girls who just want to slut it up,"* and he'd be upset if I went. Seth actually managed to convince me I should go to school with him in Ottawa too, that we would miss each other too much and long distance relationships never work. Looking back on it now, I don't know how I let him segregate me from my friends and family so much. Thank goodness I listened to Claire and applied to Brock in the end, because Seth and I didn't end things on a good note at all. And I couldn't imagine being anywhere but here.

"You're right, Claire Bear. Fuck him. I can't let him affect me. He's just being the dick I've always known him to be deep down."

"Good. Maybe we should talk to Wes and your dad, just give them the heads up and see what they say this time for real. I know Ryker dealt with him before, but he clearly isn't getting the message." I nod, agreeing with her that it is definitely time to get advice from my dad and brother. I know Wes will kick his ass if I ask him. "But for tonight, we're letting it go. You're with your Claire Bear, and you know I always have your back; it's on to fun we shall go!" I appreciate her enthusiasm and ability to make me feel better. Everyone needs a little Claire in their life I tell ya.

Chapter 27

Ryker

FUCK, I LOVE Halloween. It's by far the best holiday ever. I love getting dressed up and fucking around with people, especially the girls; they are too easy to scare. Every year the boys and I, well, since we've lived here in the Village, hold an insane costume party; which always ends the same way…me drunk, fucked hard, sated, and happy. This year will be no different. Tonight I'm planning on hibernating my cock inside the warm and willing body of some hot-ass chick.

Lucky for me, Halloween is a night where people leave their inhibitions behind and really let loose, which is just what I need considering how hard my dick has been since a certain girl has pretty much forced me to be a cock-blocker to myself, slowing my usual game. But tonight, tonight I will reclaim my game and finally get my dick wet. Man, I love Halloween.

Chapter 28

Kat

WHILE CLAIRE, THE girls, and I make our way down the street to Matt's, I have to admit I'm pretty excited at the idea of cutting loose tonight. Not dance on the bar loose, but loose enough to have a great time. Especially after that text from Seth. I shiver just thinking about that asshole. *Focus, Kat.* I get back to thoughts of getting my drink and dance on with my bestie and our friends. Yeah, that's just what I need.

Another silver lining from the fire, living so close to everything there is no need for a DD tonight as we can walk without worrying about anyone drinking and driving. It's a chilly night out, but we opt out of covering up with a jacket; mainly because we all know the chances of us forgetting it and leaving it there is pretty high. Another bonus of living in the Village is we can always make a run for it if it's too cold.

As we walk, we sing *Thriller,* as it seems to be the appropriate song to sing at the moment. We're laughing and pretty much stumbling in our heels. Of course, our little group is met with a ton of hoots and hollers from guys heading out to different Halloween activities along our street, which in turn, causes us to laugh and sing even louder. Oh man, tonight is going to be all kinds of trouble; I laugh to myself as we approach what must be Matt's house.

There is eerie music playing as we walk up to the front door, along with an array of Halloween decorations from zombies and ghosts, to pumpkins and tombstones. The place looks amazing, all lit up with orange and purple lights, which hang from the railings and eave troughs. I love how enthusiastic these guys are about their Halloween traditions. *I can't wait to see what the inside looks like,* I think as Claire leads us through the front door.

Crossing the threshold to Matt's place, I hear the familiar voice of Pete Loeffler and Chevelle singing *The Red.* Listening to one of my favourite songs playing quickly puts me at ease. I sing along as I follow Claire into the kitchen to grab what I know will be the first of many drinks. With Seth's text still heavy on my mind, I know I will be having more than a couple tonight. There is no way I want to go back to that point in time of my life. Damn, I hate how that asshole has the power to still affect me. *How did he even get my new number?*

Thankful for the reprieve, I'm brought out of my head by Claire's excitement.

"To the drinks, bitch; this devil needs her fury fuel!" she yells while laughing and looking at me over her shoulder. I trail closely behind her while the others lag a bit further behind, stopping to chat along the way. I hold her hand because it is definitely packed in here and the last thing I need is to lose sight of her.

The house is full with people dancing and crowding every corner and it's only ten thirty. I can't imagine what it will be like in another hour. Shuffling our way toward the kitchen, I have to admit, Claire was right about our costumes. We are definitely among good company with our sexy attire. I actually think Claire and I may even be overdressed compared to some of these other girls. That thought alone makes me smile to myself, as sometimes I see just why I never tell this girl no. It's because she, unfortunately, to my dismay, is often right.

Taking in my surroundings, my anxiety is slowly building, it's crowded and I can't find enough ways to exit if I needed to.

"It's all good, Kat, just try and relax. Their house is the exact replica of ours; they all are, remember? You got this. Focus on the fun we're going to have. I'm with you all night until you wanna leave. Okay?" God, I love this girl; she knows me better than I know myself sometimes, I swear.

"I'm good; you're right, piece of cake. Thanks. I just get inside my head sometimes," I whisper.

"I know, Kitty Kat, don't even stress. One day, it won't even occur to you. I'm sure of it. Besides, it's not like we're ever too far apart, right? I got your back. Always," she whispers back, and I let the uneasy feeling go for the night.

Just like I had suspected, the inside decorations are just as incredible. The place looks fantastic! Cobwebs cover the ceiling, causing us to duck in order to avoid the array of creatures lurking among the webs; ghosts, bats, and goblins are some of the ones I spied as we walked. Jack 'O Lanterns of different shapes and sizes line the many tables and shelves, as well as the mantel above the fireplace. They are pretty much scattered everywhere, sending out an orange flicker through their creative facial designs; Jack Skellington, an angry Minion, and Jason Voorhees are among the ones I recognize. The place hums with excitement and I'm giddy for a night of fun.

Approaching the kitchen, I notice a witch standing within the archway creating a narrow walking space. She's shrieking with laughter, uttering spells out to whomever dare cross her path, while she waves her wand up and down in our direction. *Jesus, do these guys go all out or what?* I gotta admit this witch is kind of freaking me out. I grab Claire a bit tighter as we pass, and turn around trying to see if that witch is a real person or simply mechanical. Not paying attention to what's in front of me, I feel Claire's hand drop from mine. As I turn back to see where she's gone, I end up screaming in horror as I smack right into the heavy chest of a hooded figure holding a scythe in his hand. After yelling at me and pretending to try and hurt me, his hands quickly dart up to grab my waist in order to steady me as I am fucking freaked out. I damn near fall to the ground.

"What the ever loving fuck?" I yell once I have my bearings back. All of a sudden, the hooded figure lifts his hood off, showing me nothing more than a big old shit-eating grin before yelling, "Happy Halloween, Kat! Gotcha! You should have heard that scream; it was priceless. Claire was right; she knew I could scare you!" Shit. *Colby of course*. Did I mention how happy I was these two were still good friends? Not!

"You sure as hell did, Colby. Jesus, I was too busy trying to figure out whether the witch is real or not, that I wasn't paying attention at all! Fuck me! You scared the piss out of me! You're lucky I didn't hurt you."

"Ha! You? Hurt me? Yeah right, dude. There was no way that was going to happen; you were freaked the fuck out!"

"Yeah okay, okay, you're right, you big jerkface. You really did have me. Awesome job, Colby, but now I think I need a drink, a very, very big, strong drink," I say while holding my hand over my chest, willing my heart to calm, while everyone around who witnessed Colby's little prank laughs at my over-exaggerated-ness. Thankfully, Colby takes me seriously and it isn't long before I have a shooter, as well as my favourite drink in my hand.

"Cheers, Kat, cheers everybody. Happy Halloween!" Colby shouts out while passing around shots of liquid goodness. There's about ten of us huddled in the kitchen now fussing over which shots to make next.

"You are forgiven, Colby," I tell him as I happily sip away at my mali-cranny he just handed me in the biggest glass he could find. Ahh, I just love my Malibu rum and cranberry juice, best drink ever.

After what feels like tasting a billion different shots, some of which were really good, while others were just bad, I need a break. My poor taste buds are getting confused. Funny how after so many, they actually all seem to just blend; honestly, I'm not even sure which ones I liked and didn't like at this point. Needless to say, well, I am feeling good, really good. From Broken Down Golf Karts, Blow Jobs, to Purple Motherfuckers, and a shit ton I can't even remember, I am one happy girl. With the alcohol creating a warm buzz travelling throughought my body, I am ready for a change in scenery. I need to dance and mingle. I move to the counter where Claire is currently the shooter chemist and convince her easily enough to come dance with me.

"Claire Bear, I need a break. That was a lot of shots in like ten minutes. My body is wired; I need to go dance. Besides, I'm sure Matt is looking for you. We've been here for like fifteen. I'm sure he knows you're here and, after all, the poor guy has been waiting all day for this, for you. He probably has blue balls from you teasing him about your costume," I add and laugh at what I think is funny.

Claire just looks at me, shaking her head. "Yeah, no more shots for you right now." We both laugh because we know it's true; I am kind of a lightweight. I don't drink too often, where I let myself lose control, for obvious reasons, and I hate hangovers.

"Okay, I'm with you, yeah. You're right, he actually just texted a few minutes ago. I guess they needed more ice, he and another buddy ran out to the store. He said he's like five minutes out. Let's go out and dance while we wait." She then adds with a devilish grin, "That way he will easily find me once he walks in the door."

I smile, having no idea what she is thinking, but nod in agreement at the plan.

"Besides, I could use a break. I definitely am starting to feel these shots, too." She laughs while grabbing my arm, leading toward the witch-guarded walkway again.

As we leave, we hear everyone chanting in the kitchen. They're excited to compete in the contest for best-shot concoction, which has just been announced; clearly the result of everyone wanting to make each other try their special shooter. Of course, the other girls stay to watch. I think the fact that the two guys from the bar the girls met last week being in there as well is what's really keeping them rooted in the kitchen. I'll be surprised if we see Laurie and Jenn for the rest of the night now.

After making it past the witch in one piece, we quickly move with our drinks in hand to the centre of the makeshift dance floor, arriving just in time to hear JT singing about "Bringing Sexy Back." A song I love!

"Woohoo, Kitty and Claire Bear in effect, y'all," I shout out to Claire and she all but snorts with laughter.

"God, you're so lame," she giggles as we begin dancing. I love music and I love to dance. It's one of the only times I feel relaxed, allowing the music to take over my body with its pulsing sensations, letting the words pierce into my soul.

As the next song kicks in, I make my way over to Claire, shimmying down in front of her in a suggestively naughty manner. Standing back up, I wrap both my arms around her neck, resting them on her shoulders. Swinging my hips to the beat of the music, my eyes meet hers and she grins back at me like the little devil she is. She pulls my arms from her neck, but doesn't let them go. Turning around, she grinds back into me, placing my hands on her hips. Our movements become synced and our hair tosses from side to side as we dance like nobody's watching. The song changes, but we continue our sexy performance. With Claire now facing me, so close I can feel her breath hitting my face, she begins ever so slowly, trailing her hands down my sides. I start to feel sexy now that I've had a few drinks; clearly my inhibitions are slipping away. I decide to continue dancing with Claire as I notice we've gained an audience, mostly male, mostly gawking at our little performance. Claire and I carry on our little tryst for a few more songs.

We're having a great time laughing and dancing. "I love you, Kitty Kat," she says to me as we finally give up our little show, "but even so much more when you let yourself go, embracing...releasing your inner sexy bitch of a self. The one I know you really are. You know, the one who needs to get fucked hard tonight while wearing that outfit. Rawr!" she ends on a yell while snorting from laughter and growling at me. Ah, yes, folks, my best friend is a funny bitch, who just will not give up. I just laugh while she attacks me with a great big hug.

Once she's done hugging me, I see from the corner of my eye a tall figure coming our way and I grin when I notice it's Matt making his way to his little devil, scooping her up from behind, spinning her around to face him, whispering in her ear. With her reaction, I have no doubt it's something which is undoubtedly dirty and x-rated. A pinkish flush immediately covers her beautiful face and exposed skin. "Matt, Jesus, what you do to me," Claire responds as he ever so slowly brings her down tight to his chest, planting his lips seductively over hers. *Geesh, get a room already,* I think and smirk in Claire's direction.

"Ahem," I clear my throat in mock annoyance at their display of affection. "Ummm, hello, people! Halloween party, not an orgy, it's time to get our party on. You two can fuck each other's brains out later," I tease, which results in me getting a 'whatever' look from Claire as she gives Matt a quick peck on the cheek while he's palming her ass.

Just as I'm about to say we need more drinks, I'm grabbed at the waist by two strong muscular hands, hands which quickly move, snaking themselves from my waist to lower stomach. Suddenly, I'm being pulled back into what can only be described as a hulking figure, a brick wall, that of a man's chest. Jesus. I manage to crane my neck back to see just who the hell this mound o' muscle belongs to, and ask who the hell he thinks he is putting his grabby hands on me. Only looking back, I'm immediately met with a pair of deep blue eyes, one hell of a sexy-ass grin, and a body that matches the rock hard chest that's sheltering my back. His smile is warm and sexy; the breath I had been holding escapes, leaving me heaving just that little bit. Matt quickly interrupts, apologizing for his friend. Explaining how he's just excited to finally meet me and that he'd like me to meet his buddy, Jay.

"Kat, this is Jay; he lives here, too. Jay, this is Kat, Claire's roommate, the dancer." He winks at me. "The one you've been dying for me to introduce you to." I smile at that comment; it's always nice to hear that someone wants to meet you, especially a hot guy like Jay. Matt goes on, "As you can see, she is not only hot, sexy, and sweet, but she's single, just how you like 'em." He grins after sharing the last part. Fucker, I see 'Operation Kat Needs a Man' has begun with Matt, too. These two are both going to be getting an ear full tomorrow, that's for certain.

"Hi there, angel," Jay whispers into the side of my face, close enough to brush along my ear, my body quickly breaking into goosebumps from his proximity. Goosebumps not necessarily breaking out because his closeness is appealing to me, it's quite the opposite. Rather, I fear it's because I feel a need to put some much-needed space between us. I feel he's too close, too fast. *Funny how this feeling overcomes me now, but not when I was being pinned to a certain ottoman,* I think as I put distance between Jay and myself. He's hot, don't get me wrong, but when I look into his eyes, they're the wrong colour. Not the colour I want looking back at me, not *honeybutter.* Just as fast as the thought seeps in, I quickly deny myself the time to let it linger. Thinking of Ryker has become a recurring habit in my daily life, one I need to kick, and fast. With this in mind, I decide piss it. Smiling at my decision, I decide to give Jay a chance *and* me the chance to let a man past my guard. Allow someone to help get Ryker out of my mind. Because it's not like he's been knocking down my door. Sure, we've spent some time together here and there, but nothing more than a few passing words on that Saturday at The Centre.

"Hi there, Jay. You want to hang out a bit? I hear you're in the market for a dance partner? I happen to love to dance." I flirt with him a bit and it feels good.

"I'd really like that. Can I just say again, you're fucking gorgeous."

I smile; I mean, what girl doesn't like hearing that?

"Not only is my girl easy on the eyes, Jay," Claire teases, "Kitty Kat is the sweetest girl you will ever meet. She is always giving and kind. You will be lucky to get to know her, if she gives you the chance," Claire interjects with a wink and I smile at her assessment.

With my mind settled and my body back at ease with my decision, I dance with Jay. We laugh, we talk, and we're actually having a great time. Jay, it turns out, isn't only hot with a great body, but he's charming, and honestly, a really nice guy. I enjoy hanging out with him, Claire, and Matt, while downing a few more shots, getting more and more tipsy as time wears on. But as we have more drinks and dance, Jay's again getting closer and closer. His hands are getting more and more exploratory, going over my hips to my ass and back making me feel uncomfortable again.

"Kat, your ass is fucking tight; I can't seem to keep my hands off you." Needing some space, I decide that maybe my initial reaction of hesitancy toward him was one I need to heed. I'm not sure what it is to be honest; it's like I can't shake this feeling that something is off with him.

"I'll be right back. I'm just going to use the washroom," I say, stepping out of his hold.

"You okay?" Claire asks, concern on her face.

"Just hot, I'm going to go powder my nose," I joke, and she nods.

"Want me to come with you?"

"No, it's fine. I'll be right back," I assert with a fake smile and then excuse myself.

I make my way to the stairs. Once at the top, I'm lucky to find the washroom empty with no one else insight. I slip in, locking the door, enjoying the silence for a moment. Moving in front of the mirror, I assess myself. Yep, still slutty looking, I laugh to myself. I apply some lip gloss, wash my hands, check the girls, and try to pull my shorts down a wee bit more before opening the door to make my way back to my friends. *He's harmless; he's having fun with me.* I decided to allow Jay to continue his flirting. I'm just being paranoid. I relax again as I walk. *I may even flirt back this time; I mean, we're at a party in a house full of people. What's the worst that can happen, right?* I'm not stupid; I won't allow myself to be alone at any time with him if things still feel off. I decide to go with the flow.

With that text from Seth still trying to force its way into my mind, Jay may just be the perfect distraction. Besides, it has been an awfully long time since I had a sexy man between my legs, and Jay is definitely hot. With my mind made up, I put a little jump in my step, hurrying to get back to my friends to continue with my newly hatched plan.

Holy fuck, Ryker! I land at the bottom of the stairs with renewed excitement only to have it dissipate immediately. *You have got to be kidding me!* Karma really is a slut-ass bitch, which is most definitely out to get me. Standing with Jay, Matt, and Claire is motherfucking Ryker Eddison, who's of course looking way beyond gorgeous and oh so edible. Who of course happens to have some blonde bimbo seemingly attached to his side. *Who the hell is she?*

I can't believe my eyes. I close them tight, breathing rapidly. I count to five before opening them; shit, I open them to find he's still standing mixed in there with *my* friends…the entity of my fantasies, the boy who creeps into my mind at night, bringing me to the brink of want and need. The very same man who plagues my days with thoughts of those eyes, stolen glances, the growl. Oh fuck! That damn growl. The majestic face behind my rabbit himself, the very same man

MY MIND'S EYE

who now owes me a shit ton of batteries—Ryker Eddison.

The very same man who I know I have a connection with, one that neither of us seems willing to admit or pursue. I haven't seen or spoken to Ryker since Robin gave me the tour of the rec centre. Maybe I imagined this pull between us.

Of all the places and all the parties, of course he's here at Matt's. Ryker is the epitome of hotness, and I know he can be beyond sweet. His costume tonight, however, just solidifies why he is the star of my fantasies. Standing, laughing it up with my friends, he's sporting the most appropriate drool-inducing costume known to women. Ryker is none other than a Chippendale! Lawd have mercy! One heck of a perfect Chippendale costume, which looks completely genuine, including a bowtie, cuff, and collar—all showcasing his perfect, naked chest and one hell of a sexy tattoo. Oh. My. God! I think I'm going to need to run home and change my panties. The effect this man has on me is dizzying. I haven't seen him around much, just in passing here and there. But he always manages to leave a lasting impression on me. And for that matter, my panties. *Jay who?*

FUCK.

Chapter 29

Ryker

ANGER AND JEALOUSY. Those are the two feelings that simultaneously take over my body, clouding my vision as well as my judgement at the sight in front of me. My shoulders tense immediately while my breathing hitches the moment I spot Kat dancing with Claire, Matt, and Jay. Fucking Jay. Asshole.

Remember that feeling of possession lying dormant, the one I've never really felt before? Well, the beast is awake.

The colour red darkens my vision immediately when my eyes fall to Jay trying to put the moves on *my* Kat, which in turn causes me to clench my jaw while my hands turn to fists without me realizing. I stand by the kitchen watching them, with my body wound tight, fists hanging balled along my side. Despite not really knowing her very well, I know enough. *I know I want her.* Seeing him all over her, whether she's mine or not yet, doesn't matter to the caveman within me. I knew the moment I tackled her in the staff room that she needed to be mine.

That she is mine.

Green is for the feelings of envy I am having toward the outfit Kat is wearing exquisitely around her body. Never in my life have I been jealous of an inanimate object as I am now, standing here seeing Kat in that sexy-as-sin angel costume. Never have I wanted so badly to be the material surrounding a titillating body, hugging it close and keeping it

180

held in tight, as I want to be that for Kat. *Fuck me.*

Man, this girl is fucking me up. I need to make my move, make her choose: fuck me or be mine. *I'm hoping she'll agree to the latter.* And I'll be damned if some fucker beats me to it. It's time for me to up my game. Who am I kidding? It's time to let the game begin. Kat will be in my bed in no time; then this little hang-up I seem to have can finally be done and she can take up a permanent residency. Either way, I need to deal with her, get her on board with my plan, and if she doesn't want me back? Well, I guess I'll go back to my old self, back to having a new chick every couple of nights, back to having no feelings, no tightness, or these thoughts of wanting more. But I'm pretty sure she wants me too. Fuck, I need to figure out what the hell we are. What we're going to be.

Yeah, this needs to end, and fast.

"Hey, hottie." *Fuck me, Sarah.*

"Hey there, Sarah. Wow, nice costume. You're one hell of a naughty looking bunny." I look her over to make her happy. She smiles and I feel myself getting annoyed; this chick is wasting my time.

"Dance with me, handsome." She puts her hands around my neck, bringing her body closer. Sarah tries to move in close to me, but I'm quick to remove her arms from my neck.

"Rain check. I need to find someone." I leave her stunned at my brush off, I can tell by her face, but she follows behind me anyway. I'm starting to think I'm going to have to be an asshole soon and tell her the score. I. Am. Not. Interested. She's chatting on and on about shit I don't even care about. I tune her out.

I need to get to Kat.

I need to get to her before Jay. I've seen him trying; trying to take what's mine. *I'm gonna break those fucking hands.* Thank God she left after that. I'm hoping she isn't into him, that she left to break the moment. *She can't be into him.* I thought I was gonna lose it when his hand reached her ass. Fuck me, I need to think of a way to make her agree to be mine. Stalking my way over to Matt, I think, *Fuck, I hate Halloween.*

Chapter 30

Kat

I STAND ROOTED at the bottom of the stairs thinking of my next move. I notice Claire looking my way, a knowing smirk on her face. I can't do this, not tonight, not with the way Ryker consumes my mind. I can't pretend anymore. I can no longer pretend I don't want him; pretend Jay would even remotely be what I want.

As a war rages on inside of me—*Go to him. Ignore him*—back and forth in my stupid mind, I don't move an inch from my spot. *Who's the girl with him? Is she with him?* I must look like an idiot, but I can't help it. It's like I'm making one of the most life-altering decisions, well it feels like it to me anyway. In the end, the chicken in me wins out...the uptight me always wins, *fucking dominant bitch*. She's the rational me, the one who knows it won't work, that I'll get hurt, the same one who knows I want more than one night.

With my decision made, I look around the house, trying to figure out where the hell to go now. I can't go over there. Being the chicken shit I am, I look to the stairs beside me. With that, I head back upstairs, back to the washroom for some solace, some time to think. Who am I kidding? I'm totally going to hide. I take the stairs fast, heading for my destination, hoping it's unoccupied, praying Ryker will be gone by the time I re-emerge. I'm praying he didn't even see me, that maybe he doesn't even know I'm here. Ha, I'm sure Claire let it be known as soon as she saw him, the traitor.

183

I feel him before I hear him. "Hot girl, stop," he says with the growl I've come to recognize. But this one is like none I've heard from him before. This growl does things to my insides. I pause in my stride, more to make sure he's actually calling to me. The next thing I know, Ryker is flush to my back. His breath a hair's whisper away from my ear, he's taking in my scent, smelling me. I stand still as an immediate case of jelly legs takes over. He's sliding his mouth and nose under my ear, burrowing into my neck, taking me in.

"You think I'm hot? Ryker, you haven't talked to me since The Centre, what, you want us to be friends?" I state, when in reality I should be asking, "What the hell do you think you're doing?"

I gasp because all of a sudden, I'm spun around, made to meet Ryker face-to-face. Eyes to eyes. Fuck me, he's beautiful. I drink him in; it's impossible not to. All those muscles, strong arms, the same ones holding my sides. God, all those muscles glistening under the dim lights of the hall. I swear I let out a moan at the heat I see staring back at me.

"Kat," he begins, "hot is nowhere near the right word to describe what I think when I look at you. Fuck, baby, hot is an understatement. You are exquisite, smart, sweet, so perfect. And no, I don't want to just be fucking friends with you. I want so much more."

Oh my! Did he just seriously say that to me? I swear my panties are beyond wet at this point; I wouldn't be surprised to see the wetness seeping down my legs.

He doesn't say anything else, and I cannot seem to find my voice at all in this moment. A moment that I know I will forever be replaying over and over in my mind. This stuff doesn't happen to me. Wordless now, we're standing there face-to-face, staring at each other, seemingly waiting for the other to make the next move. I'm about to say something, but then Ryker clasps my wrists, sending prickles of heat running down my spine. "Come with me." He begins pulling me forward toward a door a few feet away from where we're standing.

I know it sounds strange, but I'm not nervous. My heart is beating wildly in my chest, but it's all adrenaline. I'm curious, in a trance-like state, willing to follow this man wherever he guides me. Maybe I'm not the chickenshit I thought I was. Maybe this is my chance. The chance to share my feelings, the chance to tell him I want to get to know him.

"Here." He guides me through the door. I quickly notice we're in his room, spying trophies and pictures with him and his family. Fuck, of course he lives here, too. What are the chances? How did I not know this? I wonder if my sneaky little bestie knew this. I just might have to hurt the bitch.

I turn back around to face Ryker, who I find standing with his back to the door watching me. Silently, and ever so slyly, he steps toward me. His eyes trained on me intently, I feel his stare all the way down to my toes. He reaches me in no time. Bracing my hips, he turns me around until my back is toward the door. Gently, he begins to walk me backward. "You're so pretty," he rumbles, pushing me softly, while rocking me back ever so lightly until I'm up against his bedroom door.

My mind is racing on overdrive, panic taking over. No, no, I can't do this. I can't just be his for one night; not now that I know he lives here. How am I supposed to resist this—him—if he lives here, just down the street? How can I not want him all the time? How will we ever work together? How will this affect Claire and Matt? God, I need to get a grip. I tell myself to just keep it together, to breathe. *Nothing is going to happen. You can handle this.* Just ignore these feelings he's evoking. I can do it. I stand, keeping watch, anticipating Ryker's next move.

The moment he begins to speak, my resistance completely crumbles, as I register the words falling from his lips. The incredibly powerful and all-consuming words that are being uttered from the mouth belonging to this sexy man standing in front of me. Words I can't believe are aimed at me. And *Wham!* Just like that, I'm a goner. I am completely willing to give him anything he wants, without question, without hesitation, without regret; my previous plight to resist him evaporates. Fuck it. I'll take one night.

"Jesus, baby, you're my mind's eye. God, lately all I see is you. I dream of you when I sleep. I wake to thoughts of you. Then I see you and, fuck, if you're not all I need to see."

"This," he motions between us, "whatever this thing is with us—this spark, this pull—whatever the fuck you wanna call it, is gonna happen. Us, we're gonna happen, eventually," he groans, continuing, "Not tonight. You deserve much more than to be fucked in a room with a house full of people. You, Kat Rollins, need and deserve attention…worshipping." I gasp at his words. "We will fuck. Be it one night, if that's all you'll give me, I'll take it. Like a starved man I will take all you're willing to give, Kat. You're fucking me up, making me forget my rules, but for some strange reason, I like it. I think you're the girl who might be the exception to my rules. So, yeah, baby, we *will* happen."

"Ryker," is all I seem to be able to get out.

"I've wanted to be close to you again, ever since the night of that storm. God, Kat, I just want you close, baby. I can't deny it anymore. I don't want to stay away." He nuzzles his face into my neck. "Fuck, you always smell so sweet. I want to savour your delectable body, taste and touch every inch. You deserve the comfort of knowing there's no need to try and be quiet. Because, sweetheart, mark my words, when I get inside you, you will be the one growling. Growling from the pleasure I plan to inflict on your body, while you have no choice but to scream my name so loud that you'll be heard for miles around."

Holy fuck!

"Fuck, if I didn't try to deny this. I tried to leave you alone. Dammit, baby, I did. But, I can't. Seeing you tonight, dressed like the angel

I see you as in my mind, God, you're sexy as hell. I had to get to you, get to you before I ended my friendship with Jay with my fist pounding his face."

I stand there in shock at this gorgeous man's revelations. "Be ready, sweet girl, 'cause I will be coming for you. You will be mine." With that, he takes my face in his hands and slams his mouth down onto mine in a soul-shattering kiss; a kiss that I feel all the way down to the tips of my toes. A kiss that steals not only my breath, but also the last of my resolve.

I grant his tongue entrance. My legs nearly giving out, I groan into the kiss. But just as quickly as I'm ready to wrap my hands in Ryker's hair to pull him closer into me, he pulls away from me. He growls one last time, "So fucking perfect, so goddamn sweet. Fuck, you make me weak," then kisses my forehead.

"You are astoundingly gorgeous and that's probably the least interesting thing about you, I'm sure, Kat. I can only imagine you are as amazing on the inside as you are on the outside, baby. And mark my words; I am going to know all of you. I am going to consume you, as you've been consuming me. You and me, we are gonna be much more." He kisses my lips one last time.

Ryker easily moves me from the front of his door. I stand there staring up at him in what must look like a complete state of shock. Drool, I imagine, running down my face at his words.

He turns to me before leaving and grits out one last warning. "Stay away from Jay, Kat…You're mine." And with that, he leaves me standing in his room dumbfounded. Panties beyond wearable in public, my heavy breasts aching with need. *Asshole.*

Chapter 31

Ryker

FUCK, I DIDN'T mean for that to happen. I didn't mean to virtually attack her like some kind of unhinged animal. I'm sure she still thinks of me as a buffoon from the other times I've fucked up, and now I've just gone and confirmed it. *Shit*, I mutter to myself, walking to the end of the hall, intending to head back downstairs to the party to pretend like nothing happened. A stupid party that I wish wasn't even happening anymore. I really hate Hallo-fuckin'-ween. I need a fucking drink, bad, along with some space to think about what the hell is going on with me.

I needed to get away from that sweet angel before I treated her like the fucking devil I am, the one who wants to fuck her long and hard. I swear to God, I should get a medal. It took everything to walk away, leaving her in my room untouched and fucking willing. And now, no doubt, pissed off. I know she wants me. At my touch, her willingness couldn't be hidden anymore, no matter what her mind may say. Responsive to my touch, so damn pliable in my arms, I'm getting hard again just thinking about it. Fuck me sideways, fuck the medal, I should be sainted.

I end up bypassing the stairs, detouring to the bathroom. I have to get myself and my throbbing cock under control; which is impossible at this point because I can't stop fucking thinking about her. Her lips, her sounds—dammit—she even tasted better than I ever imagined she would. Locking the door, I run cold water over my face, the shock and sting of the water doing nothing to subside my thoughts.

Fuck, what this girl does to me. Man, the way she easily surrendered to my touch, allowing me to take her luscious mouth, allowing me to talk to her the way I did, crudely and matter-of-fact. Telling her—warning her really—with no uncertainty, of the things to come. And fuck if she didn't waver, not once. Rather, she simply groaned as I laid it all out for her. Fuck me. I need this girl like I need air to breathe. I know I can't wait much longer; I've given the idea of being in a committed relationship enough thought. It's what I want, what I'm ready for with Kat. For some reason, I know without a doubt, once I get inside of her mind, body, and soul, there will be no way I'm going to want to leave. Kat is who I want. I've watched her. I see her as nothing short of kind-hearted and sweet, always willing to help out above and beyond, smiling, happy. She is perfect. It's time I stop standing in my own way; it's time I go for it.

Chapter 32

Kat

FOLLOWING MY ENCOUNTER with Ryker, I stayed in his room for a while hoping he'd come back. Finally giving up on the idea, I rejoin my friends, knowing Claire is probably worried.

"Where the hell have you been? You've been gone for a long time. Are you okay? Oh lord. Please tell me you were upstairs getting it on with you-know-who." She winks before adding, "Yes, my dear. I saw Ryker follow you."

"Jesus, keep it down, would you?" I grit out, looking around, making sure no one else is listening to her big mouth.

"I may not know where you ended up all this time, or what in the hell you were doing, but I do know you, and something happened. I also know that sexy man-beast, Ryker, was with you. 'Cause he all but chased after your sexy ass once he saw you heading back up the stairs. And I know whatever went down was juicy."

At my silence, she goes on to scold me for leaving her hanging in suspense. I have to admit, sometimes it's fun to watch her squirm, trying to get the good gossip.

"Oh, okay. You wanna play like Fort Knox? Fine for now. But mark my words, missy, you will be dishing later, my friend; you can count on that. I can be very persuasive. Go on and have fun. Drink, dance, and be all secretive, but you and I *will* be talking," she quips, impressed with herself.

I have to give it to her; she is pretty relentless when she wants something.

"Okay, later. Now stop giving me shit in the middle of the bloody dance floor. I already feel on edge. Now I need a stiff drink—or five—and to get back to dancing with my bestie." I offer a smile, trying to appease her while standing in the middle of the dance floor.

"I just want to make sure you're okay. You look like you're hiding something. He didn't do anything to you, did he? 'Cause I will kick his ass if I need to."

"Claire, I'm fine. Nothing happened that I didn't want to happen. You're right. He did follow me, and we talked, although brief. But I don't want to get into it here. Not when all these people are around. I need to forget it, because in all honesty, he's an asshole who's playing with me like I'm a new untouched toy, and I am not going to be another play in his overused game book." With this, I know Claire will drop it for now. She sees I'm affected by what went down upstairs and she knows I'll open up when I'm ready to talk. Fucking Ryker and his leaving me like that for what, the second time now? There is no way I'll let him get near me like that again. That is the last time he'll leave me practically begging like a fool.

I have a few more drinks and dance the night away, trying my hardest not to keep looking for a certain someone and ignoring my thoughts about everything that happened upstairs. I can say I'm not as chipper and fun as when we'd first arrived. My world has just been thrown off its axis.

For some stupid reason like the good girl he wants me to be, I do heed Ryker's warning and stayed away from Jay. Although, I'm not really sure why, it's not like he stuck around to finish what he started upstairs, but I guess deep down, I know whatever that was; it's most certainly not over. And truth be told, despite knowing better, I'm not sure I'd even want it to be.

After I leave the party, I lie in my bed replaying over and over what happened upstairs between Ryker and me. The more I think about it, the more confused, frustrated, and angry I'm getting. Hearing him say he feels there is some strange spark between us is reassuring. I'm glad I'm not the only one feeling it, that I'm not going crazy or delusional. It's clear we have a definite attraction; there is no denying it's there. It's like a magnetic force that cannot be tamed. But with knowing his type, I cannot help but see the flashing warning signs from miles away. Wondering if I'm just another play in his game, where the goal is to fuck me like all the others I've been told about. It's no secret that Ryker is the epitome of a player, and I seriously don't need to be hurt again. Getting involved with a guy like him can only spell disaster for a girl like me. I'm not looking to be a game; I'm looking to be the game changer. In the meantime, I'm happy to wait on the sidelines for Mr. Right.

I continue to think how he's just a dick who's just been playing a game with me, who said all those sweet things to help get into my panties. Maybe he thinks he told me what I want to hear? *Would he really say all those things just to get laid?* I mean, most girls love hearing about connections, feelings, and pretty much insta-love. *Dammit,* I hate feeling like this. I hate when I get excited about a guy, and then do this to myself. What if all his talk about us, his feeling it too, an imaginary pull, us having a connection…a spark, what if it was sincere? What if he really feels something? What then?

Ryker isn't just an ordinary boy; no, he is a player. An alpha male who doesn't do more than fuck, just as I've been told on more than one occasion now anyway. Since working at Pub Fiction, I've heard more than my fair share of stories about the infamous Ryker Eddison.

Thinking back on it now, I'm more than certain Ryker is just laying the groundwork to get himself laid; he couldn't possibly change. Change for me. Once a player, always a player, right?

Brooke and Naomi themselves pretty much warned me off him and his flirtatious ways months ago. The fact that the guy needs a message bowl because he's so in demand should be all the justification I need. *Could I even compete or deal with his entourage of hoochies?*

I'm tired of being in limbo with this man. I will not allow Ryker to affect me any longer. Nor will I let him tell me the way things are going to be between us. I know he's hotter than Hades, and believe me, the visions I have created in my mind at the promises of pleasure that seeped from his mouth tonight would no doubt be unlike anything I've ever experienced. But I can't just be another name added to the bowl of women waiting for more from Ryker Eddison. Not that I wouldn't love to give into Honeybutter, even for a night. But I can't. I won't.

Especially after Seth, and how flippant he was with me, with our relationship, with my reaction to his cheating. Seth led me to truly believe it was my fault, that I was some great big bitch who was too plain for him...too boring. I know I need and deserve more now. I deserve to be worshipped inside and outside of the bedroom. I need to be with a man who wants to be with me in an actual functioning, loving relationship. I need to think about myself, my heart, as well as the fact that I can find meaningless sex with anyone. Someone who I don't feel a connection to. I know already that with Ryker, I want to get to know him so much more. I want to be important, and not just another willing body for him to bury his cock in.

Chapter 33

Kat

THINKING OF ASSHOLES all night, I reach for my phone, looking to see if I have any more messages from Seth. If I do, I know I'm going to have to call and confront him, and ask him once again to leave me alone. I'll remind him we're through, and inform him that I'll involve the police if he starts harassing me like before. Luckily, there aren't anymore.

Making my way to the kitchen, I'm surprised I'm not the first one up, especially after a night of partying like last night. As I step into the kitchen, I'm immediately assaulted with Claire's demand to talk.

"Mind telling me, now that you've slept off your mood of keeping hush-hush, what the hell happened between you and Ryker last night?" she pretty much barks as she cooks bacon and eggs for breakfast. I smile when I see a mound of food on the stove, knowing she's made some for everyone. Walking to the counter, I grab a mug and begin pouring myself some much-needed coffee. Claire has one on the go already, so I top hers off.

"We talked is all. He wanted to talk to me about some stuff coming up at work. He thought maybe I could help him out with planning a few things at Pub Fiction to raise money for the kids at the community centre," I say, knowing as soon as the lies leave my mouth that Claire will be calling me out on my bullshit and complete inability to tell a lie again.

"Really, Kat? Who do you think you're talking to here? There is no fucking way in hell that Ryker wanted to talk to you about work with you dressed like that! You didn't see his face when he spotted you by the stairs. He did *not* want to talk to you about work. I'm pretty sure he didn't want to talk at all." She stands facing me, arms crossed in front of her chest, willing me to try and lie.

"Now cut the shit and tell me the truth, Kitty Kat. I warned you last night we would be having this chat. Besides, I saw the way you were looking for him all night, and then once he finally re-emerged, the two of you were practically eye-fucking each other the rest of the time. And don't think Matt and I didn't notice how you wouldn't give Jay the time of day. I know you were upstairs together, now spill, woman," she says, all but stomping her foot.

"Okay, fuck, you're a pain in my ass," I tell her as she hands me a plate of food and sits with me at the table, settling in to eat while I fill her in on everything that really happened.

I decide to tell her the complete truth, as well as how it will not be a recurring thing.

"But in no uncertain terms will I be allowing that boy near my body again. I don't care how much I may have liked it."

"Oh, come on. It might be good for you," she challenges. "Maybe a fuck buddy, rather than a regular relationship, might do your psyche a world of good. Nothing like the cure-all of regular orgasms, you know. Endorphins…they do a body good." She singsongs the end, and laugh at how witty she is.

"Seriously Kat, seeing as Seth, the douche, kind of did a number on you in the confidence department, why not let a certain alpha hottie like Ryker help to remind you just how hot you are? Besides, with that text message last night, I'm sure Ryker might just be what you need to relax."

Isn't that the truth? I never seemed to really notice how much Seth was an asshole to me until it was too late and I found him cheating on me. Seth would always criticize my clothes and the way I wore my hair up. Telling me I looked like a child and to wear it down when around him. He disliked my friends, especially Claire, and would make me feel guilty about going out with them. So, for a really long time, I kind of ditched my friends. I choose Seth over them. Never again will I let a man make me choose like that. I need my friends, especially Claire. I can't really justify why I let him treat me the way he did, but I guess I just wasn't confident enough to argue. I think I thought I loved him.

I chomp away on my last piece of bacon, listening to her arguments supporting all the reasons I should give Ryker a chance in spite of my mind already being made up. She's sure she can convince me otherwise and she seems to have tunnel vision where he and I are concerned. She can't see the consequences of us hooking up like I can.

"I mean, you are twenty-two years old. How many one-night stands or casual sexual relationships have you had?" I just stare at her silently. "Umm, exactly, it might do your body good. Let Ryker in, see if he's worth the hype, and by the way he's been with you, I'm pretty convinced he'd even give you more than one night," Claire finishes saying while raising her brows in a *hubba hubba* gesture as she cleans up our breakfast.

Sitting at the table, finishing the last of my coffee, I think that maybe, just maybe, she has a point.

Ryker would be the perfect non-relationship. It's not like he wants more from me, right? I mean, it's not like he's contacted me, even though he has my number; I gave it to him at The Bean. *He's not really interested in more from you, Kat.*

But then, I think about all the times we have talked, the way he seems to always be there to help me. Maybe we could really be more. Then the reality of who Ryker Eddison is hits me and I'm confused all over again.

Chapter 34

Kat

November

"PARDON?" I ASKED Levi, my face clearly showing how shocked I am. Standing in his office, I'm dumbfounded at what he's telling me about the changes happening at work. I try to listen, but honestly, all I can think and hear is, *fuck me,* over and over in my head.

"I need you to learn to work the bar, Kat. I have to juggle some people around and you've done an amazing job here. I want you to think of it as a promotion. I'll need you to work the bar Friday nights, especially now with Claire's schedule needing to change as she's agreed to take on Mondays, Wednesdays, and Thursdays. I'm sure Claire has told you how much she makes in tips Friday nights," he continues, almost like he knows I need convincing. I know I need to respond, but I just don't know what to say. This was the last thing I expected; after all, I don't really have that much experience. Levi clears his throat, gaining my attention again. Dammit, I must look like an idiot. "Bartenders always make the most. I assumed you'd be excited. But judging by your face, maybe I was wrong," he says, tilting his head, his tone losing excitement.

Not wanting to come across as rude or disinterested, I decide to man up. "That's great, Levi, honestly. I'm very excited for the challenge. I really do appreciate you offering me the job. I can't wait to get started. Claire is always bragging about her tips, so yes, I'm super pumped for this opportunity."

Smiling, as if now appeased with my excitement, Levi reaches for the schedules pinned to the bulletin board and reviews them with me before giving me my own copy.

"Perfect," he says. "I've arranged for Ryker to train you a few hours this Wednesday. I've added you to the schedule for then as well. I know you typically don't work Wednesdays, but I was hoping this week you could make it in?" he asks with a cute questioning voice. I quickly try to compose myself before I answer him back, because the mere thought of working closely with Ryker has my body on high alert, almost buzzing with excitement.

"Umm, yes, sure. As long as it's okay that I'm here at seven thirty. I have class until seven," I respond.

"That's no problem; let's just make it eight. That way you're not rushing. Besides, Wednesdays aren't too busy, so that will give you lots of one-on-one training time with Ryker." *Oh yes please!* No! No! No! I scold myself as I leave Levi's office with my new schedule tightly clenched in my hand.

As I rush out of Pub Fiction, I decide this new working arrangement needs my bestie, some drinks, and a definite plan of action. I call Claire from my car as I drive home.

"Claire, pick out our outfits. Kitty Kat needs drinks, dancing, and her Claire Bear. Houston, we have a problem and I need a plan."

"You got it, Kitty Kat," she agrees without complaint. "I take it you just found out about your new job description?" Her tone tells me she's all too aware of the reason.

"I sure as hell did. What the fuck am I going to do? There is no way in hell I can avoid jumping Ryker's bones if we're working side by side. I'm freaking out!" She tells me to slow down, that it's not that bad.

"I've just been set up for failure!" I add dramatically, hoping to get

MY MIND'S EYE

sympathy, but Claire just laughs.

"I'm sorry I get that you're freaking out, but I can't say I'm feeling bad for you at all. I have to admit I'm actually excited this is happening. Ha! I can't wait to see how this new arrangement plays out. I have a feeling things are gonna get all kinds of hot at Pub Fiction. Now hang the fuck up and get here, lady."

I scoff in the phone at her before muttering a half-hearted, "See you soon."

After a few drinks to calm my nerves, and a full-blown girlie talk session with my BFF, we decide it's time for a change in scenery. We decide to go to The Beaver and Bulldog to meet up with some friends for Manic Mondays, where drinks are 2-for-1. It's a clever little scam, really, convincing us students to party on Mondays after taking Sunday off. I mean, how does one refuse 2-for-1 drinks?

We make our way into the bar, and the whole time, I'm thinking to myself that maybe I shouldn't have suggested Claire pick out our outfits. You think I would know by now that Claire is all about the formfitting, tight clothing and will always choose the same for me. Of course, the skintight jeans I've paired with my chocolate, heeled, knee-high boots are the least of my troubles. She's managed to somehow convince me to pair my sexy jeans with a deep brown, draped surplice top, which just happens to accentuate my chest, forcing one's gaze to my girls without much choice. But as Claire is always telling me, 'you got to own your shit,' so I just go with it.

Claire's response to my uneasiness of clothing choices always result in some sort of smart-ass comment that seems to make me laugh. This girl is obsessed with boobs. "Girl, you've got a pair to make Marilyn Monroe jelly. As long as they are perky and perfect, flaunt 'em while you still got 'em to flaunt. Because one day, those puppies just may need fixing."

Needless to say, yeah, my bestie is a complete ass, but yes, yes, I love her and merely laugh at her stupid comment, all the while letting her dress me, yet again. Claire has a real flare for fashion and I honestly see her as being a fashion designer, not a teacher someday. I have often told her she should consider looking into a way of doing both.

As we enter the bar, I hear Hozier singing about taking him to church, a song which is currently on heavy rotation on my iPod. I immediately grin, singing along as we scan the bar, looking for our friends. It's at that very moment, however, that my skin pricks. A knowing sensation takes over my body. My eyes instantly find exactly who my body already knew was here...*Ryker*.

As I look into those honeybutter eyes; eyes that have been taunting me in my dreams almost nightly, I falter in my steps while following Claire across the bar to where our friends are sitting waiting for us. I falter because it's as if catching Ryker's gaze instantly creates a crazy pulsing sensation that only he can seem to evoke in me, one that has my body humming while wreaking havoc on my clit. I long desperately to feel his touch, to finally give in to what it seems we both want. God, with the buzzing sensations coursing through my body as I follow behind her, I smile at the visuals my mind has managed to conjure. Holy fuck! The power behind those eyes, sweet honeybutter coloured eyes; which I know would look spectacular peering up at me while nestled nice and tightly in between my legs, surely bringing me a pleasure like I've never experienced before.

"Oh fuck, Kat, do you see who I see?" Claire asks, right on cue, a knowing smirk gracing her face.

"Of course I do," I snap unintentionally. "It's like my body has a fucking sonar machine that pulls at my goddamn vagina whenever that creature is in sight."

I smile, attempting to lace my response with some humour, but it doesn't work. Claire knows I'm full of shit, that I'm not fine at all.

"Well then, stop being a pussy and go over and talk to him. The poor guy can't seem to take his eyes off of you. Go, my friend. I give you permission to embrace your inner whore with that sex-on-a-cream pie of a man." Of course she does. Maybe she'd make more money as a pimp?

Boy, does this girl have career choices.

"No way am I going to him, fuck that. There is no way I can. Besides, he's standing with that chick Sarah again, maybe they're a thing. Maybe he's not her friend either," I quip with a bit of worry in my voice. I know Claire is about to call *bullshit.*

"Come on, Claire Bear. This Kitty Kat needs a tequila shot, a beer, a booth, and some more good ol' girl chat with my bestie about all my woes before we go dance with the rest of the hoes! You remember the whole reason why we're even here tonight, right? I need out of my mind, and like now. I need to have fun and I need a bit more of your ever-helpful advice," I half joke as I lead us to the bar.

Don't think for one minute the irony of the reason for that need being present isn't lost on me either. Oh boy, isn't it ever. I shake my head at it. Fate is a real bitch, ya know? Or is it Karma? Either way, I'm fucked. How can I sit and discuss how to handle working with Ryker when I can't stop trying to nonchalantly stare and eye-fuck him every few minutes? Pathetic. Maybe I should just say fuck it and give in.

I make the split decision that I'll simply wing it, foregoing any plan and deciding to let the 'cards fall where they may.' After all, I do actually believe the age-old saying that *everything happens for a reason.* With that school of thought, I easily decide that Ryker just might be a gift. Maybe there is an actual reason this shit with Ryker has been consuming me, mind and body, day and night. I'll take just one night.

With my new vow to just go with it set in place, waiting for whatever divine intervention to intervene, I do what any girl in my position would do.

Turning to Claire, I give her a mischievous grin before grabbing her by the hand, declaring, "Oh piss it! Let's go dance and forget about my boy trouble. I kinda wanna tempt the fates tonight."

"Oh thank the Lord!" is all I hear as I drag her behind me.

My phone vibrates in my pocket, and I check it because Naomi had mentioned she might join us tonight if she finishes early enough with her study group. Glancing down, I note Seth's number once again. For fuck sakes! Opening the screen, I opt for the ignore button. Heading straight to the setting options, I block his number, a trick I didn't even know I could do until talking to Wes over the phone the other night. During our chat, I was also reminded by my little bro that my phone is just way too much phone for a girl like me. As I was filling him in on Seth and life happenings, I reminded him why I hate having a cell phone. He ignored my phone jab, but offered his help to deal with Seth if I needed it.

Wes and I have always been close. He's seriously one of the sweetest and greatest guys ever, and not only because he's my brother either. He is too overprotective, and I know without a doubt, if I ask, he'd be more than happy to pay Seth a visit. See, my brother is also at school in Ottawa. He wants to become a lawyer as well, and Carleton University has an amazing Criminal Justice program. I have no doubt that Wes would actually enjoy getting the opportunity to have a little chat with Seth. Wes has never been a fan. I manage to convince Wes that I have it under control and not to worry. I assured him I'd keep him posted and I can handle it for now, but I just wanted him to know what was going on.

Sighing at my phone now, I know I'll most definitely need to deal with this, but not tonight. Tonight I need to try and relax.

Claire and I make it to the dance floor, and it's not long before we're swarmed by a group of guys out to have a good time. Some are pretty fucking cute, I'm not gonna lie. But then, there are also the ones who are wearing enough whore lure to gag a maggot. Like, easy on the cologne there, boys! It's supposed to be appealing, not cough inducing. Honestly, it's so bad you'd be left smelling like a cheap gigolo if you got too close. A few times while dancing, Claire and I have to move to get away from those guys, the ones who just don't get it. Chicks do *not* dig it!

As we're dancing, I scan the room for Ryker. I know he's watching me from somewhere. I can feel it. But more importantly, I know tonight's gonna be different, the start of something new. That is, if I can work up the nerve to go to him. Shaking the thought away, I concentrate on dancing and having a good time with Claire and our friends.

After a few more fast songs, the DJ switches it up. He begins to play "Only You'" by 112. It's a sexy jam that has people coming together and grinding up on one another, swaying to the lust-filled song lyrics that are blasting from the speakers. As I'm ready to head off the dance floor, my hips are quickly grabbed and I'm being swayed in time to said music. I contemplate putting my heel down on Mr. Presumptuous' foot, but I think better of it, reminding myself to be more relaxed. Deciding to just go with it rather than causing a scene or freaking out, I give in and allow myself to be taken over by the beats as well as the movements of this stranger, who not only smells divine, but can move like sex on a lazy Sunday afternoon. Just as I'm letting go, relaxing into a sexy rhythm and actually enjoying myself, I sense him. Ryker. *Shit.*

Chapter 35

Ryker

"**N**OT A FUCKING chance," I growl as I make my way through the crowds of drunken fucktards acting like idiots, who are only serving to get in my way from getting to Kat. *Assholes*. I am absolutely fucking seething. Not only am I horny as hell from this little game of cat and mouse we have going on, but now after seeing that shithead come up on Kat like he's trying to mate with her on the dance floor, I'm pissed right the fuck off. The fact that she let him near her pisses me off that much more.

In no way, shape, or form is she getting away from me, or better yet, away from us again tonight. Tonight, Kat is mine. It's time for church 'cause I am ready to worship the Goddess that is Kat Rollins. This game ends here.

Like I told Justin and Matty earlier, I'm done with this shit; it's time to make her mine. And, apparently, the time to make us happen is right the fuck now.

As the anger radiates from me, I finally make it to the centre of the dance floor. Claire sees me first, smirks, then turns in the opposite direction as if she knows I'm about to start a pissing contest. Well, let me tell you, there is no contest. I'm the guaran-goddamn-teed winner. Kat is *my* prize.

She's about to figure it out real quick that we *are* happening. I will be running off that douche-canoe grinding up on her ass in *5, 4, 3, 2,*

1..."Excuse me," I all but growl as I stand beside Kat and nimrod on the dance floor. Hell-to-the-fucking-no am I about to stand around and witness this shitshow.

Kat tenses immediately, sensing my rage as I tower over the asshat. Realizing I'm not to be messed with, the jerk flees in a hurry.

"Ryker? What the hell do you think you're doing? I'm dancing here, do you mind? Go back to your blonde friend."

"I sure as fuck do, baby. You want to dance, you dance with me. I'm done waiting, done watching. I want you, and I know you want me, too. I have no blonde friend. You are my *only* friend." There I've said it. I've shown this girl how pussy-whipped she's got me. Now I stand and wait to see how she reacts. Fuck me! I can't believe I'm acting this way willingly again. But I can't deny it; I yearn for her, and more than just her incredible body. I want her smiles; I want to know her quirks, her loves, her hates, her hopes, and her dreams. Fuck it. I want whatever she'll give me.

She nods with a sexy-as-sin smirk and that's the green light I need. My mind spins as the words *go, go, go,* chimes over and over in my head. She's fucking in. Kat is giving us the go ahead. I scan the bar, looking for a quiet secluded place. I need to get her off this crowded dance floor now! Noticing the hall, I grasp her by her hips, pulling her flush to my front, turning her so her ass is now aligned almost perfectly with what I'm about to offer her. I lead her forward to the long hall situated beside the bar. I move us past a ton of familiar faces, walk past them, ignoring them completely. I don't give a fuck who's here or what they gotta say. Pushing past the crowds, I have a one-track mind right now, and it's looped on repeat to getting this girl and getting her alone.

My brain seems to suddenly catch up with my cock and I realize there is no way we can do this here. I told her before, I need to worship her; she deserves more than a party fuck. To my amazement, I veer us back toward the way we came. I can't believe I'm actually drawing this out, risking the chance she may smarten up and change her mind. With that thought playing around in mind, I move my hand to the small of her back before leading her right out the bar's door while whispering, "Not here, baby, not here. You need better than this dive." *My bed.*

Chapter 36

Kat

I'M STUPID OR just finally realizing I can't resist this man anymore. I've tried. Like the countless of others before me, I'm caving in, tossing in the towel. Ryker Eddison wins. Tonight I will give myself over to this crazy attraction, which exists so tangibly between Ryker and me. Especially after his blatant display of caveman-like behaviour, which honestly only served to make my lady bits scream *YES!*

I follow him as he leads us to the hallway, and my heart is racing as nervousness kicks in. I can't believe I'm going to let him fuck me in this packed club. But before I can even get the words out to protest, he's pretty much purring in my ear that we're leaving. Relief instantly washes over me as he guides us out the door to the parking lot.

Of course his truck is the big-ass, jacked-up monster that screams 'I am man!' The same truck I saw that day in the lot with Seth. Luckily for me, like a gentleman, he helps me in. All the while, seriously palming my ass as he lifts me into the cab without any effort at all.

"Christ, you're fucking killing me, baby. That ass, God, it's fucking sexy and tight. It's gonna look fuckin' sexy all red with my handprint on it," he states point-blank, his jaw locked tight as he settles me in.

Clenching, I am seriously clenching now at the visions he's just inspired in my mind. *We need to get the fuck home and now.*

But, of course, Ryker doesn't stop there. No, no, of course not. He needs to slip in a few more promises to kick up my already greedy body. "God, hot girl, I can't wait to sink into your hot 'n tight pussy from behind; the view alone will be enough to drive me insane, baby. Ass up, those fucking tits jiggling all around," he grinds out, teeth clearly clenched. "I've been watching you shake that ass for way too long. It's time you shake it with me rooted to the hilt in your pussy while you grind down, milking my cock. Fuck! We need to get the hell outta here," he all out growls.

He stands there for a minute, running his hands through his hair. He demands my eye contact without a word. His presence is powerful, so I stare back at him, waiting as if he's going to say more, but he doesn't. Not right away. Rather, he stands on the outside of the truck, looking deep in thought, like he's not sure what he wants to say. After a few moments, he climbs up and stands on the running board. Grabbing my face, he holds it so he can peer directly into my eyes. He surprises me with a ghost of a kiss to the side of my mouth, then utters words that both shock and confuse me, especially with how dirty his previous ones were, the ones that have left me a needy fool.

"I think I've been waiting a long time for you, Kat. I'm going to make this amazing; I don't wanna fuck it up." Then with that, without waiting for a reaction from me, he closes the door, as if he didn't just say anything out of the ordinary. Like he didn't just skew my view of what tonight is supposed to be. Ryker makes his way around to the driver's side and hops in. All I can seem to do is sit in silence, my body humming with anticipation, my heart beating with…hope, as I sit thinking about what the implications of his last statement means, or could mean. *Will there be more than tonight?* I replay his words over and over.

Ironically enough, as we drive, the radio begins blasting a song that resonates so much with my current state that I giggle at the irony. Ryker glances over at me, a knowing smirk on his beautiful face as Queens of the Stone Age's "Make it wit Chu" croons from the speakers.

We sit in silence, both of us lost in our minds; well, at least, I know I am anyway. We may not be talking with our voices, but our bodies are having a conversation of their own. The air is crackling with anticipation of things to come. I can't fucking stand it. *I can't wait anymore,* I think as I bravely and confidently unfasten my seatbelt. With an idea so unlike me in my mind, I am actually feeling kind of giddy with how brazen I'm about to be with this boy who I don't even really know. The same boy who makes me feel spontaneous and free.

"Ryker."

Chapter 37

Ryker

I SWEAR TO all that's fuckin' holy and good that I'm going to fucking combust at any moment. After I kissed her, I knew I was done for. Fuck me, if her taste gets better and better, it's beyond my wildest fantasies. And believe me, there have been a ton of them over the last few months, and that ass, Jesus. Just standing there looking at her, thinking about her ass and all its beauty, I couldn't help the filth of my words from spewing out of my mouth about all the things I wanted—scratch that—I *will* do to her.

Kat's unlike all the other chicks I've known, and I've known a lot. It's clear beyond a shadow of doubt, this girl is different. Meaning I will have to go slow, ease into things with her. What I need is a goddamn filter really, 'cause the last thing I want to do is scare her off. I need to rein it in a bit, but fuck if I even think I know how to do that when she's around. God, my dick is throbbing at the images of this girl. I move my leg a bit, trying to discreetly shift my cock back into a comfortable position, seeing as having her beside me, knowing what's sure to happen, only fuels the power of my cock, which has been raging hard since...I don't even fucking know anymore, to be honest. All I know is that I need to sink into this girl right fucking now! Driving like this in silence is killing me; the goddamn song on the radio isn't fucking helping either. Thinking about what I said to Kat about having been waiting for her, I know my comment threw her off.

Yeah, well, welcome to my world, sugar. But I need her to know this, whatever the hell it is, I want more than one night. I want many.

We're driving, listening to the music, when suddenly I hear the click and the clank of the seatbelt and my name fall from her sweet lips.

"Ryker."

And like the crazy son of a bitch I am, the one she's made me to be, I swerve the truck over to the side of the road, even though we're less than a block away from campus. Before I even have a chance to kill the ignition, the minute the truck stops, Kat is over the console, straddled between the steering wheel and me.

"Ryker," she says again breathlessly and, Jesus, if it isn't the sounds of angels.

"Yeah, baby?"

"Ryker," she grinds down on my cock and I think I'm gonna come right there, just from the desire in her tone. Fuck this girl.

"I...I, ah, I can't wait. I need to touch you. I need contact. I'm freaking out over here," she says, almost scared that I won't understand.

Man, this girl is something else. *Believe me, baby, I can fucking relate.*

"Kat," I growl, grabbing her by the hips, pushing her down more firmly in the place that allows me to feel the sweet heat she's radiating from her hot pussy. I look up from where our bodies join as they rub, forcing her to follow my lead. We stare at each other's eyes, green to hazel, while I move her hips ever so slowly forward and back, friction increasing with each little ministration.

"Ryker, yes, that's it," she almost cries. Then suddenly, like two rabid animals, we attack each other with a fervent need so powerful I'm not sure we'll be able to stop.

"Fuck, baby you taste incredible. I can't wait to taste all of you," I all but groan as we're all lips, hands, and moans. This is definitely the best fucking car ride of my life, and I commit the image of her in this moment to my memory. God, she is the hottest thing I have ever seen. And I haven't even seen what's underneath her clothes yet.

I. AM. SO. FUCKED.

Feeling we're about to lose total control, I pull away from her mouth, my hand settling under her firm ass. "Kat, we need to go, baby. I won't fuck you in my truck. I can't. I need you sprawled out on my bed where I can see you, taste you, and fuck you properly. I need room to explore your tight as fuck body, baby." Without giving her a chance to speak, I reluctantly pick her up and place her, much to her dissatisfaction, back onto her seat. Without waiting to make sure she's even buckled in, I turn the ignition, slamming the shifter into drive, and peel out.

Chapter 38

Kat

WE FINALLY PULL into Ryker's driveway after what feels like the longest drive in the world. My body is buzzing with anticipation and wantonness like nothing I've ever known before.

The next thing I know, a brooding Ryker flings my car door open before scooping me up and basically tossing me over his shoulder as he walks up to the door.

"Ryker, I can walk, you know."

"Not fast enough, baby. Need in you now!" he asserts while walking, his hand resting on my ass. I giggle at how we must look.

"Kat," he says, before putting me down on the porch face-to-face with him. Taking my face in his hands, forcing me to look in his eyes, he asks me again to make the final decision.

"Baby, if we go inside, I need you to know I won't stop. I, er...I don't think I'll be able to hold off anymore. This," he motions from himself to me, "this, between us, has got me all fucked up. All I can think about is sinking into what I know is gonna be the sweetest pussy I have ever felt. So, baby, if we go in, we're all in. You get me?"

Holy shit, what does a girl say to that?

I stand there looking into those honeybutter eyes and I'm actually starting to freak the fuck out. This is my chance to bail, to change my mind. Can I really handle only one night? Should I even be here? Is he using me? Will he still want me? Want more?

He said things to make me feel like I might be different. That maybe, just maybe, I'm more than tonight's bed warmer. Just as I'm about to give him my decision, Ryker begins to talk. Staring at me, both our breathing heavy from the drive, but also from the connection we obviously share.

"Don't worry sweet girl, everything is going to be okay. Please give us this, give us tonight. God, baby, let me make you feel good. Give in. We can worry about the rest tomorrow. We'll figure it out, but please say you'll come in." With that, he leans down while cupping my face and kisses me.

Chapter 39

Ryker

HOLY SHIT! I sound like a fucking pussy-whipped asshole, but I can't fucking help it. I want this girl like I need my next breath. I have never felt this way before, this rush of urgency and anticipation for one woman. I need Kat to give in, to take the plunge, the chance on me. I want more with her, but first I have to fuck her within an inch of my life. I can work on sweet later.

As I stand here waiting for her choice, I decide fuck it; I can help this decision along. Ten minutes ago there wasn't any doubt of where this was heading. But because I'm deciding to try and be a nice guy all of sudden, I just might ruin my chance. What the hell was I thinking giving her an opportunity to bail? Fuck that. We are happening, decision made. Grabbing her face in my hands, I swoop in, claiming her lips. Fuck, this girl tastes goddamn sweet. I'll kiss her into submission; make her forget I even gave her the choice. I give her my all, and it isn't fucking sweet or polite. No. It's hot. It's dirty and all out needy. My kiss is laced with promises of the things to come, clues for her to guess just how good this will be.

"Ryker," she whispers breathlessly, her chest heaving from the kiss. "I want you too, Ryker, so much it hurts. Yes, let's go inside. I want to. But, Ryker, just please...please don't hurt me; I can't take it."

Nodding, before briefly resting my head on her forehead, I take her hand, unlock the door, and lead her inside, up to my room.

Things will never be the same between us again.

I might never be the same again.

Chapter 40

Kat

I FOLLOW RYKER up the stairs to his room, and I'm almost shaking. I'm nervous as hell. I can feel my heart thumping erratically in my chest. But at the same time, I'm so fucking horny and ready for him, for us. My body has been craving this for way too long. I enter his room just like the last time. I quickly take in the space, noting how masculine and very him it is. Turning back, I see him lock the door, and then he's in front of me so quickly that my breath hitches in response. He wraps those big arms of his around me while pulling me into him tightly and begins nuzzling my neck, nestling his face in the crook of my neck and shoulder, breathing me in deep, taking in my scent. Then he gently pulls my head back by my hair, forcing me to look into his eyes.

"Baby, you ignite a fire deep within me, a burning desire that drives me fucking insane with need for you. I can't explain it, it's like nothing I've ever felt before. I burn for you. I ache at the idea of you, getting to touch you. God, I ache at the idea of being inside you. Hot girl, I swear, if I don't get my cock in you soon, I'm about to fucking combust. Now, are you going to let me in, sweetheart? Are you going to save me from this fire that's killing me?"

Holy fuck!

I simply nod. I seem to be tongued-tied around this man, always nodding my replies to show my agreement because, honestly, I can't

217

even begin to think of a response to the incredible things he says. Next thing I know, Ryker growls before slamming his lips to mine, quickly invading my mouth with his. His lips sear over mine, demanding I open to him, granting his tongue the permission it seeks. The kiss is all-consuming, causing goosebumps to break out over my skin. We're literally caressing, teasing, testing, and tasting each other's mouth, and it's only serving to drive me crazy. It's not nearly close to what I'm in want of.

"Ryker, I need more. I want you. Now!"

"Fuck, if I don't already know, baby. I'm gonna make you feel so fucking good. I'm going to take such good care of you, Kat, trust me."

With that, Ryker groans and begins walking us back toward his bed. "Arms," he demands. And without question, I raise them so he can remove my shirt. I'm thankful I wore a matching purple demi bra and panty set tonight. I'm confident he'll approve.

"Fuck me, I knew these were gonna be exquisite, but holy shit, sweetheart. They're fucking perfect," he says while holding my heavy breasts in both of his hands. He's cupping them with the perfect amount of force, driving me fucking crazy. He quickly unclasps my bra, letting it fall down along my arms. It's instantly removed and discarded to the side.

"I'm gonna need to taste these for a while. Sweet Kat, I think I just may have found my new favourite pastime," he says as he lowers his head in line with my nipples and darts his tongue out, licking, sucking, and nipping at each budded tip. He's grunting and humming as he laps at my breasts. It's fucking erotic to watch...he's so erotic to watch.

"Jesus, Ryker, that feels so good," I tell him, my breath hitching from the onslaught of his mouth's attack. "Holy fuck!" He tugs on each nipple with his teeth, forcing them to become fucking erect; it sends a jolt of pleasure right to my pussy. I can't stifle the moan that falls out of my mouth at the attention he's giving to my tits.

Looking up at me, Ryker smirks; obviously aware of the effect he's having on me. "I really, really like these, baby. I've been dreaming about these sweet tits. They're perfect," he mutters with one last lick.

Suddenly he stands, looking down at me. "I'm gonna have to come back to those. Actually, I think I'm gonna have to fuck those too, sweet girl, but first, I plan on seeing if you taste as good as those titties. I need to feast on that pussy of yours, the one that I know is aching and dripping for me right now," he says, his voice turning a deep baritone from want as he guides me back to his bed. He removes his shirt before pushing me down onto the bed. Holy shit, he has the sexiest tattoo, I have ever seen. It's a beautiful Polynesian tribal tattoo that I just want to lick my way over while exploring this gorgeous specimen. I try to scoot up a bit on the bed, but I'm pulled back down to the very edge of the mattress. My jeans and boots along with my panties are gone in a flash. Ryker is now towering over me while my ass is hanging off the mattress, waiting for his touch.

Chapter 41

Ryker

FUCK ME, IF seeing Kat sprawled out, ass hanging off the foot of my bed isn't the sexiest thing I have ever seen in my life. I stand over her, taking her in, committing her to memory. Jesus, this girl is gorgeous and she's waiting for me, needing me as much as I need her. I lower myself to my knees, in perfect alignment with her sweet spot. I look up, meeting her glazed eyes. I offer a wink before spreading her open. I run my hands along her body from her shoulders to the top of her body, rubbing her breasts and torso, then back down to her thighs, passing them up and down her lithe legs over and over. I run my hands everywhere.

"Mine, Kat. You're mine. I own this body. These tits, these amazing legs that I want wrapped around my neck. This tight ass, mmm, baby," I say as I dip my hands under her body, grabbing the sexy, perfectly tight globes of her ass.

Fuck, she feels good under my touch. Licking my lips, I lean back up over her, stretching up to take her pert nipples each into my mouth one more time before hovering back over to take another kiss. Kat mewls and arches herself into my touches, seeking more. Goddammit, seeing her at my mercy is like adding fuel to a fire. Quickly, I stand, needing to remove my pants and boxers 'cause my dick is the hardest it's ever been and I'm consumed by an overwhelming need for this girl. Jesus, what she's capable of doing to me, and I haven't even gotten my cock in her yet.

With my pants off and thrown to the side, my cock springing free, I stroke it a few times before moving back over to Kat on the bed. I smirk down at her. "Like what you see here, baby?" I ask while I rub my hand up and down my shaft as I see her watching me intently, green eyes glued to my raging hard-on while she whispers her approval. "It's all for you, sweet girl; you drive me wild." Before she realizes, I'm back over her, leaning my weight on one arm as I suck in her bottom lip between my teeth, gently pulling it, causing her to moan.

"God, Ryker, ppll-lease," she spurs me on.

From her lips, I slowly move my mouth back down to offer each fantastic peak one last tug; shit, are her tits fantastic. *I'll never get enough of this girl,* I think as my hands join in my eager exploration of her lithe body. I need to calm myself down because, I swear, Kat's perfection is enough to make me come all over myself before we even get started. I dart my tongue out while making my way down to her core. Slowly, I grasp her ankles to spread her legs a bit more. The move is enough that her pretty pink pussy is now showcased in front of me.

"Fuck me, you've got the prettiest looking pussy, baby, so pink, smooth, and wet with need." I glance up at her one more time before I dive in with her eyes trained on me intently, waiting for my mouth. She needs this as much as I do, so with one last knowing smirk, I get to it.

She bucks off the bed instantly as my tongue laps between her juicy folds. Holy shit, if Kat isn't all kinds of sweet like I knew she would be. "Baby, you smell so fucking sweet, and you taste even better. God, you're fucking edible." I sit before her, pulling her legs over my shoulders. "Need you closer, hot girl. I need to feed on all I can get." With that, she begins to tremble as I slowly take her clit in my mouth, swirling my tongue all around, teasing her sweet-tasting bundle of nerves with the constant lapping of my tongue. Running my hands along the inside of her legs, I push a finger into the warmth of her pussy. She lets out a scream while she slowly begins moving her perfect hips, trying to ride my finger and face.

"You're so damn tight, I fucking love it." I push a second finger in, giving her more to ride. She bucks off the bed again as I increase the speed of both my tongue and fingers, now working in unison. I'm animalistic in my attack, which only makes her moan even more, groaning and pulling my hair that much harder. I know she's close, hearing her moan and buck under my touch is too much. I can't wait any longer.

Taking her legs from my shoulder, I wipe my mouth while staring at her beautifully flushed face. "You are too fucking sweet, I need inside of this tight pussy now, baby; I can't take it anymore. I need to feel you come wrapped around my cock."

I swear to God, she purrs at my words. "Ryker, hurry."

I quickly grab a condom, put it on, and in one hard push, my cock is thrust deep inside her. "Fuck!" I all but yell out at the pure joy I feel at her tightness taking me all in.

Chapter 42

Kat

OH MY STARS and garters! Ryker Eddison is a master with that dirty mouth and those talented hands of his. Never have I felt so many intense sensations as I have under his touch. I've lost all control of my senses and I'm on an Eddison overload. I honestly don't ever want them back. Holy fuck!

All I can hear is myself moaning and making all kinds of sounds that I never knew possible. I need him and I need him now.

"Ryker," I say as he moves from between my legs wiping his face, clearly satisfied with my reaction to him. He moves over me after putting on the condom. His warm chest grazing my nipples as he moves above me now, causing shivers to run up and down my spine, which, in turn, causes an apex of need to run straight down to my core. All in all, making me need him to the point where begging him isn't beneath me. Who gives a shit if I let this man see just how much he affects me? It's clear to me now I have the same effect on him. Looking up into his eyes, I reach for his neck, pulling him down closer to my lips and kiss him hard while telling him how badly I need him.

"I know," he all out growls before he drives home.

"Oh, God, Ryker. You feel so good. I...I..., oh, God, you're deep." Never in the past have I experienced the pleasure-pain of sex. But as Ryker thrusts into me for the first time, I welcome the experience. I relax as his cock slides in and out, rubbing me with my own

GILLIAN JONES

juices, helping to accommodate his size.

"Jesus, you're fucking sexy, so fucking tight," he hums, sinking deeper, pinning my arms above my head and running his mouth over my chest. "I'm not gonna last long, baby, not with you milking my cock the way your greedy body keeps taking me in. Oh shit!" Staring at each other intently, Ryker's movements take my breath away. I lean up, running my tongue around his tattoo, sliding my tongue over his muscles. I'm consumed with the pleasure he's giving me, the feeling of him giving me what I need, watching him pumping and thrusting, stretching me to easily take him in.

"Mmm, you're wet, so fucking tight; it's like a vice grip. Shit, sweet girl. It's so fucking good; you're fucking good." He kisses me. Ryker's movements aren't gentle, but he isn't rough either. He offers the perfect balance and it's driving me crazy. I writhe and moan his name; completely losing myself in the nirvana that is Ryker. His powerful thrusts cause me to find my own rhythm, meeting him thrust for thrust, giving myself back to him, back just as good as he gives. The constant give and take of our bodies working in tandem quickly leads me to the crest where I know I am going to explode like I have never imagined possible.

"Ryker...oh, Ryker, I'm...I'm...oh, Ryker!" I scream out his name as pure ecstasy takes over my entire being.

"Yeah, Kat, shit, that was the hottest thing. You're amazingly beautiful when you come. Christ, the way your tight pussy clenched around my cock, fuck, baby." He breathes as he picks up his movements, pumping faster and faster. "I'm gonna fucking come. I'm gonna come hard," he growls. "Oh fuck," he grits out a few seconds later.

Ryker holds me as we lie here in silent bliss.

We fall asleep. It's all perfect, *too perfect*.

I know I want more from him, and I know this is the only night he'll want from me.

It crushes me. Ryker Eddison is, after all, a player.

I wake a few hours later; he's fast asleep.

I leave.

Chapter 43

Ryker

THE MORNING AFTER Kat ditched out on me...on us, I'm fuming and in the worst mood ever. Making my way to the kitchen, I hear Matty and Justin, who were already awake cooking breakfast, chatting away about the bar last night. They both knew I was planning on laying my shit out with Kat last night. Hoping to claim her as mine.

Sighing, at what I know is coming, I decide to get the jokes and ribbing over with. I know they're sure to come, especially when they don't see Kat with me. I move into the kitchen uttering a good morning, while walking directly to the coffee maker. I'm banging shit around, making it totally obvious that I'm angry.

"Ryk, dude, what's with the mood? What, that hot piece with those pretty titties turn you down?" Justin, that fuck of a pain in my ass goes on, causing my jaw to clench at his comment. This guy needs to clamp it down and fast.

"Aww, did big bad Ryker get turned down? Did the little bitch choose that other fucktard over you? You know the one who was dancing up on her sweet ass. You need a huggy?" Now I'm seeing fucking red. Hearing him talk about her like that causes me to lose it.

Without warning, I turn, grabbing him by the scruff of the neck, positioning my face beside his ear to be sure he fucking hears what I gotta say. "What the fuck did you just say, motherfucker? I fucking think I heard you wrong, brother. You got no fuckin' clue what the hell you're talking about. You are to never speak about Kat like that again! Capiche?" Matt is quickly at us, trying to diffuse the situation. Finally I relent.

"Jesus, Ryker, I'm just messin' with ya, man. Calm the fuck down, dude," Justin says as I remove my hands from his neck, my eyes still trained on him, my body ready to pounce if need be. Justin stands in front of me, hands raised in defeat. "Ryker, man, I swear I'm only messing; it's my bad. I'm sorry. I saw y'all leave the bar together. I just assumed things went well, that she'd be here this morning."

Shaking my head, I apologize, and for the first time since shit went down with Melissa, I sit down and let loose about all the crazy shit that's been going on between Kat and me.

"This girl has got me all kinds of fucked up. I told her last night that I wanted more than just sex. I thought she understood. I dunno what the hell happened, all I know is she's fucking gone. And it pisses me off. I really don't think she's the one-night stand type. She's too damn sweet for that shit."

"Well, just give it some time, man; she'll figure it out. But just know I was only kidding with you. I'd never talk about your girl like that."

"Thanks, Justin. I'm sorry, too, man. I'm all over the place. I just reacted."

Ever since Melissa, I've never let a girl get me riled up like this. Seriously, I need to deal with Kat. I need to talk to her, convince her I want more than sex with her. I, Ryker Eddison, want all of her.

ONE WEEK. IT'S been one fucking week since Kat left my bed like a thief in the night. One week since I've officially grown that vagina, the one I've been growing over my cock ever since this damn girl walked into my life. Fuck me! Even my friends are noticing a change in me, feeling the effects of Kat on me. Clearly, I'm not as good at being nonchalant about her and my wayward feelings as I hoped. But that shit is gonna change real fast. By Tuesday, I'm more irritated and I bail on work again for the second time this week. I'm just not in the mood to deal with anyone's shit.

While I'm listening to the guys go on about letting her be, I have to question how this is the right move? I get a text back from Levi, telling me he's free for lunch, but not for a few days. I had texted him hoping he could give me some brotherly advice. Seeing as I trust him the most in this life, I'll trust his advice too.

Levi: *Meet me at Duncan's pub Thursday at noon. Be warned, I'm pissed. Just got word you called in for tonight too. You better be really sick, bud. I gotta cover.*
Me: *Sorry. See u Thursday.*

I need real advice, Levi.

Levi: *Ok. C U.*

Shit. He's never going to let me live this down. I called in sick because of a chick.

That night, the guys and I sit around playing cards and they give me their two cents about what I should do about Kat. They insist I did the right thing.

"Just leave her, dude; she'll come back. She knows where the orgasms are now. I wouldn't be surprised if she shows up begging by morning. Chicks love you, Ryk. She'll be back."

"You're an idiot, Justin. When's the last time you had a steady girl? What the fuck do you know?" Matt challenges him.

"Ryker, I think you should wait till Friday and then you can seek her out. Just tell her you've been busy. Kat will understand," Justin offers again, and I've had enough.

"I'm out. I'm heading to bed." I stand, folding my cards. Poker and beer aren't doing shit to help relax me tonight.

"Night, fellas."

"Night, Ryk. Try not to let it get to you too much, buddy. I'm sure it'll all work out."

"I hope, Matty, I really do. I've never felt like this before." With that, I head up to my room.

Chapter 44

Ryker

I MEET LEVI for lunch and, instantly, I feel like more of a tool with how I handled the situation with Kat than before. Especially after the way Levi puts things into a more realistic perspective. *Shit, I'm such a douche.* I should have called her. Gone after her.

"You idiot," Levi says, taking a pull from his beer. "I can't believe you listened to dumb and dumber. What the hell would make you think she'd want space? If anything, you probably should have gone straight to her and talked shit out. Now you've sent the message that she did the right thing by leaving, that she saved face."

Fuck. Hearing my brother say this makes me feel uneasy, like I should have gone with my gut and hunted her down. Stupid assholes, I should have known better than to listen to them. What the hell do they know? I think Claire might be Matt's only steady girl since...forever, actually.

"Dude, why the fuck didn't you tell me sooner? How long has this been going on? I've never seen you like this, Ryk. Does Mom know? She's going to lose her fucking mind." He laughs.

"Slow the fuck down, man. Of course she doesn't know. I fucking didn't know how deep I was until a week ago."

After a few beers and some more razzing, he was actually supportive and helpful.

"She's different, Levi. I've never felt like this before. Like, with

230

Melissa, it was all smoke and mirrors, you know? Nothing was really as it seemed. I didn't love her. It was lust; it was superficial. With Kat, it all feels right. Like she fills a void in me that I've had for so long. I'm not pissed off all the time; I'm excited and there isn't another chick that can hold my attention like her. Fuck, my mind is set on her. And my heart, as lame as it sounds, it's ready to let a girl in, and fuck if that doesn't scare the shit outta me. Half the time, I can't find words when I'm with her, 'cause these feelings make me fucking nervous. Nervous 'cause she actually makes me happy."

"Holy shit, Ryk. I knew you were in deep, but fuck, man, if I didn't know better, I'd say you were falling in love with her."

"God, Levi, I'm such a dick, just help me. She's going to hate me. I gotta fix this. I need this girl, man. She makes me feel good, makes me want more. Shit, man, I actually want to be there for her, like all the time. Dude, I need help. I've fucked this up."

Together we concoct a plan. Thank God for my brother, the man is a genius.

"Okay, come to work about an hour early tomorrow. I'll make sure your girl is there for you; that way you can talk in private before the others get there for their shifts. The last thing I need is a night full of drama, 'cause you're a fucking idiot," he chides before finishing his beer.

Thank fuck tomorrow is Friday. Kat and I will work together. She and I, we will be talking.

Chapter 45

Kat

IT'S BEEN OVER a week since I snuck out of Ryker's bed. One week since that unforgettable night and not a single word, text, or any attempt to contact me. The only person who seems to be relentless at getting in touch with me is Seth. I can't believe this guy. It's crazy how much time he seems willing to make for me now. How all of a sudden, I rank on his list of priorities. How he's managed to get my number again is beyond me. But again, that issue needs to take a back burner to this thing I've got going on with Ryker right now. Well, is it even a thing anymore?

God, I knew I wasn't cut out for this shit. Not with a player like Ryker Eddison. I know better. I've known better this whole time.

But fuck me if I don't think maybe it was all worth it.

Holy fudge nuggets, can that boy fuck! And he really is a good guy.

I really suck with this acting like everything's okay, that I am all right, pretending that shit with Ryker isn't affecting me. That what I experienced with him a week ago doesn't matter. Claire's been all over me, trying to get me to open up about what exactly happened between us and why I've needed to take my sleeping pills so much. She's offered to go over and kick his ass a few times this week.

As I'm studying in my room, Claire busts in. "Kat, get the fuck up and get dressed. You need to put the textbooks away and get the hell out of the house. Enough is enough. You, Radha, and I are heading to

Pub Fiction for a few drinks. Levi was able to give me the night off. Besides, you look like you could use a couple."

"Are you frickin' kidding me, Claire? I am not going there now, tonight, maybe not ever."

"Oh, don't be melodramatic, you'll get through this; it's a glitch. They happen."

"You're right, it is, and I will get over it, but you have no idea how I feel."

"I know you don't want to talk about it now, but, girl, this shit is messed up. I've never seen you so fucked up. It's like you're fine, but not. It's like you're crazy, to be honest." Claire sighs, closing the door, giving us more privacy. I know she worries, but I don't need this right now.

"Well, I'm sorry, Claire," I snap at her. "Sorry we all can't have perfect relationships with every guy we meet. I can't help it if I'm goddamn confused. I knew this shit with Ryker was going to hurt, but you know what? I'm not hurt. I'm seriously beyond it. I knew it was going to be a mistake fucking with Ryker, but I'm not upset about that. What I'm upset about is the fact that I was a chicken shit and left him. Like a fucking coward, I left. When everything we did had felt so right, I left just like he probably wanted."

"Aww, Kitty, come here. It's going to be okay," Claire states while moving onto my bed to hug me.

"No, it's not, actually. Don't you get it? I fucked up. I'm pissed off that I gave in, that I let my greedy lady bits take over my brain where Ryker was concerned. And truth be told, I want more... a lot more. I've needed my sleeping pills because I can't shut my mind off. All I do is sit and think about the way my body moulded to his, how he made me feel beautiful, wanted...different."

"Believe me when I say this. I think you are different. From what I've heard, Ryker is definitely different with you. According to Matt, he's never seen Ryker, so…so, ah…I need to say this, but don't get mad. Matt said he's never seen Ryker so alone, if you know what I mean." She cringes at the last part, knowing all too well that I won't find any comfort in that at all.

"Great! Thanks for the 'you're falling for the player' reminder; that's just what I needed!"

"Oh, for fuck sakes, you know that wasn't the goddamn point of that. The point is you are different. Maybe he's just giving you space? Maybe he thinks you don't want him? Maybe he thinks you regret it? Maybe you need to get your head out of your ass and go over and talk to him? Didn't he tell you the other night that you guys would figure it all out? Dude, I'm really thinking you might be the one who fucked this up. So why not go get what you want? If it's him that you want, Kitty Kat, go get your catnip." I laugh at this. Claire really is such an amazing friend.

We end up talking for a long time, and I gave her pretty much all the juicy details she wanted. She squealed like a slaughterhouse pig when I told her how fucking hot this man is. And how he gave me the most intense orgasm I've ever had.

It's Thursday night and I'm preparing a math lesson for my primary math class tomorrow morning, and, of course, Ryker pops into my mind. He was great about helping me with my math. I wonder how great it would be to have him around all the time to help me figure this shit out. God, I'm behind in my assignments; it's crazy. I can't believe tomorrow's December. *Where the hell did the semester go? I need to get him outta my head.* Before I know it, winter break will be here. This weekend will need to be a school focused one for sure. Sitting here working I'm too distracted and I laugh at myself.

Who would have thought that "Ms. High Strung" really just needed a good shagging, like a really, really, really amazing shaggin' actually? I never expected to feel like this. I've been stressing over this boy for months now. Trying to deny my feelings, when in the end, it seems as if being around him, one-on-one relaxes me, makes me happy. Looking back on the past few months, my focusing on Ryker has helped me to be less uptight, more spontaneous, and fun. One of the biggest things I notice is that I haven't slept that well in years as I did that night in Ryker's bed. It wasn't just from the sex either. When Ryker held me, I felt calm, my mind at ease. It was a strange feeling, one I'd give anything to feel again. Hmph, like that's going to happen. In the end, I left, saving face before Ryker dismissed me, as I'm sure he's done many times to many girls before. *You made the right decision.*

Fuck!

Tomorrow is Friday. Tomorrow I work with Ryker.

I think I'm going to vomit.

Chapter 46

Ryker

December

PULLING UP TO Pub Fiction, I immediately spot Kat's car parked in the lot. I still smile every time I see that little Beetle bug, the same one I noticed on my street all those months ago. Perfect. We're both early. Levi's plan just might work. I walk to the bar after parking my car next to hers. I've got a nervous energy buzzing around me. It's been over a week now and I'm done with this shit. We're going to get things straight right fucking now. I nearly trip over myself rushing to get inside. Levi is cleaning glasses as I approach and looks up, nodding his head at me with a knowing smirk.

He waves to me as I walk up to the bar. "Hey, buddy, your girl is waiting for you as promised. God, you're lucky to have such an awesome brother like me," he laughs as I walk past.

"Yeah, yeah, you're the shit, big man. Thanks. Oh, and don't bother coming down the hall for at least the next hour. If things go my way, there is make up sex in my future," I add with a wink.

Levi called Kat in telling her he needed some extra help with planning the Christmas auction this year. He knew she would want to help because she had offered before. This was the perfect excuse to get her in here early.

Every year, we hold a fundraiser for local community support programs. This year we are sponsoring *Food4Kids*. It's an organization that delivers food bags to school kids in need on Friday afternoons so they have healthy food over the weekend. It's a great organization, and with Kat wanting to be a teacher, he knew she'd be willing to help, no questions asked.

Little does she know, the only meeting she's going to be having is with me.

Chapter 47

Kat

MAKING MY WAY into work early had me a bit on edge to be honest. But I soon feel relief as I pull into the parking lot and see only Levi is here. Thank goodness. I'm actually excited he's taken me up on my offer to help plan the fundraising events for this year's charity night. I have some good ideas and can't wait to get started.

Walking in, I say a quick hi to Levi, letting him know I'm here and I'm just going to run and change.

"Take your time. I've got a few things to finish before we sit down and meet anyway," he tells me as I head to the staff room.

I'm standing at my locker in my bra and panties when I hear the door jiggle. Now I know for a fact I've locked it. Believe me, Claire was right; it's become a sick little habit, like some kind of OCD compulsion where I check it over and over at least five times before believing it's locked. When I hear the jiggle I shout out, "Oh sorry, Levi. I'm changing. Just give me a sec!" But there is silence. No reply, no apology, nothing! *Huh, well, that's kind of rude,* I think to myself; it's not like he didn't know I was in here. God, I hope he's not turning into a creep. I really like him and would hate to have to tell him off. Shaking that idea away, preferring to think he probably thought I was done, I continue to dress, making a mental note to talk to him about better staff room protocols when I'm finished.

I'm putting on my pantyhose when I hear a key in the lock and the door opening. What the actual fuck! We need a fucking sign on the door saying occupied or something 'cause this system is not working for me at all. I quickly throw my sweater over my head, covering my boobs. Now I'm just pissed. This is not like Levi, and to be honest, I'm a little freaked out at the moment knowing it's just him and me here. Shit.

Did I just hear a growl?

Breaking me out of my ridiculous thoughts, I shake my head. Thinking I'm being an idiot, I look up to see who the fuck would open the door when they know someone is in here. My eyes meet his and my heart jumps into my throat as I take in all his beauty...and is that anger?

Ryker.

Chapter 48

Ryker

REACHING THE DOOR, I realize I need to calm myself down. I can't barge in losing my shit, demanding all the things I want to. If I do that, I won't get the results I want, and I'm more than aware of that. Steadying myself, I take a deep breath while putting my hands on the doorknob, with every intention to walk in rationally and ask Kat to talk to me. Locked.

I know Kat is the only one inside, so I decide to use my master key to get to my girl. Perk of being the boss's brother. As I open the door, I can't fucking believe my luck.

Kat is standing by her locker in sexy-as-fuck black lace panties, pantyhose half way on one leg, while barely getting her sweater over her head in time before she sees it's me who's just walked in.

"Ryy-ker," she whispers almost inaudibly. God, my name falling from her lips affects me as if she was wrapping her mouth around my cock. I'm instantly rock hard. Maintaining eye contact, I move to close and lock the door. With the "click," I stand, leaning on the door, taking in this fucking girl. The air begins to thicken immediately as I stare at her. This girl who has been my mind's motherfucking eye for the last four God damned months. Yeah, I'm ready for this. I fucking need this girl and she is going to listen to all I have to say. Then I'm going to take up permanent residence in her pussy and her heart.

Kat Rollins is mine. Enough said.

"Kat," I all but growl, "we need to talk, baby. We need to talk right the fuck now." The command clear in my voice, but thankfully, she doesn't balk at my tone.

"Ah-umm, no, Ryker. I'm pretty sure everything between us is said and done. There isn't anything left to talk about. You got what you've been wanting from me. We've fucked; it's all good." I can see she doesn't believe her words; they lack the conviction I've heard in them before. *Thank Christ.*

Oh, hell no, she will not be dismissing me like this. I can tell by the waver in her voice that she's spewing bullshit. Telling me what she thinks I want to hear. She's letting me off the hook. *Fuck that!*

Clearing my throat, I begin to tell her how it really is; not allowing her to believe this fucked up notion she's got going on in her beautiful head.

"You see, hot girl, that's where you're wrong. Beyond fucking wrong," I deadpan as I strut forward to where she's standing. "I didn't get all I want," I say, now standing face to face. "Not by a long shot. You see, baby, I told you we were gonna talk about us," I add before moving in closer, taking her hands in mine, kissing them both before pinning her up against her locker, arms now raised above her head. Her chest is heaving; her eyes are wild with uncertainty as she tries to speak.

"B-b-b-ut you, you...It's been over a week. I...I-I thought...Ryker..." She lowers her head in defeat. I take her wrist in one hand to free the other so I can reach her chin to tilt her head to mine.

"Eyes on me, baby. I need you to see me, Kat. I need you to listen." Reluctantly, her eyes meet mine and I see it. I see that I've hurt her. Kat may act tough, but she's just as affected as I am. Shit, the last thing I wanted was to hurt her.

"Don't think that, it was a mistake not to chase you." I nuzzle her neck, licking her jawline to her ear before enunciating, "I. Am. An. Idiot. I want you, Kat. I want you so fucking bad. But this bullshit, it's your fault too, baby. You snuck out of my bed," I scold, licking along her earlobe. "Left like we were nothing, and believe me, Kat, we're fucking something," I add while moving my hand along her stomach up to her chest.

"When I'm with you, around you, it all feels real. It feels good, like this—like you—just might be my forever, and I can't stop thinking it will always be this good. That we will always be this good, and 'cause of that, I can't not see this through, Kat. Granted, I'm an asshole for not coming after you, but don't you dare think for one minute that I don't know it and haven't regretted it all week. Kat, I've never felt like this before. I'll make it up to you, my sweet girl; just give me the fucking chance." God, I'm such a fucking pussy.

"Okay, Ryker, okay," she starts softly, eyes trained on mine. "I admit you've been driving me crazy for the last few months. I don't want to want this, but I can't deny there is something pretty potent between us. But I asked you not to hurt me, and last week, in the end, you did. Maybe not on purpose, but you did, and I'm scared you're going to change your mind, or realize I'm not what you want. That I'm just a game. God, this is a risk for me too, Ryker. You're a man-whore and I'm the uptight girl who is always falling for the wrong guy. I mean, come on, Ryker, it's not like you're known for giving out too many second dates. What happens when you're over this, over us? I guess I just didn't think you'd want another with me either, or a first, for that matter." She gives me a shy smile. Seeing her vulnerable and opening up to me like this sparks something in me so profound that I look her dead in the eyes and admit for the first time what I have known all along.

"Kat," I admonish, "I'm scared, too. I'm freaked out by how in-tense my feelings are for you already. It's fucking making me crazy. But all things aside, I haven't been this fucking happy in a really long time. This fucking game we've had going has made me happy, excited again. And it hasn't just been the chase, Kat, it's you. It's you who's been making me feel things I haven't in years. Listen, I've been hurt before, and I chose to be a dick about it. Something one chick did to me. But with you, I just know I want more. Kat, I want all of you. I want to know what makes your eyes light up with joy, what makes this pulse and beat," I place my hand on her heart, "but most of all, I want to be there for you. I want your smiles, your giggles, and best of all, I want your kisses." I nudge the tip of her nose with my lips.

Staring up at me, tears running down her face, a smile slowly starts to spread across her beautiful face, and I swear to God, it's like rain in the middle of a drought. So fucking welcome and fucking needed. I release her hands and she immediately wraps them around my neck, peering her jade eyes toward mine. She brings her pouty lips to mine and begins brushing her lips against them with what feels like butterfly wings flapping ever so gently against my lips. Then with a whimper, it's like a crescendo of need takes over. Kat begins pulling at my hair where her hands are wrapped tightly around my neck, pulling me in closer and sealing our lips together.

It is so on.

Quickly, I lift her up off the ground. Instantly, she's wrapping her legs around my waist, climbing me, out of desperation as well as for the need of closeness. Fuck me, does she feel good, all lush and unbelievably sexy, moulding herself against me. Holding on to her, I pretty much bang us into the locker while we're all lips, licks, and tongues while mumbling our apologies, thank gods, and I need yous. Rubbing her bare legs, I decide screw this. I need in this girl yester-fuckin-day. I walk us over to the ottoman, and I smile thinking back to the last time we were on it.

"Christ, your legs are fucking sexy. I love feeling you up on me like this. Jesus, what you do to me." Sitting us down on the ottoman, her on my lap, I make quick work and remove her fucking hoodie from getting in my way. Needing to see, touch, and feel my girl.

"You see, Kat, you've been a bad girl," I say, nipping at her nipples, coaxing them to come out to play. "You left me and I didn't like it. Not one fucking bit. I told you, sweet girl. You. Are. Mine," I grate out in her ear, pushing our chests, fusing them together. Her breath hitches before she releases the most erotic sound I have ever heard. She reaches back and whips her bra off, taking my breath away with her boldness. Growling, I palm her sweet tits in my hand, but it isn't enough. Using my hands, I take each of her breasts. While rubbing them. I gently squeeze them close together before unleashing the onslaught of my greedy mouth, tongue, and stubble all the fuck over her glorious rack. Fuck me! I could cum all over her tits and die a very happy man. Kat is mewling, moaning; she's pretty much losing her mind. She is fucking hot with want. I make quick work of my own shirt and toss it behind me. Deciding I want her to ride me, I quickly lift her to unzip my pants. Kat, aware of my plan, helps to rid me of them completely. Sitting on the ottoman once again, Kat straddling my waist, I cup her face, as I tend to do. Looking deep into lust filled eyes, I vow, "I promise to make you happy, sweet girl. So fucking happy, every day. All I want is a fair shot. A chance to prove to you I am the man who deserves you. All of you."

She nods. "Okay, Ryker. A fair shot, you and me." She smiles, and I offer a tender kiss as she moves slowly rocking over me, teasing me with her heat.

"Now, I'm gonna need you to fuck me, baby." Yeah, I'm smooth, I know. I lift her up by the ass and grab a condom from my jeans and put it on before placing her back down. "You're fucking naughty, Kat, so naughty. I love it. Do you like it when I play with these gorgeous tits? You know what I want to see?" She swallows hard. I love seeing how my dirty words affect her. "I want you to ride me, baby. I want you to take my cock in your hands and slide it up into that greedy pussy of yours. Then I want to sit back and watch you work my cock up and down while those fucking tits of yours bounce in my face, smothering me, making me the happiest man alive."

Fuck, I'm ready to come just from talking to her about it. The visual of her riding my cock alone, is enough. With a quick nod from my girl, I rip the panties right the fuck off of her, along with the remains of her pantyhose, before she has a chance to take 'em off herself.

"Ryker! Those were one of my favourite pair!" is the last coherent set of words that fall from her mouth as she sinks down and rides us off into bliss.

Chapter 49

Kat

WE FINALLY EMERGE from the staff room hand in hand, about forty-five minutes later with matching grins. During our post make-out bliss, Ryker and I decided we would try working together on the Friday shifts like Levi needs.

"Hey, Ryk, Kat! I'm happy to see you made it back out for work." Humour laces his tone as his smile widens before delivering the rest of his comment. "I gotta say, from the sounds of it, I guess it's safe to assume things went well in there. I just hope working together won't be a problem, hey?" Immediately, I begin panicking. Oh, my God. The realization that Levi may have heard me riding Ryker like a tried and true cowgirl in the staff room makes me super uncomfortable.

Averting my eyes, my face heated with embarrassment, I begin to try and respond. "Ah, Levi, I—" But Ryker is quick to interject, bringing our twined hands to his lips before responding. *Thank God* is all I can think, well, before I hear what the idiot says anyway.

"Yep, things went amazingly well. Kat and I were able to ride out our differences," he says with a smirk and a wink my way. *What an asshole!* "But nope, no need to worry at all, Levi. Kat and I are all good, and we got this. Besides, there is no fuckin' way I'm letting Luke get any shifts with Kat now that she's officially mine. I know that asshole's type. I'm gonna need you to give me back all my usual days."

"Haha, okay, Ryker, you got it, man. I figured as much after the

246

other night. It's done."

Wait. What? Did I just hear that right?

"What do you mean your regular shifts? You mean you chose not to work with me?"

"Oh, baby, you have no idea. If we had been working together from the start, I would have been in serious trouble. I mean, look, with you dressed like that every shift, and me not able to touch you, I don't think my cock would have ever recovered. I'd most certainly be in jail from keeping all those motherfuckers away from you. I couldn't do it, baby. You were killing me. There was no way I could work here when I'd be too busy beating the shit out of all the fuckers who looked your way. At least now, I have a reason...I gotta protect what's mine." He kisses my head like he didn't just throw me off my axis with his revelation.

Later that same night, as the club fills up, I become more and more aware of how hard this might be. Maybe I need to talk to Levi and Ryker about us not working together, as I can see it spelling out trouble, especially with our regulars who have grown accustomed to treating both of us a certain way. While I receive more looks and dirty little comments, Ryker gets touches and rubs that, honestly, make me see red. He all but claims me like a Neanderthal, while I silently fume, not wanting to get into it with catty bitches. Don't get me wrong, I'll throw down if need be. But for now, I watch in silence, biding my time, while Ryker basically walks around pounding his chest.

Chapter 50

Kat

Winter Break

MAKING MY WAY down the stairs after getting ready to go Christmas shopping at the mall with my mom, I stop halfway, seeing Ryker standing in the foyer chatting up my mother, who is grinning from ear to ear.

"Oh, there you are, honey. This lovely boy is here to see if he can take you to lunch," she pretty much singsongs to me. I know she's concealing her smirk, because she and I have just spent the morning gossiping about the entity that is now standing in my childhood home. My mom knows just how strong my feelings are starting to be for this man. Clearly, she's beginning to see why.

"Uh…hi, Ryker," I mutter, pretty much tongue-tied. "I see you've met my mom, Mary."

Nodding a yes, honeybutter himself pretty much eye-fucks me from top to bottom with a hunger in his eyes, in front of my mother nonetheless, before stammering, "Hey, hot-er, um, Kat, yeah, I was in the neighbourhood; well, actually, it turns out my mom doesn't live too far from here, only about a forty-five minute drive. I decided to come see you. I was wondering if you wanted to go grab a bite to eat? Figured maybe we could go ice-skating after, too. Our real first date," he whispers once my mom is out of earshot.

Ryker Eddison is nervous and I can't believe it. I smile my best grin before nodding, as I'm still in shock that he's here. When we talked until the wee hours of the night, he never once led on that I would be seeing him this soon. I'm excited he's here.

"Um, sure, I'd like that—oh, but Mom…" I turn to face her. "Do you mind? We were supposed to go shopping after all?"

"Oh, I absolutely don't mind! You let this handsome young man take you out. We can shop anytime. Besides, I can't wait to hear how ice skating goes," she adds with a giggle.

With that, Ryker and I set out on our *first date.*

While helping me up into the cab of his truck—hand on my ass, of course—Ryker leans into my ear before hoisting me up, whispering, "Ready for our first date, sweet girl? I gotta say, I'm curious. What's with your mom and the ice skating comment?"

Huffing out a small breath, I embarrassingly admit that I've never been ice skating before. I mean, Jesus, we live in Canada, and I've never been ice skating! Turning in my seat toward the open door where Ryker stands, I expect him to make fun of me.

Rather, I'm met with a sight of his beautiful eyes and a sly smile turning up on his sexy face. Ryker leans in while brushing my nose, giving me Eskimo kisses. "That's good news, baby; that's real good news." With that, he brushes my lips with his before closing my door. *Cryptic much?*

After lunch, we make our way to Valleyview Park where they have a huge, intimidating, outdoor ice rink. Crap, one that is filled with people who look like they're floating rather than skating.

"Ryker, how about we go to a movie instead?" I ask as he's crouched in front of me tying up my skates. "Not a chance. This is an opportunity to build trust, as well as a chance for me to be your knight in shining armour as I stop that sexy ass of yours from getting bruised too much." He helps to stand me up, and then helps me onto the ice. I have to admit, he looks pretty hot in his hockey skates.

After our date of Ryker teaching me to skate, I have to admit, I love skating! Or better, I love skating with Ryker! Holy hotness. Ryker not only taught me how to skate, but he was constantly touching, rubbing, and kissing me. Never would I have imagined Ryker Eddison could be this guy.

"Jesus, baby, if that ass keeps rubbing on my cock like that, I'm gonna have to drag you over to those bushes," he moves beside me and I feel the loss of his cocoon, which had been engulfing me for the last few laps.

"Well, play your cards right, and maybe I'll take *you* over to the bushes," I sass back, deciding I want to egg him on a bit. I'm feeling a lot more comfortable; so I let go of his hand, beginning to skate faster.

"Oh, I see, hot girl, you wanna play chase? You got it. I'll give you 'til the count of twenty; then it's game the fuck on," he quips before counting.

Trying to get away, I move my legs simultaneously, faster and faster, working in tandem to move around the rink. Suddenly, I'm going way too fast and it's totally exhilarating and scary all at the same time. Then as I begin to lose my footing, on the way to making a huge face plant, big hands grip my hips, steadying me from behind.

"I got you, baby. See, I really am your knight in shining armour. I told ya I would be," he says before we land in a fresh pile of snow. Looking up while lying flat on my back in a huge snow pile, I couldn't be happier as Ryker is now hovering over me with a huge smile on his face. How the hell did we get here? He kisses my nose before speaking with a somewhat strained voice. "God, you trying to get away from me, Kat, has got me so fuckin' hard." He licks my neck up to my ear. "Watching that ass of yours moving with those sexy as fuck legs, I started to picture them wrapped around my neck as I sink into you." He looks me in the eye before laughing a deep belly laugh. "Well, that was until you almost took a face plant." He grins, waiting for my reaction. I giggle at the whole thing as Ryker swoops in, offering me a kiss that steals my breath.

Ryker and I have many more wonderful dates like this, and I swear, with each one, I fall for this man a bit more. He is full of kindness, sweetness, and goodness. I question why I ever denied myself this in the first place. I think the days we ended up being apart only helped to solidify how much we actually care about each other. Things have been going amazing, and I have never been this happy. Ryker has proven he meant every word about me and about us that day.

Chapter 51

Kat

January

As soon as we're back from the winter break, Ryker and I just seem to connect on a deeper level. We spent a lot of time really getting to know each other, voicing our insecurities where relationships are concerned, as well as sharing intimate details about our pasts.

"I can't believe we missed the movie," I say as Ryker holds the door to The Bean open for me.

"It was all your fault, sweet girl; you kept taunting me with that sweet ass of yours," the liar teases.

"Ha! You wish, buddy. All I did was try to put jeans on. It's not my fault you're a sex machine." I wink.

"Sex machine, oh, I'm hurt, that hurts." He places his hand on his heart as if he's wounded. "Well, it's not my fault my woman makes me crave her like a wild beast," Ryker growls in my ear as he brings me in for a bear hug. I nuzzle in, and then lick up his neck. "Kat," he scolds, pulling me away. "I'm not about to let these people see me fuck you like the animal I am, I suggest you stop."

"Oh, you're no fun," I joke before giving him a soft kiss on the lips.

"You go get us a table, sweet girl. I'll grab our drinks." He kisses my forehead before heading for the counter. Once I opened up to him about the fire and how it's impacted me, I felt like the last weight I'd been carrying around with me has been permanently lifted.

I guess I just worried he'd think all my little quirks meant I was crazy. Boy, was I wrong. I don't know why I waited so long to fully share that part of me with him. I know he knew something had happened to me the night of the storm when the alarm went off, but I think I needed to open up about it in my own time. And I'm glad I did. It just showed me how wonderful of a person Ryker is. He never pressured me, but always let it be known he was here whenever I was ready to share.

"I need to leave here, Ryker," I said, looking around the stuffy restaurant, sweat starting to pool on the back of my neck, the walls closing in on me. My breathing laboured as panic began to take over. Looking around, I still couldn't find a safe escape route if there were to be a fire. I just needed to get out.

"I can't... I can't sit here. It's too small. I'm so sorry. I really tried, but I can't," I blurted out as the tears I had been trying to hold in cascaded down my cheeks.

"What's wrong, Kat? Let's sit and talk about it." He motioned to our table.

Shaking my head, I managed to form a mumbled reply, "You stay. I'll catch a taxi home. I'm fine, Ryker, just forget it. I'm sorry for ruining the night." I pushed past him, around the customers crowding the place straight out the door, with Ryker following quickly, calling after me.

"Whoa, easy there," Ryker said, grasping my arm gently as he tried to stop me from running. "Sweet girl, I'm not leaving you, especially after seeing you get so upset back there." He took a hold of my hand, wiped my tears and scanned the area before he suggested, "Let's pop into Starbucks, grab a coffee, and sit over there at the park and talk."

After a few minutes and some calming breaths, I agreed to go with Ryker, "Okay, I can do that." I smiled up at his concerned face before asking, "Are you sure you don't want me to just go? I'm sure I embarrassed you back there."

"Not a chance, baby, where you go, I go. Nothing you ever do would embarrass me to the point where I'd leave you. That back there was nothing. Besides, no one noticed, sweet girl. Let's get our drinks, and you can tell me about what caused that reaction."

We talked for what felt like hours while sitting on that bench in the park, and Ryker was perfect. He even asked me to show him the Toronto Trauma Survivor Group and bookmarked it on his phone. "That way, if you're ever at my place or without your phone and need a little check-in, you can use mine." He gave me a squeeze and, I swear, my heart melted at his thoughtfulness. Okay, maybe that wasn't the way I'd planned on telling him, but regardless, it was all out in the open now, and I was grateful for that.

"Thank you for sharing that with me, baby. I can't imagine what that must have been like for you girls. I had no idea. Remind me to give Claire a big hug for helping my baby." He wipes the tears from my eyes. "What do you say we grab take-out tonight, and we'll build up to eating inside the restaurant again soon?" I nodded in agreement, still a little embarrassed at how sudden the anxiety overtook me. It was the conversation we had about the fire that really made me realize Ryker is absolutely everything I never expected him to be.

Later that same night while eating Thai food, snuggled side by side in my bed, we talked about everything; I feel like we both laid all our cards out on the table, from relationships, to the fire again, and my insomnia issues. Ryker and I talked about my relationship with Seth as well as his with Melissa at great lengths. I think both of us having been hurt before, it has only bonded us closer together. I realized Ryker will never cheat on me and I'm confident he feels the same. It's nice to know we have this in common, as it's been a sore spot for the both of us, affecting many of our relationships, or better yet, lack thereof. It was cathartic for us both.

As for the issue of Seth, Ryker has been amazing. Why I hesitated telling him is a mystery. Ryker is an incredibly understanding and protective man, and I am lucky to have him in my life.

"Again, I'm glad you shared all this with me, sweet girl. Jesus, that guy is a dick. If I had known who he was that time, I would have kicked his ass on principle alone," he admitted, intertwining our hands. "I'll deal with that loser if he ever shows his face around here again. I don't want you to worry, baby. I'll sort that fucker out."

The next day, he even took me to the police station to seek advice, but unfortunately, because nothing has been threatening in tone or there isn't a sure way to prove it's Seth, there really isn't much to be done from their end at this time. Unless he shows up again uttering threats or attempts to do me any harm. For now, I ignore the messages and share them openly with Ryker at the odd times they do come.

"Kat, it's okay; I don't want you to ever stress over that dick. I protect what's mine, and you are abso-fuckin-lutely mine," he assured me, swinging our intertwined hands.

That was the day I knew I was totally in love with Ryker Eddison.

Rykers' heavy footsteps approaching the table bring me out of my reverie. "There you are, hot girl." He puts my chai latte and scone down in front of me. "Penny for your thoughts?"

"I was just thinking about you, how amazing you are." The smell of my sweet drink has me licking my lips. Ryker notices and gives me a smirk.

"I love when you lick those lips—my sweet tasting lips," he whispers in my ear before sitting down across from me. "I should have known you'd be near the exit door," he teases me, looking around the small shop, and I know he's only joking. "I'm proud of you baby, the table right beside the door is free, but you chose this one; that's major, baby." He grabs my hand, squeezing it. *God, this man is perfect.*

Chapter 52

Kat

"KAT!" AMANDA CALLS to me from the top of the stairs.

"What? I'm just getting ready to go to the library," I yell back while putting on my shoes.

"Well, you might want to pick up the phone before you go. There's a certain hottie on the line who is demanding to speak to his woman, and if you ask me, he sounds kinda pissy."

Rolling my eyes, I jog up the stairs to grab the cordless off the kitchen table. "Hello?"

"Where's your damn phone, woman?" Ryker all but growls from the other end of the line.

"Ahem, well, that's a nice greeting, Ryker. I'm good, thanks. How are you?"

"Sorry, baby, I'm still new at this. I've not wanted to hear someone's voice like I do yours. I just wanted to talk to you and your phone's going right to voicemail. It was starting to piss me off; I didn't mean to be an ass."

"It's okay. I guess my phone died and I didn't notice. I'll start paying more attention, honeybutter."

"Honeybutter?" he questions. "Ah, Kat, did you just call me fucking honeybutter?"

"I sure did. Remember the first day we met? Well, I thought you were gorgeous and your eyes are unlike anything I've ever seen before."

"I see."

"From then on, I started to call you honeybutter, but don't worry, I've never told anyone. I keep that name all for me."

"What are you wearing?" he demands, and I'm confused.

"What? Why? What does that have to do with anything?"

"Well, now I'm on my way over, and I need to know how many layers I need to peel off my sexy girlfriend before I get to hear her scream out 'honeybutter' at the top of her lungs while I take her hard and fast. 'Cause, baby, knowing you've given me a nickname is having all kinds of effects on my cock."

I tease him. "Ah, Ryker, what doesn't turn you on?"

"With you in my life, there isn't much, baby. I am a walking horn-ball where you're concerned. Now go get ready for me, I'll be there in five."

Needless to say, I didn't make it to the library. We spent that evening in bed having amazing sex, stopping only for a few breaks; which were to eat some bad take-out and to watch a rerun of *The Big Bang Theory*, a show we've discovered we both deem as a favourite.

Chapter 53

Ryker

"HEY, MAN, WHERE ya been? Did you come home last night? I thought you were coming with me last night to pick up the beer and shit for poker night," Justin questions as I walk in the house. The smell of pizza in the air makes my stomach growl. It's poker night and we always order from Romano's. It's a bit more expensive, but it's the best in town. *I wonder if Kat's been there before. I'll have to take her either way.*

"Sorry, man, I got sidetracked." Images of Kat's smile, just before she takes my cock into her mouth, pop in my head. "I spent the night with Kat, then had classes all day... Shit, my bad, for texting you to pick up the pizzas, brother. I know I was supposed to pick them up on my way home but like I said I was really running behind." I defend before he can make a jab. "I'll grab it the next two times to make it up, buddy," I say, patting his back. I remember him asking me to do it before I left yesterday morning for school, but like I said, it totally escaped my mind. Kat has that effect on me lately; all I tend to see is her.

"Yeah, asshole. Thanks to you two douches being pussy-whipped, I had to do everything, including picking up the pizzas. You dicks each better pay your halves is all I gotta say. You're both lucky Max and Chris were around to help, or I woulda been really pissed," he says, tossing me a can of beer; nothing beats an ice cold Molson Canadian.

"I tried calling you and Matty. Answer your phones, fuckers."

"Sorry, Justin, priorities, buddy." I crack my beer, smiling as I think back to my night spent with Kat. God, that girl is amazing. Nothing like hot sex and bad take-out.

"Shit, man. You got it bad for this chick, eh? I don't think I've ever seen you like this before. Your fucking shit-eatin' grin is enough to make me sick," Justin says, opening his can.

"She's different, man. I think she just might be the one. The game changer, my motherfuckin' Holy Grail. It turns out, I'm not ruined; I was just fucked over. I feel like I just needed her. I needed Kat to come along and show me that not all chicks are Melissas and what a real relationship is like. Turns out, I'm fixable, 'cause it seems I wasn't broken, just jaded maybe. Melissa fucked with my head, my confidence, made me afraid to trust. Then Kat came along." I expel a laugh. "I know I sound like a pussy, but, man, Kat—she's amazing, man. She's repairing me. She cares about me, my dreams, goals, and opinions. Justin, I swear this girl is everything."

"As much as I wanna make fun of you right now, Ryk, I won't. I see this girl. I see how good she is for you. The way you are with each other, man, it's sweet. But I will say this, okay? Just promise me you won't become that dude who vanishes. Like, still be around, Ryk; don't forget us along the way. Okay?

"Of course not, man, you guys are my brothers, and I'm sorry about last night. I just got caught up in my girl. One day, when you decide one's enough, you'll see how easy it happens. But know that both Kat and I know how important it is to spend time with our friends. No worries there, okay, bud? We'll still have our guy time. Now enough of this girlie shit, let's grab another beer and set up the poker table. The guys will be here soon."

We spend the rest of the night drinking beer, talking shit, and having a great time. I can definitely see Justin's concern; we've basically been in the player's club together for a long time.

A beautiful thing about Kat is the love she has for her friends. I know she'll definitely not stop me from hanging out with the guys. In fact, she's always making sure she isn't taking away from my guys' time when she tries to make plans with me. Just as she knows the same goes for her. I realize the importance of keeping her time with her girls. I really meant it when I told Justin not to worry about losing me.

Chapter 54

Kat

LOOKING DOWN AT my phone, I smile at the text displayed on my screen. Yep, I've become quite the avid cell phone user since a certain honeybutter eyed boy has taken over my life.

> **Ryker:** *Be there early tonight, sweet girl. I wanna fuck you on our ottoman before work.*
>
> **Me:** *Ryker! You're so bad! Mmm, okay, can't wait! Xox*
>
> **Ryker:** *That's my dirty girl. Are you wet, baby?*
>
> **Me:** *Ryker!!!*
>
> **Ryker:** *x*

Despite my initial reluctance, I'm glad I decided to give us a chance. I have to admit, it took a few weeks for the feeling that the floor was going to fall out from beneath me to subside, but it finally did. I'm confident Ryker's player days are done. I just might be his game changer. Ryker has met my parents, and they loved him. My mom, having already met him over the break, was more smitten with him after we all went for dinner. My dad, on the other hand, took a bit longer, but as soon as he discovered Ryker had a ton of drive and ambition, he quickly saw what the rest of us already had long ago. I think the fact that they both cheer for the Jays and Raptors helped, too. Having agreed to see a game together, Ryker and my dad actually exchanged cell numbers. Talk about a surprise. My parents, like Wes,

261

hated Seth. They always felt there was something off with him. From the way he looked at me to the times he'd be a bit too demanding, even in front of them. Too many times my mother would find me crying at something Seth had said or done. Sometimes I feel I really was naïve where that jerk was concerned.

Other than Levi, I have yet to meet Ryker's family, mainly his mom, but I know that time will come one day. "My mom is the best, baby," he opened up to me one lazy Sunday while we were in bed. "I know you two are going to get along great. I want you to know that I will introduce you. We'll go spend a weekend with her, but I just need a bit more time is all." Looking me straight in the eye while kissing my chest, he added, "For me, I've never, ever brought anyone home to meet my mom before. I've never wanted to. My mom is all I have, and I never wanted to intertwine the two parts of my life. I can't really explain why, I just never felt that any girl was worthy. I know with all my heart that I'll be introducing you, Kat, 'cause, baby, I know you're worth it. I just need a little time to process that notion is all."

With that, I smiled while leaning up to grab his face. "Ryker, I get it. I respect you and the special bond you have with your mom. Believe me, I have absolutely no doubt that when the time is right, I'll be the lucky girl you take home to meet your mom. And please know, whenever the day may come, it will be an honour to meet her." No sooner than the words left my mouth, Ryker rewarded me with his mouth all over my body.

He has proven over and over to me that I'm really his girl. He is attentive, sweet, sexy, fun, and most of all, fucking supportive. He is constantly making sure we study when we're together, that I make it to class on time, and that I get a good night's sleep. Ryker making sure I sleep, well, it's by far my favourite thing about his attentiveness. He also makes sure to give me orgasms almost daily. Which, I must say, have really helped with my anxiety and insomnia. I have never been more relaxed or as well rested, and I've had a perma-smile on my face for weeks.

Chapter 55

Kat

IT'S THURSDAY NIGHT and I'm enjoying a quiet house. It doesn't happen very often around here, I'm relishing in the peace and quiet. Claire and Ryker are at work and the roomies have all gone to their study group. Ryker ended up having to work a few extra hours to help out his brother today, so he was heading in earlier than normal. This is the perfect opportunity to work on my essay about the ways schools can better integrate the use of technology in the classroom. I want to get it done before Jacob's big game Saturday, because I know we'll be gone all day. I've got my laptop open, and a ton of journal articles spread around the floor and coffee table. Just as I sit down on the couch, ready to eat my dinner, the doorbell rings. The sound startles me because it's quiet and also because I'm not expecting anyone.

Looking out the peephole, I can't contain the huge grin that spreads across my face at seeing Ryker standing on the other side of the door. Making quick work of the lock, I open the door and literally leap into his arms.

"Hi, sweet girl. I had a few minutes, and I needed to see you before work. I need to give you your goodnight kiss," he says as he walks us up the stairs into the living room, swiftly plopping me down on the couch. He begins kissing my cheek and neck. "I'm here 'cause I needed my dinner, too. I'm ravenous today."

Pointing to my Lean Cuisine on the coffee table beside my laptop,

I shrug, feeling bad that I don't have anything to give him other than the crap I've microwaved. "Sorry, babe, I didn't know you were coming. I'm eating the lazy girl's meal tonight. If I had of known—"

"No sweet girl, I didn't mean food. I'm hungry for you. I've been thinking about your sweet taste all day," he says while slipping down in front of me, taking off my yoga pants. "Scoot," he says while grabbing me by the ass, positioning me exactly where he wants me.

"Oh," is all I can muster as Ryker now has me naked from the waist down. My face flush and my now throbbing pussy is greedy with anticipation of what it knows is coming. "You're so fucking hot for me, I feel your heat," he says as he slowly begins rubbing his stubble over my mound. "I'm gonna feast on this pussy like a starved man." I buck as he begins trailing a finger between my folds, lubricating the tips of his fingers. "Always ready for me, such a greedy girl," he says before taking my clit in his mouth, tugging at the bundle of nerves, causing moans and near yelps to escape my mouth. I begin pulling his hair as a means to push his face further into my centre. Fuck! Ryker adds another finger as he laps at my pussy, eating me indeed like a starved man. Jesus Christ, this boy and his tongue.

"You're too fucking yummy, sweet girl. I can't get enough of this pussy," he says as he swirls his tongue around my clit with a perfect pressure—the one that always causes tiny pricks to run along my spine, which in turn, causes my skin to flush and break out in a sweaty sheen at Ryker's assault. An assault where he is relentlessly inflicting pure pleasure on my body with his hungry mouth and fingers. As he moves his hands to grip the globes of my ass, pushing himself deeper into my centre, I'm quickly on the brink of an all-consuming explosion that has visions of technicolored dots dancing to life behind my eyelids.

"Oh, fuck, Ryker. I'm gonna…I'm gonna, ah, shh-hit!" I yell out while tremor after tremor wracks through my core.

"Best meal ever, baby. I'll see you at work tomorrow." With that, he kisses my lips before walking out the door.

Sated and completely relaxed, I spend the rest of my night lazing on the couch thinking about Ryker. God, I am one lucky girl. During nights when we can't be together, he manages to surprise me by stopping by, even if it is for a few minutes. I grin to myself, reliving every juicy detail of what he just did to me. Shit, I guess I'll be working on my paper all day Sunday.

Chapter 56

Kat

"HOLY SHIT, THE tips are going to be epic tonight, eh, Kat?"

"God, Brooke, I was just thinking I can't believe how busy we are. I wonder what made everyone in the world come here tonight. My feet are killing me already. And it's only been three hours."

"Mine too," she pouts. "These damn boots are killer cute," she lifts one leg in the air, making sure I can see them, "but, shit, I ache."

"Ahh, the price of hotness," I tease her. "They are pretty great, so worth the pain."

"Yeah, Ben's lucky I love him. He's picking me up later and he loves me in these boots, if ya know what I mean…just the boots," she giggles.

"Too much information, chick, too much," I tell her.

"Oh, whatever, Kat. Don't you think for one second we all don't hear you and Ryker in that bloody staff room," she taunts me. "No one will even sit near that fucking ottoman anymore." Brooke laughs, and I know I blush completely.

"Don't even worry, you are too fucking cute together. We all knew Ryker just needed the right girl. I'm just glad he found you and you gave him the time of day."

"He really is something else, Brooke. God, he's terribly sweet and just so…so caring. How he is with me, my friends, and especially

267

Jacob; it just melts my heart. Who would have thought the player was really just a total front? It took a bit, but I'm really glad I let him in, too. But it's hard working together sometimes. I mean, I know he doesn't give any of them the time of day anymore, but look." I point to the group of girls perched at the bar vying for Ryker's attention. "Don't get me wrong. I know it's not a secret that we're a couple around here with the staff, but sometimes I feel these chicks have no clue that he's mine now, you know? I feel like I need to brand him or some shit."

Raising her eyebrows, she smirks at my Ryker gushing and musings. "Awe, are you a wee bit jelly? I really don't think you need to worry. Believe me, that boy only has eyes for you. He even asked me to pitch the message bowl out later as I'm on bar clean up. Out with the trash, the trash will go tonight," she giggles at her joke. "For real just try and relax and don't worry. The hoochies will all get the message soon that he isn't interested."

"I'm sure you're right. It's just hard. I've never been with a man like Ryker before. I guess I'm just scared. I know I shouldn't be; he's been perfect so far."

Brooke studies me for a moment then a huge grin breaks out across her face. "My sweet Kat, I must say, you sound pretty wrapped up in all things Ryker. I'm glad you're happy. And it sounds like you just might be falling in love with our little Ryker Eddison himself."

"I...ah, I better get over to the bar. I think I see my VIP order ready. See you in a bit. Hopefully, we manage to get breaks tonight. We can chat more then," I quip before making my way over to Ryker and the bar. I love seeing him in his element, all business in that sexy-ass t-shirt that hugs his strong arms perfectly.

I just finished dropping off the tray of drinks to Steve and his boys in the VIP section. Steve is a regular who just got into law school. He and his buddies are out for a good time. And of course on my way back to the bar, I run into this guy, the guy who's apparently looking for another type of fun. "Hey, sweet tits, why don't you come here and give me some sugar? Fuck, you're one sexy minx. I wanna see what you got under those shorts, baby," says the creep as he reaches for my hips. I cringe at the word 'baby' rolling off this asshole's tongue. With his other hand, he grabs my wrist in a tight hold before pulling me into him and rubbing his hand on my ass. Just as I'm about to let him have it, I hear a growl and can't help the smile from breaking across my face when I hear Ryker's voice.

"Buddy, I'm gonna need you to get your fucking hands off my girl, right-the-fuck now."

"Oh shit, sorry, man. I didn't know she was yours. I was…I was just trying to get some of that sweet sugar she's sportin', you know? 'Cause fuck, man, she is fine."

"Dude, did you just fucking hear me or what? Listen, fuckwad, and listen good, 'cause I will only give you this warning one time. This beautiful girl here is mine and only mine." He wraps his arms around me at the waist securely, pulling me into his front. "She will only be showing her sugar to me. I'm gonna be needing for you to back the fuck off my girl before I lose my shit all over your face."

The drunk raises his hands in surrender just as Big Jim comes over to see if Ryker needs him.

"Right, man. I got it, okay? Listen, I'm sorry. It won't happen again." With that, Big Jim escorts him to the other side of the club.

"Ryker, we need to talk for a minute." I lead him aside and down the hall away from the crowd.

"You okay, baby? That fucker hurt you at all?"

"No. God, Ryker. I'm fine. I appreciate you sticking up for me, but I could have handled him. You need to know I'm okay, that I'm capable of dealing with the assholes. You can't always save the day, you know." I look him in the eyes, trying to be stern with him. I know he means well, but I've been dealing with the jerks here just fine before he and I were together. Besides, he can't threaten to beat the shit out of all the men who bother me.

"That's where you're wrong, sweet girl. I protect what's mine, and you *are* mine." He enunciates each word in that possessive way that always makes my nipples harden and the need to clench my legs unbearable. "Ah, see. You love that, eh, baby?" He nuzzles in closer to my neck, trailing kisses.

"Well, fine then, Ryker. If you're going to protect me from assholes, tell me how am I to deal with all the whores who still think you're available. What am I supposed to do? Stand on the bar and tell them all to back off my man, that you're no longer the player they know?" He chuckles at my crazy rant, then squashes my concerns with his mouth, hands, and sweet promises.

All too suddenly, Ryker pulls away from me, leaving me panting and breathless from his kiss. "I gotta go do something, baby, something I should have done before. I'm a fucking genius. I'm gonna fix this little problem." Then he's gone, bolting back toward the bar. The music stops as I make my way back into the crowd of people, all wondering the same as me.

What the hell is this guy doing?

Ryker takes a stand on top of the bar. "Shhh, shhh, I need you all to quiet the hell down for a minute." After a few minutes, the entire bar is silent with all eyes trained on Ryker. I move in closer. "Lovely patrons of Pub Fiction, I need a moment of your time, if I may." Pointing to me he continues, "Do you all see that gorgeous shooter girl over there? Well, of course you do, how could you not? That fine-ass girl is Kat. Well, anyway, I'm standing here now to tell you all, as well as warn you, that she is MINE," he basically grits out to the listening crowd. "And just so we are clear, I am also hers. As of now, you need to all know we are together. Sorry, boys, that means you all need to watch yourselves around my girl, especially the eyes and hands. As for the ladies, the same goes for you all. I'm completely fucking gone over this girl. You needn't even bother trying."

Holy cow, I can't believe my eyes or my ears. *The* Ryker Eddison is basically hanging up his player jersey, handing in his scorecard for me. My heart is beating a million miles in my chest, but I have the biggest shit-eating grin on my face, and I don't care who sees it. God, this man makes me swoon.

With that, Ryker takes his message bowl and tosses it in the garbage before running back over to me, scooping me up and over his shoulders, and leading me to where I assume is the staff room. All I can hear are my own giggles and hoots and hollers from the bar.

Ever since that night, work has been pretty calm. My tips are a bit less, but I'm totally okay with that.

Chapter 57

Kat

February

"OH, MY GOD!"

"What is it?" Claire comes rushing to the front door where I'm holding the mail in one hand, the open letter in the other.

"That boy is just plain fucking sweet," I say, showing Claire the Valentine I found from Ryker in with the mail.

Kat,

You've been caught in my mind's eye from the moment I laid my eyes on you.

Now you're completely caught in my heart.

I can't wait to see you tonight, sweet girl.

Be ready.

Ryker x

"You're such a lucky bitch. Now don't get me wrong, Matt is amazing, but Ryker is just bloody swoony!" She beams with her hand over her heart for effect. I smile, because she honestly has no idea just how much this boy makes me feel like I've been swept off my feet on a daily basis.

It's Valentine's Day and Claire, Matt, Ryker, and I have decided to have a double date to celebrate. None of us are too keen on the holiday, but when the three of us discovered Levi was able to give us the day off, we decided we might as well go out. We've bought tickets to attend Pub Fiction's *Love is in the Air Affair*, the annual dinner and dance that the club holds to raise money for The Heart and Stroke Foundation. It's a great cause, and because it's a black tie affair, we all agreed it would most likely be a blast to get all dressed up.

I was also excited because I was busy plotting out a special after party for Ryker and me. Claire had made plans to spend the night at Matt's already. With all the others planning to stay over at Jenn and Laurie's after the bar, I had the house to myself so it worked out perfectly.

"I've just finished setting up my room for my little act tonight," I say, walking into Claire's room with all my stuff to start getting ready. Claire has agreed to help me with my hair and makeup. "I'm excited and nervous. I've never been the initiator before. I'm really hoping I can pull this off. I mean, what I have planned for Ryker is totally out of my comfort zone."

"I love it! I'm proud of you, grasshopper," Claire basically coos. "I can't believe how bold you've become, Kat. Ryker has been a really good influence on you," she beams, directing me to sit in the chair in front of her. Claire is going to put my hair up into a French twist, because she thinks it will suit my off-the-shoulder dress perfectly.

She smiles down at me before, getting to work on my updo. "I'm really happy you decided to give the guy a chance. I knew you were different to him. Besides, I'm really loving how we get all kinds of double dates now."

"Yeah, he really has. I've been noticing it myself actually. I never thought Ryker Eddison would be the reason I'm happy," I tell her honestly. Trying to ignore the emotions rising at the idea of how true that statement actually is, I'm quick to turn the talk back to tonight. "I'm way too excited for tonight! I bought the perfect pink bustier, complete with garters and stockings to wear under my dress. Ryker is gonna lose his mind, and I cannot wait!"

Claire laughs. "Jesus! Who knew you'd become such a whore? I love it, Kitty Kat. You are going to bring that boy to his knees." We laugh as we continue to ready ourselves for the night ahead.

Once we're finished, Claire and I decide to sit and enjoy a glass of wine before the boys pick us up. Just as I'm topping the glasses off, the doorbell rings.

"I'll get it!" Claire smiles before heading toward the door. We've been ready for about twenty minutes and dying for the guys to get here.

Standing up to put the drinks on the counter, I'm suddenly shocked to hear a voice that rocks jolts of fear into my body.

"Where the fuck is she? Tell me right the fuck now! I need to see my little bitch of a girl. I'm fuckin' done with her ignoring me."

"No, Seth!" I hear Claire yell as a bumping sound echoes through the hall.

Hands shaking, I'm standing, feeling almost paralyzed with my back to the counter, wine glasses in hand, liquid spilling all over the floor, listening for sounds of Claire. But all I hear is the sounds of heavy footsteps coming up the stairs. I try to compose myself, as I know Seth has clearly made his way past Claire. God, he better not have hurt her. Putting the glasses on the countertop, I turn back around and I'm all too quickly met face-to-face with an angry Seth Cooper. *Shit!*

Chapter 58

Ryker

"MATTY, I THINK the girls are gonna love these flowers. I'm full of great ideas, eh? Stick with me, buddy, and I'll teach you all the tricks to making your girl smile 24/7, all the while getting you laid as a thank you." I slap his back as we're leaving the florist.

"Okay, Casanova, like you've ever bought flowers for a chick before, or done anything sweet like this," he smarts me back as we exit the shop.

"You're right, Matty. None of the chicks I've been with have ever made me want to do nice things like this anyway. Actually, none of them have made me want more than a quick fuck and a 'see ya later.'" Matt nods knowingly. "Melissa just used to demand I do what boyfriends do. It's nice to want to do these things on my own for a change. I know Kat appreciates it, and honestly, I really like seeing that sexy-ass smile of hers when I do something she doesn't expect."

I actually buy Kat flowers every week, along with a little note including a song lyric or lines from a poem. Yep, my *vagina* has fully grown in and, honestly, I'm okay with it as long as I make my girl smile. I'm not sure if Claire knows or not, but she definitely hasn't told Matty 'cause I know I'd be razzed by the guys for sure. Not that I'd give a shit anyway. Kat's my girl and I'm all about making sure every fucker out there knows it.

Matty reaches in his pocket to retrieve his cell that's been blasting

AC/DC's "You Shook Me All Night Long." Just as we reach my truck, I laugh at the ringtone. "Claire," he says with a smirk. "She's probably calling to find out where the hell we are. We were supposed to be there fifteen minutes ago," he tells me before answering as we hop in my truck. Good thing the florist is about five-minutes away. We'll have our girls in no time.

"Hey, sunshine, I know, I kno—What? Baby, breathe, calm down. What…Seth?" As soon as Matt drops that fucker's name, ice seeps into my veins. I know we need to get the fuck outta here right the fuck now.

"Matty, dude, I need you to tell me what the fuck is going on and now, brother!" I spew as I drive off toward Kat's. He lowers the phone to give me what he's gathered so far. While I'm listening, I call campus police to meet us there. This shit ends today.

"Claire said they were having a drink, waiting for us to get there, when the doorbell rang and it was Kat's ex, Seth. She tried to hold him off, but he pushed past her, knocking her down."

"What the ever-loving fuck?" I say, slamming my hand down on the steering wheel. I knew this asshole was going to make a move eventually. Looking over, I see Matt is losing control as fast as I am. While he's listening to Claire and relaying information, his legs are moving constantly in agitation as he tells me what's going on.

"She hit her head on the ground pretty good when he pushed her, but she says she's all right. Claire says Kat was in the kitchen before Seth pushed his way in. She thinks they're still there. She called us as soon as she got her bearings." Matt covers the phone again. "Sorry, Ryk, man, but I'm telling her to stay put until we get there. I can't have her getting involved with this guy; he's already hurt her."

"No, no, of course, Matt. You tell Claire to go wait outside. Tell her we're nearly there and not to worry."

After what feels like the longest drive of my life, I barely get the truck in park before I'm through the door of Kat's house.

Chapter 59

Kat

STANDING IN FRONT of me, Seth is seething, anger radiating from him to the point where his body has a slight tremble. "Kathleen, Happy Valentine's Day, baby. Will you be mine?" he sneers, and it's the most revolting words I have ever heard in my life. This person standing in front of me is not the boy I once knew; the boy I thought I loved. I know now what real love is, and it's what Ryker Eddison gives me on a daily basis. This version of a man is nothing more than a psycho and a stalker. I'm petrified of what his next move will be.

"What's the matter, whore? Cat got your tongue? You look surprised to see me, Kathleen," he draws out my name and it's like nails on a chalkboard. I hate my full name, and this asshole damn well knows it.

"What the hell are you doing here, Seth?"

"It was time I checked in on you. You've been a real skank since you've moved into this new place. Dancing on bars, spreading your legs for that dick." He refers to Ryker with disgust in his voice. "Did you get the flowers I sent? Oh yeah, right, you tossed them out in the trash, you ungrateful bitch."

Holy shit is all I can think as the realization hits me. Seth has been watching me for months. My pulse rate starts to pick up and I begin to panic. *Oh, God, please not now.*

"Again, Seth, why are you here? Why aren't you in Ottawa at

school?"

"I dropped out. I needed to come here, fuck school!" he shouts. "I came to get what's mine, sugar, and that's you," he says with a smirk and a look of lust in his eyes as he takes in my dress.

"Aww, did you dress up for me? I gotta tell ya, Kat, I fucking love it. I will love it more when it's in a heaping pile on the floor." With that, he moves in closer. *Breathe, Kat, just keep breathing.*

"Not a fucking chance, asshole," I mutter more to myself than to him, but of course he hears me. Shit.

"Listen here, you fucking whore. You *will* be getting naked and you *will* be begging for me to take you and your slut ways back. You stupid cunt. Did you think I'd let that asshole have what's mine? Hell the fuck no. I'm back just in time for that shit to stop. I see the way you look at that guy, and I DON'T FUCKING LIKE IT," he comes up and yells in my face. Stepping back to look down at me, he begins to really lose it, and it's clear that Seth is not mentally stable at all. I'm honestly afraid. "I see the way he thinks you're his. Too fucking bad I'm back now, sweetheart—back for what's mine, for what will always be mine," he spits while coming closer to me. I'd like to think he won't hurt me. He never has before, but I can't take the chance, so I decide to try and reason with him.

"Seth, please, I've told you we're over. You chose that whore over me." *Idiot Kat,* I think as the words slip from my mouth. I should keep my stupid comments to myself. The last thing I need to do is piss him off more. Like the stupid person I am, I continue on anyway. "You made that choice, not me. You decided we were done, that I wasn't enough. You're the asshole, not me!" With that, he backhands me hard across the face before grabbing me and, shoving me up against the fridge. I cry out in shock and pain from the impact of the pressure he's putting on my body with his own. Suddenly, he's whispering he's sorry in my ear, trailing kisses along my jaw and face. I think I'm going to be sick.

"You always smell so sweet, Kathleen. I need you. I'm going to make you forgive me, sweetheart. I'm going to make you remember how good we are."

No, No, No. He grips my breasts before he starts slide his hands down to my ass.

"Please, Seth, don't do this," I beg. But it falls on deaf ears as he begins trying to pull up my dress; using a force that tells me he's got a one-track mind. Bile rises in my throat and tears stream down my face now as I prepare for what's to come. Seth is too strong and has me pinned against the fridge. I can't seem to budge, no matter how hard I try. *Ryker,* is all I can think as a loud sob escapes my mouth before closing my eyes, willing what's to come next to be over as fast as it possibly can.

"*Get your fucking hands off my girl.*" Those seven words are all I need to hear before I visibly relax, knowing everything is going to be okay.

Ryker.

Chapter 60

Ryker

"KAT? KAT, BABY, where are you?" I say as I make my way up the stairs. What I see makes the hairs on the back of my neck stand as fury takes over my entire being. I see that asshat has my sweet girl pinned against the fridge. His body is flush to hers, with one hand holding her two smaller ones above her head, his other hand roaming her body while he kisses her face, muttering words I can only imagine.

I'm like a raging bull in Pamplona at the sight.

I charge.

"I will fucking kill you, motherfucker!" I say, grabbing him by the scruff of the neck, getting in his face. "You see that beautiful fucking girl you were touching? That girl, asshole, is mine! And I swear to Christ, you need to fucking learn that fact real fucking quick!" Headbutting him, I give him the lines I want him to recite out loud. "Now repeat after me, asshole: Kat belongs to Ryker. Now say it, dickwad." I hold him by the hair, forcing him to look up at me, to see the rage behind my words... "Fucking say it, dick," I slap him upside the head. "You fuckin learnin' it yet?" I ask while I stand him up, pinning him against the fridge. Using my leg as leverage, I move it between his to squish his balls, and like the pussy he is, he begins to beg.

"I get it. I-I-I geeet it, asshole!"

Are you fucking kidding me?

280

"Did you just call me asshole, asshole?" *Punch, whack, punch.* With these last relentless bouts, Kat's screaming for me to stop wailing on him, but I can't. He needs to know he's no longer welcome in our lives. Ever. By the time the campus police arrive, Seth is a bloody mess, crying and whimpering like the pansy ass bitch he is.

Chapter 61

Ryker

August

IT'S BEEN SIX months since that asshead fucked with my girl. Thank God she's so fucking resilient. Kat never let that piece of shit get inside her head. She bounced back pretty much immediately, never letting him stop her from moving forward with her life. I'm proud of my girl. I know she was more worried about Claire than anything. I swear to Christ, I have never been that pissed before in my life, as I was that day when I rounded the corner, seeing that asshole with his hands all over my sweet girl. It was scary as hell, because in all honesty, I have never in my life had such strong feelings like I do for Kat. Never have I been this happily consumed with thoughts, feelings, and amazement like I am for this woman. Love isn't nearly the right word to even begin to describe the way this girl makes me feel. And knowing that asshole was threatening the very thing I've come to hold the closest to me, just about destroyed me. I really felt I was going to kill that son of a bitch.

Believe me, no one in my position would have thought any different. Seth had better be counting his lucky stars every single day that campus police showed up when they did. Seeing Kat pinned up against that fridge with that fucktard's hands trying to violate her did something to me that took me a real long time to come to terms with. I would have gladly gone to jail for my girl if that would have meant I kept her safe. I think it was shortly after this incident that I realized how much I'd fallen in love with her. When I grabbed him off her, it was like I became this crazy adrenaline junkie who just couldn't stop.

The last we heard, Seth had been charged with assault, stalking, and a slew of other offences that would keep him tied up in jail or court proceedings for years to come. According to the police, Seth had flunked out of law school and had been exhibiting a series of unstable behaviours for months. A restraining order has been put in effect just in case, and he is not permitted within a thousand meters of my girl.

Tonight I'm taking Kat out to celebrate. We've graduated University and quit our jobs at Pub Fiction, not that we won't help Levi out from time to time. I mean, after all, that fucking place holds a special place in our lives. Mainly, we're heading out on the town to celebrate our new adventures. Kat has been offered a job teaching third grade here in the city at Highview Elementary. As for me, I'm just waiting to close on the purchase of my new building. It's a few blocks away from Kat's school and where I plan to start my dream. The Locker Room is no longer a pipe dream, baby! Needless to say, the last six months have been amazing, and I am ready to move forward with Kat and our lives.

Boy, do I have a surprise for her.

Chapter 62

Kat

IT'S BEEN SIX months since Seth tried to destroy my life and happiness. I count my lucky stars every day that no one was hurt. Claire, thank goodness, only suffered a little bump on the back of her head. She was having a harder time letting go of the feeling of guilt that seemed to be consuming her because she let Seth get to me, but also because she didn't come after him once she got her bearings. Claire feels she is responsible for the fact that Seth even got near me. She says she should have looked out the peephole and she let me down by not having my back when I needed it the most. She can't seem to get past thinking what could have happened to me. It wasn't until one drunken night about a month after the incident, that I finally convinced Claire to let it go and reminded her she is, in fact, the best friend a girl could ever have.

That night, I took Claire to our favourite Italian restaurant, *Spazzo,* because we were in desperate need of girl time. Over the last few weeks, Claire had been avoiding me and that shit was not okay.

It was time to fix this shit.

"Claire," I peered at her over my menu, "we are having the deep fried Ravioli and a bottle of red to start." Matty and Ryker told me they would pick us up, so we could have a good time, which according to them includes lots of alcohol, food, and girlie talk. "Okay, sound good?"

Looking up, with the first genuine smile I've seen on her face in way too long, she agreed, "Sounds perfect. But we need to add the calamari; I love it here."

We ended up having three bottles of wine over the course of four hours, along with a few more appetizers before deciding to share a bowl of spaghetti and meatballs. We had the best chat, and I knew things would be back to normal between us.

"Never again, never again," I reaffirmed to her as we waited on the curbside for the guys while holding onto each other. Claire tried to hide a tear as I faced her, placing my hand on her shoulder, just like the night of the fire. "That shit was no way your fault, just like you told me at the fire, remember? God, Claire, it was you who saved me. You called Matt. Do you remember what you said to me the night of the fire? I mean, they are after all pretty ingenious words to live by, but now I think it's your turn to heed them."

Claire smiled while wiping her face. "Yeah, I think I remember saying something genius, like I usually do." She laughed and I joined her, before making sure she actually remembered.

"You basically told me, and I quote, 'We are both safe, and that's all that matters. From this moment on, don't ever think about anything other than that!'" With that, we hugged and cried just in time for our two incredible guys to arrive.

LOOKING BACK ON that day, even now, all I can think is thank God Ryker got to me when he did. It took me a while to get past the what-ifs of that night, just like it did with the fire. But in the end, I've managed to work through all the thoughts, feelings, and emotions associated with those two traumatic events, and I can actually smile at how far I've come.

Today I know I've made it through and I'm moving forward, not dwelling on a past I can't control. I've got amazing friends, I've graduated University, gotten a job, and best of all, I have Ryker. I know without a doubt that Ryker Eddison is my rock. He's been an amazing support system, and I could not have gotten past any of this without him.

Tonight, I am planning on bringing that boy to his knees like I had planned many months ago.

"You ready for me to style your hair now, Kitty Kat?" Claire asks from the vanity where she's pointing to the chair in front of her.

"Yeah, one sec," I call out, peering at her from the en suite where I've just put on the pretty pink bustier Ryker still has yet to see. "I just gotta throw on my dress."

"Okay, but hurry up! Ryker said he'd be here by seven o'clock sharp, and it's not like I can keep him out when it's his own place, ya know? Besides, I need to get out of here before you start this little sexcapade of yours."

I smile at her comment as I slip my heels on my feet. Yep, Ryker and I have moved in together! Eeeppp! We bought a beautiful condo just on the outskirts of the city, and I've loved every minute of my new life with this man. Despite our parents being reluctant of our decision, we didn't care. We know without a doubt we are in this life together. I have to say, Ryker's mom has actually been on our side from the get-go. She even helped to convince my parents that her son would absolutely do right by their little girl, not that they ever doubted it. Ryker's mom is truly amazing and we've become very close.

Patricia is very sweet. I can see why Ryker never introduced her to his randoms before. I'm honoured that right was reserved for me.

I smile at the memory of him finally inviting me home to meet his mom...

"*Fuck,* hot girl, you keep smothering those titties down and around my cock like that and I'm fuckin' gonna come—ahh, shit—all over the fucking place," Ryker uttered as I sat on my knees in front of him with his hard cock sliding between my oiled up chest like he loves so much. I discovered his fascination with my tits after the first time we had sex. Ryker Eddison is one hundred percent a boob man.

"Fuck, baby, take me in your mouth now," he demanded in the gravelly voice I've come to term in my mind as the 'I'm gonna come soon' signal. Glancing up at him, I moved a bit higher on my knees, pulled my hands behind my back, arched it so my tits were on display, before I began rubbing my face along his hard cock, teasing and tormenting him with little flicks and licks of my tongue. "Jesus Christ, I'm gonna embarrass myself soon if you don't put that fucking sexy-ass mouth of yours around my cock," Ryker groaned, his tone dripping impatience. I love when he's at my mercy like that.

Deciding to play nice, I pushed my chest out to rub his exposed legs as I slowly slid his smooth, hard cock into my mouth. "God, ohhhh shit, yeah," he said, as I looked up and caught Ryker's eyes before I begin to swirl my tongue around the head of his hardness, lapping, quickening my pace before I started my hands in on the action, pushing him closer to the edge. As swift as a hurricane, I was pushed back, bouncing onto Ryker's bed.

"Gotta be in you, sweet girl. You're fucking teasing me with that mouth and these titties." He popped each of my nipples into his mouth. "Fuck me, I can't take it. I need your tight pussy wrapped around me," he all but growled. "You ready for my cock now, baby?" he asked while trailing his fingers along the lips of my pussy.

"Fuck yes," I squealed as he pushed two fingers into my core. "Ryker, please!" The next thing I knew, Ryker was thrusting into me, pushing and pumping. Thrusting so fucking deep, I swore he was hitting my cervix. "Oh, umm…oh fuck. God, yeah, yeah," I chanted. With Ryker increasing his pace, it wasn't long before I was a quivering mess under the man I love.

Ryker pinned my hands above my head while slowing. "Kat," he murmured in my ear, and then stopped moving, becoming dead serious. "Kat, I need you to look at me." I stilled my hips and looked to find him staring at me, his honeybutter eyes intense as he was still inside me. "Hot girl,"—he cleared his throat—"I need you to know something, baby." My nose started to twitch as my tears threatened in preparation of the moment I knew we were about to have. Skimming my nose with his, giving me an Eskimo kiss, he pulled back again, looked deep into my eyes before uttering the words I knew without a doubt meant he loved me. "I'd like you to come home with me and meet my mom this weekend." I couldn't help but laugh and cry at the same time. I was laughing because this crazy alpha male was buried inside me while he brought up his mother, all the while confirming for me that my love was, indeed, reciprocated.

Later that night, I laid in Ryker's cocoon, with his muscular arms wrapped tightly around me from behind. While nestling in for the night, he whispered ever so softly into my ear, "I love you with my mind's eye and my heart's soul, Kat Rollins. Now go to sleep before I have you ride my cock that you've just stirred to life with that fine ass of yours rubbing on it."

"Ryker!"

I laugh every time I think back on that day. Ryker never ceases to amaze me.

After saying bye to Claire, I make my way back to our bedroom, positioning my purple and black armchair in the middle of the floor. I check that my song is in queue, and then, taking a deep breath, I sit on the edge of the bed and wait.

Twenty-five minutes later, I hear the door click open.

Ryker.

Chapter 63

Ryker

MAKING QUICK WORK of the door, I expect to find Kat ready on the other side. I'm actually a few minutes late and our reservation is for 7:30 p.m. at *August 8*. I half expect her to sass me about my tardiness, especially since I sent her a little reminder text to be ready at seven sharp. She's nowhere to be found.

"Kat, I'm home, baby. We'd better get going or we're gonna be late," I call, making my way further inside the house. She's not in the kitchen or living room. My heart rate begins to increase as I race up the stairs, feeling the protective instinct that seems to have taken up residence ever since Valentine's Day. "Kat!" I shout a bit louder this time.

Reaching our door, I take a deep breath, calming myself before I go in. The last thing I want her to see is how worried I am or to even know I was worrying. With my luck, Kat would most likely take to calling me the 'worry wart.' We know Seth is long gone, and we honestly have nothing to fear. With a renewed calm, armed with a witty comment about her not being ready, I turn the knob, opening the door. Jesus! Nothing could have prepared me for the sight before me. This girl is gonna be the death of me.

"Holy fucking shit." I stop in my tracks at the vision of my sexy girl.

Here I thought my heart rate was erratic before I opened the bedroom door, but finding Kat waiting for me in our room has my heart rate increasing as well as my skin prickling with wonderment and excitement. Kat isn't late. No, she's clearly ready, and by the looks of her, she's been ready and waiting for me. The moment my eyes land on her, taking her in as she's sprawled out before me, brings my cock to immediate attention. Clearly my cock is one smart fucker, having received the message of what's happening before my brain fully registers the scene.

I guess we really do think with the wrong head.

Fuck me, Kat lying across that bloody armchair she loves so much, the same one that just might be my new favourite piece of furniture—well, besides the ottoman I stole from Pub Fiction, which is now a part of our living room.

Legs, which go on for miles, draped over the side with those sexy 'fuck me' heels of hers—ah, God, are those garters I see? I gulp, clearly not able to hide my curiosity.

"Hi, I've been waiting for you, honeybutter," she says, almost breathlessly, as she rises from the chair, so elegant in her motions that I can't take my eyes off her. Her hair is all wavy, long, and sultry, begging for me to grip it in my hands. It takes everything in my being not to go claim her. Fuck! I'm a lucky bastard. I gasp audibly as I take in what she's wearing. It's the sexiest little black dress I've ever seen. It hugs my baby in all the right places; sleeveless, exposing a ton of smooth skin, cinched at the waist with a belt, which serves to make me think of unwrapping her like a present. Her tits are spilling out just enough to make me drool, proving to me even more just how much I fucking need this girl as much as my next breathe. Fuck, what she does to me.

With a click of the remote, Ed Sheeran's "Thinking Out Loud" comes through the speakers, blaring the words that have become infinitely ours. Striding up to stand in front of me, Kat looks me in the eye before giving me one of the most beautiful smiles I have ever seen. God, my girl is stunning.

"Ryker, would you dance with me?"

Abso-fuckin-lutley.

"If it means touching you, baby, a million men couldn't keep me away." I grip her hips, bringing her flush to me as we begin to sway to our song. I start singing softly into her ear like I have a thousand times before. The words speaking volumes to the way this girl makes me think, feel, live, and best of all, love. I hold her close to me as we move in time to the music. Nuzzling her neck, I whisper over her skin, "God, I love you," before taking her lips between my teeth and dipping her, before kissing up and down her neck and jawline.

"We found love, baby, right here, you and me," I end on an over-dramatic note before cupping my hands on each side of her gorgeous face and kissing her with all that I am.

Suddenly, ending our kiss, Kat pushes away from me.

"Now, Mr. Eddison, enough of that sweetness. I have a little surprise for you. I'm going to bring you to your knees, big boy. Go sit that fine-ass of yours in the armchair, and under no circumstances are you allowed to get up." She begins pushing me as I walk backward, while hitting the dim feature of the light remote while passing the bed.

"Oh really? Will this surprise let me see what'cha got on under that sexy-as-fuck dress of yours?" I growl, trying to cop a feel before she pushes me down to the chair.

Paula Cole starts belting out "Feelin' Love" and I swear I come in my pants as I instantly have an idea of where this is going.

Fuck, Kat.

Chapter 64

Kat

BACKING AWAY FROM Ryker, who I've left sitting in that chair, I revel in his gaze heavy with anticipation. I sway my hips suggestively in succession with the music that's beginning to filter from the speakers. Smiling, I glide my fingertips up and down the sides of my body, stroking my neck and collarbone in time as Ms. Cole quickly gets her groove on about how she's *feelin' love*. I can't believe I'm doing this, but I am, and it feels liberating, and oh so fucking right. Ryker Eddison has changed me. Gone is the high-strung girl, and in her place is a woman who knows what she wants, which at this point, is to give her man a show he will never forget.

With that, I turn my back to Ryker and hear his gasp as I slowly raise the hem of my dress, revealing my pink garters. "Kat," he growls, I turn my head back and offer him a wink as I shake my ass, all the while continuing to pull the hem up more and more. Turning, ever so slowly, I flip my hair around a few times before moving my hands smoothly over my breasts, along my sides, and through my wavy locks. I catch Ryker's eyes, maintaining contact as I shimmy down low, opening my legs wide and inviting, as I slide my fingertips gently across my inner thighs.

"I fucking swear to Christ..." With that, he attempts to stand, and I feel a surge of power at his reaction to my performance. I know I'm testing him here, big time, but hell if I'm not loving it.

"Sit down, Ryker," I command with a smile to my tone. "Patience, honey, I'm just getting started, but you'll get what you want."

"It's not what I want, baby. God, it's what I need. My cock is fucking hard, Kat. Baby, when I get my hands on you, I'm gonna fuck you so deep; you're going to feel it in your throat." At his dirty promise, I waver a bit and I know Ryker sees it as he grins, knowing he's affecting me now, too.

As Paula's lusty voice croons the chorus line over and over, I begin to unclasp the belt to the dress, which has been concealing the pink bustier. At an agonizing pace, I pull the belt loose. After removing it, I twirl it around a few times before dropping it to the floor.

"Fucking hell. *Jesus, baby,*" is all I hear fall from Ryker's lips before I resume my swaying, gyrating, and dancing with perfect synchronicity to the sexy lyrics being heard. I strut closer to him, giving him a better view of my outfit, allowing him to see it as well as its sheerness. I pull at my nipples as I dance around him in the chair, leaning in closer at times, taking turns moving my ass and my tits in front of him. I tease him by tugging the back of his hair, running my hands along his jawline. More than once he tries to reach me, causing me to utter out a few "tsk, tsks" and "uh-uhs" as I swat his hands away.

"Kat," is all he can seem to verbalize as I continue my assault.

I drop onto all fours as the song is proving to be the perfect background noise to up the ante for my performance. I start crawling toward Ryker as he continues to sit in the armchair, showing no emotions on his face, unusually quiet except for his moans, growls, and curses, which are all the signs I need. I can tell my plan is working. He can't take those beautiful eyes off me. He's been gripping the chair's arms, and I'm pretty sure it's to keep him in his seat.

"Jesus. Fuck me. You are breathtakingly beautiful. I'm not gonna last much longer over here without you, baby." It's an admission that I take pleasure in hearing.

With this plea, I crawl the rest of the way to him. "Take that big cock out for me, Ryker. I need you in my mouth." With my intention clear, I land between his welcoming legs.

Chapter 65

Ryker

NEVER IN MY life have I been this hard or this horny. I swear, hearing Kat telling me to whip my cock out almost made me weep like a baby. How the hell did I get this fucking lucky? God, watching her crawling to me on her knees just about undoes me. When she's finally close enough, she begins rubbing her hands up and down my legs, avoiding my pulsing cock. "Kat, no more teasing," is all I can seem to muster. Resting on her knees, she arches her back then pushes the front of that sexy-as-sin bustier thing down, giving me access to her perfect tits. Palming them, I slide closer to the edge of the chair to maintain a better position so I can suck her sweet nipples. Fuck me, if the sight of her doesn't cause my cock to bounce, begging to be tended to. With a smirk, Kat grips me in her hand before swirling her tongue around my tip, lapping up the pool of pre-cum that has been sitting there waiting for her. I hiss, deciding I can't take it anymore. I need her.

"Kat, stop. I need you to stand up, baby." She listens, which surprises me, but I think she realizes I'm at my breaking point.

"Legs," I command. Instantly, she wraps her hands around my neck before jumping up to straddle me, wrapping her legs around me tightly. With my hands on her ass, I begin moving her up and down on me, causing friction where we both crave it the most.

"Ryker, please."

295

I awkwardly walk us over to the bed as my pants are now pooling at my feet. "I can't wait any longer, Kat. I need to feel your sweet pussy milking my cock." I lay her on the bed, then begin the process of removing everything on her that's standing in my way from feasting on every inch of her delectable body. "My sexy, sweet girl," I murmur as I lick between her thighs. "I fucking loved that show, baby," I tell her before licking up to her stomach, stopping to give some much-needed attention to her gorgeous tits. "I love these, baby. I need to fuck 'em again real soon. But there's no time now. I can't be sweet, Kat. I need you too fucking much. This is going to be hard and fast, baby. Like I said, you're going to feel me in your throat," I say as I lick along her throat before sliding in-between her welcoming folds. "Fuck. I can feel your heat. God, so fucking hot, so fucking wet. I glance down where we're connected, marvelling at my cock, loving the glistening sheen of Kat's juices as they coat me every time I pump in and out. Pulling out, I grip my cock then begin rubbing it up and around her clit, causing her to buck, moan, and curse. Her body is covered in the prettiest pink flush I have ever seen, and the sight is too much. Flipping us to get a better view, I'm completely mesmerized by how amazing this woman feels.

"Ride me. Make me come so fucking hard. Rub those titties on me." I command while she hovers over me, kissing me anywhere and everywhere. She rides me hard and fast, bringing us both to the crest in no time.

Chapter 66

Kat

LYING ON RYKER, trying to catch my breath, I'm shocked when he flips our positions. He's now above me. He sprawls out, linking our hands together above my head as he kisses me fervently. I close my eyes, allowing the feeling of his kisses to consume me. "Kat," he says softly after pulling away, stopping one hell of an amazing kiss. I pretty much pout at the loss of his lips as I lay there still, eyes closed, hoping he kisses me again soon. "I need you to look at me." Opening my eyes, I see him spooned up close beside me, staring. His eyes are that intense colour they get every now and again.

"Kat," he clears his throat as if he's getting emotional, "I need to ask you something, baby."

"What is it? Is everything okay?" I ask, because at this moment, he looks serious. Skimming my nose with his, giving me an Eskimo kiss, like he's done in the past, he pulls back again, looking deep into my eyes before moving to reach for something from the drawer of his nightstand.

"Ryker?" I say, getting a little anxious. Turning back, he lays over me while pushing my legs apart, hinting at what he wants. He begins kissing me again, but this time it's slow, passionate, filled with emotion. Slipping inside me again, we begin to move in perfect rhythm. Not rushed or demanding like before. No, this time, it's melodic and sweet. Taking my hands in his, he brings them to his mouth, kissing each one before holding them above my head.

As the words fall from his lips, I feel him slip a cold object onto my finger, which after a moment, I register to be a ring. Oh, my God!

"Kat, I need you to be my wife, baby. I love you so fucking much. You're my everything. My Holy fucking Grail, baby. I fall more and more in love with you every day. You're a gift, and I want to treasure you, always."

I laugh and cry at the same time. I cry tears of joy, and I laugh at the fact that, for the second time, Ryker has asked me a monumental question while being buried inside of me. Wrapping my hands around his neck, I pull him in, resting my forehead to his. I'm silent for a few seconds, allowing this to all sink in. I relish the fact that this confidant man is waiting patiently with bated breath for my answer to his question.

"Hot girl, you're killing me."

With tears streaming down my face, I finally find my voice. Looking at my finger, I find the most beautiful emerald cut diamond ring I have ever seen. I place my hand over his heart and the other on his face. Looking into those amazing honey eyes, I smile as pure happiness seeps out of my soul.

"Ryker Eddison, I love you so much. Of course I'll marry you!" I say, not being able to stop the little giggle from escaping.

"Something funny here, baby? Are you laughing at me?" Ryker asks as he moves in me. "That little giggle felt good on my cock. How's about I make you laugh some more?" He begins tickling along my sides.

"Okay, Ryker, ah, Ryker." I move my hips faster and faster, and he's right, it feels so good. "Oh shit, baby, that, ohh…"

Ryker begins tugging on my nipples, ceasing all laughter with his assault on my sensitive tips. "Now, my sweet girl, tell me what the hell is funny?" he demands.

I take this time to share my thoughts with him. "I was just wondering if we do this, are you always going to ask me such important things when your cock is inside me? I mean, this is the second time now. I'm kind of seeing a pattern here."

He just smirks down at me "Oh fuck. You lost me when the word 'cock' fell from that sexy mouth of yours. Do you know how hard it makes me when you're innocent mouth says shit like that? It's so fucking hot." He grunts and begins moving more rapidly. I giggle some more. Of course, that's all he got from that.

Pulling him in closer to me, I whisper, "Now, Ryker, move that cock hard and fast right fucking now. We need to consummate this engagement." I tease my fiancé, "Yeah, that's it Ryker. I like your cock moving in me like that. I'm going to fuck you into next week, Honeybutter." I giggle at how corny the last bit of my dirty talk sounds, but it doesn't matter. He's too worked up at this point. It doesn't even faze him.

Once Ryker cleans us both up, he slips back into the bed and snuggles me into the Ryker cocoon I love.

"Guess we're having take-out tonight, seeing as you've made us miss our reservation," he adds with a grin before whispering a sweet kiss over my lips.

"Well, if you ask me, eating is overrated anyway." I wink before pulling him back down to me.

"Fuck, you're perfect," he tells me before taking me deliberately to the precipice once again.

Holy shit!

I'm engaged to Ryker Eddison.

Epilogue

Kat

3 years later...

OPENING THE DOOR, I smile with excitement and purpose. I can't believe how happy I am. Never did I think one man would have such an impact on my life. Considering the last thing I was looking for was love, especially from the likes of Ryker Eddison, I'd say I hit the proverbial jackpot. Ryker and I were married a year ago, and it's been incredible! Ryker is always kind and attentive. Despite owning his own business, he makes sure he's home with me every night and he's still always full of surprises. Ryker will often wake me up with breakfast in bed followed with him as dessert. I think him bringing me fresh flowers once a week is still the sweetest thing. I smile at the beautiful bouquet of lilies he brought me yesterday. He was an amazing boyfriend before, and if it's even possible, he's morphed into the most incredible husband. It's with that thought alone that I can't stop the huge grin from spreading across my face as I enter The Locker Room.

"Hey, Kat, you here to work out or to see Ryk?" Deanna, the front desk clerk, asks with a welcoming smile.

"Hey, Deanna. I'm actually here to see Ryker. Is he around?"

"Why don't you head up to his office and I'll page him to head there, too. I know he was working on the floor this morning, helping a few patients with getting their exercises down pat."

"Sounds perfect, thanks." I quickly make my way to the office. I

MY MIND'S EYE

feel a surge of pride every time I'm here. Ryker has made his dreams come true and The Locker Room has been voted best physiotherapy and sports medicine facility every year since its opening.

I slip into Ryker's office, and draw the blinds before giving Deanna a quick call. "Hey, Dee, I forgot to ask you to hold all calls or pages for Ryker for the next half an hour, please."

"Not a problem, he actually doesn't have any appointments for the rest of the day, so he's all yours. I'll be sure to take messages."

"Perfect," I reply before hanging up. I loosen a few buttons on my blouse, revealing the cleavage my husband loves so much before positioning myself on the edge of his desk. Ryker and I always seem to end our visits the same way; with me pinned to the desk while he takes me from behind. God, I love this man. I giggle at the plan I've devised in order to surprise him today, and I smile with excitement.

Ryker

I CAN'T HIDE the smile or surge of excitement that beams from me at hearing Deanna announcing over the paging system that Kat is here and waiting in my office. Her surprise visits always manage to send a jolt of excitement straight through to my cock. I think that's mainly because these visits always end on a high note, which is most often me taking her over my desk and burying my cock to the hilt inside my sexy-as-fuck wife. Who the hell am I kidding? I get that same jolt of excitement every time I look at Kat, let alone think of her. Since we've gotten married, it's been like a permanent state of honeymoon for my girl and me, and honestly, I don't think I'll ever get enough of her.

"Hi, sweet girl." I smile to Kat before locking the door behind me.

"Hey, baby, a little presumptuous locking the door, don't you think? I just saw Matty and Justin walk into Matt's office on my way up, so don't you go thinking for a second you're getting any with them right next door," Kat says with a sheepish grin, trying to deter my focus as I'm stalking toward her. My eyes catch the tops of those luscious tits of hers and it's suddenly obvious where I shall strike first. Fuck, am I ever hot for teacher.

"Hot girl, you better not be wearing that shirt open at work," I say as I'm now standing in front of her. I smirk down at her before brushing my face along her jaw to her ear and neck before ripping her blouse open with my hands.

"Ryker!" Kat tries to sound mad, but I know as well as she does, that she knew damn well what was going to happen once I caught sight of her skin, no matter how much of it is on display. Ignoring her attempt to scold me, I cup her face like always and kiss her.

Breaking the kiss, I step back in admiration. "Fuck, I missed these today, baby," I utter before releasing my beauties from the cups which confine them. *Stupid bra.* I toss it, along with her ripped shirt, behind my head. "Sorry, what were you saying, sweet girl? No what today? I think I sort of got sidetracked?" Despite rolling her eyes, Kat leans back on the desk, resting back on her arms, which causes her to arch further into my onslaught of her gorgeous tits. "Yeah, that's it, baby. Give me those titties," I thank her as I lap at one nipple then the other.

"Ryker, please," Kat all but moans as I'm basically standing in my office motorboating my wife, while sucking, tugging, nipping, and pretty much ravishing her like a starved man while she sits on my desk groaning and becoming more and more turned on from my actions. "Ryker, now, I need more," Kat's needy voice brings awareness that my girl needs her pussy touched.

"Lay down." It comes out more of a command than a request, but she doesn't seem to mind. I've learnt by now all the little things that turn my girl on and make her pant with desire. Kat quickly sprawls herself out on top of my desk. "Yeah, that's it, sweet girl." I position her heels to rest at the edge, while grabbing her ass. I push her down in a position so that her fine ass is hanging off at the perfect angle, allowing me to feast. "Christ, you're sexy, baby."

I kiss her stomach before ridding her of her skirt. I gasp, noticing she isn't wearing any panties. "Fuck, hot girl, are you trying to kill me? I swear, I'm going to come in my pants seeing your pussy all fucking ready for me like that."

Standing between her legs, I hover over her body as she's lying, anticipating my touch. I lick my lips before trailing my nose from her belly button down over to her exposed skin. "You smell so fucking good, Kat," I say as I insert a finger, then another, into her core. She gasps and the sound alone is enough to bring me to my knees. Pushing them in, then pulling them out again, I lick my fingers clean as the need to taste her increases by the second. Her reactions to my touch are always enough to drive me mad. Fuck, what my wife does to me.

"Ryker, enough! Now, please."

"Yeah, baby, beg. God, Kat. That turns me on so fucking much, hearing you beg me to lick you, to fuck you with my mouth." With that, I slide my tongue between her overheated folds, inhaling her scent, licking, lapping, and nuzzling my face in as close as I can get to her centre. As I find my rhythm, repeating the movements she loves over and over, Kat's body nearly launches up off the desk, and I relish in the fact I affect her as much as she does me. "Mmmore, Ryker," she pants as it's clear she's reaching the pinnacle.

"I want you to ride me, sweet girl. I'm fucking hard." I stand, immediately reaching to help pull her off the desktop, helping to guide her around to the huge leather chair that sits behind my desk.

Springing my cock free from the confines of my pants, I sit in the chair, beckoning my girl to come.

"Come sit on my cock, wifey." I chuckle a bit as I've recently become a fan of referring to Kat as wifey when making sexual demands. Without missing a beat, my girl puts me in my place.

"Oh, why? Is my husband ready?" she saucily asks, glaring down at my throbbing cock.

"Wifey," I growl before she relents, finally joining me on the chair.

"Husband," she calls breathlessly, before she finally sinks her tight pussy down on my cock.

"Fuck, yes." I smile, looking up at the beautiful woman rocking my world. "You look good with my cock filling you," I say, gripping her hips, helping to push myself in as deep as humanly possible. Fuck, does she feel good, sliding her juices all over me. Jesus, I'm not going to last. "Faster, baby, ah, fuck, Kat. That's it, aww, fuck, right there."

"Oh, God, Ryker." Within seconds, we're both catapulted into nirvana. Fuck, I love my wife. My Holy fuckin' Grail.

Kat

"HUSBAND," I CALL, all snuggled up to Ryker's chest, our bodies still connected. I decide it's the perfect time to execute the final stage of my plan.

"Yeah, sweet girl? You need help getting up? You want me out?"

I smile at the reference of him still inside me. "Umm, no. I actually, ah, I need to ask you something."

"What is it, baby? Is everything okay?"

"Oh yeah, everything is perfect, actually." With that, Ryker squeezes me closer.

"I was wondering, how do you feel about a new name?" I ask, not looking at him. Our faces mere inches apart.

He gives me an Eskimo kiss and laughs a bit before answering in a less than serious tone. *Fuck, I love this man.* "Ah, well, I'm kind of partial to Ryker. I really love when you call me 'babe' or 'honeybutter.' But I really love it most when you call me 'husband,'" he nuzzles my neck. "Why? What did you have in mind? It better not be 'asshole' or 'player,' baby. I've outgrown those I'd say, yeah?" He smiles wide at his joke, and I laugh with him before leaning up to speak into his ear.

Steeling my nerves, I whisper one of the most important questions I will ever ask into Ryker's ear.

"What about the name 'Daddy'?"

The End

Coming December 14, 2015

On the Rock (Pub Fiction Book 2)

Acknowledgements

I honestly have so many amazing people to thank because I feel truly blessed to have had all of these wonderful people in my corner.

Please bear with me while I gush at them in no particular order, because they are all equally amazing.

Karl – My amazing hubby! You are my everything and I can't thank you enough for supporting this crazy idea I had thinking that I could write a book. But you encouraged me and let me try it out. For that, and for holding down the fort, I am eternally grateful.

Radha – Dude, it's because you are relentless that this even started!! You little book writing pusher!!!! I love your face and how you pushed and pushed me. You never let me give up and your feedback and questioning of what the hell I was writing sometimes makes me so grateful that you are my friend. With that bloody blurb thank god you are the way you are! I love you B! (You get the B-right?) lol xox

Kymmie – You kept me, me! Your constant reminders to be me, and not to lose my story were so needed. I can't thank you enough for being such an incredible friend and wingwoman. I really value our friendship and appreciate how you laid it all out for me to see each side. Thank you for always letting me vent and for putting up with my crazy!

Amanda – Honestly lobby…you killed me. Kat is yours, she's all for you. My goal was to make you her because dude, you HATED her!! Lol. And the day you told me you liked her I almost died!!! Thank you sooooo much for talking to me like Kat and Ryker were real life people who needed us to get their story straight! You're an incredible sounding board, friend and crazy life partner!!! xox

Deanna – I don't really have the words to articulate to you how grateful I am to you, Deanna. I am thankful that you read MME over and over and over and over again. I bet you could recite that shit. Thank you for using your mad skills to help fix all my wordly issues. And being so willing to give up your time for me. I love you hard lady!! xox

Cassia Brightmore – OMG!! We did it!! It feels like forever ago when we started chatting about doing this, and now it's done. From many chats, to the "Can you read this part?" and the constant encouragement, you're amazing and I can't imagine having taken this crazy journey without you by my side. I have to add just how much of an amazing person you are to do what you did for me. Your friendship is a gift and I am so humble to have you in my corner. I honestly don't have the words to articulate how much you saved my ass. Did I mention…we did it!! I have loved getting to know you and I love you hard, WHORE2! You're stuck with me for life, my fellow Canadian. xxxo

Toni Thompson – I love you! You are one hell of a crazy woman and I am so happy to call you my friend, my beta, my PA. You are in a class of your own and you read MME so many times without hesitation and for that I am grateful. I love the little messages questioning how things were possible and how you called me out when I needed it. I love you Best, WHORE!

Alissa Evanson – My book twin. God I needed you! When you agreed to read my little story you made my day! You are my target audience and you gave me such valuable feedback and you pushed me to make MME better, pushed me to SHOW more of Ryker. You are my book twin and friend for life and I promise not to send you the next one 22 times!! Hehe!

River Savage – I don't have enough thank yous, to tell you how grateful I am for your kind words and encouragement. You are an amazing woman and I have so much respect for all you do. Your insight and feedback has been incredible. You are an inspiration to authors like me and go out of your way to help. You really are something special. Xx

KC Lynn – You're such an inspiration! I just can't thank you enough for just being such an influential and truly kind and approachable person. Thank you so much for taking time out of your day to answer questions and offer feedback about that damn blurb. You're a class act through and through. xx

Aly Martinez – Just wow! Thank you for being down to earth and helping me when I was stuck. Still can't believe you let me send you pieces to look at. I was very confused and making myself worse. Thank you for the intervention and taking the time to sort me out.

Laurie Carrier – Thank you for being my friend, my beta, my "Can I send it again?" My cheering squad for loving and supporting me while I did this crazy thing! xox

Leanne Tilston – Thank you for taking time out and beta reading for me over and over. Your feedback was perfect and soooooo appreciated!

Jen Jones – ESM!!!! I don't have the right words to express my gratitude. Thank you for taking a chance and reading my story. I loved your comments and concerns when they would strike you. I added little bits just to calm you, Panda, lol. I am very lucky to have you in my corner, your encouragement and kind words made a huge difference. xox

Jenny Newell – Thank you for being you! And taking the chance and reading my story. I was excited when I got the message saying you liked it!!! xox

Mom – I love you! You supported and encouraged me from the beginning; you really are the best mom I ever had! I am lucky to have a mom like you! From chats about plot to reworking pieces you were an amazing support system! xox

Dad – Thanks for cheering me on and supporting me! I still love that you shared my dirty teasers on your Facebook page! I love you!

Jeneane Johnson – Thank you for reading over my story and giving me feedback! It meant a lot! xo

Laura S – Thank you for always being excited about my book and encouraging me! xx

Ashley at Book Cover by Ashbee Designs: Thank you for your patience, communication, and creating a cover I love!

Kylie at Give Me Books – Thank you so much for all your support and for helping MME to get out there.

Made in the USA
Middletown, DE
29 December 2018